Hunter of Legends

Books by Clayton Taylor Wood:

The Runic Series
Runic Awakening
Runic Revelation
Runic Vengeance
Runic Revolt
Runic War

The Fate of Legends Series
Hunter of Legends
Seeker of Legends
Destroyer of Legends
Avenger of Legends

Magic of Havenwood Series
The Magic Collector
The Lost Gemini
The Magic Redeemer

The Magic of Magic Series
Inappropriate Magic
Ridiculously Inappropriate Magic
Ludicrously Inappropriate Magic
Absurdly Inappropriate Magic

The Masks of Eternity Series
Elazar the Magician

Hunter of Legends

Book I of the Fate of Legends Series

Clayton Taylor Wood

Published by Clayton T. Wood.

ISBN: 978-0-9980818-9-2

Cover designed by James T. Egan, Bookfly Design, LLC

Printed in the United States of America.

To my wife, who is legendary in her own right, alive within each character in this book. And to my son Hunter, for whom this book was written.

Special thanks to my brothers and my father, and of course my wife, for their invaluable advice.

Table of Contents

Hunter of Legends

PROLOGUE

Taylor stood in a small cavern a hundred feet below the surface, looking up at the uneven, rocky ceiling above. There was a dark, narrow vertical shaft there, with a rope dangling through it, just long enough to reach the cavern floor. He pointed his flashlight up the shaft, seeing his wife Neesha rappelling down the shaft toward him. He aimed the flashlight just below her, so she could see where she was going.

"You okay?" he asked as she continued downward. At a faster pace than he had, he noted with dismay. She smirked at him.

"Better than you were," she replied. Five foot one, with chocolate-colored skin and big, beautiful eyes, she was a sight to behold. He'd been damn lucky to find her...and even luckier that she'd said "yes" so many years ago.

"Show-off," he grumbled. Neesha reached the bottom, disconnecting her harness from the rope. She brushed past him, checking him with her shoulder as she did so. He stumbled to the side, catching her smirking as she strode forward through the small cavern beyond. Lanterns had already been set up in the cavern by her grad student, Mark. Taylor spotted a small tunnel ahead, extending beyond the cavern.

"Try to keep up," Neesha quipped, striding toward the tunnel. Taylor hesitated.

"Hey, let's take a picture," he proposed. She stopped, turning to give him a look.

1

"Really?"

"For Hunter," Taylor explained. Neesha sighed.

"Fine," she grumbled.

She pulled out her phone, leaning in next to Taylor and snapping a picture. Then she put her phone in her back pocket, striding toward the tunnel again. Taylor followed behind, admiring his wife's well-shaped buttocks as she walked. An amateur powerlifter, her posterior was damn-near perfect…and she knew it.

"I know you're staring at my ass," Neesha said, not even bothering to turn around.

"Can you blame me?"

"Not really," she conceded. "Come on baby, try to focus on your work."

"Right now," he replied, "…I'm focusing on what I'll be doing *after* work."

"Dirty boy," she murmured. But the way she said it, he could tell she was smiling.

They continued down the tunnel, using their flashlights to illuminate the way ahead. After a few minutes, the tunnel opened up into another small cavern. Lanterns lit the cavern as before, and two men were standing by the far wall, talking to each other. They stopped in mid-conversation, turning to face Taylor and Neesha.

"Oh, hey professors," one of the men greeted. It was Mark; tall and lanky, he was the best archaeology grad student Neesha had ever had. The shorter, beefier man beside Mark was Corey, a linguistics grad student.

"Whatcha got?" Neesha asked, stopping before the two men. Taylor studied the wall before them. It was mostly composed of rough granite. But embedded in the far-left side of the wall was a thick black stripe of what looked like metal extending from the floor to the ceiling, its surface perfectly smooth save for small symbols carved into it. The stripe was about a foot thick, and curved away from them as it went upward, vanishing into the wall.

"I'm not sure," Mark admitted. "We've been excavating this thing all morning. Or trying to, anyway."

"Do you recognize the symbols?" Taylor asked. Corey shook his head.

"They're not like anything I've ever seen," he confessed. "I took some pictures," he added. "I'll have to do a database search once we get back to the surface."

"Interesting," Neesha murmured. She reached out with one gloved hand, touching the black metal. It was obvious that the two students had spent a great deal of effort digging a few yards to the right of it, a large gouge in the wall present there, with rubble moved to one side of it. "Keep digging."

"Yes professor," Mark replied. He grabbed a pickaxe resting against the wall, and Neesha and Taylor backed away. Mark got to work, swinging the pickaxe at the wall, without much effect. After a few swings, Neesha stopped him.

"Let me do it," she stated, grabbing the pickaxe from him. Mark stepped back, and Neesha planted her feet, then swung the pickaxe in one smooth motion, slamming it into the wall. The rock crumbled with the force of the blow, and Neesha swung again, striking the wall a second time. A hole appeared in the wall, about the size of a fist. Inky blackness lay beyond.

"Damn," Corey breathed, staring at Neesha in admiration. Taylor grinned.

"Yeah," he replied. "My wife's a badass."

Neesha lowered the pickaxe, peering through the hole, using her flashlight to illuminate what lay beyond.

"What do you see?" Taylor asked.

"There's another chamber beyond," she answered. "I can't get a good look at it yet. We need to widen this hole." She handed the pickaxe to Mark. "Come on buttercup, put some muscle into it."

"What muscle?" Corey quipped. Mark rolled his eyes, but got to work, widening the hole swing by swing. After a few minutes, the hole was large enough to fit a leg through. Taylor took over, taking a few swings himself. No stranger to lifting weights, he was in almost as good shape as his wife. He made quick work of the wall, broadening the hole. When he tired, Neesha took over, making them all look bad, as usual.

"Not bad for being eleven weeks pregnant, eh?" Taylor quipped. He swiped Neesha's phone from her back pocket, snapping a few pictures. Mark and Corey didn't respond, no doubt feeling utterly emasculated.

When Neesha dropped the pickaxe at last, the hole was large enough for a person to squeeze through. Taylor peered into it, seeing nothing but blackness beyond.

"I can't see much," he said.

"I'll go first," Neesha offered. Being the shortest of them, it was the most logical choice. Taylor nodded, and Neesha stepped through the hole, vanishing into the darkness. Moments later, her head poked through. "Mark, hand me a couple of lanterns."

"Yes professor," Mark replied, retrieving a few and handing them to her. She vanished from sight again.

"Holy shit," they heard Neesha blurt out.

"Hon, you okay?" Taylor asked. A few seconds later, Neesha's head poked back through the hole. She gestured for them to follow.

"Come on," she urged. "You've *got* to see this!"

Taylor gestured for Mark to go in first, followed by Corey. Then he followed them, barely squeezing through the narrow opening. He straightened up, then froze, his eyes widening. There, illuminated by the lanterns, was a tunnel running left to right. A *huge* tunnel. The ceiling was over twenty feet high, the walls curving inward in a perfect upside-down U-shape. To the right, the tunnel ended abruptly in an irregular rock wall. To the left...

"Holy shit," he blurted out.

There, not five feet from where he stood, was a huge arch of the same black metal they'd seen earlier, matching the curvature of the ceiling perfectly. Small symbols were carved into the arch along its entire length. And while the tunnel ended at the arch, it was not with a stone wall like he would've expected. Rather, there was a perfectly smooth wall of utter blackness.

"I know, right?" Neesha stated.

"What the hell *is* that?" Corey asked. Neesha shook her head.

"I have no idea," she admitted.

"Do you recognize any of these symbols?" Mark asked Corey. Corey walked up to the arch, peering at the symbols carved into the jet-black metal. Then he shook his head.

"Afraid not."

"Look at the walls," Neesha said, gesturing at the curved rock walls around them. Mark's eyebrows furrowed.

"What about them?"

"They're perfectly smooth," Taylor answered for Neesha, walking up to one of the walls and running a gloved hand across it. The granite was as polished and smooth as a countertop. As was the ceiling...but not the floor.

"This is so weird," Mark murmured, running his own hand over the wall. "What is this doing a hundred feet below the surface?"

Taylor glanced at Neesha. She was staring at the black wall bordered by the metal arch, pointing her flashlight right at it.

"Guys," she called out. "Check this out."

4

"What?" Taylor asked, walking up to her side.

"It's not reflecting any light," Neesha explained, scanning the wall with her flashlight. She was right; no matter where she shined her light on that utter blackness, no light was reflected.

"A wall that doesn't reflect any light?" Taylor asked. "That doesn't make any sense." He'd heard of materials that could absorb any light that shined on them, but they were incredibly high-tech, made of carbon nanotubes ten thousand times smaller than a human hair. Certainly not something that would be found in a cave.

"Interesting," Neesha murmured.

"How old do you think this thing is?" Mark asked her.

"I have no idea," she admitted. She pointed her flashlight at the arch bordering the darkness, peering at the symbols. "The first step is to figure out these symbols." She grabbed her smartphone from Taylor, walking up to the arch and taking some pictures.

"That arch is metal," Mark observed. "But I don't know what kind. Whatever it is, it's really strong."

"What makes you say that?" Taylor asked. Mark gave a sheepish grin.

"I…may have hit it by accident a few times when I was trying to make that hole earlier," he admitted. "Before you guys came." He shook his head. "The pickaxe bounced right off. Didn't even make a scratch on it."

"Really?" Taylor pressed. "A full swing?" Mark nodded.

"I hit it pretty damn hard," he confirmed. "Not a scratch."

"Yeah, well we've both seen you try to swing a pickaxe," Neesha teased. Mark blushed. "Alright, so it's made of metal," she stated, snapping a few more pictures. "Building it would've involved smelting and molding. South Americans had that capability maybe two and a half thousand years ago."

"You mean the Mocha," Mark deduced.

"Right. But they were in Peru," she said. "Smelting wasn't used in North America in pre-Columbian times."

"So you're saying this is at most what, five hundred years old?" Corey asked. "That doesn't make sense…these symbols aren't like anything I've ever seen."

"And neither is this wall," Taylor added, eyeing the wall's utter blackness. Neesha finished taking pictures of the arch, and turned to focus on the wall. She stared at it for a long, silent moment.

"What are you thinking, hon?" he asked.

"That we have a lot of work to do," she answered. "We need to excavate this whole thing. We're going to need more people to do that."

"We could call in the MCX-CMAC," Taylor offered. That was the U.S. Army Corps of Engineers' Mandatory Center of Expertise for the Curation and Management of Archaeological Collections. Neesha glared at him.

"Day one and you're ready to bring the damn government in," she grumbled. "No thanks."

"Just a thought," Taylor stated. "They have better toys than we do."

"Think of something else," Neesha shot back.

Corey grabbed one of the lanterns by the hole they'd made in the granite wall, bringing it up to the inky black wall. Again, no light reflected off of its surface. He put one gloved hand on the wall, sliding it side to side.

"It's so smooth," he murmured. "And cold."

"We *are* in a cave," Neesha reminded him. "It's like fifty degrees in here."

"Yeah, but it's colder than the arch," Corey countered.

"Probably just a better conductor of heat, like metal," Taylor ventured. "So it feels colder." Corey hesitated, then took off his glove, placing his bare hand on the black wall.

It passed right through.

"What the…" he exclaimed. His hand had vanished *into* the wall, up to his wrist. Beyond his wrist, there was only blackness…as if he'd dipped his hand into a pool of black liquid. But no ripples appeared on the wall's surface.

"Woah," Taylor blurted out. "How in the hell…?"

"It went right through," Corey stated in disbelief, staring at his exposed wrist. "Like it wasn't even there!"

"But you just put your hand on it earlier," Mark protested. "It was solid."

"Well it isn't now," Corey countered.

"You were wearing your glove the first time," Neesha recalled.

"You're right," Corey replied. He dipped his arm further in, until it was up to the elbow. "Weird," he stated. "It feels cold at my elbow, but I can't feel anything past that." He concentrated for a moment. "I can't feel my hand," he added. "It's like it isn't even there."

"Really?" Mark asked.

6

"Yeah," Corey replied. "In fact, I…" He frowned then.

"What?" Mark pressed. Corey grimaced.

"My arm's stuck," he answered. "I'm trying to pull it out, but it won't come."

"What do you mean it won't come?" Neesha demanded, taking one more picture, then lowering her phone.

"I'm pulling on it," Corey explained. He jerked his whole shoulder back, but still his arm remained elbow-deep in the inky blackness. Neesha set her phone down on the ground, then walked up behind him, grabbing his shoulders and pulling backward.

He didn't budge.

"Hold on," she told him.

She grabbed Corey around his flanks, planting her feet wide and pulling backward. Her arm muscles tensed, the veins at her temples bulging with the effort. But still, his elbow remained stuck. She let go, beads of sweat glittering on her forehead.

"Well shit," she swore. She glanced at Taylor. "Want to lend me a hand?"

"Uh guys," Corey interjected. "My arm…"

They turned to look at Corey's arm, and saw that his elbow was no longer visible. He was up to his mid-bicep in the wall now.

"Damn," Neesha swore. "Don't put your arm any further in."

"I didn't," Corey retorted.

"Are you sure?"

"Pretty damn sure," he insisted. He tugged again at his arm, then stopped, staring at it for a moment. His face paled. "Aw, shit!"

"What?"

"It's being pulled in!" Corey exclaimed. Taylor stared at the student's arm, realizing that he was right. As Taylor watched, Corey's arm sank slowly but steadily into the wall.

"You're not leaning into it?" Neesha pressed.

"No, I'm not fucking leaning into it," Corey retorted, his voice rising in panic. "Pull me out!"

"Grab his waist on the left," Neesha ordered, nodding at Taylor. "I'll get the right. Mark, you pull his shoulders from behind."

"Got it," Taylor said. He wrapped his arms around Corey's waist, as did Neesha. He planted his feet, then pulled backward, as did Mark. They strained, but it was no use…Corey didn't budge. In fact, he'd been pulled in even further; he was up to his shoulder now.

"Come on guys!" Corey shouted. "Get me out!"

7

"Grab his legs," Neesha ordered. "Pull him by his legs!"

Taylor grabbed Corey's left leg, and Neesha tore off her gloves, grabbing his right leg. They lifted Corey's legs off of the ground, leaning backward and pulling as hard as they could.

Nothing.

"Damn it!" Neesha swore.

"Guys!" Corey yelled. His shoulder passed through the wall, his upper chest sinking slowly into the blackness. His face was only inches away from the inky surface now. He twisted his head away from it. "Guys!"

"Pull damn it!" Neesha shouted. She heaved backward, and Taylor followed suit, straining as hard as he could. Sweat trickled down his forehead, stinging his eyes, his biceps burning. But it was no use.

Corey screamed as the right side of his face touched the blackness, sinking into it.

Then his eyes rolled in the back of his head, and his left arm and leg began to jerk uncontrollably. Taylor's grip on Corey's leg slipped, and he stumbled backward, falling onto his butt on the stone floor.

"Come on!" Neesha urged, yanking on Corey's leg again. "Mark, help me!" Mark rushed up to Corey's still-spasming leg, trying to grab it. But he was kicked in the chest, and fell backward as well. Neesha swore, grabbing both of Corey's legs and leaning backward, the muscles of her arms going taut.

The rest of Corey's head was sucked into the blackness, and then *both* legs started jerking, yanking Neesha forward. She stumbled, letting go of Corey's legs and falling onto her belly on the ground.

"Neesha!" Taylor exclaimed, rushing to her side. "You okay?" She was pregnant after all, and had fallen right on her belly. But she waved him away.

"Grab him!" she ordered, struggling to get on her hands and knees. Taylor grabbed one of Corey's legs, realizing that the poor guy's head and neck had passed all the way into the blackness. And that he was being drawn in faster now, the darkness greedily consuming him.

"Shit," Taylor swore, pulling backward as hard as he could. But it was no use…Corey's upper body vanished through the wall, his waist passing through rapidly, and then his upper legs. When Corey's knees passed through, Taylor let go, backing away from the wall quickly.

Corey's legs and feet vanished into the wall, the blackness swallowing him whole.

"Well shit," Neesha swore. Taylor stared at the spot where Corey had been, unable to believe his eyes.

"What the hell just happened?" he asked.

"Babe," Neesha said.

"I can't believe he just…"

"Babe!" Neesha repeated, louder this time. Taylor looked down at her. She was still on her hands and knees near the wall, staring at her left hand.

The tip of her index finger was touching the wall.

Taylor rushed to her side, dropping to his knees. His blood went cold.

"Can you pull it out?" he asked. Neesha ignored the question.

"Get out your knife," she ordered. Taylor stared at her blankly. She glared at him. "Your knife!" He hesitated, then reached for his belt, for the hunting knife there. He unsheathed it. Neesha twisted to the side, exposing her stuck finger.

"What do you…"

"Cut it off," Neesha ordered.

"What?"

"Cut my finger off," she clarified, her voice icy calm. He just stared at her. She grabbed the knife from his hand, then pressed the blade against her index finger, just beyond the last knuckle.

"Babe!"

"Shut up," she commanded. Her jaw rippled, and she slid the blade across her finger, blood welling up immediately, the skin parting easily. Yellow fat was exposed beneath, blood pouring out of the wound. She bit back a scream as she sawed into her own flesh, the sound of metal grating on bone echoed through the large tunnel.

And then her finger began to suck into the wall.

"Babe!" Taylor repeated. But Neesha ignored him, biting back another scream, sawing faster. Blood began spurting out in regular intervals, spraying the blade and Neesha's other hand. Mark backed away, his face turning deathly pale, and promptly vomited.

"God *damn* it!" Neesha shouted.

"What?"

"I hit the goddamn wall with my goddamn knife!" she exclaimed. She was right; the tip of the knife had plunged into the wall. She pulled on it frantically, but it didn't budge.

9

"Move your finger against the blade," Taylor offered. Neesha glared at him.

"I *can't* move my finger!"

"Can you move the blade at all?" he pressed.

"No," she answered. She leaned back, jerking her left arm from the wall. Her partially-severed finger continued to spurt blood, but it held. "Oh come on!"

Then the finger was sucked further into the blackness, the wounded part vanishing beyond it.

"Mark, do you have a knife?" Taylor asked. Mark fumbled through his equipment, then shook his head. Taylor swore, turning back to Neesha. Her finger was now entirely engulfed by the blackness…and as he watched, her hand joined it. "Baby, grab my hand," he ordered, reaching out to her. She swatted his hand away.

"Get back," she told him. Taylor stared at her uncomprehendingly.

"What?"

"Get away from the wall," she clarified. "You can't get trapped too."

"Babe, we have to…"

"You're not getting me out," she interrupted, her tone icy calm. "You need to be there for our son."

"We can still…"

"I love you hon," she said, reaching out and touching his cheek. She gave him a sad smile. "I'll always love you."

"Baby, no!" Taylor insisted, grabbing her hand and pulling it back, trying to pull her free. It was no use…the blackness consumed her, pulling her in past the wrist now. Her forearm vanished, then her elbow.

"Let go babe," Neesha requested, her tone gentler. Her shoulder passed through, her head only inches from the wall now.

"No," Taylor shot back, his vision blurring as tears welled up in his eyes. "No baby, no."

"Take care of our son," she pleaded. "He can't lose both of us."

"Baby, please…"

"Kiss me," she demanded. He hesitated, then leaned in, pressing his lips against hers. He felt the soft crush of her lips, smelled the sweetness of her breath, of her skin. That intoxicating scent that meant everything was going to be okay…that he was home.

She pushed him away, staring into his eyes.

"Goodbye love," she murmured, smiling at him again, tears dripping down her cheeks.

And then the back of her head passed into the darkness.

"*No!*" Taylor shouted.

Her face stiffened, her eyes rolling into the back of her head. Her arm spasmed, then her legs, convulsing rhythmically. Her face passed through the blackness, then her right shoulder, her arm sucking inward rapidly. Her hand reached out for him, her fingers spreading wide.

And then she was gone.

Chapter 1

Hunter sighed, drumming his fingers on his desk. He watched as a young woman got up from her chair, walking up to Mr. Stanson's desk to pass in her test. It was Tiffany, easily the hottest girl in school. She had the kind of body that kept a guy up at night…in more ways than one. Tall, slender, with a cute butt and long, luscious golden hair, she was like a magnet for the eyes…and his eyes tracked her as she walked back to her desk to sit down.

God damn, he thought.

He glanced at the clock on the wall; it'd been over twenty minutes since he'd finished the exam, being the first to do so, as usual. He'd always been pretty good at tests, even if he didn't know the material that well. A gift he'd gotten from his father…one of the few.

Hunter fidgeted in his chair. There were still another ten minutes left before class ended. His mind wandered, and he found himself gazing at Tiffany again. Not only was she easy on the eyes, she was also one of the nicest people he'd ever met.

Man, he mused. *What I wouldn't give to be with her.*

Fat chance of that ever happening, of course. He'd pined after Tiffany for years now, always from afar, never quite having the guts to ask her out on the rare occasions that she'd been single. And she certainly wasn't single now; she was dating a dumb jock in class called Tyler. But hey, a guy could dream…and he planned on doing just that later on tonight. Among other things.

More students got up to pass in their exams, and eventually the bell rang, signaling the end of class. A tall, muscular guy in the back row hurried up to Mr. Stanson's desk to drop off his test, and Hunter found with no small amount of satisfaction that it was Tyler, Tiffany's boyfriend. The colossal prick was usually the last to finish. God only knew how he managed to stay on the football team with his lousy grades.

"Alright," Mr. Stanson declared. "Class dismissed."

Everyone bolted from their chairs, and Hunter got up as well, joining the rush toward the exit. But Mr. Stanson caught his eye, gesturing for him to come up to the front desk. Hunter hesitated, waiting for the last of the students to leave, then walked up to his teacher's desk.

"What's up?" he asked. Mr. Stanson, a short, middle-aged man with reading glasses, handed Hunter some papers. Hunter took them, realizing that it was his test.

"I graded yours already," Mr. Stanson declared, leaning back in his chair and eyeing Hunter disapprovingly. "Almost as quickly as you took it."

"Thanks," Hunter mumbled. He glanced at the score, written in bold red marker on the top of the page. 82%…not bad.

"You made some pretty stupid errors," Mr. Stanson told him. "If you'd taken your time, you might have gotten a better score."

"Not bad for not studying," Hunter countered. Mr. Stanson sighed, leaning forward and propping his elbows on his desk.

"You know Hunter," he began, "…every year I get someone like you. Smart, but lazy. I used to think it was because they weren't stimulated enough…that things were just too easy for them." He took a sip from a glass of water on his desk. "You wanna know what I think now?"

Hunter just stared at him.

"I think you," Mr. Stanson stated, jabbing a finger at Hunter, "…are afraid."

"Of what, getting an A?"

"Of what you might be able to accomplish if you actually tried," Mr. Stanson corrected.

Hunter glanced down at his test, then back at Mr. Stanson. He felt a familiar bitterness rise up within him.

"My parents tried," he replied at last. "It didn't work out so well for them."

Mr. Stanson sighed, leaning back in his chair.

"You can't use that as an excuse forever, you know," he retorted. "You've had it rough, I get it. But sooner or later you're going to have to take a chance, Hunter. You're a good kid, and you have a lot of potential…don't waste it."

"It's not an excuse," Hunter countered.

"Yeah, well next time, don't hand in your test until time's up," Mr. Stanson ordered. "Now go on, get out of here."

Hunter was all-too-happy to oblige, walking out of the classroom and into the hallway. He trudged toward his locker at the far end, spotting his friend Sam there. Short, with black curly hair and glasses, he was a total geek…and one of the awesomest, most loyal people Hunter had ever met.

"What did Mr. Stanson want?" Sam asked, opening his own locker – which happened to be next to Hunter's – and dropping his books into it.

"Just busting my balls," Hunter answered. "He was mad I got a B."

"What a douche," Sam muttered.

"Nah," Hunter replied. "He's pretty cool, actually." And it was true; as much of a hard-ass as Mr. Stanson was, he was the only teacher who actually seemed to give a damn about his students. He was also the only teacher who knew the truth about Hunter's dad…and his mom.

"You want to hang out later?" Sam asked.

"Sure," Hunter agreed, dropping his pre-calc textbook into his own locker.

"Hey Hunter," he heard a voice say. He looked up, seeing Tyler – Tiffany's boyfriend – walking up to him.

Great, he thought. *This again.*

"Finished early again, huh?" Tyler asked.

"Uh huh."

"Heard that was a problem for you," Tyler quipped, smirking at him. "Caught you staring at my girlfriend again," he added. "Need to change your underwear?"

Hunter ignored him. He felt more eyes staring at him, and knew that Tyler's buddies had swooped in to enjoy the show. As usual.

"Get lost Tyler," Sam interjected. But Tyler ignored him.

"Aww, it's okay man," he continued, patting Hunter on the shoulder. "You'll get laid someday. Somewhere out there, I'm sure there's a guy that's *perfect* for you." Tyler's friends laughed at that, and Hunter rolled his eyes.

14

"You volunteering sweetheart?" he asked, not even bothering to look up. He shut his locker, spinning the lock.

"Oh damn," one of Tyler's friends blurted out. "Tyler, I think he wants you!" Tyler laughed.

"Yeah, you know what," he said, "...I think I *did* catch him trying to sneak a peek at my dick in the bathroom." He sneered at Hunter. "You a faggot, *boy?*"

Hunter froze.

"I asked you a question," Tyler pressed. Hunter turned to face him.

"You sure had a hard time finishing that test," Hunter replied coolly. "Maybe you should switch to the special needs class."

Tyler stared at Hunter for a long moment, then stepped in closer. He was a good eight inches taller than Hunter, and a whole lot bigger.

"You calling me a retard?" he shot back. "Careful boy," he added, "...or I'll hit you so hard I'll make *you* a retard."

"Right," Hunter muttered, turning back to his locker. "Is that what you did to Tiffany?" he asked. "That explains why she's going out with you."

Tyler stepped in even closer, glaring down at him.

"What did you say, boy?"

Hunter ignored him, zipping up his backpack and closing his locker door. Tyler shoved him backward, and Hunter slammed into Sam, knocking his friend over. Sam fell to the floor, his glasses flying off his face. Hunter managed to keep his balance, and looked down, seeing Sam's glasses on the floor.

They were broken.

Hunter helped Sam up, handing him his glasses, then turned to see Tyler stepping toward them again.

"I asked you what you said," Tyler growled. Hunter clenched his fists, feeling anger rising within him.

"Need me to talk slower so you can understand?"

Tyler went to shove Hunter again, but this time Hunter pushed back, and they both moved back a step. Tyler's face turned red.

"You little black piece of shit," he spat. Hunter smirked.

"Dumb *and* racist," he shot back. "You're nothing but white trash, Tyler." Tyler shoved him again, pushing him back a few steps.

"At least my white trash dad didn't knock up some dirty nigger *ho*," he spat.

The rage was instant.

15

Hunter burst forward, swinging his fist at Tyler's face as hard as he could, his knuckles slamming into the jock's nose with a loud *crack*. Tyler dropped like a stone, landing on his back on the floor. Blood spurted from his nose, gushing over his face and onto the floor.

He was out. Cold.

"Jesus!" one of Tyler's friends blurted out.

"Anyone else wanna talk shit about my mom?" Hunter asked, stepping toward one of Tyler's friends. Then he felt arms grab him from behind, pulling him away. He resisted, trying to break free.

"Stop it!" he heard a man shout. "Stop *now!*"

It was Mr. Stanson, he realized. Holding him from behind.

Well shit.

* * *

Hunter slumped into the passenger seat of his dad's car, putting his seat belt on. He felt Dad's eyes on him, and avoided making eye contact, staring straight ahead. Dad sighed, starting the engine and pulling out of the high school parking lot. They drove in silence for a while, and Hunter turned to stare out of his side window glumly.

"What happened?" Dad asked at last.

"Some kid dressed up as a punching bag," he answered. "It wasn't my fault," he added. "The costume was so realistic. How was I supposed to know?"

Dad just glared at him.

"Some douchebag started pushing me and Sam around," he admitted. When Dad didn't say anything, Hunter turned away from the window to look at him. "He broke Sam's glasses."

"You broke his nose, Hunter," Dad countered.

"He started it," Hunter insisted. "I tried to talk my way out of it, but he kept going after me."

"Okay," Dad replied. "But now you're suspended."

Hunter said nothing, lowering his gaze. He *was* suspended…for a week. He was damn lucky he hadn't been expelled. With only a year left, that wasn't a mistake he could afford to make. Even his suspension might cost him dearly. With his dad's salary, he *had* to get a good scholarship if he wanted to have any chance of going to college with Sam and the rest of his friends.

"Sorry Dad," he muttered.

"I am too," Dad replied. "That was really stupid, Hunter."

16

"I know."

"You can't just hit people when they piss you off," he continued. "You have to learn how to control your temper."

"I *know*," Hunter repeated. He'd heard the lecture a thousand times.

"If you *knew* it," Dad pressed, "...you'd *do* it."

Hunter sighed, staring out of his side window, at the houses whizzing by. They were close to home now, only a half-mile away. He swallowed past a lump in his throat.

"He made fun of Mom."

Dad slowed, then stopped at a red light. His jawline rippled, and he accelerated rapidly when the light turned green, his tires squealing a bit.

"He called her a..."

"I don't want to know," Dad interjected. "I *really* don't want to know."

"He used the N-word," Hunter continued. Dad grimaced.

"I understand why you got upset," he conceded. "But it isn't an excuse to hit someone." He turned down a side street. "You could've gone to a teacher, you know. Then you wouldn't have gotten suspended."

"Yeah, well," Hunter muttered, still gazing out of his window. They were passing a few greenhouses now. "Mom would've hit him."

Dad slowed down, then turned into their driveway, parking the car in the garage. He pulled his keys from the ignition, getting out of the car without saying anything. Hunter sighed, opening his own door and getting out. They both went into the house, taking off their shoes and walking into the kitchen.

"She would've," Hunter insisted. Dad turned to glare at him.

"I know she would've," he replied. "That doesn't make it right."

"Yeah, but..." Hunter began, but Dad put up a hand.

"Stop," he ordered. Hunter obeyed, glaring at his father silently. "You screwed up," he stated. "And now this suspension is going on your permanent record. Think about that," he added. "You wanted to go to college with your friends? Too bad. You wanted to get into a good college at all? Good luck." He turned away from Hunter, his jawline rippling. "I need to cool down for a bit," he stated. "We'll finish this conversation later." He walked to one of the kitchen cupboards, retrieving a tall glass. "Go to your room."

17

Hunter complied, walking out of the kitchen and into the foyer, then taking the stairs up to the second floor. He went into his room, closing the door behind him and throwing himself onto his belly on the bed. He buried his head in his pillow, taking a deep breath in, then letting it out.

Great.

Dad was right, of course…and Hunter knew it. Tyler deserved what he got, there was no doubt about it. But it sure hadn't been worth getting suspended over. He'd screwed himself over…again. And without a scholarship, he wouldn't be able to afford to go to college with Sam and the rest of his friends. All the plans he'd been making for the last year had just been destroyed. His future was gone. His life as he knew it was over.

Just great.

He felt a heavy paw on his back, and rolled onto his side, seeing a black cat standing there. It meowed, rubbing the side of its head against his shoulder, purring loudly.

"Hey Charlie," he mumbled, petting the cat absently. He'd named her after his mom's old black cat. She purred louder, and he scratched around Charlie's ears, earning a truly blissful look. He sighed, rolling onto his back and letting her walk onto his belly and sit down, positioning herself perfectly for maximum petting.

Turning his head to the side, he spotted a framed photo on his nightstand. It was a picture of him and his mom when he'd been nine. The last picture they'd taken together, before she'd died. Dad was white Mom had been black, but Hunter mostly took after his mother, being just slightly less brown. It wasn't exactly an advantage. White kids at school shunned him for being black – while pretending not to – and black people shunned him for not being black enough…and didn't bother pretending otherwise. Points for honesty, he supposed.

Hunter stared at the picture, trying to remember what she'd been like, his mom. She'd died about eight years ago, and each year he had a harder time recalling memories of her. He'd have already forgotten her voice if it hadn't been for the videos Dad had saved of her.

Like everything else in his life, she was slipping away. And there wasn't a thing he could do about it.

He felt his eyes growing moist, and wiped them dry with his sleeve. He turned back to Charlie, running a hand over her back.

Her butt rose in the air as he reached her tail, and she continued to purr, her eyes nearly shut.

"You're the only one here who isn't broken, Charlie," Hunter told her.

He turned back to the picture of his mom, staring at it. Mom had died on a work site, according to his father. Her and Dad had been rappelling down a tunnel when her equipment had failed, and she'd plummeted to her death. After that, Dad had quit being a professor at the university, going to work as a consultant for the Army Corps of Engineers.

Hunter felt suddenly antsy, and turned onto his side, causing Charlie to hop off his belly and onto the floor. He got out of bed, walking out of his room and into the hallway. The pull cord to the attic was right outside of his bedroom door; he pulled it slowly, so as not to alert his dad, watching as the folded wooden stairway descended. He unfolded the stairs, then climbed up to the attic, flipping the light switch on the wall as he went up. Charlie joined him, following close behind. The attic smelled musty, and was oppressively hot; he ignored this, stepping onto the plywood floor. He turned toward the far end of the attic, spotting a few boxes there.

Mom's stuff.

He walked up to one of the boxes, kneeling before it and opening it. There was a stack of old photos inside, ones he'd long since memorized. A few of her favorite books. A bottle of Egyptian musk, her favorite perfume. He paused, grabbing this and opening it. Taking a whiff, he closed his eyes, feeling an immediate sense of peace.

It smelled like *her*.

He held the feeling for as long as he could, but it slipped away as quickly as it'd come, and he sighed, capping the perfume and setting it down. Charlie rubbed against his leg, and he smiled at her.

"*You'd* never leave me," he said, scratching under her chin. Then he turned back to the box. There were a pair of workout gloves, still reeking of sweat and dust. Her favorite jacket – pink, a color she'd hated, strangely enough. A notebook. An old smartphone.

He paused, staring at the phone, then picking it up. It was practically ancient, at least nine years old. Blowing the dust off the screen, he turned it around in his hands. He'd never really paid the phone much mind. He tried pressing the power button, but of course it didn't turn on. And he didn't recognize the port for the phone charger. He sighed, and was about to put the phone back in the box when an idea struck him.

There was a box of old cords in the spare bedroom.

Hunter stood, going back down the attic stairs. He waited for Charlie to come down, then folded the stairs back up, pushing the trapdoor to the attic shut. Walking into the spare bedroom, he found a few boxes stacked to one side in the closet. He rummaged through them, eventually finding the box of cords.

He checked each cord methodically, trying to plug each of them into the phone's charging port one-by-one. After a few minutes, he found one that matched.

Bingo.

He plugged the cord into the wall, then stared at the phone. Nothing happened.

Come on…

He waited a few seconds, but the screen remained blank. He shouldn't have been surprised. The phone was so old that the battery must have died. He was about to unplug it when the screen suddenly turned on.

Yes!

He smiled, watching as the phone booted up. Rows of icons appeared on the screen. He scrolled through them, then found what he assumed was the icon for camera photos. Tapping it made row after row of thumbnails appear. He scrolled through them, then clicked on a random one. It was a picture of Mom and Dad in their old office at the university, along with a tall, lanky younger man Hunter didn't recognize. He swiped the screen, seeing the next picture…a dirt path leading up a hill, with a sign on the side of the path.

Welcome to Smuggler's Cave, it read.

Hunter swiped again, seeing another picture of the path, this time showing it lead to the mouth of a cave ahead. Dad was ahead, his muscles bulging out of his t-shirt. Those were back in his bodybuilding days, before Mom had died. He sure as hell didn't look like that anymore. The only thing bulging out of his shirt now was his belly.

Hunter swiped again. Now they were inside the cave. A few more pictures of Dad walking, which meant Mom must've taken them. Then a picture of Dad standing in a cramped cavern, pointing his flashlight down a large hole in the ground. It was a long vertical shaft, descending as far as the eye could see. A rope had been tied to a large rocky outcropping near the hole, and was dangling down the shaft.

Hunter hesitated then, realizing that he was almost certainly looking at the pictures Mom and Dad had taken right before her death. She'd fallen down a shaft, after all. It had to be *this* shaft. His finger hovered over the screen, and he felt a twinge of fear in his gut.

He took a deep breath in, then swiped again…and frowned.

For they'd clearly reached the bottom of the tunnel…both of them. They were smiling into the camera, Mom having taken a rare selfie with Dad.

What the hell?

The next picture was of Mom swinging a pickaxe at a rock wall. A tall, lanky guy and a shorter man were off to one side, and to their left was a thick band of black metal that extended halfway to the ceiling. Strange symbols were carved into the metal.

The next picture showed Mom standing beside a hole in the rock wall with a rather satisfied smile on her face. He found himself smiling back, and swiped again.

He frowned, trying to understand what he was looking at.

There was a large tunnel, that he could tell. It looked to be made of pure rock. Ahead, there was a huge black metal arch, shaped like an upside-down "U." It looked to be a continuation of the black metal he'd seen earlier. The arch surrounded a perfectly flat wall of utter blackness. To one side, he saw his dad and the two other men standing by the arch; Dad was pointing to one of the symbols there.

He swiped again.

More pictures of the symbols, close-ups now. He swiped through them quickly, until he found a photo of the arch again. This time, the shorter man had his hand on the black wall, and his dad and the tall guy were watching him. Hunter swiped again, then blinked.

The next picture showed the shorter guy touching the wall again. But this time his hand was going *through* the wall. Or rather, it had disappeared *into* the blackness.

That's weird.

The next picture showed the man again, but this time his arm had vanished into the wall all the way up to the elbow. Hunter's eyebrows furrowed, and he stared at the man's face.

He looked terrified.

Hunter hesitated, then swiped again. But that was the end of it…there were no more pictures. He stared at the final picture, at the man with his arm in the wall. It looked like he was trying to pull his arm back…and obviously not succeeding. Dad and the taller guy looked alarmed.

Hunter stared at the picture for a long moment, then shut the phone off. He left it where it was, letting it charge. Then he went back to his own room, sitting down at his desk and booting up his laptop. Charlie hopped on his desk, trying to sit on his keyboard, as usual. He put her on his lap instead, then waited for his computer to boot up.

Welcome to Smuggler's Cave.

He did a quick search for the cave, and found a web page about it within seconds, along with a street address. It was about an hour's drive from here. He got the directions, printing them out. The whirring of the printer spooked Charlie, who hopped off his lap and bolted out of the room. He grabbed the printout when it was done, folding it and stuffing it in his pocket. Then he went back into the spare room, waiting for the phone to charge for a bit longer, then unplugging it and walking out of the room to go downstairs.

There Dad was, in his usual spot on the couch, watching TV with a tall glass of brown liquid in his hand. Whiskey, as usual. It was already half-empty.

"Dad," he called out. Dad turned to face Hunter. His eyes were glassy.

"What?" he slurred. Then he frowned. "You're supposed to be in your room."

"And you're not supposed to drink anymore," Hunter shot back, reaching for Dad's glass. Dad pulled it away just in time, cradling it to his chest. "Come on Dad," he insisted. "Give it to me."

"What do you want?" Dad demanded, refusing to give it up. Hunter grit his teeth, then gave up, crossing his arms over his chest.

"What happened to Mom?" he demanded. Dad's brow furrowed.

"What?"

"What happened to Mom?" Hunter repeated. He held up Mom's phone. Dad stared at it.

"What are you…"

22

"You know exactly what I'm talking about," Hunter interjected. He turned on the phone, the last picture appearing on the screen, and tossed the phone at his father. It bounced off Dad's chest, landing in his lap. Dad flinched, then set his glass down on the coffee table carefully – far away from Hunter – and picked up the phone.

His face paled.

"You told me Mom died falling down that tunnel," Hunter accused, pointing at the phone. Dad stared at the picture, his Adam's apple bobbing up and down. Then he glanced back up at Hunter.

"Hunter…"

"How did she die?" he demanded. "Tell me the truth."

"She fell after we were climbing back up…"

"Don't lie to me Dad," Hunter interjected. "She's my mom. You *owe* me the truth."

Dad stared at Hunter mutely, then glanced back down at the phone. At the photo of the man's arm in the wall. At the panic in the man's face. Then he sighed, his shoulders slumping.

"Alright," he muttered. "She…she didn't fall down the tunnel."

"Then what happened?"

Dad shook his head mutely, staring at the TV. *Through* the TV.

"I don't know," he admitted at last. "She…it happened so fast."

"What happened?"

"That damn wall," Dad answered. "It took her."

Hunter stared at him uncomprehendingly.

"What do you mean?"

"It sucked her in," Dad explained. "Just like it sucked Corey in."

"Corey?"

"The guy with his arm in the wall," Dad clarified. "He touched the wall, and his arm went right through. He tried to pull it out, but he couldn't. Then it pulled him in, and he never came back."

Hunter processed this for a moment, hardly believing what he was hearing.

"And Mom?" he pressed. Dad sighed, lowering his gaze to his lap.

"She got caught in the wall trying to save Corey," he replied. He raised a finger. "One damn finger was all it took."

"Wait," Hunter stated. "She got caught in the wall too?" Dad nodded, swallowing visibly. He reached for his drink then, taking a big gulp, then setting it back down.

"One finger," he muttered. He took another gulp. "One *goddamn* finger."

"Why didn't you pull her out?" Hunter pressed. Dad turned to glare at him.

"You think I didn't try?" he shot back. "I couldn't save her. It was too late. There was nothing I could do." His eyes turned moist, tears dripped down his cheeks. "I watched her die."

"How do you know?" Hunter asked. Dad frowned, glancing up at him.

"How do I know what?"

"That she's dead?" Hunter pressed. "You don't even know what happened to her."

Dad didn't answer.

"She could still be alive!" Hunter exclaimed, his heart racing. He walked forward, grabbing the phone and pointing at it. "We could go here and..."

"No," Dad interrupted, his tone cold. "We can't."

"But..."

"The government's all over that place now," Dad interrupted. "The Army Corps of Engineers took over after I called them." He shook his head in disgust. "I asked them to help me find Neesha, and instead they took over and blocked me from ever going there again...even after I started working for them."

"But she's *there*," Hunter insisted. Dad raised his eyebrows.

"Where?" he asked. "In the wall?" He shook his head. "She's gone, Hunter."

"Well, why didn't you go after her then?" Hunter pressed. "You just watched her get sucked in, then *left*?"

"I didn't just *watch* her get sucked in!" Dad shouted. Hunter flinched, staring at his dad, who glared at him furiously. "You act so high-and-mighty, thinking you know what you're talking about. But you don't know *shit* Hunter."

Hunter stared at his father silently for a long moment, resisting the urge to snap at the man. He crossed his arms over his chest.

"You should've gone after her," he insisted. Dad just stared at him mutely, his jawline rippling. "*I* would've gone after her."

"You think I didn't want to?" Dad retorted, his voice cracking. He stood up from the couch, swaying slightly. "Is that what you think?"

Hunter said nothing, glaring at his father.

"I was *going* to go after her," Dad insisted. "But she told me not to." He took a deep, shaky breath in, letting it out, then pointed one finger at Hunter. "The only reason I didn't go after her was because of *you*," he spat.

Hunter felt his blood go cold.

Dad lowered his finger, grabbing his glass and taking another gulp. He stared at Hunter for a long moment, his mouth quivering. More tears spilled down his cheeks.

"She was the love of my life," he said, his voice cracking again. "But I stayed for you."

Hunter stared at Dad, then at the mostly-empty glass in the man's hand. He thought back to every after-school game Dad had missed, every party Hunter hadn't been able to go to because he had to stay home and make sure Dad didn't fall and kill himself. Or drive and kill someone else.

"I wish you hadn't," Hunter muttered at last. "You could've been a hero," he added. "But now you're just a lousy drunk."

Dad's eyes widened, and he shot up from the couch, lunging at Hunter and whipping the glass at Hunter's head. Hunter dodged at the last minute, and the glass hurtled through the air, smashing into a framed photo on the wall behind him. It shattered, sending the photo crashing to the floor, glass spilling outward in all directions. Hunter backpedaled, half-expecting Dad to come after him and beat him. But instead, the man froze in place, his eyes on the ruined photo on the floor.

It was a blown-up photo from Mom and Dad's wedding.

Dad stared at it, his face turning deathly pale. He stumbled backward, landing on the couch and sitting there, his eyes unblinking. Then he looked up at Hunter.

"You're right," he muttered at last. "I *should* have left you behind."

CHAPTER 2

Hunter slammed the door to the garage behind him, staring at the two cars parked there. One was a new SUV – his dad's car – and the other was a beat-up sedan. He stood there for a long moment, clenching and unclenching his fists. His father had stormed off upstairs a few minutes ago, going to his bedroom and locking the door. Which was fine with Hunter; the bastard could stay there the whole weekend for all he cared.

Lousy drunk.

He wiped moisture from his eyes, taking a deep breath in, then letting it out, staring at the cars. He reached into his pants pocket, fingering the keys there. He was supposed to be grounded because of the suspension, but it wasn't like Dad was about to stop him from going out. He was probably drinking himself into oblivion now anyway, like he did every day. He'd gone upstairs, which meant there was a chance he might fall down the stairs again later tonight. Which would mean another visit to the hospital.

Hunter grit his teeth.

I'm done babysitting him.

He reached into his other pocket, feeling the paper he'd printed out earlier there. He took it out, unfolding it and staring at it. Directions to Smuggler's Cave.

To Mom.

He stared at it, then at the two cars.

I can make it there in an hour, he reasoned. *Dad would never know.*

He walked toward the beat-up sedan, unlocking the door and getting inside. He turned it on, then swore. The gas tank was almost empty, and he didn't have any money on him. He could go back inside the house and steal some money from his dad's wallet after the guy passed out, but that might take a while, and Dad had locked his door anyway.

But his keys are on the kitchen island.

Hunter went back into the house, finding the keys there and grabbing them. Then he hesitated. If he was going to try to get to Mom, he'd need rappelling equipment. Luckily Mom had taught him how to use it when he was a kid. Dad's old equipment was probably in the basement. He grabbed his backpack, then went downstairs, finding a bunch of dusty old boxes in the corner labeled "work." He searched through them, and after a few minutes found what he was looking for. Harness, clips, rope…everything he needed, except gloves. He stuffed these in his backpack, bringing it back upstairs and into the garage. He threw the backpack into the front passenger seat, then got in, turning the keys in the ignition. The engine roared to life; to his relief, there was a full tank of gas.

He hesitated then, staring at the steering wheel, feeling doubt trickle in. If he was going to do this…if he was going to go after Mom, then it might very well be a one-way trip. Hell, there was a possibility that Mom had even died getting sucked into that thing, whatever it was. If so, and he tried to go after her, then he'd be next. But it wasn't as if he had much to live for here. A drunkard for a dad, no mom, no girlfriend. A future in shambles. Even a chance of getting his mom back was worth the risk.

He took a deep breath in, then let it out, gripping the steering wheel with both hands.

All right, he told himself. *Let's do this.*

Hunter hesitated then, opening the car door and stepping out. He went back into the house, making a clucking sound. He'd hardly needed to; Charlie was already trotting up to him. He picked her up, cradling her against his chest, feeling her warmth, and the steady vibration as she purred. He felt a burst of affection for her, for the one thing in his life he could love without being punished for it.

"Bye Charlie," he whispered.

He set her down then, walking back into the garage and getting into the car. Then he looked around the cabin. He might need some cash for the tolls, after all. He found a couple of dollars in the center

27

console, then popped the glove compartment, reaching inside. He froze.

There was a gun inside.

He grabbed it, pulling it out. A silver revolver. It felt heavy, and very real. He turned it over in his hands, vaguely recalling going to the range with his mother so many years ago. He hadn't shot a gun since she'd died. He popped the cylinder, spinning it around. There was a single bullet inside.

He stared at it, feeling a chill run through him.

Jesus Dad.

Glancing back at the glove compartment, he saw another few bills laying there. He grabbed them, then shut the compartment, looking for the safety on the gun. He couldn't find one, of course. Revolvers didn't have safeties. But it did have a hammer...he vaguely remembered that he had to cock the hammer first before he could fire. He hesitated, then stuffed the revolver in his backpack.

Opening the garage door, he pulled out of the garage and down the driveway. Then he accelerated forward down the street, following the signs for the highway.

* * *

The sun was hovering over the hills in the distance by the time Hunter pulled up in front of a tall chain-link fence blocking the dirt road. He glanced at the directions he'd printed out, then at his phone. Both said he'd come to the right place...Smuggler's Cave. Past the fence, the road continued forward toward a large hill perhaps a quarter mile away. Deep tire-marks ran through the dirt road ahead, as if heavy construction equipment had rolled over it. But that must've been a long time ago; grass had partially overtaken the road, along with a few gangly shrubs.

Hunter got out of the car, slinging his backpack over his shoulder and walking up to the fence. A sign on one side of the fence said: "DO NOT ENTER" in big red letters, and the chain-link double-doors blocking the path ahead had been chained and padlocked shut. But the padlock was rusty, the fence in disrepair, much like the road.

Interesting.

He tested the padlock, pulling on it vigorously, but it held. Looking upward, he spotted razor-wire at the top of the fence. He sure as hell wasn't going to be able to climb over. He walked back to the car, popping the trunk. Dad occasionally still went to dig sites. He always kept random equipment in boxes in his car just in case he needed it. Hunter searched through one of the boxes, finding exactly what he'd been hoping to find: a pair of heavy-duty bolt cutters. He grabbed them, walking back to the fence. He looked around, suddenly nervous that someone might spot him. After all, if his dad was right, the place had been taken over by the government. If they caught him now, he probably wouldn't get another chance at finding Mom.

But there was no one around...the place was deserted.

Hunter used the bolt cutters on the padlock. With a little effort, the padlock snapped, and Hunter pulled it from the chain looping around the fence doors. Unwrapping the chain, he opened one of the doors, stepping through to the path beyond. He decided to leave the door open. If someone caught him here before he could get to that thing that took Mom, he needed to make sure his escape route was clear. And if he wasn't caught, it hardly mattered if someone discovered the open door afterward. If he managed to find Mom and bring her back, he'd deal with the consequences of his trespassing later.

Alright then.

He continued forward down the path, following it as it wound gently to the right. The path rose upward at a slight angle ahead, just as it had in the pictures he'd seen on Mom's old phone. In the distance, he saw a sign by the side of the road. As he drew closer, he saw its familiar greeting: "Welcome to Smuggler's Cave."

He slowed his pace, staring at the sign, feeling a chill come over him. This was where *she'd* been. Walking on this very path, seeing this very sign. He imagined her snapping a picture, Dad a few steps ahead. Probably laughing at one of Dad's silly jokes. Back when Dad used to tell jokes.

He sighed, trudging past the sign, continuing forward and upward.

The path narrowed a bit, squat rocky walls rising some five to six feet high on either side. A strong breeze blew up the path, pushing him from behind. He switched his backpack to his other shoulder, his back starting to ache from the weight of it. After a few minutes, he saw the path end abruptly, blocked by a tall rock wall. And there, in the middle of the wall, was the opening to a small cave...just like Mom's photo.

He glanced back, seeing the path winding down the hill. Far in the distance, he could see his dad's car beyond the fence.

Hunter continued up the path, reaching the entrance to the cave. A few feet into it, the path was plunged into utter darkness. He retrieved his phone, turning on its flashlight and checking its battery. It was at 42%. Running out of juice while rappelling into the bowels of the earth wouldn't just be inconvenient...it'd be deadly. And he needed enough battery life for the trip back, assuming he ever got back. He'd have to be quick.

He aimed the light into the cave, then strode inside.

There was a narrow tunnel beyond, the ceiling just high enough that he didn't have to stoop. The light from his phone was barely bright enough to guide his way, sending inky black shadows like long fingers across the irregular walls on either side. He strode forward, glancing from side to side as he went. The photos from Mom's phone had shown a hole in the wall...the one that had led to the long shaft traveling downward.

The cave wound through the earth, twisting left, then right, angling slightly downward. He followed it, moving quickly. He glanced at his phone...40% battery left. It was draining pretty quickly. He switched it to power-saving mode, turning off wi-fi and putting it into airplane mode.

Onward he went, the tunnel widening a little ahead. He tread carefully, not wanting to roll an ankle on rocks littering the cave floor. While the temperature outside must have been in the 70's, the air here was much cooler, and he shivered, suddenly wishing he'd brought a jacket.

Minutes passed.

Suddenly the tunnel ended, a rock wall blocking his way. Hunter stared at it, then shined his light on the walls on either side. There was no hole in the wall like he'd seen in his mother's photos...just a dead end.

The hell?

He turned back the way he'd come, shining the light down the length of the tunnel. Shadows stretched across the walls on either side. He moved forward, the shadows shifting as he went. He angled the light side-to-side as he walked, and after a few minutes, he saw what he'd missed the way in: a waist-high hole in the wall to the left. The shadows thrown by his light must have hidden it earlier. He squatted in front of it, shining his light through. Beyond, there was a small cavern, with a hole in the ground. A rope hung from a hook embedded in the ceiling, extending downward through the hole.

Bingo.

He crawled through the hole, his backpack scraping against the top of it. Squeezing through, he stopped before the vertical shaft. Slipping his backpack off and setting it to the side, he took the rappelling equipment out, putting it on. That done, he clipped his harness to the rope, picking up his phone and glancing at the screen. 36% left.

He grimaced, aiming the light down the shaft. It plunged downward as far as he could see, vanishing into the shadows. He retrieved his backpack, then grabbed the rope with one hand, lowering himself into the hole, bracing his feet against the walls of the shaft. He hesitated then, staring downward, realizing just how long it'd been since he'd done something like this. He took a deep breath in, then let it out.

Here goes…

Downward he went, slowly at first, then more quickly as his muscle-memory kicked in. It wasn't long before he saw the bottom of the shaft below. He dropped toward it, his feet striking the rocky floor a few moments later. Unclipping his harness from the rope, he shined his light forward. He was in a cavern, exactly the same as he'd seen on his mother's phone. At the far end of the cavern was a tunnel; it was bigger than he remembered from the pictures; tall enough for him to walk through without stooping, and wide enough to fit two people side-by-side.

Hunter strode forward into the tunnel, glancing at his phone again. 32% battery left…he'd managed to make it using only a quarter of the phone's charge. It'd take longer to climb back up the shaft, but he could probably get away with not using the light while doing so. So far, so good.

Suddenly, he heard voices in the distance.

He froze, quickly turning off his light. He stood there in the tunnel, pressing himself against the wall and straining his ears. He heard the voices again, echoing through the tunnel. They were coming from ahead, unintelligible but clearly male.

Shit.

Hunter hesitated, then turned on his light again, aiming it downward so it wouldn't travel as far. If there were people ahead, he didn't want them to know he was coming. If he got caught, he'd have to pretend he was just some stupid kid spelunking. He'd have to get past them somehow, and make a run for the archway his mother had vanished through. But what if he *couldn't* get past them?

He stood there in the darkness, hearing the voices again in the distance, and had the sudden urge to turn back. Then he pictured his mother the last time he'd seen her. Her big brown eyes, high cheekbones. Long curly hair tied back into a ponytail. Her laugh.

She'd been the strongest woman he'd ever known, the glue that had held their family together. She would have done anything for him, and for his father. And his father had abandoned her.

If Hunter didn't do this, he'd be no better than his dad.

He took off his backpack, setting it on the ground, then unzipping the main compartment. Reaching in, he felt cold metal under his fingertips. He grabbed it, pulling it out.

It was Dad's revolver.

He stared at it, then glanced down the tunnel. If the people ahead were armed, it was game over. But if they weren't, and they gave him trouble, the revolver would give him the upper hand. But there'd be no coming back from that…his future here would be over.

If he was really going to do this, he had to commit.

Hunter glanced at the revolver one more time, then stuffed it in his pants, hiding it under his shirt.

Here goes…

He slid his backpack on again, then moved forward through the tunnel. The voices got progressively louder as he continued down the tunnel, which soon led to a small chamber ahead. It was well-lit with electric lanterns set on the rocky floor, and a large hole carved into the far wall leading to another room beyond. Hunter turned off the light on his cell phone, shoving it in his pocket and ducking low. He was still far enough away from the light to be invisible in the darkness…he hoped.

Suddenly a man ducked through the hole into the chamber, carrying a few boxes stacked on top of each other. He was middle-aged and overweight, and wore a red jacket with the words "Bridge Corporation" on the back of it.

"Come on Gus," the man urged. "We're almost done."

A younger man ducked through the hole, also carrying a few boxes. They lowered these onto a large pallet on the floor of the chamber.

"Yeah yeah Harvey," the younger man grumbled. "What is this shit anyway?"

"Bunch of leftover equipment from the Corps," Harvey answered, stretching his back. "Company wants this crap outta here."

"Why the Bridge Corporation would want this place is beyond me," Gus muttered. "We're a goddamn tech company!"

"Who cares?" Harvey shot back. "Two more boxes to go," he added, gesturing at Gus. "Go get 'em."

"Your back hurting old man?" Gus teased. But he did as he was told, vanishing through the archway and returning moments later. He set these on the pallet with the rest. "This is stupid," he stated, gesturing at the pallet. "Why don't we just throw this shit into that black wall?"

"Won't work," Harvey replied. "Unless one of us touches it first. They say it's activated by living things touching it. You volunteering?"

"Uh…no."

"That's what I thought," Harvey replied with a smirk.

"That wall creeps me out," Gus confessed. "I heard the people who found this place got sucked into it. Never came back."

"That's what I heard too."

"You think it's real?" Gus asked.

"You can test it if you like."

"Yeah right," Gus muttered. "Age before beauty old man."

"Let's just get the hell outta here," Harvey grumbled. "I gotta get up early tomorrow to drive to the Cape."

"Weekend with the wife?"

"Yeah," Harvey confirmed. He picked up one of the lanterns, as did Gus, and the two men started walking toward the tunnel.

Toward Hunter.

Hunter cursed under his breath, backtracking as quickly as he could, until he reached the chamber he'd climbed down into earlier. He glanced at the rope dangling down from the vertical shaft above. *I could climb it,* he thought.

He glanced back, seeing the light from the men's lanterns in the tunnel growing brighter as they approached. There was no time to climb the rope…they'd almost certainly see him, and then the jig would be up. He walked to the wall just beside the tunnel, pressing his back against it…and reaching down to touch the revolver stuffed into his pants.

He heard footsteps behind him, getting louder.

Maybe they won't see me, he thought. *Maybe…*

And then Harvey and Gus stepped into the cavern, stopping a few feet from the dangling rope.

Hunter froze, staring at their backs…and then bolted down the tunnel!

"What the…" he heard Harvey say from behind. "Hey!"

Hunter sprinted down the tunnel as fast as he could, soon plunging into total darkness. He cursed, grabbing his phone and fumbling to turn on its flashlight. His right shoulder scraped against the tunnel wall, and he stumbled, nearly dropping his phone.

"Hey you!" a voice from behind shouted, footsteps clambering after him. "Stop!"

Hunter ran as fast as he could, keeping one hand on the wall to his right so he wouldn't slam into it again. He spotted light ahead – the chamber with the pallet and a few remaining lanterns.

"I said stop!" Harvey shouted. The footsteps were getting closer, Hunter realized. He resisted the urge to turn around and look, focusing on the chamber ahead. Moments later, he burst into it, leaping over the pallet and ducking into the hole in the wall beyond.

And found himself in a huge underground room.

He skidded to a stop, looking around quickly. The room was long, with a tall arched ceiling high above his head. To his right was a flat stone wall in the distance, illuminated by a few more of the electric lanterns. To his left…

His blood went cold.

For there, a few yards away from him, was an inky black wall bordered by a dark metal archway, runes inscribed into the archway's surface. It was just as he'd seen in the pictures from Mom's phone…except that a few feet in front of the wall stood a long wooden fence, a sign with huge red block letters in the center of it.

DO NOT PASS, it read. *DO NOT TOUCH WALL.*

He hesitated, glancing back, seeing Harvey and Gus sprinting down the tunnel and into the smaller chamber. They ran around the pallet, ducking through the hole after him.

Hunter ran to the left toward the fence, vaulting over it, then stopping. He was only a few feet away from the black wall now; he turned, seeing Harvey and Gus skidding to a stop, turning to stare at him.

"Hey kid!" Harvey yelled. "Get the hell away from there!"

"Don't touch the wall!" Gus added.

34

Hunter glanced at the wall, then at the two men, his heart pounding in his chest. He was struck with the sudden realization that this was it. That if he did this, there was no going back. And that these could very well be the last moments of his life.

"Come on kid," Harvey insisted, stepping toward Hunter slowly. "Come back over the fence."

"I can't," Hunter retorted.

"Why not?"

"My mom went through," he explained. "I have to get her back."

Harvey glanced at Gus, then turned back to Hunter. He grimaced, shaking his head.

"Aw shit kid, I'm really sorry," he said. "Really, I am. But you gotta understand, no one comes back. Once they go in...." He trailed off, shrugging helplessly.

"I have to try," Hunter insisted.

"What's your name?" Harvey asked. Hunter hesitated; if he told them, they'd know his identity. Which meant that they'd at least be able to tell Dad what'd happened to him.

He owed Dad that much.

"Hunter," he admitted.

"Okay Hunter," Harvey replied. "I understand you miss your mom, but I can guarantee you she wouldn't want you going through that wall."

Hunter said nothing, knowing damn well that Harvey was right. Mom hadn't wanted Dad to go through either.

"Come with us," Harvey pleaded, taking another step toward him. "We'll help you get home. You won't get in trouble, I promise."

Hunter glanced at the wall again, then lowered his gaze to the floor. His resolve wavered, and he was struck with the sudden realization that he could be making a terrible mistake. That he might be throwing his life away for nothing…and leaving his dad – and Charlie – alone, with no one to care for them.

"Come on Hunter," Harvey urged. "You mom's not coming back."

Hunter looked up at the man, swallowing past a lump in his throat. He imagined himself stepping over the fence, joining these two men. Going back to the surface, then back home. Living the rest of his life taking care of Dad, until the guy died of liver failure, or a fall that Hunter wasn't there to prevent. A life without Mom.

35

He took a deep breath in, then let it out, squaring his shoulders.

"Then I'm going to her," he replied.

And plunged his left hand into the wall.

Hunter felt his left hand go instantly numb as it vanished into the darkness, feeling as if it had been instantly and painlessly severed. He pulled back reflexively, but the wall resisted, his arm not moving an inch. Panic seized him.

Oh shit.

He yanked his left arm again, and again it didn't budge. He tried clenching his left fist, but felt nothing. It was as if his hand was gone. Maybe it *was* gone. Maybe the wall had dissolved it, and the rest of him was next.

Oh shit oh shit!

He glanced back at Harvey and Gus. Both were staring at him, their eyes – and mouths – wide open.

Something *pulled* on him.

Hunter turned back to face the wall, realizing that he was moving forward. Slowly but surely, the wall was sucking his arm into it. He saw the bump at the end of his wrist pass through, felt it vanish from his awareness just as his hand had.

What have I done?

He jerked his arm back a third time, but it was pointless. His forearm gradually disappeared into that utter darkness. The wall was consuming him more quickly now, pulling him into its unholy maw.

"Help!" he cried, turning back to the two men. "Help me!"

They just stared at him.

"Damn it!" he swore, yanking at his arm again and again. He felt his elbow pass through, vanishing from existence, and then his left bicep. He nearly lost his balance, stepping back with his left foot...and feeling it go numb as it passed through the wall.

No!

The wall tugged at him relentlessly, sucking his arm and leg into it. He was nearly shoulder-deep into the darkness now, his head mere inches from the deadly void.

"Help me!" he pleaded, glancing back at Harvey and Gus. The older one shook his head.

"Sorry kid," he apologized. "No one can help you now."

Hunter cursed, pulling his head as far away from the wall as possible. He felt his left shoulder become non-existent, then his left calf. He continued to struggle, but it was futile.

He was going to die.

Hunter felt the left side of his chest go numb, and his left thigh. He stopped struggling, feeling the darkness consuming him, pulling him into its nothingness. In another few seconds, his head would be pulled in. He turned to face that horrible void, that utter nothingness, and felt terror grip him. He grit his teeth, pulling the revolver from his pants and pressing the barrel against his own temple.

I'm coming Mom.

Then he threw himself into the darkness.

CHAPTER 3

Hunter groaned.

He opened his eyes, and immediately regretted it. Brilliant blue light assaulted him, so intense that it made his head pound. He squeezed his eyes shut, turning his head away from the light, waiting for the pounding to subside. He was lying on his back on something hard…dirt he realized as he slid his hand across it. His throat was parched, the right side of his tongue throbbing. It felt swollen.

He shielded his face with one hand, facing upward and opening his eyes again. He squinted against the light, seeing bright blue sky above, scattered wisps of clouds floating serenely in that sea of blue. He frowned, then struggled to sit up, his limbs feeling like jelly. His head swam with the movement, and he closed his eyes, steeling himself against a sudden wave of nausea.

Jesus.

He swallowed, feeling the nausea pass. Then he opened his eyes…and froze.

A huge expanse of sunbaked dirt and rubble stretched out before him, as far as the eye could see.

He stared, then rose to his feet unsteadily, feeling another wave of nausea come over him. He stood there motionlessly, waiting for the sensation to pass again. Then he turned in a slow circle. More dirt and rocks, extending outward to meet the sky. A hill rose upward at a shallow angle in the distance to his left. Other than that, the landscape was utterly flat. It was like a desert, no grass or trees. No hint of life whatsoever.

Where am I?

Hunter stuck out his tongue, feeling the swollen side of it with his finger. When he withdrew his finger, there was a little blood on it.

What the hell happened?

He closed his eyes, thinking back. He remembered leaving the house, remembered driving up to the fence. Even remembered using the bolt cutters on the padlock. And then…and then…

He couldn't remember.

Opening his eyes, he stared outward at the bleak landscape, then looked down, spotting something on the ground, gleaming in the sunlight. It was his dad's revolver. He picked it up, then looked around, spotting his backpack nearby. He put the gun inside, then slung the backpack over his shoulders, looking upward. The sun was directly overhead…it had to be around noontime. But it'd been late when he'd made it to the fence…at least six o'clock. That meant it had to be a whole day later.

He stared up at the sky, then felt his breath catch in his throat. There, to the right of the sun, was the moon. And further to the right, there was…another moon. And by the horizon, a *third* moon.

The hell?

He stared at the three moons, feeling the hairs on the back of his neck stand on end. His heart began to race, and closed his eyes, taking a deep, steadying breath in, then letting it out.

Don't freak out, he told himself. *Maybe you're just dreaming.*

He opened his eyes, staring at the three moons, then pinched himself, feeling a sharp pain on his forearm as he did so. The air was warm and dry, the sun baking his scalp and shoulders. He could still feel the throbbing pain on the side of his tongue. It was all very real. Too real to be a dream.

So what happened?

He looked around, searching for some clue as to how he'd gotten here. A path maybe, or a road. But there was nothing. He certainly wasn't anywhere near Smuggler's Cave, that was for sure. Hell, with three moons in the sky…

You must've made it to the cave, he reasoned. That was the only explanation. He'd made it to the cave, then gone through the black wall. And then he'd ended up here…wherever that was. And Mom had gone through the wall too, so many years ago. Which meant…

She's here.

His heart skipped a beat, and he felt a surge of hope, something he hadn't allowed himself to feel in years.

She's here!

He collected himself, suppressing his excitement. She'd ended up here, just as he had. And she must have been as disoriented as he was. But eventually she would have started moving…would've tried to find other people, and shelter. Which meant he had to do the same thing. But where would she have gone?

Hunter looked around, thinking through the possibilities.

Mom had been incredibly practical. Street smart *and* book smart. She would've looked for a clue, some evidence that people had been here. Assuming that there were other people here at all, of course. This place could be one huge wasteland. What if there was no water, no food? He would starve to death. He felt a pang of fear, and grit his teeth.

Stay focused.

He looked around. Ahead the terrain was flat, and there was nothing remotely resembling a road or a building. Far in the distance, he could make out barren hills, tall enough to prevent him from seeing anything past them. Behind him, the terrain angled upward, and he couldn't see anything past a hundred feet or so. But if he walked up the shallow incline, he'd reach higher ground, and might get a better view of his surroundings. He strode up the incline, his shoes crunching on the dirt and small pebbles underfoot. After a few minutes, the terrain leveled off, revealing what lay beyond.

He stopped abruptly.

There, maybe a quarter mile ahead, a long row of huge wooden pillars rose from the ground. They looked to be twenty feet tall, and sitting on top of them were big, flat stone slabs. These slabs were rectangular, and joined together to form an unbroken ceiling above the wooden pillars. The structure extended to the left and right like a crude bridge as far as he could see, curving slightly with the terrain. There was enough space between the pillars for him to easily walk through.

He strode toward the bridge-like structure, looking left and right. It looked like it was deserted, but the fact that it even existed meant that someone had to have built it. That meant there *were* people here.

People who might have met Mom.

Hunter walked up to one of the huge wooden pillars, putting a hand on it. It was warm and dry, with countless splinters sticking out of it. The stone slabs twenty feet above sent a broad shadow across the ground, making it significantly cooler here. The structure was maybe forty feet wide, supported by four rows of the wooden pillars, and beyond these he saw more lifeless terrain. He frowned. It didn't make any sense…why would someone build a structure like this? It couldn't be a wall, not with the gaps in between the pillars. So what was it?

Strange.

He walked between the first row of pillars, then the second, reaching the third row.

Then heard a *thump*.

He froze, staring straight ahead, between the rows of pillars. Someone was sprinting toward him. A dark figure against the bright blue sky.

Hunter backpedaled quickly, then felt his back strike the pillar behind him. The shadowy figure bounding toward him grew larger as it got closer, maybe a hundred feet from the pillars and closing in fast. Hunter backtracked between the pillars behind him, then through the first pair of pillars. The figure was gaining on him quickly, almost at the other side of the structure now. Hunter continued to backpedal, watching as the figure reached the closest pillar. Whoever it was was *huge*. Easily eight feet tall, with shoulders so broad they scraped against the pillars on either side as it squeezed past them. It was wearing some kind of suit, he realized…black armor that covered it from head to toe. Except something was wrong…just below its arms were a *second* pair of arms. It reached the second set of pillars quickly, squeezing past them…and behind the figure, *another* armored figure was sprinting toward him.

Shit!

Hunter's heart leapt in his throat, and he turned away from the two, breaking into an all-out run.

There was shouting from above and behind, and he ran faster, pushing his legs to the limit. He heard a high-pitched whistling sound, and then a piercing scream far behind him. The *thump, thump* of heavy footsteps grew louder, and Hunter glanced back, seeing the two armored figures not fifty feet from him now, and closing in fast, moving across the packed dirt with terrifying speed.

Shit shit shit!

He heard more shouting from behind, and looked past the two figures, at the structure behind them. There, standing on top of the stone slabs supported by the pillars, were several men shouting and gesturing frantically.

Then the nearest armored figure caught up with him, ramming him from behind.

Hunter cried out, falling headlong into the packed dirt. His shoulder struck the ground, pain shooting through it. The world spun around him madly as he went into a roll, stopping at last on his belly in the dirt. He scrambled onto his hands and knees, then felt cool arms encircling his waist. He looked down, seeing black hands clutching at his belly, attached to forearms with long, thick black armored plates. He felt himself being lifted upward, his hands and knees rising off the ground.

"Get off me!" he yelled, flailing wildly. He kicked back as hard as he could, feeling his foot strike something as hard as rock. He didn't even hear a grunt. The arms around him squeezed painfully tight, and then the thing holding him turned around, running back toward the structure.

The men on top of the structure shouted again, and Hunter heard a high-pitched whizzing sound to his left. The armored figure flanking the one carrying him jerked backward, an arrow sticking out of its eye. It tumbled to the ground.

"Got him!" he heard one of the men on the structure shout.

The thing holding Hunter bent over, bounding on all fours now, its second pair of arms carrying Hunter less than a foot off the ground. It tucked its head down, aiming for the gap between two of the pillars ahead. More *whizzing* sounds shot through the air, and Hunter heard a dull *thunk* as an arrow struck whoever was holding him. He heard a loud grunt, but the thing continued forward, racing between the first two pillars.

"Help!" Hunter cried.

And then something slammed into his captor's right side, sending them flying to the left...right into a wooden pillar.

Hunter felt the arms around his waist let go, heard a loud *thump* as the thing slammed head-first into the pillar. He was thrown to the side, landing on his back and sliding to one side of the pillar, his back scraping against the packed dirt below. He slid to a stop, then scrambled to his feet, running toward the other end of the structure.

"STOP!" he heard a guttural voice cry.

He glanced backward, spotting the armored figure rising to its feet.

Then it sprinted toward him.

He swore, pumping his legs harder, his lungs burning with the effort. But the thing caught up to him easily, reaching out with one hand to grab him. He feinted to the left, then angled sharply to the right, avoiding its grasp. But it was no use; it tracked him easily, reaching out again and yanking on his backpack. He lost his balance, his legs shooting forward from underneath him, and landed on his butt on the hard earth. Pain shot up his tailbone, and he cried out, pulling against his backpack straps. He managed to slip out of them, and shot to his feet…but not before something slammed into his upper back, throwing him onto his belly on the ground.

He rolled over onto his back, his eyes going wide.

The armored figure towered over him, monstrously huge. It stared down at him with jet-black eyes. Its skin was equally black, with a wide nose, prominent cheekbones, and wide, thick lips. Black armor extended from the sides of its head downward to the backs of its shoulders and neck, and long, tubular antennae sprouted from in front of its small ears, extending upward. A thick, translucent membrane ran like a mohawk from the top of its head down its spine, terminating in a short, broad tail. The membrane appeared to be filled with a blue, glowing, gel-like substance.

The creature tossed Hunter's backpack at him, then reached down to grab him.

Hunter shoved its hand away, scrambling up to his backpack and fumbling with the zipper. He managed to open it, and reached inside, feeling cool metal under his fingertips…Dad's revolver.

"Get back!" he shouted, pulling the revolver out and pointing it right at the thing's face. But it swung one hand, slapping the revolver out of Hunter's grasp. He backpedaled, turning to run again.

And then he heard a loud grunt.

He glanced backward, seeing an arrow sticking out of the thing's temple.

It turned to the side, just as a shadow appeared behind it. A man, swinging a massive hammer at the back of its head. The hammer struck the thing, and it lurched forward, falling onto its belly on the ground.

"Get him!" the man shouted.

More men rushed toward the thing, also carrying huge hammers. The first man swung again, smashing the thing's head with a loud *crack*. But the hammer bounced off, leaving only a small dent in the thick black armor encasing its skull. The creature rolled onto its back just as one of the other men swung their hammer at its head, and it grabbed the falling hammer with two of its left hands, yanking on it hard. The man flew over the creature, falling head-first onto the ground with a sickening *crunch*.

"Use the pointy end, idiots!" one man shouted.

The men rotated their hammers 180 degrees, revealing a long spike tapering to a sharp point opposite the blunt end of the hammer. One of them swung the vicious spike at the creature's head…but not before it got to its feet.

The thing swung one huge arm, knocking the hammer away, then grabbed the man by the throat, tossing him aside. The man flew through the air, smashing the back of his head against one of the wooden pillars. He fell to the ground, motionless.

Dead.

Another arrow slammed into the creature's armored back, barely penetrating it. The creature lunged for another one of the men, grabbing his hammer and ripping it out of his hands. Then the thing swung the hammer in a tight arc, taking the man's head clean off his shoulders in a spray of blood.

Shit!

Hunter backpedaled, then spotted his revolver lying on the ground nearby. He reached down and grabbed it.

One of the men swung their hammer at the creature's abdomen, the spiked end striking the black metal plates there. But the spike bounced off, knocking the creature back a few steps. It roared, grabbing the man's arms with its bottom pair of hands, then reaching forward with its top pair, plunging its thumbs into the man's eye sockets.

The man *shrieked*.

The creature lifted the man up above its head, then slammed him down onto the ground so hard that he bounced nearly a foot off of it. It turned its grotesque head toward Hunter then, taking a step toward him.

Hunter cocked the hammer of his revolver, then pointed the gun right at the thing's face, pulling the trigger.

The revolver kicked back violently, a loud *bang* echoing through the air. Hunter stumbled backward, falling onto his butt on the hard ground. The creature's head jerked backward, a chunk of its face blowing off. It fell onto its back with a loud *thump*.

One of the men rushed in, swinging their hammer, striking the thing's face with the spiked end of it. Its face caved in, bright red blood squirting out of the wound. The man yanked the spike out, rotating the hammer, then swinging the blunt end of it at the thing's face again. Its entire head crumpled, chunky yellow stuff oozing out of either side of the hammer, spilling over the dirt and mixing with a rapidly expanding pool of blood.

The thing's limbs jerked, then went still.

"Finish off the others," one of the men ordered, gesturing at a few of his companions. They nodded silently, running back toward the structure. "Don't forget the runner," he shouted after them. The man lowered his gaze to the dead creature, shaking his head. "Never seen one that looks like this," he muttered, kneeling before it. He poked at the glowing, gel-filled membrane on top of its head. "What is this shit?"

He poked at it a bit more, then glanced up at Hunter, eyeing him warily. The man was older, perhaps in his forties, and bald. He was very tall, and heavily muscled, with scars crisscrossing his face. His clothes appeared to be made of some sort of thick, tough brown hide.

The man stood up, smirking at Hunter.

"Almost got yourself turned into lunch, kid," he declared. He slid the butt of his hammer on the dirt, scraping blood and flesh from it. "Lucky we came in time."

Hunter stared at the man silently.

"You're welcome, by the way," the man added. He reached out with one hand. Hunter hesitated, then realized the man wanted him to shake it. He switched his revolver to his left hand, then tried to grasp the man's hand with his right, but the guy leaned in too far, grabbing Hunter by the forearm. Hunter paused, then did the same, gripping the man's forearm. The man grinned. "I'm Alasar," he introduced. "Sergeant Alasar."

"Uh, I'm Hunter."

"Nice meeting you," Alasar replied. He looked Hunter up and down. "Not from around here, are you?"

"I don't think so," Hunter replied. "Where is here, anyway?"

"You came through the Gate," Alasar declared. He shook his head, giving a low whistle. "Never thought I'd live to see an Original."

45

"A what?"

"What's that thing you used?" Alasar asked, gesturing at Hunter's revolver.

"A gun," Hunter answered. When Alasar just stared at him blankly, Hunter cleared his throat. "Like a little crossbow," he clarified. This seemed to satisfy the man.

"Well it certainly helped," Alasar stated. "Would've lost a lot more men if you hadn't used it." He smiled, giving Hunter a curt nod. "Thanks."

"Thanks for saving *me*," Hunter countered.

"Come on," Alasar prompted, picking up Hunter's backpack and handing it to him, then turning back toward the structure and walking toward it. "We better get going before more of these bastards come."

Hunter looked up, seeing a few men – dressed like Alasar – on top of the structure. They were lowering something to the ground…a ladder. Alasar started climbing up, and Hunter put the gun in his backpack, zipping it up and slinging it onto his back. He followed Alasar up the ladder, and within moments, they reached the top. The stone plates forming the floor upon which he stood were as wide as the structure itself, and rectangular in shape. It was a bridge, Hunter realized; though why it was running across a veritable desert was beyond him. A half-dozen men stood before them on the bridge, all looking remarkably similar to Alasar. Each was tall, muscular, and middle-aged, each carrying various weapons. Including a few bows.

"He's an Original," Alasar declared, gesturing at Hunter. "What's your name again, kid?"

"Hunter," Hunter answered.

"Right," Alasar replied. "Did we kill that runner?" he asked one of the men, who nodded.

"Yup."

"You sure?" Alasar pressed. The man nodded a second time. "Good," he stated. "We don't need those assholes sending reinforcements." He turned to Hunter. "Let's get you home, kid."

"Home?"

"Not your home," Alasar clarified. "Ours." He began walking to the left along the path made by the bridge's stone slabs, gesturing for Hunter to follow. "Come on."

Hunter followed behind the man. Two other men walked behind Hunter, while the others stayed where they were.

"Who are you guys?" Hunter asked.

"We're the Gate patrol," Alasar answered. "These are my men."

"What is this place?" Hunter pressed, quickening his stride until he was walking beside Alasar.

"This?" Alasar replied. "These are the Deadlands." He gestured at the barren landscape all around them. "Used to be part of the kingdom," he added. "Not anymore."

"The kingdom?"

"You'll see," Alasar replied. He glanced at Hunter. "So you're really from the Gate, huh?"

"The Gate?"

"Yeah," Alasar replied. "From the other side," he added. Hunter frowned…the man must be referring to the black wall Mom had gone through…and that apparently he'd gone through too.

"I guess so."

"Damn," Alasar murmured. "Can't believe I'm looking at an honest-to-god Original!"

"An Original?"

"Someone who comes from the other side," Alasar clarified. "Now I know why we posted so many men near the Gate. Used to think we were daft to post soldiers there."

Hunter glanced behind him, seeing a few men on the ground below, standing around one of the fallen creatures.

"What were those things?" he asked.

"Those beasts?" Alasar asked. Hunter nodded. "Those are Ironclad," he answered. "Strong fuckers, aren't they?" He shook his head. "You're damn lucky they didn't get you," he added darkly. "Who knows what they would've done to you."

"Why did they attack us?" Hunter pressed.

"They hate humans," Alasar answered. "If the Ironclad had their way, they'd kill every last one of us, let me tell you. We've been fighting them off for over twenty years." He glanced at Hunter. "One of the damn things murdered my father when I was a kid. I joined the military just to get a chance to kill a few of 'em."

The path angled upward, following the gentle slope of a large hill. They strode up it, and Hunter had to struggle to keep up with Alasar's quicker pace. The sun beat down on his back, making him sweat.

"Has anyone else come through like me?" he asked. "A woman, about eight years ago?"

"Eight years ago?" Alasar asked. "No."

"You're sure?" Hunter pressed. Mom should have ended up here just like him, after all.

"I'm pretty sure."

After a few minutes, the incline ended at the top of the hill a few dozen feet ahead.

"Get ready for it," Alasar warned. Hunter frowned, glancing at him.

"Ready for what?"

Alasar smiled, but said nothing, continuing forward up the path. Hunter followed, reaching the top of the incline. Ahead, the path leveled out, then dipped down, following the slope of the terrain. Beyond the hill was a huge valley that extended for miles ahead. And beyond that...

Hunter stopped dead in his tracks, his eyes widening.

There, beyond the valley, built at the foot of a huge hill in the distance, was a massive stone wall. It was easily fifty feet tall and forty feet thick, and extended to the left and right for what seemed like miles. It went back to form a giant rectangle, beyond which Hunter saw the sparkling waters of the ocean. And, completely surrounded by the giant wall, was something that took Hunter's breath away.

Alasar stopped, glancing back at Hunter.

"Told you to get ready," he said with a smirk. Hunter just stared, unable to believe his eyes.

There, encircled by the wall in the distance, was a massive, sprawling city. Tall buildings rose up toward the sky, built on the upward sloping side of the hill. And in the middle of the city was *another* wall, one nearly as tall as the first. One that surrounded a building larger than any Hunter had ever seen. It was a veritable fortress made of white stone. To call it a castle was an understatement; it was far larger than any castle he could imagine, with countless spires with golden domed roofs rising far above the city. It'd been built on the very top of the hill, rising from the rock itself as if it had grown from it. The white and gold fortress contrasted sharply with the deep blue of the ocean far beyond, gleaming in the light of the sun.

It was quite easily the most incredible thing Hunter had ever seen.

"Welcome to the kingdom of Tykus," Alasar stated, spreading his arms out wide. "And welcome home."

CHAPTER 4

Dominus gripped his cane tightly, grimacing at the gnawing pain in his calves as he made the long walk through his gardens, the discomfort worsening with each step he took. After a few minutes, he stopped to kneel before a pallet lying on the grass, feeling the pain slowly – mercifully – abate. The pallet was one of many, and set upon each were numerous wooden boxes. He set his cane down on the grass, then took the top cover off of the box nearest him, peering inside. There were eight wooden frames stacked front-to-back inside; he pulled one of the frames out, disturbing a few bees as he did so. They buzzed around him, some landing on him. He ignored them, hardly fearing their sting. For he was dressed in a protective white suit from head to toe, his face protected by a veil. He pulled the frame all the way out, staring at the flawless array of hexagonal cells constructed of beeswax within.

Perfect, he thought. An expression of the bees' particular nature, every hive the same.

He studied the cells, spotting worker bees milling about. The young workers, he knew, were nursery bees, taking care of the eggs that the queen laid, and the very young. Older worker bees secreted the wax, creating those perfect hexagonal cells. Still others collected nectar from the flowers, transforming that sweet substance into one sweeter still: honey.

And then, of course, there was the queen.

A singular creature, the queen bee. The undisputed leader of her hive. She laid all of the eggs, choosing whether to create males or females. She directed her workers, ensuring the survival of her hive. No hive could thrive for long without a robust queen, one fit for her duties. Her presence ensured that bees – their very identity and way of life – would survive the passage of time.

Dominus lowered the frame back in its proper place, then chose another, lifting it upward. This one had what he was looking for...empty cells. But they were in a spotty configuration...and there were too many drone bees. He peered at the cells closely, spotting eggs there...but laid on the side of the cell instead of the center. The worker bees were starting to lay eggs.

All signs of a failing queen.

He searched for the telltale sign of the queen – worker bees surrounding a larger bee, one with a longer body – but she wasn't there. She must have fled, sensing danger. Either that, or she was dead.

Lowering the frame into the box, he was about to pull another when he heard footsteps behind him. He twisted around, seeing his servant Farkus walking through the garden toward him. A tall, slender man nearly as old as Dominus himself, Farkus's back was slightly bent, his white hair short and his face smooth-shaven in the manner of all servants.

"Your Grace," Farkus greeted, stopping to bow deeply – while keeping well clear of the hive. "Your visitor has arrived."

Dominus sighed, rising slowly to his feet, then turning away from the row of boxes and walking up to Farkus. He took off the hood of his beekeeping suit, handing it to the man. Much to Farkus's dismay, as there were still a few bees crawling on it.

"My nephew, I presume," Dominus guessed.

"Obviously, your Grace," Farkus confirmed, holding the hood at arm's length. Dominus smirked; the man was possessed of the same distaste for wasted speech as Dominus was...a product of them having spent so many decades together, no doubt.

"Bring him to me," he ordered. Farkus bowed again.

"Of course, your Grace."

He left, and a few moments later he returned, a boy walking at his side. Nearly six feet tall, with long blond hair and blue eyes, he was a near-perfect representation of the kingdom's royal line, an ancient family borne of the greatest of the Legends. The two stopped, and Farkus bowed again, gesturing at Dominus.

"His Grace, the Duke of Wexford," he introduced. Axio bowed. "Your Grace," he greeted. Dominus said nothing, studying the boy. He'd never met Axio before, which was a shame. For one reason or another, Dominus had always found himself too busy to entertain the boy whenever he'd happened to be visiting the Acropolis. Axio was perhaps sixteen, and well-groomed, with clear attention to detail. He was also wearing the uniform Dominus had given as a gift earlier that year. A sign of thoughtfulness and consideration, assuming he'd dressed himself. With the way the youth were these days, that was hardly a given.

"Welcome," Dominus replied at last. "I trust your trip was uneventful?" He spotted Farkus's grimace, and suppressed a smile. It was a stupid question, a banal conversation-starter. The boy had traveled from the kingdom along the King's Road…a journey involving considerable risk. If it'd been eventful, the boy would've been dead.

"Yes, your Grace."

"I take it you know why you're here," Dominus pressed. Axio nodded.

"I do."

Dominus clasped his hands behind his back, staring at Axio silently for a long moment. He was curious about the boy; he'd of course heard a great deal about Axio from the boy's family. They'd spoken very highly of him. But of course they would; it wasn't every day one had the chance at their son becoming the next Duke of Wexford. A chance at power and extraordinary wealth had a tendency to make people abandon their honesty…and any other inconvenient morals.

The boy stood silently, eyes slightly downcast. Waiting.

Dominus regarded the boy approvingly. The boy was patient…another rare quality in young men. No fidgeting. No betrayal of nerves whatsoever. Whoever had trained him had done so well. It was too much to hope that such calmness was the boy's natural predisposition, but if it was…

Dominus limped up to the boy, a dull ache in his right calf growing more intense with every step. He ignored the discomfort, stopping only a foot away, far closer than one should find comfortable, staring down at Axio. He waited, focusing inwardly. Moments passed, and he felt a slight trepidation, but that was all.

Interesting, he thought.

"Do you want to become Duke of Wexford when I die?" Dominus inquired. Axio hesitated.

"My family does," he answered. Dominus arched an eyebrow. Answering the question without answering the question. The boy was nuanced.

"And what do *you* want?" Dominus pressed.

"To serve the king," Axio replied. Dominus sighed inwardly. A typical answer, devoid of information. Blind loyalty was mandatory in the common folk and idiocy in the aristocracy. Patriotism – love of one's nation – was far nobler, as long as it wasn't blind.

"And who does the king serve?" Dominus inquired. Axio gave him a confused look.

"The king is the king," he answered. "His role is to rule, not to serve."

Dominus grimaced, feeling suddenly annoyed. Another rote answer. Not that he could blame the boy; the educational system was designed to raise compliant, obedient citizens. Couldn't have people thinking for themselves, after all. Far more useful to have their beliefs given to them.

"Everyone serves," he corrected. "Even the king. *Especially* the king."

"Please explain," Axio requested.

"I may," Dominus replied, "…in time." He glanced at the boxes again. "What do you know about bees?" he inquired. Axio followed Dominus's gaze.

"Not much," he admitted. Dominus gestured at the boxes.

"Do you know what these are?" he asked.

"I assume they're beehives, your Grace."

"They are," Dominus confirmed. "*My* beehives, to be precise." Axio frowned.

"Of course, your Grace," he stated. "Everything here is yours." Dominus smirked.

"True," he replied. "But I built these hives myself," he added. "I enticed swarms to these frames, and I extract their honey from the comb. I maintain the hives, and nurture them."

"I see," Axio murmured. Dominus eyed the boy.

"Do you now?" he replied. "I sincerely doubt it."

Axio gave him a questioning look, and Dominus sighed.

52

"What," he asked, "…is the question that is on your mind right now? Be honest," he added. Axio hesitated, then gestured at Dominus.

"Why are you taking care of bees?" he asked.

"Exactly," Dominus agreed. "Why would the Duke of Wexford, second only in power to the king himself, waste his time as a lowly beekeeper?"

Axio shrugged, clearly at a loss.

"What type of government do we have?" Dominus inquired.

"A kingdom, your Grace."

"Partially correct," Dominus agreed. "More generally, a caste system." He eyed the boy. "And what is a caste system?"

"A society where class is determined at birth, your Grace."

Dominus nodded in approval. The boy was well-educated…and well-mannered. Already he was clearly an improvement on Dominus's own son. A fickle thing, heredity. Even the best of men could breed a fool. And god, was his son a fool…the miserable, cocky prick.

"Bees also employ a caste system," he lectured. "In a hive, there are drones, workers, and of course the queen…just as we have the peasants, the merchant class, the aristocracy, and the king."

Axio nodded, but remained politely silent. A good listener…another rare quality, and not just in the young. Most men pretended to listen, all the while merely waiting for a turn to speak.

"The drones," Dominus explained, "…are the lowest caste, serving only to mate with the queen. After they mate, they die." He gestured at the bees buzzing around the boxes. "The workers serve the queen, secrete the wax for the cells of the hive, collect nectar and make honey of it, store the honey in the cells, and maintain the temperature of the hive and defend it."

"And the queen, your Grace?"

"The queen," Dominus answered, "…creates life. All of the workers and drones are her children. She maintains the hive, and directs it. Without a queen, the hive will fail."

"Yes, your Grace."

"So why," Dominus asked, "…am I droning on about bees?" Axio hesitated, clearly mulling it over. Then he shook his head.

"I don't know, your Grace."

"Because," Dominus answered, "…to understand bees is to understand society." He gestured at his beekeeping suit. "I tend to my bees not for the honey, but for the perspective."

"To understand our caste system?" Axio guessed.

"In a way," Dominus replied. "The king rules, the nobles manage the common folk, and the common folk work the land and maintain the kingdom."

"Like a beehive," Axio deduced.

"Very much so," Dominus agreed. "But who," he inquired, "...is the beekeeper?"

Axio stared at Dominus, his expression blank.

"I don't understand," the boy confessed.

"Who stands outside of the kingdom," Dominus clarified, "...and tends to it, ensuring that it maintains its integrity?"

Axio swallowed visibly, clearly uncomfortable with this line of questioning.

"The king?" he guessed.

Dominus sighed. He turned then, gazing across his gardens, at the inner curtain – the high stone wall surrounding his castle keep. The castle Wexford was some seventy kilometers from the kingdom, the King's Road the only path connecting the two. Far enough away to avoid the inanities of the court, while close enough to know its secrets.

"The king's duty is to give himself fully to his nation," Dominus stated. "And to preserve the identity of his people...their customs, the noblest of their bloodlines, and their lands."

"Yes, your Grace."

"So as you must see, the king serves just as do the common folk," Dominus explained. "But in far grander a fashion."

"I understand, your Grace."

"You do not," Dominus retorted. "But you will."

Dominus turned to his hives, gesturing for Farkus to hand him his beekeeper hood. The servant complied, and Dominus took it, holding it in one arm. Then he turned to Axio.

"One of my hives has a failing queen," he declared. Axio frowned.

"Pardon?"

"A queen that is failing her duties," Dominus clarified. "I must provide a new queen so that the hive may flourish."

"I see, your Grace."

Dominus stared at Axio for a long moment. He had potential, there was no doubt about it. He was as good a candidate as Dominus had ever interviewed. The risk of bringing him into his confidence was high, but he had the means to ensure the boy would conform to his will.

His will was, after all, almost legendary.

"What I am going to teach you," Dominus declared, "…is forbidden knowledge." He stared Axio down, his eyes suddenly hard. "You will not repeat it to another soul."

Axio swallowed visibly, lowering his eyes and bowing deeply.

"I swear I will not, your Grace."

"Of course you won't," Dominus agreed. He placed his hood over his head, securing it carefully. He gestured to Farkus. "Show my nephew to his room," he ordered. "See to his every comfort."

"With joy, your Grace," Farkus replied, his tone flat, as usual. Dominus turned to Axio.

"Now, if you will excuse me," he stated, "…I have work to do."

The two left, and Dominus walked back to the box he'd tended to earlier, kneeling with difficulty and pulling the wooden frames out one-by-one. Eventually he found what he was looking for…a long bee, larger than the workers. But smaller than she should be.

A failed queen.

He studied her, knowing what must be done. A strong queen was needed to salvage the hive. He needed a new queen…but he also wanted to preserve the hive's bloodline. Without a queen, the worker bees would begin to feed royal jelly to the younger eggs, making queens of them. The worthiest queen would rise to rule the hive.

He reached into the honeycomb, grabbing the failed queen between his thumb and index finger, watching her squirm in his grasp. Worker bees swarmed around him, flying at his suit and stinging it. Protected as he was, he felt nothing.

Dominus stared at the queen, watching her struggle against her inevitable fate. Then he pinched his fingers together, crushing the life out of her. He placed the frame back in the box, grabbing his cane, then walking away from the hive, toward the castle keep in the distance. The bees attacking his suit gradually dwindled, then faded entirely, their stingers embedded harmlessly in his suit while they lay dying from their ultimate sacrifice.

"For the hive," he murmured.

* * *

Hunter wiped the sweat off his forehead as he walked alongside Alasar, the sun beating down on them mercilessly. They continued down the raised stone path toward the huge, walled-off city in the distance. They were close now, maybe a half mile away. The path ended ahead, merging into the slight incline of the upcoming hill. A wide dirt path continued past this, up the gradual incline of the hill to the massive stone wall in the distance. A huge metal gate was set into the wall, nearly twenty feet high and just as wide.

"What did you say this place was called again?" Hunter asked, gesturing at the city.

"Tykus," Alasar answered. "Named after the man who founded it. A true legend."

They walked steadily toward the end of the path, the ground rising up to meet them. After a few minutes, they reached the end, stepping onto the packed dirt beyond and continuing toward the huge wall ahead. Hunter glanced back over his shoulder at the stone bridge-like path they'd been walking on.

"What's with the bridge?" he asked.

"What bridge?" Alasar inquired. Hunter gestured at the bridge. "That one."

"Oh, that's the King's Road," he answered. Hunter frowned. "A road? Why is it so far off the ground?" he asked. Alasar hesitated.

"That," he answered, "…is complicated." He gestured at the wall in the distance. "Come on, we're almost there. Let me talk to the guards. Don't talk unless they ask you a question."

Hunter peered at the wall ahead, spotting two guards stationed just outside, standing on either side of the massive gate. He nodded, following beside Alasar silently. He stared at the wall, studying it. It was made of stone, and was at least fifty feet tall. Intricate designs had been carved into the wall's surface, with occasional clusters of white objects embedded into the stone. As they drew closer, he realized that the white objects were bones.

Human bones.

He stared at them, spotting a skull inset into the wall, a curved spinal column below it. Other skulls merged with the intricate carvings in the wall, forming a morbid collage.

Ooookay, he thought. *That's not creepy at all.*

Hunter looked down from the wall, realizing he'd slowed down a bit, and was trailing Alasar now. The man stopped before the two guards, and they nodded at Alasar, eyeing Hunter suspiciously.

"Afternoon," Alasar greeted.

"Afternoon sergeant," one of the guards replied. "Who's he?" the guard demanded, putting a hand on the hilt of a sword strapped to his waist. Alasar glanced back at Hunter.

"An Original," he answered. "Ironclad came for him right after he passed through the Gate. Killed a few of my men, but we managed to kill the bastards, with his help."

"Is that so," the guard muttered. He looked Hunter up and down, his hand still on his sword. "You say he's an Original?"

"He is."

The guard hardly seemed convinced.

"Prove it," he shot back. Alasar nodded, gesturing for Hunter to give him his backpack. Hunter slipped it off his shoulders, handing it to Alasar.

"He has this," Alasar stated, handing the backpack to the guard, who hesitated, then took it. Alasar turned to Hunter. "How do you open it?"

"There's a metal piece attached to some teeth on the side there," Hunter explained, pointing to the zipper. "If you pull on it, it'll open up."

The guard did so, unzipping the largest compartment.

"Pull out that silver thing there," Alasar instructed. The guard pulled out Hunter's revolver. "That's what took down one of the Ironclad."

The soldier turned the revolver in his hands, holding it as if it were contaminated with something.

"It's like a small crossbow," Alasar explained. "Hell of a weapon," he added. "Went right through the Ironclad's armor."

The guard nodded, putting the gun back into the backpack. He lowered it to the ground, pulling out Hunter's harness, then unzipping the other compartments and searching them. When he was done, he placed the items back in the backpack, zipping the compartments back up. He handed the backpack to the other guard, who carried it back to the gate, making a series of gestures with one hand. There was a loud *thunk*, and suddenly the massive gate began to rise, revealing a large tunnel beyond. The guard strode through, vanishing beyond.

"We good?" Alasar asked. The remaining guard glanced at Hunter, then nodded.

"I'll take it from here sergeant," the guard stated. "I'll notify the authorities of the attack on your post." He glanced at Hunter, then

57

back at Alasar. "You and your men should return to the base for cleansing," the guard added.

"I'll bring them back at shift change," Alasar promised. He paused then. "One other thing," he added. "One of the Ironclad was…different. Had a mane and a tail filled with some sort of blue gel. Never seen one like that before."

"We'll notify the authorities," the guard promised. Alasar nodded, then turned to Hunter.

"Good luck kid."

"Thanks," Hunter replied.

Alasar left then, walking back toward the King's Road in the distance. Hunter waited with the guard, standing there in awkward silence. Minutes passed, and then the other guard appeared again, no longer carrying Hunter's backpack. He gestured for them to come in.

"Come on, boy," the first guard prompted, walking toward the gate. "Follow three meters behind me, no closer."

Hunter complied, and the second guard followed a good ten feet behind Hunter, striding into the tunnel beyond the gate. More guards stood by either wall of the tunnel, their hands on their hilts. They stared as Hunter passed, taking a step back when he drew close. At the far end of the tunnel, some forty feet away, was another gate identical to the first, which was closed.

"This way," the guard in front of him prompted, turning to the left down a small side-hallway. Hunter followed obediently, finding himself in a long hallway with closed doors on either side. Eventually it ended, turning right. Stone steps led upward, and the guard led Hunter up them to another hallway beyond, one with more doors on either side. The guard stopped at one of these, knocking on it. The door opened, and the guard gestured for Hunter to step through, moving further down the hallway to maintain the ten-foot distance between them.

Hunter hesitated, then obeyed, finding himself in a small room with a long table in the center, with a chair on either end. Sitting on the chair at the far end was an older man in a white and gold uniform. He had long gray hair, with a gray beard and sharp blue eyes that glanced up at Hunter as he stepped into the room. Someone was standing behind this man…a tall man with short blond hair dressed in a black and gold uniform, a silver medallion resting on his chest.

"Have a seat," the older man requested, gesturing at the empty chair. The door closed behind Hunter, who hesitated, then sat down in the chair, facing the old man. "My name is Ekrin," the man greeted. "I'll be doing your intake. What's your name?"

"Uh, Hunter."

Ekrin dipped a feather quill into a bowl of ink, then wrote something down on a piece of paper in front of him.

"What nation do you come from?"

"The United States," Hunter answered. Ekrin glanced up at Hunter, frowning slightly.

"And what is that, a city?"

"A country," Hunter corrected.

"Ah," Ekrin replied. "And where in the United States are you from?"

"Massachusetts."

"And that is…?"

"A state," Hunter explained.

"How did you get here?"

"I uh, can't really remember," he admitted. "I think I went through a black wall in a cave."

"And what was bordering the black wall?" Ekrin pressed. Hunter frowned, recalling the photos on his mother's phone.

"A black metal arch," he answered. "With symbols on it."

"And what happened after you went through this wall?"

Hunter described how he woke up in the Deadlands, and his harrowing battle with the Ironclad. Ekrin listened without interruption, writing on the page, until at last Hunter was done.

"Thank you," Ekrin stated, finishing his writing. Then he lowered the quill, leaning back in his chair and glancing at the man standing beside him…the stranger in the black and gold uniform. "If you would," Ekrin prompted.

The stranger walked up to Hunter, putting a hand on Hunter's shoulder. Hunter resisted the urge to pull away from the man's touch. The stranger stood there for a long moment, then let go of Hunter's shoulder, walking back to Ekrin.

"He's an Original," the man confirmed.

"Excellent," Ekrin replied, glancing at the man. "You may leave us now."

The stranger inclined his head, then left the room closing the door behind him. Ekrin smiled at Hunter.

59

"Well then," he declared. "You must have questions. Feel free to ask me anything you'd like."

"Where am I?" Hunter asked.

"Right now, in a processing room within the Wall," Ekrin answered. "But more generally, in Tykus, the most powerful kingdom in the world." He leaned forward. "You've passed through the Gate, a door from your world to ours."

"You call that black wall the Gate?"

"That's right," Ekrin confirmed. "It's the only way into this world."

"And how do I get out?" Hunter inquired.

"You don't," Ekrin answered. "The Gate is one-way only. Once you're here, there's no going back."

Hunter stared at him, a chill running down his spine.

"You're joking, right?"

"Afraid not," Ekrin replied. "Our ancestors searched for a way back for thousands of years. There isn't one."

Hunter felt his heart beat faster. If there was no way back home, that meant that he was stuck here forever.

"I regret having to give you such terrible news," Ekrin stated. Hunter nodded absently, only half-hearing the man.

No going back!

He felt dazed, as if this wasn't happening to him. If he couldn't go back, that meant he'd never see his friends again…or his father. Or Charlie.

"Do you need a minute alone?" Ekrin inquired. Hunter blinked, then shook his head.

"No," he muttered. He took a deep breath in, trying to focus. "So what happens now?"

"Well, normally, we don't allow immigrants into Tykus," Ekrin answered. "But your case is a special one."

"What do you mean?"

"You're an Original," Ekrin explained. "You come from the source world, the world our ancestors came from so long ago."

"You mean Earth," Hunter clarified. Ekrin shrugged.

"We've heard Originals call it by many different names over the years," he replied. "Suffice it to say, being an Original makes you exceptional. You see, for us, Originals only come through the Gate maybe once a lifetime, if that."

"My mother came through about eight years ago," Hunter stated. "I came here to find her. Have you seen her?"

"Eight years ago?" Ekrin asked, his brow furrowing. "No, I'm afraid not. We haven't had an Original for about fifty years now."

"But my mother..."

"I'm sorry," Ekrin interjected. "If she came through the gate eight years ago, she didn't come here." He hesitated for a moment, looking as if he was about to say something more.

"What?" Hunter pressed.

"If your mother came eight years ago, she didn't come to Tykus," Ekrin answered. "It's very likely the Ironclad got to her."

"Those...things?"

"They patrol the Gate," Ekrin explained. "And attack anyone that comes through, as they attacked you." He sighed again. "Frankly, you're lucky to be alive. I heard that several of our men were killed trying to save you."

Hunter lowered his gaze to the tabletop, hardly believing his ears. If the Ironclad had gotten to Mom first, then she was dead. He'd given up everything for a chance to find her...and it had all been for nothing.

Tears welled up in his eyes, and he blinked rapidly, taking a deep, steadying breath.

"They saved you because you're an Original," Ekrin explained. "That makes you very special..." He glanced at his notes. "Hunter." He leaned forward. "We want to help you," he added. "Normally immigrants are not allowed, but for you we'll make an exception." He reached down below the table, lifting up something familiar: Hunter's backpack. He set it on the table. "I hear you used a very interesting weapon against the Ironclad." He reached into the backpack, pulling out the revolver. "What is it called again?"

"A gun."

"A gun," Ekrin repeated. "How does it work?"

"It shoots bullets," Hunter answered. When Ekrin gave him a blank look, he cleared his throat. "Small pieces of metal."

"By what mechanism?" Ekrin pressed.

"There's a metal piece at the base of each bullet," Hunter explained. "It has gunpowder in it."

"Gunpowder?"

"Powder that explodes," Hunter clarified. "The explosion shoots the bullet out of the end there," he added. Ekrin frowned.

"And where does one put these...bullets?"

"In the cylinder in the middle," Hunter answered. "If you pull that cylinder latch, it pops open. The bullets go in the tubes there."

"Fascinating," Ekrin murmured. He stared at the revolver, then returned his gaze to Hunter. "How many of these bullets do you have?"

"None," Hunter admitted. "There was only one in the gun, and I used it."

"Can you make more?" Ekrin pressed. Hunter shook his head. "I don't know how."

"I see," Ekrin murmured, obviously disappointed. "Can you make this gunpowder?" Hunter shook his head. He had no idea what gunpowder was made of, embarrassingly enough.

Ekrin pushed the backpack to the side, folding his arms in front of him.

"We understand your situation and are sympathetic to it," he stated. "We want to help you. For the time being, we'll house you and feed you, and eventually we'll find a more…permanent residence for you. All I ask for in exchange are these items," he added, gesturing at the backpack and the revolver, "…and information about your world."

"Okay," Hunter agreed. He certainly had no use for an unloaded gun, or a backpack for that matter. "Thank you…that's very generous of you." Ekrin smiled.

"You're an Original," he replied, as if that explained it. "Tykus himself was an Original," he added. "The founder of this great city."

Hunter nodded, not knowing what else to say.

"Stay here," Ekrin ordered, standing up from his chair. "I'll send a guide to come and show you around the city. They'll bring you to your apartment as well."

"Thank you again, Ekrin," Hunter said. "I appreciate it."

"You're welcome," Ekrin replied. "I'll send the same guide back to you tomorrow evening, and every evening thereafter. She will take you to me for nightly meetings."

Ekrin walked down the length of the table toward Hunter, opening the door. He paused outside of it, looking down at Hunter.

"Good luck," he offered. Then he stepped through the door, closing it behind him. Hunter stared at the door, then lowered his gaze to the table, feeling despair come over him.

Mom didn't come here.

There were only two possibilities, of course. Either she arrived in this world, then went somewhere else…or the Ironclad had gotten to her. In which case she was almost certainly dead. He'd spent most of his life believing that she'd died, and today was the first time he'd allowed himself to feel hope, to believe that she was still alive somehow. And now he had no idea where she was…or if she was even still alive.

And now I'm here, he thought darkly. *And I'm never going home.*

The door opened suddenly, and Hunter sat up straighter, glancing up from the table. A young woman stood in the doorway, looking down at him. She had long blond hair and striking blue eyes, her skin pale and flawless. Quite pretty, but not as attractive as Tiffany back at school. She wore a simple sleeveless shirt, low-cut enough to catch his interest, and short brown shorts that showed off pale, slender legs.

"Are you Hunter?" she asked. Hunter nodded, standing up from his seat hurriedly.

"That's me," he answered. She smiled at him, revealing perfect white teeth.

"Oh good," she replied. "I'm Trixie."

"Nice to meet you."

"Do you want to come with me?" Trixie asked. "I can show you the city."

"Um…sure," Hunter replied.

She took a few steps back into the hallway, holding the door open for him, and he followed her. She turned her back to him, walking down the hallway, and he followed behind, unable to help glancing at her butt. It was small, but cute. Her shirt didn't quite reach all the way down to her shorts, leaving her lower back exposed.

They headed down a flight of stairs, eventually reaching the wide tunnel past the main gate. Trixie stood before the second, interior gate, and the guards standing before it smiled at her. Moments later, there was a *clunk*, and the gate rose slowly. At length it stopped; beyond the gate was a long, wide street, with walls rising several stories on either side. And walking atop these were men with bows, staring down at them.

Trixie stepped onto the street beyond, and Hunter followed beside her, glancing up at the bowmen on either wall. Eventually the corridor ended, the walls on either side giving way to broad city streets to the left and right. And before them were stairs as wide as a highway, leading up the hillside toward a huge, white stone wall on the top of the hill, at least a mile away. It was, he realized, the wall surrounding the massive fortress he'd seen from afar earlier. In the middle of the stairway was a wide stone ramp. Guards stood on the steps on either side of the ramp at regular intervals. On either side of the steps were rows of white buildings built on the steep surface of the hill, each row built higher than the last.

"Where do those stairs go?" he asked.

"To Hightown," she answered. "And the Acropolis."

"The Acropolis?"

"The fortress beyond the wall," she explained. She gestured to their right and left. "This is Lowtown, the lowest part of the city."

"Hope this isn't the nice part of town," he grumbled. Unlike the buildings flanking the stairs ahead, the buildings to their left and right were rather shabby.

"Oh no," Trixie replied. "Hightown is much nicer." She hesitated. "We can't go there right now," she added apologetically. "I have to bring you to your apartment."

"Where's that?"

"I'll bring you there," she promised. "Come on."

She turned to the right, and he followed behind her, passing building after building on the left. To their right, the fifty-foot wall surrounding the city extended forward as far as he could see. They passed a few side streets on their left, and Trixie turned down one of them. It wove between irregularly spaced buildings on either side, eventually leading to a wide-open area ahead. The cobblestone road gave way to rectangular stone pavers some seven feet long and three feet wide, forming a large plaza. In the center of the plaza, about fifty feet ahead, was a huge building. It looked like a gothic cathedral, with imposing stone walls and tall spires.

"What's that?" Hunter asked.

"The Church," she answered. "We can't go there right now," she added. "I have…"

"To bring me to my apartment," Hunter interjected. "Got it."

She continued forward, aiming rightward of the church, passing it. The plaza ended abruptly, with steep wooden stairs taking them down to a small valley of sorts below. A large body of water stood at the bottom of the valley, a wide pier going from the street to a large cluster of buildings that had been built over the water, each suspended a foot above its surface on thick wooden posts. It was an entire neighborhood on the water; Hunter stared at it, impressed and dismayed at the same time.

This looked like a slum.

The buildings were two to four stories tall, but extremely narrow, like houses he'd seen in San Francisco. To say they were run-down was an understatement. A series of docks connected the buildings to each other, forming streets suspended above the water. A few people standing on those docks turned to look at them, stopping to stare.

"Let me guess," Hunter ventured. "My apartment is here."

"That's right," Trixie confirmed rather cheerfully, clearly not sensing his sarcasm. "How did you know?"

"Lucky guess," he muttered.

"We're almost there," she stated eagerly, turning left down a narrow street between the rickety buildings. They were apartments, he realized; people stood at their windows – which had no glass, he observed – and stared down at them. Or rather, at *him*.

Jesus, he thought. *It's like they've never seen a black person before.*

That, he realized, might very well be the case. Everywhere he looked, the people were white. They all had some variation of blond hair, and the same blue eyes as Trixie. It was like he'd arrived in a bizarre version of medieval Sweden.

"Here we are," Trixie exclaimed, stopping before a three-story building that looked just as run-down as the rest. "I can show you inside," she offered.

"Sure, thanks."

"Okay," Trixie agreed. Hunter let her go first, opening a flimsy-looking front door. It revealed an equally flimsy-looking staircase that led upward. He followed Trixie up the stairs to the third-floor landing, and a closed door beyond. Trixie took a key from her pocket, unlocking the door and opening it, then handing him the key. "Before I forget," she explained. Then she stepped into the room beyond, and Hunter followed her in. To call it a studio apartment would have been generous. The apartment was eight feet square, with one window and a bed in the corner. A few hooks had been nailed into the wall facing the bed. There was no stove, no refrigerator, no sink…and no shower. Nothing but a bed.

"Uh…" Hunter began, at a loss for words. "Where is…?"

"Where is what?" Trixie asked.

"Everything," he replied, gesturing at the room.

"The bed's right there," she answered, pointing at it.

"I know," he stated. "But how do I cook food?" he asked. "Or wash my clothes?" he added. Or go to the bathroom, for that matter.

"Oh, you do that at the community center," Trixie answered. "It's the big building in the center of the Outskirts."

"The what?"

"This part of the kingdom," Trixie clarified. "It's called the Outskirts."

"Oh."

Trixie paused, glancing around the room, then back up at Hunter. She picked at her fingernails for a moment. "Do you have any more questions?" she asked. Hunter sighed, shaking his head.

"Guess not."

"Okay," she replied. She hesitated again. "Do you want me to stay with you tonight?"

"What?"

"I can stay with you tonight," she repeated. "Or I can come in the morning."

Hunter glanced at the bed. It was barely a twin-size, and he wasn't about to have her – or himself – sleep on the floor.

"I'll see you tomorrow," he answered. "Thanks again, Trixie."

"Oh," she mumbled. She hesitated, then gave a weak smile. "I'll see you then."

She turned about and left, closing the door behind her. Hunter watched her leave, then shook his head.

Well that *was awkward.*

He glanced about his room, then sighed, hanging his key on one of the hooks on the wall, then sitting down on the edge of his bed. The mattress was stiff, the pillow dusty. He started to take off his shirt, then thought better of it, lying down on the bed and staring up at the ceiling. He could hear people talking through the walls, their voices muffled.

So this is it, he thought. Ekrin was going to get him a job eventually. Then it was going to be work…and this.

"Great," he grumbled.

He rolled onto his side, staring at the door to his room. He half-expected Charlie to hop up onto his bed, but of course she didn't. If only he'd brought her, she'd be curled up at his side right now, purring contentedly. All she'd ever needed was *him* to be happy…and now he'd left her just like Mom had left him. Dad wouldn't take care of her, not well anyway. He'd probably send her to a shelter.

Hunter sighed, feeling monumentally depressed. He rolled onto his other side, facing the wall.

To think that he'd woken up this morning in his own comfortable bed at home on Earth, preparing for just another day at school. And then the suspension, and his fight with Dad. Then one stupid, impulsive decision, to go after Mom, to do what Dad had failed to do. There was a very real chance that it'd all been for nothing...for *less* than nothing. Because now his life as he knew it was over, everyone and everything he cared about back home a thing of the past. He was stuck in this strange world, and his mother was probably long dead.

Just great.

He closed his eyes, feeling suddenly exhausted. Although it was still mid-afternoon here judging by the sunlight, it'd almost been nighttime when he'd driven to Smuggler's Cave. And so it was, that despite the muffled voices coming through the walls, and the stiffness of his mattress, he soon drifted off to sleep.

CHAPTER 5

Hunter groaned, rolling onto his side and grabbing his pillow, putting it over his head. There were loud voices coming from outside, followed by the sound of footsteps. The sounds faded gradually. He was nearly asleep again when he heard more voices.

"God damn it," he blurted out, tossing the pillow to the side and rolling onto his back. Who the hell had Dad invited over this early in the morning? He rubbed his eyes, feeling supremely annoyed. Then he frowned, staring up at the ceiling. Instead of the nice, white painted ceiling of his bedroom, he saw bare wooden planks. It took him a moment to remember where he was.

Shit.

He glanced at the lone window in his tiny room, seeing sunlight shining through it. More voices came from outside, and he realized with dismay that he wasn't going to get any more sleep. And not just because of the noise. He had to take a piss…and badly. But there was no toilet in this apartment. Trixie had mentioned that there was a big building nearby for eating and bathing; hopefully it had toilets. If not, he swore to God he was going to piss out the window. He imagined himself doing so, his stream hitting the people who'd woken him up, and couldn't help but smile. He was just like Mom, after all…terribly grouchy when he woke up.

Hunter sighed, grabbing his key from its hook and leaving the apartment, locking the door behind him. He went downstairs, emerging onto the dock-like street just outside. He looked around, spotting people walking from their apartments, all going in the same direction…almost certainly to the community center Trixie had spoken of yesterday. He followed them, weaving between narrow buildings, until at last he saw a large, one-story wooden building in the distance. A line of people had formed before the front double-doors of the place, and he got into line…or tried to. The man in front of him turned to look at him, then jerked away, backpedaling rapidly.

"Whoa," the man blurted out. "What the hell do you think *you're* doing?"

Hunter stared at the man, realizing that more people had turned to face him. *Everyone* backed away from him then, staring at him with something that looked like horror.

"Uh, sorry," Hunter replied, "…did I choose the wrong line?"

"Stay the hell away from me!" the man snapped, backing away another couple of steps. Hunter stayed where he was, glancing about. The people around him had backed away as well, forming a circle around him. All of them were staring at him, clearly unnerved.

No, they were downright freaking *out*.

"Why are you looking at me like that?" he asked. "I'm just trying to get something to eat." No one said anything. He pointed to the building. "This is the community center, isn't it?"

"Sure is," a voice replied from behind.

Hunter turned around, seeing a young woman walking toward him. She was barely over five feet tall, with lightly bronzed skin and long dirty-blonde hair tied into thick braids. She had striking blue eyes, and she smirked at him as she approached. She wore heavy boots and a tight black shirt and pants, revealing that she wasn't lacking in the curves department. She stopped a few feet from him, looking him up and down.

"Well ain't you crispy," she murmured, still smirking. She extended a hand. "Name's Sukri," she introduced.

"Hunter," Hunter replied, shaking her hand. Her grip was firm, and even a little painful, and he was glad when she let go.

"These lily-white wanna-be's giving you trouble?" she inquired, glancing at the people around them. Most of whom were, Hunter realized, similar to Trixie…not quite as pale, but still blonde-haired and blue-eyed.

"Little bit," he confirmed.

"Don't mind 'em," Sukri instructed, glaring at the crowd. "Just pretend they're not there. None of them has the balls to go near

69

you." She grabbed Hunter's hand, pulling him toward the double doors. The people ahead of them parted to either side, giving both of them a wide berth. Sukri stopped by the doors, glancing at Hunter. She cleared her throat then, glancing at the door handles. Hunter hesitated, then pulled one of the doors open. Sukri smiled at him, stepping through. He followed behind her, finding himself in a large room. It resembled a run-down cafeteria, with rows of what looked like picnic tables bolted to the floors. Tables covered with food lined the walls.

"Best part about being you," Sukri declared, gesturing at some empty tables, "…is you get any table you want." She glanced at him again. "So where we gonna sit, Crispy?"

"They're all the same to me," Hunter replied. She smirked.

"Ain't that the truth."

She led him toward one of the tables, gesturing for him to sit down. Then she left for the tables filled with food, making two plates and bringing them back, setting one in front of him. She sat opposite him then, eyeing him critically.

"Never seen you around before," she stated, digging in to her food.

"I came through the Gate," Hunter answered. Her eyebrows rose.

"No shit," she said, chewing absently. "Really?"

"Yup."

"You're an Original?" she asked. "Damn." Then she frowned at him. "You gonna eat or what?"

Hunter glanced down at his plate. There was meat there that looked like chicken, and something that resembled rice, but with much longer grains. He went for the meat, finding it bland but palatable. No seasoning at all, which wasn't exactly surprising.

"So what's the deal with them?" he inquired, gesturing at the double-doors in the distance. A few people had ventured inside, and were staring at both of them. Sukri gave them a sour look.

"Those assholes?" she asked. "They're afraid we're contagious."

"Contagious?"

"Yeah," she said. Then she flashed him a conspiratorial grin. "We are, you know."

"We're what?"

"Contagious," she answered.

70

Hunter heard footsteps approaching from behind. He twisted around, seeing a very large man approaching their table, a plate of food in each hand.

"Hey Sukri," the man greeted, sitting beside Sukri, facing Hunter. He glanced at Sukri, then at Hunter. "Who's this?"

"This is...what's your name again?" Sukri asked.

"Hunter."

"Right," she agreed. "Hunter, this is Gammon," she added, gesturing at the big man. He was easily over six feet tall, and built like a sumo wrestler. He had short blond hair and blue eyes, with slightly tanned skin. He smiled at Hunter, his clean-shaven cheeks dimpling.

"Nice to meet you," he greeted. "You're very dark," he added, staring at Hunter.

"Uh, thanks?"

"Where's Kris?" Gammon asked Sukri.

"Late as usual," Sukri answered, giving Gammon a wry smirk. "Probably slamming the brains outta that whore he brought home last night."

"Right," Gammon replied. "Forgot about her." He smiled. "She was nice."

"She's paid to be," Sukri retorted.

"Oh, I don't think he paid," Gammon countered. "He never pays. He doesn't have the money."

Just then, a second man approached their table. He was of average height, but broad-shouldered, with short dark hair and lightly tanned skin. He had a well-manicured beard, with a huge tattoo running from his right shoulder all the way down to his wrist. He grinned, sitting down at Sukri's other side and setting his plate of food on the table.

"God I'm starving," he declared, digging into his food.

"You just ate last night Kris," Gammon protested. Kris grinned impishly.

"Sure did."

"Kris," Sukri interjected, gesturing at Hunter. "This is Hunter." Kris turned to Hunter, then did a double take.

"Damn you're dark," he blurted out. Then he held up one hand. "Not that there's anything wrong with that."

"Jesus," Hunter grumbled. "Has *anyone* here ever seen a black guy before?" Kris paused, then shook his head...as did Gammon and Sukri.

"You're the darkest person I've ever seen," Gammon admitted. "But I wouldn't say you're black," he added. "More like a nice brown." He smiled. "Like toasted bread."

"Gee thanks."

"It looks cool," Kris opined. "I like it."

"So," Hunter said, taking another bite of his food. "What's wrong with all these people? And why are you guys sitting with me?"

"Oh, we're not sitting with you," Gammon countered, gesturing at Sukri. "We're sitting with her." He smiled. "*She's* sitting with you."

"We're together," Sukri explained to Hunter. "But not like that," she added hastily when Kris arched an eyebrow at her. "We work together."

"We're going to be Seekers," Gammon stated rather proudly. He shoveled food into his mouth then, chowing down with unfettered glee.

"It's not going to run away from you, you know," Kris stated, staring at Gammon with a mixture of awe and disgust. Gammon swallowed.

"I've never given it time to try," he replied with a grin.

"So what exactly are Seekers?" Hunter asked. Kris frowned at him.

"You don't know?"

"He's an Original," Sukri explained. Kris's eyes widened.

"Whoa, really?"

"Yeah," Hunter confirmed. Kris gave a low whistle.

"Damn man," he murmured. "An Original!"

"To answer your question," Sukri interjected, returning to the original subject, "...it's complicated. But suffice it to say it's the only way outta this dump," she added, gesturing around her.

"Damn right," Kris agreed. "The Outskirts are a dead end for people like us."

"What do you mean?"

"People that don't fit in," he answered. Then he gestured at Hunter. "Like you."

"Finish up guys," Sukri ordered, finishing the last of her meal. Gammon obeyed with remarkable speed, leaving Kris to struggle to finish his. By that point, Hunter was done. All three of them stood, while Hunter stayed seated. Kris arched an eyebrow at him. "You coming or what?"

"With you guys?"

"You wanna go with them instead?" she pressed, gesturing at the other people around them. The tables closest to them were empty, the other residents having given them plenty of room.

"Where we going?" Hunter inquired, standing up.

"To our place," Sukri answered. "Come on."

"I gotta take a piss," Hunter said, his bladder near to bursting now.

"That way," Sukri stated, pointing to a door at the other end of the room. He hurried to it, opening it to find a large room beyond, with a long row of holes in the floor.

"Classy," he muttered, stepping through the doorway. He did his business, then returned to the others. Sukri led the way, Gammon and Kris following behind, and Hunter taking up the rear. They left the community center, exiting the double doors and walking across the docks to a large apartment complex on the other side of the Outskirts. Hunter noticed a few men in chain-mail armor patrolling the area, one of them exiting an apartment, then going into another.

"What's with them?" Hunter asked, nodding at the guards.

"They're searching the Outskirts," Sukri answered. "Couple of nobles from Hightown went missing recently." She gave a sour look. "Of course this is the first place they'd look."

"What, they think someone here kidnapped them?"

"We're always the first to be blamed when anything goes wrong," Sukri explained. She reached a door in the large apartment complex, unlocking it and leading them inside. Hunter found himself in a large room – easily four times as big as his entire apartment. There were three bedrooms off the main room, but again, no kitchen or bathroom.

"This is our place," Sukri stated, gesturing at the room.

"Nice," Hunter murmured. "A lot nicer than mine."

"We split the rent," Sukri explained. She sat down on a large U-shaped couch in the center of the room, and Kris flopped down next to her. She shoved him away, and he moved to the opposite end of the couch. Sukri patted the center cushion. "Come on Hunter," she said. "Sit with us."

Hunter complied, sitting down between the two. Gammon sat down cross-legged on the floor, facing them.

"So what's your story?" Sukri asked Hunter. He gave a quick recap of his journey, starting with his mother's disappearance. All three listened to him, remaining silent until he was done. Then Gammon shook his head slowly.

"Wow," he breathed. "You really *are* an Original."

"Guess so," Hunter conceded. Then he sighed. "And now I have no idea where my mom is, or if she's even alive." He glanced at Sukri. "If she isn't here, where could she be?"

"Hell if I know," Sukri answered. "No one is allowed to leave the city but the nobles and the Seekers. And the military, of course."

"Wait, I can't just go out and find her?" Hunter pressed. Sukri shook her head.

"Sorry."

He lowered his gaze, staring at the floor. So even if Mom *was* still alive, there was no way for him to get to her. He was trapped.

"Never thought I'd live to see an Original," Kris piped in. "It's been what, half a century since the last one?" He grinned at Hunter. "Nobles must be shitting their pants right about now." Hunter snapped out of his morbid thoughts, glancing up at him.

"Why do you call us 'Originals?'"

"Because you're from the original world," Kris explained. "Like Tykus."

"Tykus?" Hunter asked. "That's the name of the city, isn't it?"

"And the guy who founded it," Kris added. "The city was named after him. He was an Original, like you…and a legend."

"Yeah," Gammon agreed. "Everyone here worships him."

"You mean they want to *be* him," Sukri added, her expression souring. "Which leaves people like us shit out of luck."

"Why's that?" Hunter asked.

"We got no money," she answered. "And no way to *make* money…not enough to leave this dump."

"Well, there is *one* way," Gammon corrected. They turned to him. "The try-outs tomorrow," he explained.

"Yeah," Sukri conceded, "…but even if we become Seekers, we're still not gonna be allowed in the Acropolis. And there's no guarantee we'll pass the test."

"You nervous, Sukri?" Kris teased. Sukri rolled her eyes at him. "Do I look like I'm nervous?"

"I am," Gammon admitted. They both turned to the big man.

"Why are *you* nervous?" Kris retorted. "You don't even want to be a Seeker."

74

"Yes I do," Gammon insisted. "And I might not make it," he added. "Even if I do, all of us might not," he continued, glancing at Sukri.

"Wait," Hunter interjected. "Make what?"

"The Seeker try-outs," Kris explained. "The Seekers are having their annual try-outs for new recruits tomorrow. We're all going now that we're old enough."

"So what exactly are Seekers again?" Hunter asked.

"They're friggin' awesome is what they are," Kris replied with a grin. "They're basically bad-ass bounty hunters." He winked. "And they get all the pussy."

"Ignore him," Sukri grumbled. "Seekers mostly go out and find artifacts for the kingdom," she explained. Hunter frowned.

"Wait, they get to go out of the city?" he asked, feeling a glimmer of hope. "I thought you said…"

"No one can go out but nobles and Seekers," she interjected. "Seekers can go outside whenever they want."

Hunter sat up straighter.

"So they're having tryouts for people who want to be Seekers tomorrow?"

"Yup," Gammon confirmed.

"It pays really well if you're good," Kris added. Sukri nodded.

"And the best part is," she said, "…you get to spend some quality time with the artifacts before you drop them off."

"Okay," Hunter stated. If becoming a Seeker was the only way he'd be allowed to go find Mom, then that's what he'd have to do. "So…what do you do at these try-outs?"

"Well," Gammon answered, "…first they test your will. That's where most people fail." He crossed his arms over his huge chest. "Not us, though."

"That's for damn sure," Sukri agreed. "That's why we can hang out together and still be our awesome selves." Then she turned to Hunter. "After they test your will, they'll bring you into the guild compound and finish the testing there."

"Then they have the Trials," Kris piped in. "No one knows what they are," he added. He gave a sour look. "But anything is worth getting out of the shitty jobs we have now."

"Ain't that the truth," Sukri agreed.

"What jobs do you have now?" Hunter inquired.

"We're all in waste management," Sukri answered. "It's exactly like Kris said…shitty."

"Ekrin said he'd find a job for me today," Hunter offered. "The guy who met with me when I first got here."

"Yeah, good luck with that," Sukri muttered. "Guarantee they put you in waste management too. Everyone like us works there."

"Awesome," Hunter grumbled. "My life just keeps getting better and better."

"Hey," Gammon interjected, putting a meaty hand on Hunter's shoulder. "Why don't you come with us?"

"Where?"

"To the Seeker try-outs," Gammon clarified. Sukri nodded.

"Not a bad idea," she agreed. "It's not like you have any other prospects. You up for it?"

"Yeah, I'll do it," he replied. After all, if Seekers could leave the city at will, that meant he could go after Mom. "What do I have to do?"

"Just come with us," Gammon answered.

"The try-outs are tomorrow," Sukri said. "Why don't you meet us for breakfast at sunrise, and we'll all go together from there?"

"Sounds good."

"Well guys," Gammon stated suddenly, standing up. "We'd better get to work."

"Oh, right," Kris said, glancing at something on the windowsill. It looked like a sundial. "Shit, we're gonna be late."

"All right," Sukri declared, standing up from the couch. "Nice meeting you Hunter," she added. "But we're kicking you out. See you tomorrow?"

"Sure thing," he agreed. "And…thanks, Sukri." She grinned at him.

"Don't mention it Crispy."

They all said their goodbyes, Gammon giving Hunter a hearty – and bone-crushing – handshake, and then they pushed Hunter out of their apartment, hurriedly making their way to wherever it was they had to go. Hunter watched them leave, then looked around. The docks were mostly empty, only a handful of people walking to and fro. Anyone who happened to make eye contact with him gave him a nasty look, hurrying away.

Hunter sighed, walking across the docks, eventually finding his way back to his apartment. He would've liked to explore the rest of the city – and not just hang out in the Outskirts – but he had a feeling no one there would be particularly happy to see him. Thank god that Sukri and her friends had taken him in, otherwise he probably wouldn't have had the guts to get breakfast at the community center.

He climbed the stairs to his door, unlocking it and walking in to flop unceremoniously on his bed. According to Ekrin, that girl – Trixie – was supposed to stop by later on today. With nothing else to do, he might as well just sleep. Luckily, sleep was something he was extremely good at…like his mother. Dad said he got most of his personality from Mom, for which Hunter was grateful. Hunter vaguely remembered Dad before Mom left them. Before he'd become an alcoholic. Hunter felt an all-too familiar bitterness rise within him, and shoved it down, remembering what Dad had said.

The only reason I didn't go after her was because of you.

He tried to imagine what that would feel like, to have to decide between your wife and your son. To have to make the decision in a matter of seconds. It was an impossible choice; Mom would never have forgiven Dad if he'd gone after her, leaving Hunter behind. And Hunter had attacked him for leaving Mom behind.

Dad had chosen to stay for Hunter, and that choice had destroyed the man.

He felt a lump rise in his throat, and he swallowed it down, wiping moisture from his eyes.

I'm sorry, Dad.

He remembered all the times he'd lambasted Dad for drinking, insulting the man. The contempt he'd felt for so many years. And now he'd never have the opportunity to apologize, to tell Dad that he forgave him. To thank him for everything he'd done. Everything he'd sacrificed. Not only that, but now Dad would be truly alone, wondering if Hunter was still alive.

Hunter thought of the gun he'd found in Dad's glove compartment. Of the single bullet left in the chamber.

I'm sorry.

Hunter sighed, wiping his eyes again, then rolling onto his side. Maybe Dad would realize where he'd gone. Maybe he'd come after Hunter. Hunter had left Dad's car by Smuggler's Cave, after all. Unless the government tried to cover it all up, Dad would *have* to know what had happened.

Hunter closed his eyes, curling up into the fetal position. His guts squirmed, fear gnawing at him. He took a deep breath in, then let it out, waiting for sleep to come. Waiting for it to take him away from his pain.

And, after a long, long time, it did.

CHAPTER 6

There was a knock on the door.

Hunter groaned, lifting his head off his pillow and peering at the door to his apartment. He must've slept for quite a while; the room was darker than before, and he was starving. He heard a second knock, and sighed, sitting up. His back was aching from the overly-firm mattress, and the rest of him was sore, probably from running away from those monsters – the Ironclad – yesterday.

"Coming," he called out.

He got up and walked to the door, opening it. It was Trixie; she smiled at him.

"Good evening," she greeted. "Can I come in?"

"Uh yeah, sure," Hunter mumbled. He stepped to the side, and she walked in. She was wearing a tight black shirt, low cut and sleeveless as before, and tight black shorts. Her hair was pulled back in a long ponytail.

"Did you take a nap?" she inquired. Hunter nodded, then yawned. "That's good," she stated, stifling a yawn of her own. "Are you hungry?" she pressed. "I can take you to the community center to get dinner."

"Yeah, that'd be great," he answered. His stomach growled in agreement.

Trixie led the way, going downstairs. Hunter followed, almost forgetting to lock his door. They walked out of the apartment building and across the docks. It was night-time, the three moons shining bright silver in the starry sky. Hunter looked around, noticing that there was nobody around. It was like a ghost town.

"Where is everybody?" he asked.

"At church," Trixie answered. "Most people cleanse at night."

"What about you?" he pressed.

"Oh, they don't want *me* there," Trixie replied. "I worship at the house with the rest of the girls."

"So uh, what does everyone worship?" he inquired. Not that he was particularly interested. He'd never been religious himself, after all. His dad hadn't brought him to church growing up, and his mother had been a bit of a pagan.

"Tykus," Trixie answered.

"The guy who founded the city?"

"Yes," she confirmed. "Tykus was a legend, the greatest one of all. He created our people, and His will lives on in the city. His will is powerful in the churches."

"Okay."

"If we expose ourselves to His soul, He will grace us with His will, and cleanse us of impurities," she explained.

"Nice," Hunter mumbled. Sounded suspiciously like a cult. He hesitated. "We're not going there, are we?"

"No."

They headed across the docks toward the community center, eventually reaching its double-doors. This time there was no line to get in, and Trixie opened one of the doors for Hunter, gesturing for him to go in. He did so, and she followed after him. As before, there was food on the tables lining the perimeter of the room. Hunter filled his plate, then sat down, Trixie sitting opposite him. He noticed a few people eating at other tables, all of whom turned to give him dirty looks.

"Why is everyone looking at me like that?" he asked, feeling terribly self-conscious.

"You're dark," Trixie answered matter-of-factly. "You make them nervous, that's all." He raised an eyebrow at her.

"Do I make you nervous?" he asked. She shook her head.

"Oh no," she replied. "I like you. Besides, they have me cleanse twice a day. I'm very lucky."

"Huh," Hunter mumbled. "Speaking of cleansing, how can I take a shower?"

"A shower?" she asked, giving him a confused look.

"Uh, to bathe," he added. "You know, get clean."

"Oh, you mean the bathhouses," she realized. "Yes, there are lots of them in town. There's one nearby. Do you want to do that after meeting with Ekrin?"

"Sure," Hunter replied. He dug into his food then. It was bland, as before. He finished quickly, and Trixie hurried to keep up with him. She stood then, guiding Hunter out of the community center and across the docks. They left the Outskirts altogether, reaching the streets of Lowtown beyond, and climbed the wooden stairs leading up to the church plaza. As expected, throngs of people were surrounding the church, a long line waiting at the front doors. Trixie led Hunter past the church and down a few winding roads, and eventually he saw the huge wall surrounding the city ahead. The wall was on their left…which meant Trixie was taking him back toward the gate. He glanced at her as they walked, admiring her slender body. She did have a cute butt, and small, perky breasts. Her clothing was almost skintight, leaving very little to the imagination. He found his imagination doing quite a bit with what little it'd been given.

Hunter realized she was staring at him, and he jerked his gaze up, forcing himself to look her in the eyes.

"So uh, this is Lowtown?" he asked, glad that his skin was dark enough to hide his blushing cheeks.

"Oh yes," she agreed with a smile. "There's lots to do," she added. "But we can't do it now. I have to take you to Ekrin first."

After a few minutes, they reached the wide corridor leading to the inner gate, which was to their left. To their right, he saw various shops and other rather run-down buildings built into the rising slope of the hill. They were still better-kept than the Outskirts, however. There were only a few pedestrians, who reacted to him by crossing to the other side of the street hurriedly.

She led him to the wide corridor leading to the interior gate. This opened shortly after Trixie spoke to a guard, and they walked into the tunnel beyond. Trixie led him back upstairs to the room Ekrin had met him in yesterday. She opened the door, stepping into the room beyond, and Hunter followed, finding Ekrin sitting in his usual spot at the far end of the table. Hunter sat down opposite him, while Trixie remained standing.

"Good evening Hunter," Ekrin greeted. "I trust you slept well?"

"I did," Hunter replied.

"Good," Ekrin stated. "Now, as we discussed yesterday, I'd like to pick your brain about your world, and the…technology you possessed."

"Alright."

Ekrin pulled out the revolver Hunter had given him, and began asking all sorts of questions about it. How it worked, what it was made of specifically…down to the exact materials. And the components to gunpowder, and so on and so forth. Of course, Hunter had no idea about most of the specifics, only able to provide a general understanding…a fact that clearly didn't satisfy Ekrin.

"Thank you for the information," he stated. "Do you have any questions for me?"

"Yes, actually," Hunter replied. "Why does everyone here hate me?" Ekrin grimaced, leaning forward and propping his elbows on the table.

"That's complicated," he admitted. "Where to start?" He paused, thinking it over. "Did Trixie tell you about our founder, Tykus?"

"A little."

"Yes, well, He was a legend," Ekrin explained. "The greatest man in our history. His will was unparalleled, so powerful that He united our people, creating the most powerful kingdom in the world. Every person you've met here has been shaped by His will."

"By going to church," Hunter recalled.

"Not just that," Ekrin countered. "You see, Tykus's will is everywhere. In the churches, in the streets. In every corner of the kingdom. It *is* concentrated in the churches," he added. "And that is why people worship there, so that they can feel Tykus's will, and have it cleanse them of impurities."

"What impurities?" Hunter inquired. "Impure thoughts?" He glanced at Trixie, recalling the impure thoughts he'd had earlier.

"Not just thoughts," Ekrin corrected. He paused, leaning forward and propping his elbows on the table, as if choosing his words. "You see, Tykus was the pinnacle of human achievement, the greatest man who has ever lived. We give ourselves to His will so that we can continue His legacy, and so that His will lives through us." He smiled. "We keep Tykus alive, and Tykus makes us who we are, along with the other great men of the past."

"Okay," Hunter replied. "But what does that have to do with my question?"

81

"Well," Ekrin answered, "...our people are...sensitive to anything that might take them astray from Tykus's will." He gestured at Hunter. "You represent an...undesirable alternative to our peoples' identity."

"Because I'm black," Hunter stated bluntly.

"Because you're brown," Ekrin corrected. "Yes, that's part of it. Appearance is part of one's identity, after all," he added. "And shared traits symbolize the identity of a nation, of a people brought together by shared ancestry. A nation is a family of sorts...and shared traits – personality, appearance, customs, beliefs – are what bind a family together." He paused for a moment. "Tykus is the father of our nation, if you will. We want His essence to continue through our bloodlines. You, unfortunately, represent an undesirable alternative to that."

"So it's a religious thing."

"In part, yes."

"Oh good," Hunter replied. "That makes it okay then."

"In any case," Ekrin stated, ignoring Hunter's sarcasm, "...I recommend you keep to yourself for the time being. Stay in the Outskirts as much as possible. There are some people like you there, after all, and you'll be safer among them."

"People like me?"

"Outsiders," Ekrin clarified. He stood then. "Thank you again for the information. I'll have Trixie escort you out...and I'll have a job for you within the next few days."

"Will it pay good enough to get an apartment that doesn't suck?" Hunter joked. Ekrin raised an eyebrow.

"Yes," he replied. "With time. But I suggest you appreciate the apartment you have," he added. "Our government does not typically give handouts to people. They have to earn their possessions. Be thankful that we took pity on you and offered to clothe and shelter you at all."

Hunter lowered his gaze, realizing he'd been an ass. Ekrin was right...they owed him nothing.

"Sorry," he mumbled. "I'm just...having a hard time getting used to everything." He glanced up at Ekrin. "Thank you," he added. "I appreciate everything you've done for me."

"You're welcome," Ekrin replied. He nodded at Trixie. "Take Hunter back to his apartment as we discussed." He gave Hunter one more look, then walked past them, opening the door and stepping out of the room. The door closed behind him, and Hunter stared at it, then glanced at Trixie.

"So what now?"

"We can go back into the city if you want," she offered. "I can show you around."

"Sure," he agreed. It wasn't like he had anything else to do. Besides, he actually didn't mind spending time with her. Trixie walked to the door, holding it open for him. He got up from his seat, following her out of the door and into the hallway. She led him back into the city, passing through Lowtown once again. As they walked, more passers-by were switching to the other side of the street when they saw him...or straight up turning around and going the other way. He shook his head.

"I still don't get it," he admitted.

"What?"

"Why no one wants to be near me," Hunter clarified. Even after Ekrin's explanation, it still didn't make much sense. Despite what he'd experienced at school – the taunting from guys like Tyler, and the occasional racial slur – he'd never really been treated like *this* before.

"You're brown," she replied. "They just don't want to turn brown too."

"What?" Hunter blurted out, stopping in his tracks. Trixie stopped as well, facing him. "That's the silliest thing I've ever heard. Being black...uh, brown...isn't contagious, you know."

"It isn't?" Trixie asked, clearly taken aback. Hunter stared at her.

"No, it isn't."

"Oh," she mumbled, frowning prettily. She glanced up at him. "I didn't know that." She grimaced. "I'm sorry," she added. "I've never met someone like you before."

"You seriously thought it was contagious?" Hunter pressed. Trixie nodded. "Then why aren't you freaking out like everyone else?"

"I think it looks nice," she confessed, putting a warm hand on his bare arm. Her touch sent a shiver through him. She had an effect on him, there was no doubt about it. Her touch – and even her very presence – was magical. He suddenly forgot why he'd been upset.

"Where are we going now?" he asked.

"I can show you the bathhouses," she offered. Hunter considered this; he'd have to bathe at some point. He hadn't worn

83

deodorant since yesterday, after all. He pulled his arms in close to his sides, not wanting her to smell his funk.

"All right."

After a few minutes, they arrived at a large bakery, the smell of freshly baked goods hanging in the air. Attached to this was another building…one with no windows.

"That's a bathhouse," she explained.

"Attached to a bakery?" Hunter asked. "Interesting combo."

"They use the heat from the ovens to warm the water," Trixie explained. "Come on," she added, pulling him through the front door of the place. Inside, there was a woman sitting behind a desk, a long hallway behind her with doors on either side. The woman glanced up at them as they came in, her eyes settling on Hunter. Her expression soured.

"Use the back room," she snapped. "Don't take long." She reached into something in the desk, then tossed a keyring with a single key at Trixie, who caught it deftly. Trixie thanked the woman politely, then led Hunter to the back of the building. She stopped before a door there, using the key – wooden, Hunter noted – to unlock it. They stepped through into a room with a large wooden tub filled with water. The room was quite warm, like a sauna.

Trixie closed the door, and immediately began to pull her shirt off.

"Whoa," Hunter blurted out, turning away quickly. "What are you doing?"

"Taking a bath," she replied.

"I thought *I* was taking a bath," he protested.

"Can I take a bath too?"

"No!" he answered.

"Oh, okay," he heard her reply.

He hesitated, then turned around, glancing at her. To his relief – and at the same time, disappointment – she'd put her shirt back on. He immediately regretted his decision.

"You can bathe then," she prompted.

He nodded, standing there for a long moment. She just stood there, staring back at him.

"Uh, can I have some privacy?" he asked. She blinked.

"Why?"

"I'm…" he began, then stopped. He shrugged. "I just want privacy."

"Are you shy?" she pressed.

"No," he retorted, a little too defensively.

"I can help you bathe," she offered. "That way I can clean your back." Hunter was about to protest when she interrupted him. "I'll turn around while you undress," she decided. "You can get in the water, and then I'll face you." Hunter considered this, then nodded grudgingly.

"Fine."

She did just that, turning away from him, and he hurriedly undressed, stepping into the water. It was as hot as a hot tub back home, and he hesitated before lowering himself all the way in, glancing furtively at Trixie to make sure she was still facing away from him. True to her word, she was. He lowered himself belly-deep into the water, finding an underwater bench to sit on. Then he cleared his throat.

"Okay."

Trixie turned around, smiling at him, then walking up to the side of the wooden tub. She grabbed a small washcloth, soaping it up and pressing it on his back, scrubbing firmly.

"You don't have to..." he began, but she shushed him. His mouth snapped shut, and she continued, scrubbing his back in small circles, going from one shoulder to the other. Then she shifted her weight, and began scrubbing his chest. He tolerated this with some difficulty, feeling extraordinarily awkward. He was, as Tyler back in school had so kindly reminded him, still a virgin, and had never had a girl – much less a girl like Trixie – tend to him in such a way.

"Relax," she murmured.

He tried to do so, resting back against the tub wall. She continued, scrubbing his chest and arms, then bringing the washcloth down to his upper belly. He stiffened, then forced himself to relax again, closing his eyes. She continued to scrub him, traveling downward again, now at his mid-belly. He felt his body reacting, his member rising rapidly in response. A very real problem, given that at full height, it would most definitely block the path of her washcloth. He jerked away from her, clearing his throat.

"Uh, thanks," he mumbled. She said nothing, moving so she was directly behind him now, draping one arm over his chest, holding him tight. Her other hand, clutching the washcloth, descended to his belly, and she slid it gently across his skin.

"Relax," she murmured, moving the washcloth in slow circles on his belly. He stiffened, and despite his terror he felt himself stiffening below as well. He tried to move away, but Trixie held him in place gently but firmly with her other arm, sliding the washcloth downward…scandalously low. It passed to the right of his member, grazing it.

"Uh…" he began, but Trixie ignored him, sliding the washcloth down his right thigh, then bringing it back up. It grazed him again, and he stiffened in response. She brought her lips to his ear, brushing against it.

"You want to go to your apartment?" she murmured. He swallowed in a dry throat, feeling the heat from her breath, and of her body pressed against his upper back. Her hand slid up to his belly, then back down, grazing him again on the left, making his breath catch in his throat.

"Uh, sure," he mumbled. She smiled, dropping the washcloth, then placing her hand on his belly, a fraction of an inch from obscenity.

"You want me to stay with you tonight?" she inquired. "Or should I come in the morning?"

Hunter swallowed again, feeling the heat from her hand on his belly, his heart pounding in his chest.

"Both," he replied.

CHAPTER 7

Dominus eased himself into his oversized chair, sitting at his desk in his study. He stared at the long piece of parchment before him, a detailed legal document penned in perfect handwriting. He leaned forward, dipping his quill pen in an inkwell, then bringing its tip to the end of the document, where his signature was to go. Pressing the tip on the page, he watched as a small circle of ink spread from it.

He hesitated.

There was a sudden burning, tingling pain in his right foot, and Dominus set the quill down, pushing himself back from the desk and slipping his right foot out of its boot. Pulling the sock off, he stared at his foot.

Or rather, what remained of it.

The great toe was gone, a blackened nub all that remained. Bone protruded from the nub, a bit of white amongst the black. His foot was mottled, a large ulcer on the right side of his ankle, over the bony prominence there. It was dying, his foot. A trickle of his lifeblood still flowed to it, barely enough to sustain its vitality. He spotted a few black spots on his pinky toe, and grimaced. Soon it would be dead. Then his foot would blacken, and it too would die.

And so too, in time, would he.

Dominus heard a knock on the door to his study, and looked up, slipping his sock back on and stuffing his foot into his boot again. He sighed, grabbing his quill pen and setting it in a small jar of water, rinsing the tip. Then he dipped his fingers into a bowl of sand, sprinkling it lightly over the page.

"Come in," he called out at last.

The door opened, and Farkus stepped in.

"Your Grace," the servant greeted, bowing before him.

"What is it Farkus?"

"The shipment that you arranged for," Farkus replied. "It's been…intercepted, your Grace."

Dominus leaned forward, staring at Farkus incredulously.

"Intercepted?"

"By the Ironclad," Farkus clarified. "They attacked the carriage and the guards accompanying it. One of the survivors just returned to the castle Wexford, your Grace."

Dominus grimaced, leaning back in his chair. He resisted the urge to snap at the man, rubbing his face with his hands, then taking a deep breath in and letting it out. That shipment had cost him a fortune…and its loss was going to cost him far more.

"Anything else?" he inquired, his voice deceptively calm. Farkus nodded.

"Your nephew, the good sir Axio, is here as you requested."

"Send him in," Dominus ordered.

"At once, your Grace."

Farkus bowed again, turning about sharply and leaving the study. Dominus watched him go, waiting until the door to his study was closed. Then he slammed his fist on his desk, the sand on the page before him jumping.

Damn it!

He took another deep breath in, then folded his hands before him. Moments later, Axio strode into his study, stopping before the desk and bowing sharply. Dominus regarded Axio silently for a moment, using the time to collect himself. The boy had bathed and had lunch after their first meeting, and had dressed himself in another uniform…also one that Dominus had given as a gift previously. The boy was thoughtful indeed.

"I trust you found your room and amenities acceptable?" Dominus inquired. Axio nodded.

"Yes your Grace."

"Axio," he stated. "I want you to promise me something."

"If I can promise it, I will," Axio replied. Dominus gave a slight smile.

"I want you to be utterly honest with me from now on," he requested. "Exercise proper decorum, of course, but do not hold back your thoughts on my account…or your questions." Axio considered this for a moment, then nodded.

"I will do my best, your Grace."

"I suspect you will," Dominus agreed. He gestured at a chair to one side of the study. "Pull up a chair and sit." Axio obeyed, sitting opposite Dominus. "You of course recall our conversation about my bees."

"I do."

"As we discussed, the Acropolis – and Tykus as a whole – employs a similar caste system. Each caste plays a vital role in our government, from the lowliest peasant to the king himself. Each is necessary to preserve the integrity of the kingdom, just as each type of bee is integral to the health of the hive."

"Yes, your Grace," Axio replied. Then he hesitated.

"Yes?"

"I do not see how the peasants are vital to the kingdom," he confessed. "They are crude and intellectually inferior, and impure."

"That is why they are peasants," Dominus stated. "But I daresay they are as important to our kingdom as the king himself."

Axio stared at Dominus, clearly unconvinced.

"I cannot believe that," he stated bluntly. Dominus smirked.

"Very good," he replied. "Your honesty is appreciated." He sighed then, turning to gaze out of the window of his study, at his gardens beyond. "Peasants," he declared, "…built this castle. They built Tykus, and maintain it. Yes, engineers and architects designed these structures, and left to themselves the peasants would not have had the knowledge or wisdom to do such things. But while the architects are the brains, the peasants are the hands that, obeying the will of their masters, bring everything you see around you into being."

"Granted."

"Labor is vital to a government," Dominus explained. "Ideas without execution are worthless."

"Yes your Grace," Axio murmured. Then he hesitated again. "But the peasants are ignorant," he pressed. "Uneducated. They know next to nothing of philosophy or ethics, or the sciences."

"True."

"They have little intellectual curiosity," Axio continued. "They hold to their primitive beliefs, scoffing at facts and reason."

"To a large extent, yes," Dominus agreed. "Thankfully so."

Axio frowned.

"What?"

"When your parents raised you," Dominus stated, "...did they instill a respect for authority?"

"Of course."

"Why?"

"Because those in authority are wiser than I," Axio answered.

Dominus raised an eyebrow.

"Do not confuse authority with wisdom," he countered. "One does not necessarily imply the other." He leaned back in his chair. "Tell me...do peasants obey their Lord just as you obey your parents?"

"I suppose so, your Grace."

"They are subservient by choice?" Dominus pressed. Axio considered this.

"The Lords have soldiers," he countered. "The peasants *have* no choice."

"Mmm," Dominus murmured. He glanced out of the window again. "So you would think...and so we groom the peasants to believe." He remained silent for some time, and to his credit, Axio did not succumb to the urge to fill this void. A characteristic of lesser men, to find silence unbearable.

At long last, Dominus returned his gaze to Axio.

"The only man without a choice," he said at last, "...is a dead man." He smiled grimly. "Remember that Axio."

"I don't believe I understand," Axio confessed. Dominus sighed.

"You will."

There was a knock at the door.

"Come in," Dominus ordered. Farkus opened the study door, stepping inside and bowing deeply. "What is it?"

"A courier from the Acropolis, your Grace," Farkus replied, giving a knowing look.

"Send him in."

Farkus disappeared, and moments later he returned accompanied by another man. Tall, with long blond hair and blue eyes, his features nearly as perfect as Axio's. Clearly the man was from the Acropolis...and a courier for someone very important. He wore the white and gold uniform of a noble, lightweight fabric that allowed for quick movements. Sewn into the fabric were innumerable objects that, to an untrained eye, looked like beads. They were, in actuality, teeth.

"My Duke," the courier stated, bowing before Dominus. "Sir," he added, bowing less deeply at Axio. "I bring terrible news."

"Be quick and concise in telling it," Dominus commanded. "I will not suffer dramatics."

"The king is dead," the courier declared.

Dominus's eyebrows rose, and he leaned forward in his chair. That *was* unfortunate news…but not unexpected.

"When did he die?" he inquired.

"This morning."

"Of natural causes?" Dominus pressed.

"Yes your Grace."

Dominus sighed, leaning back in his chair and glancing at Axio. The boy was staring at him, clearly shocked. And suddenly very uneasy. He couldn't blame the boy. The king had never sired an heir, after all. In a cruel twist of fate, he'd only sired girls. Which meant that the highest-ranking aristocrat in the kingdom was in line for the throne.

Which was, of course, Dominus.

"Very well," Dominus stated, turning to Farkus. "Prepare my chariot, and triple my usual entourage."

"Yes your Grace," Farkus replied, bowing and then exiting the room immediately. Dominus turned to Axio.

"You will accompany me to the Acropolis," he notified the boy. Axio bowed his head.

"As you command, my liege."

"Leave me now," he ordered. Axio obeyed, standing up and bowing one more time before leaving the study, and the courier followed behind him. Dominus watched them leave, then sighed, staring out of the window, at the familiar rows of wooden boxes resting on their pallets in his garden. He'd put the hives there purposefully, always visible from his study. A reminder of his grand role.

The king is dead.

He looked down at the parchment on his desk, at the sand strewn across it. He paused, then picked it up, sand streaming off the paper. He blew on it, getting the residual sand off, then set the page down. He picked up the quill pen, dabbing the tip on a cloth, then dipping its tip in the inkwell. Taking a deep breath in, he placed the tip on the parchment, signing his name in large, clear strokes.

91

Time to crown a king.

* * *

Hunter opened his eyes, rubbing the crust from them. Faint light streamed through the lone window by his bed, bathing the floor in a soft glow. He rolled onto his side…or at least he tried to. An arm was draped over his chest, a warm body pressed against his.

Trixie.

She stirred slightly with his movement, but didn't waken. Her long hair, freed from its ponytail, fell over her lovely face, a few golden strands cascading over her bare breasts. Her pale skin had a slight tan from spending so much time in the sun with him yesterday. He stared at her, taking in her beauty, savoring it. Savoring *her*, with his eyes now, just as he had with his body the night before…and early into the morning.

It'd been, in a word, incredible.

He'd had no idea what to do at first, of course, bumbling around like an idiot. Thankfully she'd had no problem taking control, showing him how things worked in the most pleasant of ways. After a few rounds, she'd let him take over, encouraging him rather vocally. He felt a stirring in his groin as he played the night over in his head, marveling that, despite the fact that he'd had her so many times so recently, he still wanted more. He'd never felt such desire before, such unbridled lust. She made him insatiable…and apparently he had the same effect on her. They'd gone at it again and again, until they'd collapsed from sheer exhaustion.

And staring at her, feeling her soft body against his, he wanted nothing more than to do it again.

He glanced at the window, at the pale light streaming through, struck with the sudden urge to wake her. He should let her sleep, he knew. They'd been up all night, and it was barely sunrise, after all.

Sunrise!

He sat up abruptly, Trixie's arm falling from his chest. He'd almost forgotten about the Seeker tryouts!

He scrambled out of bed, finding his new clothes strewn across the floor, along with Trixie's. He pulled on his shirt, then heard the bed creak behind him. He turned around, seeing Trixie lying there on the bed on her side, gazing up at him.

92

"Morning," she murmured, her gaze dropping to his chest, then to his naked groin. He was still at full mast, of course. Her eyes lingered there, a smirk on her lips. "A good morning," she added.

"Morning," Hunter replied.

"Where are you going?" she inquired, meeting his gaze once more.

"I have to go to a meeting," he explained. "Sorry I woke you."

"No problem," she reassured. She held out one hand then, gesturing for him to come closer. He obeyed, walking up to the edge of the bed. She reached for his groin, cupping him in her hand gently. Then she sat up, still holding him, and leaned forward to kiss his belly, her chin brushing up against his member. She gazed up at him. "Enjoy yourself last night?"

"Thought I made it pretty obvious," he said with a grin. She smirked.

"Sure did," she murmured. She got out of bed then, standing before him, nude and utterly unconcerned about it. She stared into his eyes, her hand cupping him. From here, he could see slight flecks of green in her blue eyes...something he'd never noticed before. It made her all the more beautiful. "When will you be back?"

"I'm not sure," he admitted. "Should be by tonight."

"Good," she replied. She put a hand on his chest. "Don't tire yourself out today," she added. "You're going to need all the energy you can get tonight."

"That a promise?"

"Mmm hmm," she murmured. "Go on," she added, pushing him back playfully. "Put on your clothes." She smiled, releasing his...lower parts. "I'll watch."

He obeyed, getting dressed, then getting a kiss from Trixie. Then he left, bounding down the stairs and rushing across the docks. He made it to the community center in less than a minute, cutting through the line there easily. All it took was walking right through...everyone backed away from him, of course. He ignored them, passing through the double doors and into the community center. Looking around the large room, he spotted Gammon's huge form at one of the tables. He felt immediate relief...he'd made it on time.

"Hey guys," he called out, walking up to their table. "Sorry I'm late."

"Oh hey," Kris greeted. "Thought I'd been stood up."

"Sure as hell wouldn't be the first time," Sukri piped in.

"I'm glad you came," Gammon said, smiling at Hunter. "You should hurry up and get something to eat."

Hunter nodded, doing just that. He grabbed the usual fare, sitting down beside Sukri. She eyed him critically.

"You look like shit," she observed. "Get any sleep?"

"Not really," he admitted, holding back a grin. He didn't really care to brag about losing his virginity. It would cheapen what had happened, reducing Trixie to a conquest. She was anything but.

"Aww Hunter," she said with a smirk. "You nervous about the tryouts?"

"Nah," he replied. "Noisy neighbors."

"Did you hear a woman moaning?" Kris asked with a grin. "If so, I apologize."

"Yeah," Sukri agreed. "He sounds like a girl when he cries himself to sleep."

"Now that's just cold," Kris muttered. Sukri grinned at him.

"We'd better get going guys," Gammon interjected, slurping up the last bits of food from his second plate, then standing up, towering over the table. Everyone else finished, then stood, walking out of the community center. The line of people still outside parted before them, treating them all like lepers, as usual. Sukri led the way out of the Outskirts and into Lowtown, weaving through the streets with confident ease.

"So where are we going again?" Hunter asked her.

"The Guild of Seekers," she answered. "It's in Lowtown," she added. "The only major guild in Lowtown."

"So Seekers find stuff and bring it back to the city?" Hunter pressed. Sukri shook her head.

"Not that simple, sweetheart," she replied. "You know anything about your will?"

"Are these tryouts so dangerous I'd need one?" Hunter quipped. Sukri rolled her eyes.

"I mean your willpower," she clarified. "Has anyone told you about it?"

"Nope."

"Well shit," she grumbled. She glanced at Kris, who shrugged. "We don't have time to go over it," she told Hunter. "Guess you'll have to learn as you go."

With that, the street opened up to a large courtyard, nearly as big as the plaza by the church. A huge, gothic-appearing building stood in the center. Seven stories tall at its highest, it was made of blackened wood, but was in far better condition than any of the other buildings in Lowtown. A five-foot-wide moat surrounded the large building, with a single wooden bridge spanning it, leading to a set of double-doors. Three long lines of people stood in the courtyard, a dozen or so feet before the moat.

"And there we are," Kris declared, gesturing at the building. "The Guild of Seekers!" He stopped staring at the building. "I wonder what it looks like on the inside."

"I'll let you know," Sukri replied with a smirk. She kept going, leaving Kris behind. He hurried behind them, and they eventually reached the end of one of the lines.

"Big turnout this year," Gammon noted. Sukri clapped him on the back.

"Most of these jokers will be turned away before long," she reassured. "It happens every year. Look," she added, gesturing at the front of the line. Hunter did so, spotting a tall, middle-aged man in a gold and black uniform facing the front of the line. He said something to the first person in line – a middle-aged man – and then shook his head. The man exited the line, walking away from the guild.

"What are their criteria?" Hunter asked, suddenly nervous. If he was turned away…

"Nobody knows for sure," Sukri admitted. "Best I can tell, they don't take anyone too young or too old. And they don't care for the pure."

"The pure?"

"Blond hair, blue eyes," she explained. "Like Tykus."

"Thank god for that," Hunter replied with a grin. "We don't have anything to worry about then."

Sure enough, Sukri was right. The lines moved surprisingly quickly, most being turned away by the men in the black and gold uniforms. Perhaps one out of every five were allowed to stand to the side, clearly passing whatever test the uniformed men were conducting. It wasn't long before Sukri – the first in line of their group – was next to be tested. Gammon put a hand on her shoulder, and she smiled up at the big guy, stepping forward to stand before one of the testers. The man looked Sukri up and down, then had her stand within a foot of him, putting a hand on her shoulder. She tolerated this without question. After nearly a minute, the man nodded, and gestured for Sukri to step to the side.

"Way to go, Sukri!" Kris whispered at her as she left. She winked at him, then stood to the side.

Gammon was next. The huge man stepped forward, towering over the tester. Gammon stared down at the man expressionlessly, his arms crossed in front of his chest. The tester observed him much as he'd done for Sukri, then again put a hand on the man's arm, holding it for nearly a minute.

"Come on…" Kris whispered, grabbing Hunter's arm.

The tester nodded once, then gestured for Gammon to step to the side. Kris grinned, giving Hunter's arm a squeeze. Then he let go, stepping forward when the tester gestured for him to approach. They went through the same process, but this time the tester held Kris's shoulder for much longer. Finally, he nodded, and Kris stepped to the side.

The man in the gold and black uniform turned to Hunter, staring at him expressionlessly for a long moment. The guy was middle-aged, with a salt-and pepper goatee and light brown hair, and a long scar ran down his left cheek.

He gestured for Hunter to approach.

Hunter took a couple steps forward, stopping when the man held up his hand. The man stared at Hunter for a long moment – much longer than he had for the others – then gestured for Hunter to step forward. He did so, and the man reached for Hunter's shoulder, grasping it tightly and closing his eyes.

They stood there, motionless.

Hunter stared at the man, noticing a large silver medallion resting on his chest, a metallic triangle with symbols etched into its surface. He stood there, feeling a bit uncomfortable. Not just nervous, though. Something didn't feel right…something was *off*. He frowned, his curiosity piqued. He studied the sensation, trying to figure out what it was. Over a minute passed, and still the man held onto his shoulder.

Something's wrong, he thought.

Suddenly the man let go of his shoulder, staring at Hunter for a long moment. Then he nodded, gesturing for Hunter to join the others.

"All right!" Kris exclaimed, slapping Hunter on the shoulder as he joined them. Sukri flashed him a grin, and Gammon beamed at him.

"Congratulations," the big man said. "I was nervous for you."

"Thanks big guy," Hunter replied, grinning back. He felt a wave of relief…he'd made it past the first test. He had a chance now…a chance to become a Seeker, and to find Mom.

They waited, watching as the lines grew smaller and smaller, until at last every candidate had been either rejected or allowed to stay. Of the hundreds of people who'd come, only a few dozen had been chosen.

"What now?" Hunter asked Sukri. She shrugged.

"Hell if I know," she answered.

"I have a feeling we're about to find out," Kris said, gesturing ahead. The three men in gold and black uniforms – Hunter assumed they were Seeker uniforms – faced the three groups. One of them was the man who'd tested Hunter; he motioned for everyone to form one large group, then stood in front of the other testers, gazing at the small crowd.

"Good morning," he greeted in a deep, gravelly voice. "I am Thorius, Master Trainer for the guild." He gestured at the crowd. "You all have passed the first stage of our screening process for Seeker candidates. Congratulations."

There was scattered applause at that, but Thorius raised his hand, and the crowd went silent.

"The second stage of the screening process will begin shortly," he stated. "You will each be escorted into the guild, three at a time. You will wait here until directed by a Seeker to go inside."

With that, Thorius turned, nodding at the other two Seekers. Three people at the front of the crowd were chosen, and were led across the bridge over the moat and into the double-doors of the guild by the Seekers. The doors closed behind them, leaving the rest of the candidates outside.

Minutes passed.

"Wonder what they're doing in there," Kris muttered, breaking the silence. Sukri shrugged.

"I don't give a damn," she replied. "We're either gonna pass or fail. I'm guessing knowing ahead of time won't help."

"Agreed," Gammon piped in. "We'll have to wait and see."

"Relax," Kris grumbled. "I'm just curious."

A few more minutes passed, until finally the double doors opened, three candidates stepping out. All three walked over the bridge, leaving the courtyard without saying a word. The Seekers came out soon afterward, choosing another three candidates and bringing them inside.

"Well shit," Sukri murmured. "No one made it."

"This is gonna take a while," Kris lamented. Sukri raised an eyebrow at him.

"Got someplace better to be?" she inquired.

Kris didn't answer, not that he had to. It was clear to Hunter from their conversation earlier that joining the Seekers was the only way out of their dead-end jobs…and Hunter's only chance at avoiding a lifetime slinging crap around in waste management, or whatever it was he'd be forced to do. If he had to wait all day, he would.

Eventually, the double-doors opened again…and again, three candidates left. Two more people were chosen…along with Sukri.

"Good luck," Gammon whispered to her as she left, putting a hand on her shoulder. She flashed him a smile, then went with the Seeker, following the other two people into the guild. Hunter watched her go, suddenly apprehensive. He glanced at Kris, who was biting a fingernail.

Minutes passed, until finally the doors opened again. A single candidate walked out, striding across the courtyard…and it wasn't Sukri. The three Seekers followed soon afterward.

"She made it!" Kris exclaimed, punching Gammon on the shoulder. Gammon smiled at him, punching him back…and nearly sending him tumbling to the ground.

"I thought she would," Gammon proclaimed.

The process continued, the Seekers choosing three more candidates, all of whom failed. Another three were chosen, then another, only a few chosen to remain within. By the time the Seekers took Kris and Gammon – along with a third person – the sun was nearly overhead.

"Good luck," Hunter offered as the two men followed the Seekers into the guild. Gammon waved at him, and Kris just gave a nervous-looking smile. They disappeared beyond the double-doors, leaving Hunter with five other people standing in the courtyard. He glanced around, unable to help noticing that the others were standing a good ten feet from him.

Nothing new there.

They waited, and perhaps ten minutes later, the doors opened again, and a man walked out. A tall man with dirty-blond hair.

Hunter let out a breath he hadn't realized he'd been holding. The man wasn't Gammon, and he wasn't Kris. They'd both made it!

The three Seekers came out, and Thorius glanced at Hunter, gesturing for him to come forward. Hunter obeyed, standing before the Seeker while two more people were chosen. Thorius led them across the small bridge over the moat then, opening one of the double-doors and leading them into a large foyer. The floor was made of dark cherry, the walls made of translucent paper-like material, like a traditional Japanese home. The foyer was simple, with barely any furniture to speak of. It was well-made and clearly well-maintained, but hardly what Hunter had been expecting based on the exterior.

"This way," Thorius prompted.

They turned left into a long, wide hallway, with closed doors on either side. Thorius stopped then, turning to face the candidates. The two other Seekers handed out a sheet of paper to each candidate. Hunter glanced down at his; there was writing on it, but he couldn't really read it. Strange that everyone here spoke perfect English, but the written language was so foreign.

"You must sign this contract before going further," Thorius explained. "Understand that the process you are about to undertake involves substantial risk. You may suffer significant, even fatal injury. You may do things you will never forgive yourself for. You may lose your mind, or your very soul...the very essence of who you are." He crossed his arms over his chest. "The only way forward is to accept these risks."

Hunter stared at Thorius, then down at the paper in his hands. Sounded like an idle threat, probably part of the test. Whoever didn't have the guts to sign would leave, and the brave would pass. Thorius handed him a quill, and he signed the paper. Simple enough.

"Proceed," Thorius told him, opening one of the doors and directing Hunter through it. He found himself in a small room, barely bigger than his apartment. There was no furniture in the room of any kind...only another door ahead, opposite the first.

The door closed behind him.

Hunter stood there, glancing around the room. Again, there was nothing but a bare wooden floor, the paper walls, and a bare wooden ceiling.

"Okay," he muttered. "This isn't so bad."

Then the door opposite him opened, and a man stepped through.

He was perhaps fifty, this man, with long, unkempt graying hair and heavily tanned skin. A scruffy beard lay draped over his chest. He was wearing a simple white shirt and pants, which were stained yellow at the armpits. He approached Hunter slowly, accompanied by the stench of body odor and urine.

"Who're you?" the man demanded, glaring at him suspiciously. "Who sent you here?"

"Who're you?" Hunter countered. The man's eyes narrowed.

"I asked you first."

"I'm Hunter," he answered, wrinkling his nose. "Is the smell part of the test?"

"What?"

"You smell like…shit," Hunter confessed. And in fact the man did.

"I don't bathe," the man declared, somewhat defensively. "You can't trust the water, you know," he added. "They put things in it. You're from the Outskirts, aren't you?"

"Yeah," Hunter answered.

"You ever wonder why they built it over the water?" the man asked. Hunter paused, then nodded. He *had* wondered about that. "They put things in the water," the man revealed. "The vapors rise up from the water, and get into the buildings. Makes everyone like sheep, doing whatever the nobles in the Acropolis want."

"Uh huh."

"It's true," the man insisted, stepping closer. Hunter resisted the urge to take a step back. The man's stench was almost overpowering. "They keep people like us passive, so we work the sewers all our lives, never asking questions."

Hunter gave in, taking a step back. He felt suddenly irritated at the man for invading his personal space, and resisted the urge to push him away. The man jabbed a finger at Hunter's chest.

"You're the slave, you know," he continued. "Doing whatever they say. Doing anything you can to look like them, to talk like them." He gave a toothless sneer. "You want to *be* them, don't you?"

"Be who?"

"Like the people in the Acropolis," the man clarified. "You all do." He grinned proudly. "But not me," he added. "I don't drink the water…don't go near it. You drink it, you end up like everyone else."

Hunter stared at the man, breathing through his mouth. There was no doubt that everyone around him *had* looked similar, at least outside of the Outskirts. And Ekrin and Trixie had made it clear that everyone wanted to be like this Tykus guy.

"You see it, don't you," the man pressed. "They're controlling us, making us do whatever they want." He shook his head. "They think I'm crazy, but it's not crazy to fight for your soul, is it?"

"Not at all," Hunter replied.

"Don't patronize me!" the man snapped. "You're just like the others, aren't you? Going to take me away, lock me in a cell! I know what you're up to," he added. "I was like you once, until they put me in that cell." He grinned, tapping his temple. "That's when I realized the truth. A little time alone in prison and you'll see things you didn't see before. You see how the world *really* works, and then…"

The door behind the man opened, and a man in a Seeker uniform strode in. He grabbed the old man's arms, hauling him backward through the doorway. The man shrieked, spinning around to claw at the Seeker's face, but the Seeker grappled the man, subduing him with unnerving ease. He dragged the man out of the room, kicking and screaming. Moments later, the door closed, the man's screams fading away.

"Well then," Hunter muttered. Nearly a minute passed, the man's stench leaving much more slowly than he had. Then the door opened again, and someone else stepped through. A slender woman with long blond hair tied back into a ponytail, wearing tight black pants and a tight shirt. Hunter's breath caught in his throat…it was Trixie!

She walked up to him wordlessly, stopping a few feet in front of him. He smiled at her.

"Hey Trixie," he greeted. "What are you doing here?" She frowned at him.

"I'm here for you," she answered. "But my name isn't Trixie. It's Kala."

"What?" Hunter replied. He stared at her incredulously. She *was* Trixie…she even walked and talked like her. "You're kidding, right?"

"No," the woman said. She put a hand on his shoulder, stepping in closer. "I'm feeling lonely," she murmured, staring into his eyes, a slight smile on her lips. He felt his groin awaken with her touch.

"What are you, her twin?" Hunter pressed, taking a step back. Her hand slid off his shoulder.

"What are you talking about?" she asked. He stared at her, realizing that her eyes were perfectly blue...no green flecks like Trixie had. And her skin was utterly white, not slightly tanned like Trixie's.

"You're not her," Hunter realized. She stepped toward him again, putting both hands on his shoulders, her face inches from his.

"No," she replied. "But I could be yours."

Hunter stared at her, feeling his groin stirring again. She smelled amazing, her perfume subtle but tantalizing. He took a deep breath in, his gaze lowering to her cleavage, her pale breasts straining against that tight shirt. She smiled, leaning forward until her lips were inches from his, giving him a better view. She slid one hand down his chest, then his belly, her fingertips resting just above his groin. He felt himself rising to meet that hand, growing until it slid underneath it. She rested her hand there, tilting her head to the side and pressing her lips against his cheek, just to the left of his lips. His skin tingled with her touch, and she pulled away a little, placing her other hand on his cheek and turning his head slightly to face her. She leaned in again, pressing her lips against his...and letting her fingertips slide down the front of his pants.

His breath caught in his throat, and before he knew it he felt himself kissing her back.

What the hell are you doing?

He turned his head to one side, breaking their kiss, then pushed her away gently but firmly.

"Sorry," he muttered, pulling her hand from his groin. "I'm taken." She ignored him, leaning in again. But he held her back with one hand.

"You don't know what you're missing," she pressed, giving him a hungry look. He shook his head.

"I know who I'd miss if I did anything with you," he shot back.

She stared at him for a moment longer, then turned away, opening the door and leaving the room silently. Hunter watched her go, feeling suddenly uneasy.

Jesus.

That'd been a hell of a test. Somehow, they'd found someone who looked exactly like Trixie, and tried to seduce him. The first test had been easy, but *that*...

He heard a door open behind him, the door he'd come into the room through. He turned to face it, seeing Thorius step through. The Seeker gave a curt nod.

"Congratulations," he stated. "Come with me."

The man led him out of the small room and back into the hallway. The other two candidates had already come out of their rooms, their heads bowed. Obviously they hadn't done as well as he had.

"Escort these two outside," Thorius ordered the other two Seekers. They obeyed, and Thorius turned to Hunter, gesturing for him to go down the hallway in the opposite direction. Hunter complied, walking to the end of the hallway. The only way to go was right, and he did so, the hallway continuing until it opened up into a large room. Eight other candidates were standing there in the middle of the room...including Sukri, Gammon, and Kris. Sukri noticed Hunter, and gave him a big grin as he walked up to her.

"Hey, you made it!" she exclaimed, shoving his shoulder playfully. Gammon smiled down at him.

"Good job, Hunter," he congratulated. "I'm proud of you buddy."

"Thanks guys," Hunter replied, grinning at them. "I'm glad we all made it."

"I know, right?" Kris agreed. "I mean, what are the chances?"

"That *you'd* make it?" Sukri replied. "Not great."

Thorius entered the room then. The room went quiet, all of the candidates turning to face the man. Thorius regarded the nine candidates silently for a moment, then cleared his throat.

"You have passed the screening examination," he declared. "Well done. You are now Initiates of the Guild of Seekers." He smiled with his lips, but not his eyes. "This is a great honor. You should regard it as such."

The two other Seekers entered the room, each carrying a stack of neatly folded white uniforms. They lowered the stacks to the floor before the candidates, then left the room.

"These are your uniforms," Thorius explained. "They are white, signifying the purity of your being. You are as much yourself today as you ever will be." He gave a grim smile. "I suggest you enjoy yourself today. Treasure your final moments as you. I guarantee you they are your last."

He turned away then, walking toward the hallway they'd entered through.

"You will return here at noon tomorrow," he declared, disappearing down the hallway.

The room was silent.

Hunter glanced at Sukri, who shrugged.

"Well, guess that's it then," she stated. "We did it."

"Yeah," Gammon agreed. He looked troubled, however. "Are you guys feeling the way I'm feeling?"

"If you mean kinda freaked out," Kris replied. "Yeah."

"I wonder what he meant by all that," Sukri stated. Gammon shook his head.

"I don't know," he admitted. "But I don't think I like it."

"Well," Kris declared, putting an arm around Sukri's shoulders...and around Gammon's waist. "I for one am going to take his advice."

"What's that?" Sukri asked.

"I'm gonna enjoy myself," he replied with a grin. "Who's with me?"

CHAPTER 8

Dominus gazed out of the window of his carriage, watching as the trees passed slowly by. The clopping of horses' hooves at the front of the carriage was soothing, a gentle rhythm that usually lulled him to sleep. But this was no occasion for a nap. His shipment had been intercepted by the Ironclad, necessitating that he have it retrieved, assuming it had not been destroyed. That presented its own complications, of course. The shipment had been of a highly illegal artifact. There was only one person he trusted to have both the skill and discretion to retrieve it.

The carriage rolled smoothly over the King's Road, suspended twenty feet from the forest floor below. It was a marvelous feat of engineering, his carriage, designed to minimize the influence of the outside world. Its exterior was fashioned of thick, insulating wood, while the interior was made of a thin layer of cleansed stone. A block of King's stone had been set just beneath the cushions of the carriage seats, providing further protection against corruption. A necessary precaution when traveling through the forest. Nature was a cruel, insidious thing, sinking its roots into every corner of the world. It was constantly seeking to break down the order of things, to reduce humanity to a mere animal, a lowly savage.

The technology of the carriage, and of the King's Road, was the only protection against such corruption.

The clopping of the horses' hooves continued as the carriage moved ever forward, and Dominus found himself contemplating the beasts. He'd read from the histories that people used to ride horses…that is, until they'd began to absorb the horses' traits, and vice-versa. Now horses only moved humans via carriage, staying a few feet ahead to avoid corrupting the carriages and the driver. In addition, horses – as with all other domesticated animals – were bred and trained with minimal human contact. By peasants, of course. And domesticated animals were always kept together as much as possible, separated from other species to help preserve their unique qualities.

Dominus heard a cough, turned to see Axio sitting in the seat beside him. The boy had ridden in silence for the first few hours of the trip, for which Dominus was grateful. Axio's silence was yet more evidence of his virtue. He was, Dominus decided, a suitable replacement.

"What's on your mind, Axio?" he inquired. The boy stirred.

"The succession, my liege," he answered.

"Ah yes," Dominus murmured. As with bees, so with men. His hive's queen had died, and a new one would rise, fed of the royal jelly by its nurse bee, the glorious substance that had the power to make it the queen. The power to give it dominion over its hive, to control it utterly.

Hail to the royal jelly, the humble queenmaker. So much like the bones of Tykus, that would recreate the king.

"When will you be crowned, my liege?" Axio inquired. Dominus sighed.

"We shall see, Axio," he replied. "Better for you to concentrate on things you can control than those you cannot," he added. "You'll know far greater success in your life if you follow that advice."

"Yes my liege."

The forest gave way suddenly, the forest replaced by a vast stretch of barren wasteland. Yellow, cracked dirt as far as the eye could see, not a plant in sight.

The Deadlands.

He saw Axio turn to look out of the window, saw him gazing at the ruined land. Miles and miles of wasteland, a reminder of darker days. Of a war that had nearly destroyed them.

"Half a century ago," Dominus stated, "…when I was in my twenties, Tykus was a much larger city. Nearly three times its current size, in fact."

"Before the war," Axio ventured.

106

"Indeed," Dominus confirmed. "My father was duke, and I was as you are. Much of the Deadlands was once known as the Outskirts, a place similar to the slum of the same name you know of today."

"So I've learned, my liege."

Dominus smiled. No doubt Axio had learned of the great civil war during his schooling. But learning history from a book was far different than having lived it. Lessons were far more poignant when they were experienced.

"We made the mistake of allowing a relatively large population of immigrants into the city," Dominus explained. "They provided a cheap source of labor, of course. And we never allowed them in the Acropolis, as is true today."

"But what of the threat they posed?" Axio inquired.

"Indeed," Dominus agreed. "Their influence threatened our identity as it does today. Why would we ever have been stupid enough to allow them within our city, even at the Outskirts?"

Axio hesitated, then shook his head.

"I don't know, sire."

"People," Dominus explained, "…are tools. Each has a role, a purpose. Humans crave purpose, Axio. Remember that."

"Yes my liege."

"Our ancestors believed that the threat posed by the Outskirts was containable," Dominus continued. "Controllable. Indeed, it was the very threat the Outskirts posed that your ancestors hoped to use to their advantage."

"I don't follow," Axio admitted.

"People are tribal, Axio," Dominus lectured. "They have loyalty first to their family, then their friends. Then their nation, their people. These constitute the 'us.'" He gazed out of the window. "Beyond these psychic borders are the 'them,' those that do not belong."

"Yes, my liege."

"The very existence of peoples, of nations, of national identity, and customs, and everything that makes human society work," Dominus continued, "…depends on an 'us' and a 'them.'" He turned to Axio. "Without this distinction, there would be no nations, no borders, no patriotism, no national identity, no racial identity. Shared customs would vanish after a generation or two."

"Indeed," Axio agreed.

"There is no social animal in existence that does not recognize an 'us' and a 'them,'" Dominus declared. "Animals have territories that they defend, sometimes dying to protect them. Even the humble honeybee has its hive, a family so pure that every member shares the same mother, the queen."

"I see."

"This is the essence of Tykus," Dominus explained. "It is a kingdom in which every pure citizen has a shared identity...that of its first king, its very founder. A bloodline thousands of years old, preserved perfectly even today through Tykus's very flesh."

"The Ossae."

"Correct," Dominus replied. "The bones of Tykus, preserved in the heart of the kingdom. His will lives within them. Each king must give himself to the Ossae, surrender his very self to them. In that way, each successor to the crown will essentially *become* Tykus, and continue his rule."

"But what of the Outskirts?" Axio pressed. "You said our ancestors hoped to use the threat they posed as an advantage?"

"Indeed," Dominus confirmed. "Our citizens must always be reminded of who they are. Of the value of their identity. They must see the 'us,' and the 'them.' Our ancestors, my father among them, believed quite correctly that in allowing outsiders to live in the Outskirts, that it would remind our citizens of the constant threat they imposed." He smiled. "There is no greater tool to a government than providing its people with an enemy. A 'them' they can band together with their brethren against. A threat to their identity, their way of life."

"To what end?"

"To maintain control over the populace," Dominus explained. "To preserve patriotism, and to remind citizens of the value of their government, of their way of life. Without such a threat, the people would become complacent, no longer fearing the loss of their identity. The government, and its people, would slowly collapse."

"So they allowed the outsiders to live at the edge of the city," Axio deduced. Dominus nodded.

"And the constant threat of corruption...of the will of all of those outsiders...drove Tykus's true citizens further into the love of Tykus, clinging desperately to the shared traits that made them a great people."

"But it didn't work," Axio protested.

"It did," Dominus countered. "As it does today. The error was in allowing too great a population of immigrants within the kingdom. Recall what I said about peasants, Axio."

"That they are subservient by choice?"

"Correct," Dominus replied. "You believed that they have no choice but to be subservient to their lords."

"And you said the only man without a choice is a dead man," Axio recalled.

"You paid attention," Dominus noted approvingly. "Again, correct. All it takes for peasants to have power is for a man – or woman – with a formidable will to show them that they *do* have a choice. That they have power." He sighed. "This is exactly what happened fifty years ago."

"The Original," Axio murmured.

"Yes," Dominus agreed. "The Original showed the peasants their true power. And their population was large enough that their power was considerable."

"So we allow the Outskirts," Axio concluded, "…but keep their population small."

"That's right," Dominus agreed. "Too small to pose a real threat, while maintaining the value of their perceived threat."

"I understand, my liege."

"Good," Dominus replied. He sighed then, leaning back in his seat and closing his eyes, knowing that Axio would recognize this as the end of their conversation. He had a great deal of thinking to do before they reached the Acropolis. He'd been planning this trip since long before the king had died. Since the moment the great man had fallen ill years ago. Transitions were always dangerous times. There was a great deal he needed to accomplish, and it would not be easy…particularly the matter of his wayward son.

The fate of Tykus hung in the balance.

* * *

Hunter sighed, flopping unceremoniously onto his narrow bed. He stared up at the ceiling, his head swimming a little. Everyone had gone out to have a few drinks to celebrate after becoming initiates of the guild, and while Hunter had of course stolen a few swigs from his dad's considerable stash in the past, he was a lightweight compared to his new friends. Thank god Gammon had helped him get home, otherwise he was pretty sure he'd have stumbled off the docks and into the water. The big guy apparently didn't drink, which was fortunate.

Hunter yawned, rolling onto his side, facing the door. The sun was already low in the sky, the light fading as night approached. Trixie was supposed to be here soon, for which he was immensely grateful. He'd missed her the whole day, wanting nothing more than to be with her again, to feel her gentle touch, her soft kiss. He wanted to tell her all about how he'd made it through the try-outs…and how he was that much closer to being able to find Mom.

He closed his eyes, picturing her. Or trying to. Instead, the woman who'd approached him in the Guild of Seekers came to his mind's eye, a spitting image of Trixie. If she'd pretended to *be* Trixie, he probably wouldn't have known any better. And then he might have done something he would've regretted.

Maybe that was the test, he thought. *Maybe they knew about Trixie, and were trying to fool me.*

But that couldn't possibly be true, he knew. There'd been so many candidates that day that they couldn't possibly have researched all of them. And besides, he'd only been here for a couple days, and had slept with Trixie just last night. There was no way the Seekers could've know about that.

So why had that woman been at his test?

Suddenly there was a knock on the door.

Hunter groaned, getting up out of bed and unlocking and opening the door. Sure enough, Trixie was there. She smiled at him, stepping into the room and leaning in to give him a kiss. He allowed this, but didn't exactly kiss her back. For while he'd stopped himself from doing anything terrible with that other woman, he'd still kissed her. He couldn't help but feel guilty about it.

Trixie pulled away, frowning at him.

"Is something wrong?" she asked.

"No," Hunter replied automatically. Then he grimaced. "Or actually, yes. Maybe."

"Do you want to talk about it?" she pressed. He sighed, walking up to his bed and sitting down on the edge. She sat down next to him, putting a warm hand on his knee.

"I went…somewhere today," he said. "The Guild of Seekers," he added.

"Oh," Trixie replied. She stared at him silently, looking radiant, as usual. She was wearing a gray shirt, low cut and baring her belly. He didn't even bother to pretend he wasn't looking.

110

"I uh, met someone there," he continued. "Someone who looked like you."

"Really?" she asked. "What was her name? Maybe I know her."

"I don't remember," he replied. "But she didn't just look a little like you," he continued. "She looked almost *exactly* like you."

"Okay..."

"It kinda freaked me out," he admitted. She smiled at him.

"You don't have to be freaked out," she soothed, patting his knee. "A lot of people in Tykus look alike."

"I noticed," Hunter muttered. She was right, of course. Seemed like everyone here was the picture of Aryan perfection: tall, blond, blue-eyed, and rather generically attractive. He'd seen twins who'd looked less alike.

"Was that what was bothering you?" she pressed. Hunter hesitated, considering telling her about the kiss. He decided against it...no point in hurting her feelings.

"Yeah."

"Aww," she murmured, leaning in and kissing him again. This time, he gave into it, feeling his body respond to her. She reached a hand behind his head, pulling him into a kiss, her tongue searching for his...and finding it.

God damn, he thought. *But this girl can kiss.*

She stood then, pushing him onto his back on the bed, then straddling his lap. She leaned over, kissing him again, her body pressing against his. He felt her hand sliding down his chest, felt her hips lift off of his, her palm sliding over his groin.

His breath caught in his throat.

She pulled her lips from his then, her hand stopping there, resting with gentle pressure. He grew against her, and she smiled at him.

"I don't have to take you to Ekrin today," she said. "It's his day off."

"Mmm."

"You're very big," she murmured. "I've never seen one as big as yours."

"You know just what to say," he replied with a smirk.

"It's true," she insisted.

"I don't doubt it," he replied. Stereotypes weren't always true, but in this one case, he'd been blessed.

"I was nervous at first," she confessed, sliding her hand up and down.

111

"So was I," he replied. "It was my first time." She arched an eyebrow.

"And your second, and your third, and…"

He pulled her down onto him, kissing her. She allowed it, but pulled away soon after, smiling down at him.

"Pace yourself," she warned. "It's going to be a long night." She leaned in again, touching the tip of her nose to his. He grinned at her, staring into her lovely eyes.

And froze.

Her eyes were perfectly blue. Not a single speck of green in them. And the tan she'd had earlier was gone, her skin as white as snow.

"What's wrong?" she asked, pulling back. "You tensed up."

"Nothing," he blurted out. He stared at her, picturing the woman at the guild, the woman who'd looked – and sounded – exactly like her. Hell, she'd even *moved* like Trixie. In fact, Hunter had told the woman Trixie's name. Which meant that the woman on top of him might not be Trixie at all…it could be the woman from the guild.

A chill went through him.

"Relax," the woman murmured, leaning in and kissing him again. He didn't respond, but his body did, and her hand continued to massage his groin, more urgently now. He moaned, his focus wavering, and he found himself kissing her back.

This isn't Trixie, he told himself, turning his head to the side, breaking their kiss. She kissed his neck, biting it a little, her breath hot on his skin. Then she slid her hand under his underwear, grabbing him gently but firmly, continuing to work on him. His breath caught in his throat.

This isn't Trixie!

He grabbed her shoulders, gripping them tightly. She ignored him, going faster now. She pulled his head toward hers with her free hand, crushing her lips against his. Her tongue snaked into his mouth, and despite everything, he let it happen. She felt amazing on him, her hot skin pressed against his, her hand guiding him expertly toward inevitable bliss. All he had to do was let it happen.

She looks exactly like Trixie, he told himself. *You can say it was an honest mistake.*

Her hand continued its magic, and his hips bucked, pleasure rising within him. It was coming quickly now, the end in sight.

There would be no turning back soon. He stiffened, his conscience stirring within him.

Don't do this.

But she was too skilled, her hand never stopping, her technique perfect. He felt his pleasure peak, felt his whole body go tense, his mouth locking on hers. She guided him expertly to the point of no return, blasting past it, the ecstasy continuing to mount, more powerful than he'd ever felt before. More powerful than he could have imagined possible. The release came quickly and violently, aided by her ever-moving hand. She brought him through the finish and past it, until at last he was spent, with nothing more to give. She slowed, then stopped, holding him in her hand, releasing her lips from his. She pulled her face back then, smiling down at him, her blue eyes twinkling.

"My goodness," she murmured, gazing down at his belly and chest. "You had a lot in you."

He said nothing, staring at her, feeling an immediate shame come over him.

You could've stopped her.

He watched as she sat up straight, pulling her shirt off, exposing her perfect breasts. She threw her shirt to the floor, lowering herself back onto him, and turned his head to the side gently, kissing his neck. Then her lips brushed up against his ear.

"Did that feel good baby?" she murmured, biting her earlobe gently. He swallowed past a lump in his throat, staring up at the ceiling, feeling suddenly empty.

"It did," he answered. And it was the truth, as much as he hated to admit it. It *had* felt good, while it was happening. Hell, it'd felt *amazing.*

But now it just felt like betrayal.

CHAPTER 9

Alasar stood at the edge of the King's Road, gazing across the vast emptiness of the Deadlands, at the innumerable tiny yellow lights beyond the great wall in the distance. It was Tykus, of course, its streets lit by countless lanterns, their light growing more and more visible in the steadily darkening sky. Sundown was coming...and with it, the end of his shift.

He sighed, lifting his giant hammer from where it rested on the road beside him, securing it on his back.

"I'm headed home," he called out. A few of the overnight shift soldiers nodded at him, saying goodnight. Half of the evening shift had left for the military base southwest of Tykus, at the far edge of the Deadlands. The other half had to stay with Alasar until the overnight commanding officer arrived to take Alasar's place. Barek had arrived late once again, the lazy bastard. Making a fuss about it wouldn't accomplish anything, either. Sergeants working the overnight shift were expected to have a warm body and a pulse...and that was about it.

"Night," Barek muttered, nodding at Alasar, who nodded back, heading south down the King's Road, his soldiers in tow.

"Prick," he muttered under his breath.

He strode quickly down the road, passing lit torches on either side. There were torches spaced every two hundred meters down the length of the road, as far as the eye could see. The night shift lit them on their way to the Gate, every night without fail. Just in case the Ironclad attacked, and they needed to escape back to the base. Which never happened, of course.

He sighed, his boots *clunking* on the stone below in a hypnotic cadence. His soldiers didn't bother trying to talk to him, knowing how moody he got when he was tired.

Five years working this shift, and he'd only had one run-in with the Ironclad, when that boy had arrived at the Gate. The dark boy. The Original. It was, of course, why Alasar had applied for the job in the first place. Sure it was boring, but working the Gate had a benefit that was hard to resist: not getting his ass killed. He'd seen enough action during his previous deployments to last two lifetimes, after all. And he'd been damn lucky not to get killed a dozen times over.

No, the Ironclad usually kept to themselves. Just standing there in the Deadlands, patrolling the Gate. What for, he had no idea. Probably to stop the kingdom from getting access to the Originals' strange technology. Like that...thing the boy had used. The gun, or whatever he'd called it.

If we could produce more of those...

It would turn the tide, that was for sure. The damn Ironclad were aptly named, covered from head to toe in a black carapace so thick and strong that it was like steel plate mail. Vicious creatures, living in caves, eating anything they could find. Just one of nature's many abominations...and like so many of nature's creations, the Ironclad hated humanity with a passion. It was a peculiar quality of the forest, the vast untamed wilderness of this forsaken world, that hatred. A twisted darkness that corrupted everything it touched.

Alasar passed another set of torches, seeing a split in the road ahead. One path went right, the other left. He chose the rightward path, heading southwest to the military base. To home.

"You going out for drinks later, Sergeant?" one of the soldiers asked. A relatively new recruit, too new to know any better. Or maybe his fellows hadn't warned him on purpose, hoping for a good show. While it was certainly tempting bait, Alasar wasn't about to give them what they wanted.

"I got a new kid, son," he replied. "So no."

"Aw, why not?" the soldier pressed. Alasar turned to glare at him.

"So I don't kill the damn kid," he answered. "You ever wake up to a newborn screaming his brains out?" He smirked. "Try it with a hangover."

"Ain't you too old to be making babies?" another soldier asked, grinning at him. Alasar sighed. Now they really *were* testing his patience.

"If you had a wife that looked like mine," he replied, "…you wouldn't be able to help yourself."

The soldiers laughed, then mercifully left him alone. He continued down the King's Road, quickening his pace. The sun was setting quickly, the sky steadily darkening. He wanted to get home before the Ironclad would be too difficult to spot in the darkness. The beasts were more nocturnal than not, their black carapaces blending in seamlessly with the night.

Except for that weird one, he thought. The tall one with the glowing mane the Original had helped kill. After Alasar had dropped the kid off at Tykus, he'd returned to take care of the corpses. The glowing one's body had been missing…which meant there must've been another Ironclad hiding somewhere nearby. The things usually didn't bother retrieving their dead, though. That glowing one must've been special.

He sighed, gazing across the Deadlands as he walked. It was getting steadily darker now. The Ironclad wouldn't dare attempt to attack humans on the King's Road, but there was a good half-kilometer from the road to the outer wall of the military base. Better to make the trek when visibility was still fair. They were making decent time…he spotted the telltale glow of torchlight a half-kilometer away, from the torches lining the wall surrounding the base. Beyond that, he could see the black line of the forest in the distance. The end of the Deadlands, the edge of the forest.

The Fringe.

The military base was a kilometer from the Fringe, far enough away to avoid the danger of the forest, but close enough for the kingdom to keep an eye on it. If there was any threat to Tykus, it would come from the Fringe. No one dared enter the forest, not for long. No one except for the Seekers, the crazy bastards.

He gazed at that dark tree line, knowing that somewhere, deep in the forest, the Ironclad lurked. And horrors far worse, no doubt. He'd read stories of the world of the Originals, of a benign world. Forests a man could walk through without fear. Without the constant threat of corruption, of a man's soul being twisted into something vile and monstrous.

"Hey sergeant," one of the soldiers asked. The new one. He turned to the guy, then spotted something moving in his peripheral vision. A dark shape within the shadows seven meters below the King's Road. He stopped abruptly, holding up one hand. The soldiers stopped with him.

Alasar peered over the edge of the road, seeing nothing but darkness…at first. Then he spotted more movement, another shadow moving quickly across the terrain, in the same direction they were going.

Shit.

He put a finger to his lips, seeing another shadowy figure, then another. All of them moving southwest, toward the military base in the distance. Gliding through the darkness like inky ghosts, moving across the barren terrain with unnerving speed.

Shit!

The ghostly figures moved ever forward, and in the distance Alasar saw a few of them emerge from the shadows, into the light cast by the torches lining the wall of the base. Huge, black creatures with two pairs of arms bounding toward that wall, spilling out of the darkness. Dozens of them. No…*hundreds* of them. All converging on the base.

"Run," Alasar ordered, turning around and breaking out into a sprint back the way they'd come. The other soldiers hesitated.

"But we have…"

"I said *run*, damn it!" Alasar hissed.

The soldiers obeyed, sprinting behind him, their boots *clunking* loudly on the King's Road. He glanced back, seeing the Ironclad swarming toward the military base, blanketing the earth with their unholy bodies. They reached the wall, climbing on top of each other, scaling the seven-meter-tall barrier with terrifying ease. Hundreds of them, maybe thousands, dropping into the base from the top of the wall.

"We have to go back!" a soldier protested.

"It's gone," Alasar retorted, picking up speed, his hammer bouncing painfully on his back. There was no way the base would be able to fight off that many Ironclad. Just one of the damn things could kill a dozen men; an army of them could threaten the kingdom itself. He had to get back to Tykus to warn them. They'd only ever seen a few dozen Ironclad at a time, never imagining that there could be so many of them. The kingdom had to know.

He glanced back again, spotting an endless stream of Ironclad scaling the walls, dropping into the base. Like beetles swarming over a corpse. And he knew in that moment that his wife and newborn son were about to die.

Take them in their sleep, he prayed, feeling grief well up inside of him...and heart-wrenching guilt. For he knew that he was leaving them to die.

He pushed the thought away, focusing on the road ahead of him. He saw it converging with another path ahead, knew he was halfway to the Gate. He ran faster, his breath coming in short gasps now, his lungs burning. Sweat poured down his sides.

Come on...

He heard a shout behind him, and turned, looking past his soldiers, spotting black arms reaching over the side of the road. A massive Ironclad pulled itself over the ledge.

Alasar's blood went cold, terror gripping him.

They can climb the King's Road!

The Ironclad rose to its feet, now only thirty meters from the last soldier. Another climbed up one of the wooden pillars, using its four arms to scale it easily. It pulled itself up onto the King's Road, followed by yet another.

Shit!

"Go go go!" Alasar cried, feeling a burst of adrenaline course through him. He picked up speed, his lungs on fire now. Sweat poured into his eyes, making them sting. He turned, seeing a pair of torches on either side of the road ahead, and the silhouettes of the overnight Gate patrol. "Hey!" he screamed, waving his arms wildly at them. "Hey!"

He heard a *thump* behind him, and then a shrill scream.

Alasar resisted the urge to look back, pumping his legs as fast as he could. He reached back for his giant hammer tossing it over the side of the road. He ran even faster then, unburdened by its formidable weight. He was only a couple hundred meters from the Gate patrol now.

"The Ironclad!" he shouted at them. "They're here!"

But the soldiers didn't move, their inky black silhouettes facing him silently.

"Hey!" he shouted.

And then he realized that the soldiers were far too tall...and that they had two pairs of arms silhouetted by the torches beyond them.

"Aw *shit*," he swore, skidding to a halt. He felt his fellow soldiers slam into him from behind, catapulting him forward. He landed flat on his belly, his breath blasting from his lungs. He gasped for air, pushing himself onto his hands and knees, seeing his men rushing past him. He gestured ahead, trying desperately to take a breath in.

"Not…" he gasped, "…ours."

He saw the soldiers who'd passed him reach the Ironclad ahead, then skidded to a stop, shouting in alarm. One of the Ironclad grabbed a soldier, tossing him through the air like a rag doll, right over the edge of the road.

Alasar scrambled to his feet, taking a deep breath in at last, his head swimming sickeningly. He watched helplessly as another one of his men swung his hammer at an Ironclad, only to have it torn out of his hands. As the soldier was thrown bodily off of the King's Road, falling seven meters to the ground below.

Then Alasar felt powerful hands grip the backs of his arms, hauling him backward. He looked down, seeing huge black fingers curling around his biceps, squeezing him with bone-crushing strength. They jerked backward, and pain ripped through his shoulders as they dislocated. He screamed, feeling himself rise up from the road, his feet dangling in mid-air.

He knew then that he was going to die.

Alasar watched, suspended in the air, as his men fought the Ironclad. Watched as the beasts tore his men's arms from their sockets, flinging their bodies over the edge of the road. Watched as his men were slaughtered, until there was no one left but him.

I'm coming for you baby, he thought, picturing his lovely wife, their tiny son cradled in her arms.

One of the Ironclad strode toward him, its four hands dripping with blood. It stopped before him, staring down at him with its unholy black eyes. It was taller than the others, with a thick, gel-filled membrane forming a glowing blue mane from the top of its head down its spine, to a broad tail that hung between its legs.

Alasar stared back, his shoulders in agony, the muscles spasming uncontrollably. He tried not to think of his wife and son, of what these monsters had done to them.

I'm coming baby.

The creature raised one massive hand, gripping the front of Alasar's uniform. He felt the hands gripping him from behind fall away, felt himself rising up even higher as the thing in front of him lifted him upward with one hand, until its eyes were level with his. It stared at him, its black mouth opening, revealing misshapen gray teeth.

"WHERE," it growled, the word barely intelligible. "...IS...HE."

Alasar stared at the thing, his jaw dropping.

They can speak!

"WHERE?" it repeated, its lips curling in a snarl. Alasar shook his head.

"Who?" he asked.

The Ironclad pulled him forward, until its gruesome face was inches from his. He could feel its hot breath on his face, the putrid smell making him gag.

"THE...ORIGINAL."

* * *

Hunter opened his eyes, squinting against the sunlight streaming through his window. He groaned, reaching up to rub his eyes, but his right arm was pinned down by something warm and soft. He frowned, glancing to his right, and saw a woman lying next to him on his bed. She was nude, her lower half covered by a thin blanket, blond hair streaming down over her breasts. He felt his guts squirm as the events of the previous night came to him, memories of what he'd done.

Shit.

He stared at her, sleeping peacefully beside him. Whoever she was. She stirred, murmuring something in her sleep, then going still.

How did I get myself into this?

She had to be the woman from his test earlier. The woman who'd come at him, trying to seduce him. It was the only explanation. This must have been the *real* test...a test of his loyalty. Thorius had figured out where he lived, and sent this imposter to test him. And if that was true, that meant he'd almost certainly failed...and that he'd ruined his one chance at getting out of the city to find his mother.

He grit his teeth, sitting up in bed and swinging his legs over the edge, no longer able to stand the idea of being next to this woman. He'd betrayed Trixie, and forsaken his mother...all for some cheap thrills.

You're a damn fool.

She stirred behind him, and he felt a warm hand on his shoulder.

"Morning," she murmured, resting her chin on his shoulder, her lips by his ear. She pulled him backward, and he fell onto his back on the bed. She got to her hands and knees, gazing down at him. "How'd you sleep?"

"Not great," he muttered.

"Aww," she replied, smiling at him. "My poor baby. I kept you up all night."

Hunter said nothing, feeling a now familiar emptiness inside. He wanted nothing more than for her to leave, but after everything they'd done together, telling her to go felt incredibly awkward.

"How about one more before I go?" she inquired, sliding her hand down his belly. He twisted to face her, seeing her eyes twinkling mischievously.

Blue eyes, with faint green speckles. And her skin with a slight golden hue.

He pulled away from her, standing up and staring down at her, his jaw dropping.

"Trixie?" he blurted out.

"Last time I checked," she replied. He continued to stare at her, hardly believing his eyes.

"But last night," he protested. "That was...you?" She frowned at him.

"Of course," she replied. "Who else would it be?"

He stood there, his mouth agape, then shut it with a *click*. He hesitated, then sat down beside her. It *was* Trixie!

"I thought..." he began, then stopped himself. "But your eyes were pure blue yesterday," he protested. "And you didn't have a tan."

"I cleansed last night before I came here," she explained.

"You what?"

"I cleansed," Trixie repeated. "Remember how I said I was lucky 'cause I get to cleanse twice a day?" Hunter hesitated, then nodded. She *had* said that.

"What does that mean?"

"I go to the altar where I work," Trixie answered. "We have a special altar there, like at church. It cleanses us of impurities."

"Impurities?"

"Remember how I said you were contagious?" she asked.

"Uh, yeah."

"That's why people are afraid of you," she explained. "They don't want to be brown." She sighed. "It's silly really," she added. "If they cleanse, it's no big deal."

121

"Wait," Hunter blurted out. "You're saying my…brownness is contagious?" She nodded.

"That's right. That's why I have a tan now."

"That's…" he began, then shook his head. "That's impossible!" She frowned.

"What do you mean?"

"My skin color can't be contagious," he protested. "It's not a frickin' *disease*."

"Oh no," she replied. "I didn't say it was a disease. It's just…well, that's just the way things are." She gave him a concerned look. "You mean you didn't know?"

"Didn't know what?" he asked. She put a hand on his cheek, giving him a look that was almost pitying.

"Oh baby," she murmured. "I'm so sorry, I didn't realize."

"What?"

"It didn't even occur to me that you wouldn't know," she continued. "I mean, that it might be different where you're from."

Suddenly there was a knock at the door.

"Who is it?" Hunter asked, pulling the sheet over his lap. Trixie, however, didn't bother to cover herself.

"Gammon," a deep, muffled voice replied.

"Oh *damn*," Hunter blurted out. He'd forgotten that he was supposed to be at the Guild of Seekers at noon. He must've overslept…luckily Gammon had taken him home last night, and knew where his apartment was. "Hold on a sec." He got up, slipping on a pair of underwear and his Seeker pants, then opening the door. Gammon stepped into the apartment, glancing at Trixie, who was still nude…and unabashedly so.

"Oh, hey," Gammon greeted, his cheeks flushing. "Uh, you need a little time?" he asked.

"No, it's okay," Hunter answered. "Is it almost noon?"

"Yeah," Gammon replied. "I thought you might be a little hung over, so I came to wake you up."

"Thanks big guy," Hunter said. He pulled on the rest of his new uniform, then glanced at Trixie. "I'm really sorry," he told her. "I've gotta go…"

"That's okay," she replied with a smile. "I'm sure I'll see you later."

"Let's go," he told the big guy, stepping out of the apartment and closing the door behind him. They went downstairs, making their way through the Outskirts to Lowtown, eventually reaching

122

the Guild of Seekers. They crossed the bridge over the moat, finding Sukri, Kris, and the other initiates standing in front of the double-doors. One of them was a tall guy with curly blond hair and a wispy mustache named Donahue, a nice enough fellow who'd accompanied them to the bar the night before. Another was Lucus, a far more serious and earnest man. Sukri had asked him to join them last night, but he'd declined.

"Hey guys," Hunter greeted. Sukri and Kris grinned at him.

"Thought you weren't coming," Kris said, clapping him on the shoulder. "Rough night?"

"Something like that," Hunter replied.

"He brought a girl home," Gammon revealed, a big smile on his face. "She looked expensive."

"Went all out, eh?" Kris stated. "Good for you, man!" He leaned in then. "But just a piece of advice...never pay for something you can get for free."

"I didn't pay her anything," Hunter retorted. Kris grinned, slapping him on the shoulder.

"That's my man!"

"Looks like we have another man-whore in the group," Sukri grumbled, eyeing them both. "You two will have a lot to talk about."

"Hardly," Hunter retorted. "I'm a one-woman man."

"You've clearly never had two at a time," Kris quipped. Sukri rolled her eyes.

"Pffft. Overrated."

Kris stared at her.

"Wait, you've..."

Just then, the door opened, revealing a Seeker on the other side, one of the ones from yesterday. The man gestured for them to come in, and everyone did, following the Seeker to the room they'd ended up in previously. Moments later, Thorius arrived, standing before the group.

"Good afternoon," he greeted brusquely, his eyes moving from candidate to candidate. "I trust you enjoyed your selves last night."

"Oh yeah," Kris replied. Everyone else remained silent, and he cleared his throat, lowering his gaze. Thorius smirked.

"I hope so," he stated. "It was your last opportunity to do so."

Just then, a few more Seekers entered the room, each carrying a bunch of black medallions with golden ribbons. They set these on the floor in front of the candidates, then left as silently as they'd come. Thorius gestured at the medallions.

"Each of you, pick up a medallion," he ordered. The other initiates hesitated, and Hunter shrugged, stepping forward and picking one up. It was surprisingly heavy, and appeared to be made of obsidian, with unfamiliar symbols carved into its surface. He stepped back, watching as the others picked up theirs. "You will wear your medallion wherever you go. You will bring it home, sleep with it, and bring it back here during training. It will accompany you everywhere. Treat it as your own flesh."

"Yes sir," the candidates replied, almost in unison.

"Call me Master Thorius," Thorius instructed. "Master will also do." He smirked. "Thorius will not."

"Yes Master Thorius."

"If you have...company during sleep," he continued, "...you may not wear the medallion."

"Yes Master Thorius."

"You will each be assigned a trainer," Thorius continued. "They will work with you one-on-one, and you will return here for group training sessions." He glanced from student to student. "This is not a competition," he added. "You will not become a Seeker by besting your peers. If all of you are deemed qualified, you will all become Seekers. And if none of you are qualified, none of you will."

"Yes Master Thorius."

"You will be paid an allowance daily, equal to your previous wages," Thorius stated. "Pay will be distributed at the end of class."

He paused then, sweeping his gaze over the gathered initiates.

"One more thing," Thorius added, his tone darkening. "If you reveal any information about your training, or about the guild in general, you will be terminated." He gave a grim smile. "And by that I mean that I will kill you. Personally."

Everyone glanced at each other, but no one said anything.

"Likewise," Thorius continued, "...an attack on you is an attack on the guild. Wear your uniforms in public at all times. If someone should assault you, or threaten to, notify the guild immediately."

"Yes Master Thorius."

"Do not abuse this," Thorius warned. "We will know if you are lying. And if you lie to us, we will kill you." He raised an eyebrow. "Any questions?"

No one had any.

"Good."

As if on cue, a group of Seekers entered the room, standing behind him. "Pair up as we discussed," he instructed them. The Seekers stepped forward, each grabbing an initiate and directing them through a door to the left. One by one they left, until only Hunter remained. Hunter glanced at the door, then at Thorius. "Where's my trainer?" he inquired. Thorius crossed his arms over his chest, eyeing him critically.

"You're looking at him."

* * *

Unlike the other Seekers, Thorius did not bring Hunter through the door, instead staying in the room after everyone else had left. The man retrieved a clear, orange-sized orb from his pocket.

"Hold this," he added, handing Hunter the orb. It was surprisingly heavy, its surface smooth and cool to the touch. "Put it in your pocket."

"Why?" Hunter asked.

"Because I told you to," Thorius answered. Hunter hesitated, then complied, putting the sphere in his pants pocket. "Now," Thorius stated, crossing his arms over his chest. "...you're clearly not from around here."

"I'm an Original," Hunter told him.

"I know," Thorius replied. "That's why I have to start from scratch. You're going to take a long time to express your potential, and you know nothing of our world, which puts you at a significant disadvantage. That's why I chose to train you...you're going to need all the help you can get."

Hunter frowned at that, not liking the tone of Thorius's voice.

"What is that supposed to mean?" he demanded. "I'm not stupid, you know."

"I didn't say you were," Thorius countered. "But you *are* ignorant."

"Ignorant?" Hunter pressed. Thorius had said it like it was an insult.

"You are."

"Yeah, well I'm not the only one," he retorted. Thorius raised an eyebrow.

"Oh really?"

"Yeah really," Hunter shot back. "You think I'm ignorant? You don't have a goddamn clue how ignorant *you* are." He scoffed at

Thorius. "You're a bunch of primitives compared to me," he added. "Talking about how great your city is. But hey, no running water, no electricity."

Thorius just stood there, giving him a smug look.

"Guess what?" Hunter continued. "You're living in the dark ages, pal. You guys don't even have *showers*, for Christ's sake. You wanna call me ignorant? Tell me what you know about physics, about biology." He waited, but Thorius said nothing. He smirked. "Exactly," he muttered.

Thorius crossed his arms over his chest, giving Hunter a patient look. As if he was tolerating a child.

"This whole city's filled with a bunch of racist assholes living in shacks," Hunter continued.

"Is that so."

"Damn right it is," Hunter replied.

"Now you're just being insulting," Thorius stated coolly.

"Yeah, well you started it," Hunter retorted. "I'm sick of being treated like a leper just because I've got a fucking tan. You're all just a bunch of goddamn Nazi white nationalist hillbilly morons, treating me like I'm fucking contagious. Like being different is a *disease.*"

Thorius raised an eyebrow.

"We don't think it's a disease," he countered. "It just makes you inferior."

"Inferior?" Hunter blurted out. Suddenly he wanted to wipe that smug look right off the man's face. "If I'm so goddamn inferior, why did I beat out all those other lily-white assholes to get here?"

"Perhaps we made a mistake."

"Yeah, maybe I did too," Hunter spat. "You know what? I'd rather deal with shit in the sewers than deal with shit like you."

"You'd better watch your tone," Thorius warned. Hunter raised his eyebrows, taking a step toward the man. He was taller than Thorius, and a lot younger and almost certainly a hell of a lot stronger.

"Make me," he growled.

Thorius didn't budge, staring up at Hunter with that smug look on his face.

"You have a big mouth," he said. "Why don't we practice keeping it shut."

"Fuck you," Hunter spat, shoving Thorius backward. Or at least he tried to. Before he knew it, the world was spinning around him, and suddenly he felt his back slam into the floor below, the air blasting from his lungs. He gasped, trying to suck air in, realizing that Thorius was standing above him, gazing down at him. He scrambled to his feet, and Thorius shoved him back onto the ground with one boot, grinding his heel into Hunter's chest. Hunter gripped the boot, trying to shove it off him, but Thorius just leaned more weight on him, forcing the air out of his lungs.

"Take the orb out of your pocket," Thorius ordered.

"Go…to hell," Hunter gasped.

Thorius knelt down, reaching into Hunter's pocket and retrieving the orb, rolling it across the floor away from them. It struck the wall on the other end of the room, stopping there.

"Calm down," Thorius ordered, easing off on Hunter's chest. He rose to his feet. "Get up."

Hunter stared at the man, then got up, rubbing his aching chest.

"That," Thorius stated calmly, "…was your first lesson."

"What, that you can beat the crap out of me?" Hunter retorted, glaring at the man. Thorius smirked.

"That was your second lesson," he corrected. "Your first was the sphere."

"The sphere?" Hunter asked, glancing at the thing. "What about it?"

"There once was a middle-aged man," Thorius explained. "A drunk. Alcohol didn't exactly bring out the best in him."

"Oh, so now it's story-time," Hunter muttered.

"One day, he went drinking after work, as he normally did," Thorius continued, ignoring him. "He came home to find his wife in bed with another man. Turns out she'd gotten sick of his drinking, and decided to head for greener pastures." Thorius smirked. "He didn't take it well. You see, drinking made him angry. Made him violent."

"What does…"

"Don't interrupt," Thorius interjected. Hunter felt a twinge of irritation, but complied. "The man came home, found his wife being serviced by this other gentleman, and was understandably upset. What was less understandable was the fact that he beat the man's head in, then strangled his wife to death."

"Jesus."

"And then he threw their two-year-old son out of the third-story window," Thorius concluded. He glanced at the sphere at the other end of the room. "That," he declared, pointing at it, "…was in his pocket the night he killed them. He'd bought it at the store as a present for his wife before going to the bar for a few drinks."

Hunter stared down at the sphere, then looked back up at Thorius.

"That crystal," Thorius continued, "…witnessed a triple-murder. Rage beyond description." He turned his gaze back to Hunter. "It hasn't forgotten. It may never forget."

"Wait," Hunter protested. "It can't remember anything, it's just a…"

"Why did you attack me?" Thorius interjected calmly. Hunter glared at him.

"You provoked me."

"Did I?" Thorius pressed. "What did I say that made you assault your teacher?"

"You said…" he began, then frowned. "You said I was inferior."

"True," Thorius agreed. "You needed a little push, but you were already furious before I said that."

"You called me ignorant," Hunter reminded him. Thorius shrugged.

"Your ignorance is no fault of your own," he countered. "And it is the easiest thing to cure." He gestured at the sphere. "The sphere has never forgotten our drunk murderer's rage. It absorbed that emotion, was corrupted by it. And now it in turn corrupts anything and anyone near it." He gestured at Hunter. "Such as yourself."

"You're saying that thing made me attack you?"

"That's correct," Thorius confirmed.

"Bullshit."

"Is it?" Thorius pressed. "Tell me, how do you feel now?"

Hunter focused inward, realizing that he wasn't angry anymore. Irritated yes, but only mildly so.

"Would you like me to hand you the sphere again?" Thorius inquired. Hunter eyed it warily, then shook his head. "Your first lesson is this," Thorius stated. "Objects absorb intense emotions, and the more intense the emotion, the more completely an object will absorb it. This emotion can then be transmitted to you, or anyone else, merely by being close enough to the object to be corrupted by it."

"You're serious about this," Hunter realized.

"Yes," Thorius confirmed. He walked over to the sphere, picking it up and putting it back in his pocket, then walking back up to Hunter. Hunter eyed him warily.

"Aren't you worried about being close to that thing?" he asked.

"Excellent question," Thorius replied. "The answer is no."

"But why not?" Hunter pressed. Given how easily Thorius had beaten him, if that sphere really did what the man said it did, then Hunter wouldn't stand a chance if Thorius decided to beat the crap out of him…or worse.

"A Seeker must learn to sense the corruption in the world around them," Thorius answered. "To understand the danger, and to sense that corruption in himself. You must learn to resist that corruption, to accept that it exists but not fall prey to acting on it."

"How do I do that?"

"By developing introspection," he replied. "You must learn who *you* are to know what feelings are yours and what are not." He gestured at Hunter. "For example, right now I am extraordinarily angry with you. In fact, I could kill you right now, and not regret a thing. No one would question me."

Hunter felt the blood drain from his face, and took a step back from the man. Thorius smirked.

"The only reason I haven't," he continued, "…is because of my training…and willpower. And we're going to have to spend a great deal of time developing yours."

"How do we do that?"

"You'll see," Thorius replied.

Hunter glanced down at the pocket where Thorius had put the sphere.

"So that sphere can absorb emotions," he stated. "Is it because it's a crystal?" Thorius shook his head.

"All objects can absorb emotions," he countered. "And animals, and people. Even plants, and water."

"You're kidding."

"I'm afraid not," Thorius replied. "I've read that in your world, this is not the case."

"It's not," Hunter agreed.

"You can imagine how dangerous this might be," Thorius stated. "Imagine a man wanted to force an enemy to commit murder. It would be as simple as putting this sphere in his pocket." He gave a grim smile. "Very few people have as strong a will as I do."

"So *everything* around me stores emotions like this?"

"Correct."

"But…" he began, glancing around the room. "Why don't people just walk around getting pissed off all the time?"

"Some objects absorb emotion better than others," Thorius explained. "In general, the greater the density of an object, the better it absorbs. And weak emotions transmit weakly, while strong emotions transmit powerfully."

"So if I get pissed, the floor will absorb that?" Hunter asked. It sounded ridiculous.

"Not well," Thorius answered. "Wood does not absorb or transmit emotions efficiently. That is why most structures in the city are made of wood, and not stone."

"Oh," Hunter mumbled. He'd wondered about that. "Is that why the walls are made of paper?"

"Correct."

"Wow," Hunter murmured. He glanced around the room, then down at the medallion resting on his chest. "What emotion has *this* thing absorbed?" Thorius gave a tight smile.

"Nothing of consequence," he answered. Hunter frowned.

"So what does it do?" he pressed.

"You'll find out soon enough," Thorius replied.

CHAPTER 10

The sun hung low in the sky by the time Hunter stepped out of the double-doors of the Guild of Seekers with Sukri, Gammon, and Kris. Donahue and Lucus had decided to tag along, walking behind the others. No one said very much about what they'd done that day, particularly after Thorius's warning that doing so in public would get them murdered. For his part, Hunter had spent the rest of the day having Thorius hand him various objects, all supposedly "corrupted" by various emotions. At first, Hunter couldn't help being skeptical, still attributing his anger to his teacher's smug attitude.

It hadn't taken long for him to realize how wrong he was.

First Thorius had handed him a small locket, an anniversary gift from a man to the woman he'd loved for years. He'd died before her, and she'd worn it on the day he'd died, sitting with him, remembering their life together. Sure enough, he'd started to feel rather sentimental after holding it for a few minutes. Another object – a book owned by a notorious shut-in – made him feel profoundly anxious, fearful of even leaving the room. Each time Thorius had handed him a new object, he'd felt something different. It'd become all too clear that the Master Trainer had been correct. Objects were indeed corrupted by the emotions of people around them, and carried the memory of those emotions with them, infecting anyone who drew near. Apparently it didn't even require physical contact to transmit these emotions...just proximity. And the stronger the emotion, the farther the distance it could transmit.

He couldn't help but feel a little paranoid of everything around him now, knowing that he might be infected by their emotions. That they might be warping his mind. *Controlling* him.

"Man," Gammon said, rubbing his belly. "I'm starving." Kris gave him a skeptical look.

"You've got a long way to go before you starve big guy," he observed. Donahue grinned at Gammon.

"He's got you there."

"Let's go get dinner," Sukri said, leading the way back to the Outskirts. They reached the community center within a few minutes, and as usual the long line to the front doors parted before them like the Red Sea. No one in the line gave them any trouble this time, almost certainly because of their uniforms. Apparently everyone here was aware of the consequences of messing with the Guild of Seekers.

This he could get used to.

They made it into the community center, grabbing their food and sitting down at a table. They all dug in to their food, no one saying much of anything at first. It wasn't until Gammon had polished off his first plate – which didn't take long – that anyone broke the silence.

"We should go have some fun after this," the big man stated, eyeing his second plate as if strategizing its dismemberment.

"Sounds good to me," Kris agreed. "I don't know about you guys, but I need a drink."

"I second that," Donahue piped up. "You in, Lucus?" Lucus hesitated, then shook his head. Like Gammon, he didn't drink. But at least Gammon was still fun when he was sober. Hunter wondered why Lucus even bothered tagging along with them.

"I need more than one," Sukri muttered. "Seeker Draken kicked my ass today." She glanced at Hunter. "How you holding up, Crispy?"

"Not bad," he replied. "Still trying to process everything."

"Yeah, sorry 'bout that," she apologized. "I meant to tell you more about your will and stuff, but we didn't have time."

"That's alright."

"Wanna go drinking with us?" she asked.

"I'll bring you home again," Gammon offered, perking up. Hunter smiled.

"Thanks big guy," he replied. "Sure, why not."

"I'll make sure you don't drink too much," Gammon stated, finishing his second plate. "You need to be home on time for your girl."

"Ooo," Kris piped in, his interest clearly piqued. "Got a hot date Hunter?"

"Sure do," Hunter confirmed. He felt much better after realizing it'd been Trixie all along last night, and not that girl from the guild.

"Nice, Crispy," Sukri stated. "Hope to hell I find a nice hunk of meat to take me to his apartment tonight," she added. "I love living with you guys, but having to be quiet sucks."

"Yeah, please don't bring anyone back to our apartment," Kris pleaded. Gammon nodded in agreement.

"If she's not sleeping, no one is."

"Ooo, there's a story there," Donahue interjected, raising an eyebrow at Sukri. She ignored him.

"All right," she declared, standing up. "Let's go."

They left the community center, passing through the Outskirts and into Lowtown. They reached the shops near where Trixie had taken Hunter to buy his clothes…and where Hunter had gone drinking the night before. The bar was at the end of the street, a small black wooden building. A large, burly man was standing at the front door, blocking it. Sukri walked up to the guy, fearless as usual. Having Gammon behind her probably helped.

"We're closed," the man stated, crossing his arms over his chest.

"What do you mean you're closed?" Sukri asked. "It's the weekend."

"There's a curfew tonight," the man explained gruffly. "Haven't you heard?"

"Heard what?" Sukri pressed.

"The king died," the man stated. "One day of mourning. No alcohol." His expression darkened. "Ironclad took out the Gate patrol last night too," he added.

"Wait, what?" Kris blurted out. "The Ironclad attacked us?"

"That's right."

"Well shit," Sukri muttered. She glanced up at the guy. "Thanks anyway." She turned around, walking back the way they came. "Guess we're going home."

"That sucks," Kris muttered.

"The king died?" Hunter asked. Sukri nodded.

133

"Yeah, he was really old," she replied. "He would've been eight-three this year."

"He ruled for sixty years," Gammon added. "That's almost a record."

"So what happens now?"

"Well, he never did have a son," Gammon answered. "That means the next in line for the throne is the Duke of Wexford."

"Who?"

"He's the second-most powerful man in the kingdom," Sukri explained. "He's old as hell though. Got to be in his seventies."

"Yeah," Gammon agreed. Then he frowned. "Watch how you talk about him Sukri," he warned. "You should be more respectful."

"Sorry big guy," Sukri mumbled. For the first time, Hunter saw her look chastised. She noticed him looking at her. "Need to be careful what you say around here," she explained. "A lot of people really don't like you talking shit about anyone in the Acropolis."

"A few years ago," Gammon said, "…Sukri made a joke about the duke at a bar." He shook his head. "She got death threats for weeks. We've never been to that bar again."

"It was a nice bar too," Kris added wistfully.

"Lot of patriots here, if you know what I mean," Sukri stated. "Best if you don't talk politics."

"Got it," Hunter replied.

"I can't believe the Ironclad attacked us," Kris commented, shaking his head. "That scares the crap outta me."

"Yeah," Gammon agreed. "They haven't attacked Tykus in years."

"They attacked me," Hunter interjected. Everyone turned to look at him. "When I came through the Gate. Two of them attacked me. They killed a couple of soldiers before we managed to kill them."

"Damn," Kris swore. "You actually *saw* one? What was it like?"

"Terrifying," Hunter admitted, remembering the massive creatures. "Wait, that guy said they killed the Gate patrol?" he pressed. That was the group of soldiers Alasar had been with.

"Yeah," Sukri confirmed. Hunter felt a pang of fear. What if Alasar had been there when the things attacked? The guy had saved Hunter's life, after all…and had treated him like a human being, unlike most of the people here. He felt suddenly depressed.

"Guess we're going back to the apartment," Kris muttered.

"We could use the extra sleep," Gammon ventured. Donahue raised a hand.

"I've got alcohol at my place," he offered. "Wanna come?"

"We don't need sleep *that* much," Gammon decided. Sukri grinned at Donahue, punching him playfully in the shoulder.

"I knew I liked you," she declared. She grabbed his arm. "Show me the way, bartender!"

Gammon turned to Hunter.

"Are you coming with us?" he asked. Hunter considered it, then shook his head. He didn't feel like socializing all of a sudden. He just wanted to go home and go to sleep. Trixie had kept him up two nights in a row, after all.

"I'm beat," he replied. "Maybe tomorrow."

They walked back to the Outskirts, and Hunter parted with his friends, going back to his apartment. It was still the weekend, so he didn't have to meet up with Ekrin tonight, for which he was grateful. He climbed the stairs to his apartment, unlocking the door and stepping in. He flopped himself on his bed, his medallion resting heavily on his chest. He stared at it, remembering what Thorius had told him; he was supposed to wear it when he slept at night, but not if anyone else was going to be in the bed with him. He sighed, rolling off the bed and laying on his belly on the floor, peering under the bed. He was about to place the medallion there when he froze.

There was already something there. An obsidian cube.

He stared at it, then pulled it out. It had symbols carved into each of its six sides. He got up from the floor, sitting down at the edge of the bed, twirling it in his hands.

What the hell is this?

He took off the medallion, placing it on the floor. Then he closed his eyes, holding the cube close to his chest. Thorius had told him that stone absorbed emotions extremely well, and transmitted them powerfully.

Someone put it under my bed, he thought. *Were they trying to control my emotions?*

He held the cube, waiting to feel something. But other than feeling tired, nothing obvious came to him. He opened his eyes, staring at the cube. How long had it been there? Why was it there?

Trixie.

He felt a chill go down his spine. Had *she* put it there? She'd had access to his apartment, after all. And she'd still been here when

135

he'd gone to the Guild of Seekers this morning. But he'd already been wrong about her once…he didn't want to seem like he was paranoid.

Maybe it was there before I got the apartment.

It was a definite possibility. And he didn't really feel anything holding the cube, so it must not be that corrupted. Still, he didn't like the idea that it was here. He'd have to bring it to Thorius tomorrow, and see what the Master Trainer thought about it. If anyone would know, it was Thorius.

Hunter sighed, placing the cube on the floor near the bed. Then he grabbed his medallion, and hesitated. Trixie was coming tonight, so he shouldn't put it under the bed. He placed it in one corner of the apartment, then sat down on the bed again, thinking of Trixie. He still felt guilty about allowing her to do what she did when he didn't realize it was her, but the sting wasn't as bad as it'd been this morning. He supposed that Trixie just had that effect on him…he simply couldn't resist her. Hell, even thinking about her now made his body react. He closed his eyes, picturing her as she'd been last night, when she'd had her way with him that first time. When he'd given in to her, despite his mind's protests, and allowed her to bring him to ecstasy.

Damn, he thought, feeling himself growing steadily, straining against his pants.

There was a knock on the door.

"Come in," he called out, sitting up quickly and putting his arms in front of his groin. The door opened, but it wasn't Trixie that stepped through. It was Sukri. "Oh, hey," he greeted.

"Heya Crispy," she replied. "You got a minute?"

"Yeah, what's up?" he asked. "I thought you were going out drinking."

"Oh I am," she confirmed. "I just wanted to talk to you in private first. Nice place by the way," she added, looking around. Hunter grimaced.

"Ha ha."

"What's that?" she asked, gesturing at the cube near his bed. Hunter shrugged.

"Hell if I know," he replied. "I found it under the bed earlier." Sukri frowned, walking up to it and kneeling down, staring at its symbols.

"Well damn," she said, picking it up and rotating it slowly, looking at the symbols carved on its sides. "Holy shit."

"What?"

"This is a Temple Stone," she replied. "I can't believe this."

"What's that?"

"It's from the Acropolis," Sukri explained. "A block of obsidian from the Temple of Tykus," she added. "I've never actually seen one in real life before." She glanced at him. "These are incredibly rare. People here would kill to have one of these."

"What's it doing here?" he asked. Sukri shook her head.

"I have no idea," she admitted. "But someone really important must have put it here."

"Why?"

"Each Temple Stone is kept by the Alter of Tykus," she explained. "They're exposed to the most devout worshippers at the Temple, absorbing their wills. We're talking nobles here, not peasants like us. Tykus is strong with them."

"I don't get it," he admitted. "Why would someone put it under my bed?"

"To expose you to the will of the devout," Sukri answered. "They want to make you loyal to the kingdom...to Tykus."

"What?"

"You're an Original," Sukri explained. "They worship Originals, like Tykus. But they don't want to end up with another civil war."

"I don't understand," Hunter admitted. Sukri sighed, sitting down on his bed. He sat down next to her.

"Fifty years ago," she began, "...an Original came through the Gate. The kingdom took her in, and she lived in the Outskirts." She ran a hand through her hair. "The Outskirts were a lot bigger back then, covering the Deadlands."

"Wait, the Deadlands were..."

"Hold on," Sukri interrupted. "Let me finish." Hunter nodded. "There were a ton of people like us back then, immigrants the kingdom allowed to enter the city. People from other kingdoms coming to Tykus to try to live a better life."

"Okay."

"Tykus was, and is, the richest kingdom in the world," she continued. "Back then, the Lords were more generous, sometimes even allowing more wealthy peasants to rent land from them. People in the Outskirts could have homes, not just shitty apartments like this."

"Gee, thanks."

"Anyway, this Original, she lived in the Outskirts, at the very edge, near the Fringe."

"The what?"

"The edge of the forest," Sukri explained. "People who lived there were corrupted over time by the forest."

"Like corrupted with emotions?" Hunter pressed. Sukri hesitated.

"Sort of," she replied. "The forest hates us, so people who live near it started to hate the kingdom too. And they started to…change."

"Change how?"

"Well, you know how objects absorb emotions?" Sukri asked. Hunter nodded. "That's not all they absorb," she continued. "See, they absorb *everything* around them. Emotions, appearances, personalities…everything."

Hunter just stared at her.

"The forest changed the people near the Fringe, made them start to look different. A little darker, a little stranger. Just…not quite right. The Acropolis sent soldiers out regularly to examine the peasants, and if they thought a peasant was becoming too corrupted by the forest, they'd either throw them out of the city…or kill them."

"Wow."

"Yeah," Sukri muttered. "The Acropolis didn't want the peasants to turn against them, so they had to keep people from being too corrupted by the forest."

"How can the forest hate us?" Hunter asked. "I mean, it's just trees." Trees didn't have emotions, after all.

"I don't know," she admitted. "But it does. That's one of the reasons Tykus created the Deadlands," she added. "The forest is so far away now that it can't corrupt anyone in the city." She paused, putting the Temple Stone down, then putting her hands in her lap, glancing sidelong at him. "Anyway, the Original, she lived near the Fringe. One day, when the soldiers from the Acropolis came to take away corrupted peasants, she and a crowd of other peasants stopped them. They fought back, killing the soldiers, then starting a massive revolt in the city."

"Why?"

"They say she was corrupted by the forest too," Sukri answered. "And she was very strong-willed…a born leader. The peasants rallied around her, and she led them against Tykus, starting the Civil War."

"What happened?"

"The peasant army attacked the city, killing many of the nobles. Some even got past the inner wall, around the Acropolis itself. The Acropolis fought back, eventually killing most of the peasants. The survivors fled into the forest."

"What happened to the Original?" Hunter pressed. Sukri shrugged.

"No one knows," she answered. "She fled with the surviving peasants. No one ever saw them again." She sighed. "After that, the Outskirts were...significantly downsized. The king ordered most of it demolished, turning it into the Deadlands. Then one of the dukes had the wall built around the city to keep out any immigrants...anyone corrupted by the forest, and anyone who wasn't like them. Like Tykus."

"Damn."

"People like me," she continued, "...and Gammon and Kris, we're descendants of the original peasants. That's why we look different than everybody else." She sighed. "They let us live here, but we'll never be anything but peasants. Becoming a Seeker is the only way out for us."

"I get it," Hunter muttered. It was the only way out of here for him, too...literally and figuratively. She smiled at him, putting a hand on his knee.

"I know you do," she replied. "You're one of us now."

"Thanks for taking me in," Hunter stated, smiling back.

"Aw, no problem Crispy," Sukri replied. She leaned against him, resting her head against his shoulder, her hair tickling the side of his face. He was suddenly reminded of Trixie, of how her hair had done the same the night before. Even the thought of it made him shift uneasily on the bed. If it hadn't been for Sukri's hand on his knee, he would've put his hands in his lap. "I'm glad I did, you know."

"Huh?"

"I'm glad I took you in," she clarified, turning her head to look at him. He'd never really noticed her eyes before. They were bright blue, almond-shaped, and slightly slanted...quite stunning, actually. Her lips were much fuller than Trixie's, he couldn't help but wonder what it would feel like to kiss them.

"Me too," he murmured, pushing the thought away.

"You're almost as much of an ass as I am," she added with a grin. He had to smile at that.

"Yeah, you're probably right about that."

"Of course I am," she agreed. She sighed, staring at him for a long moment, then shaking her head. "Damn," she muttered.

"What?"

"I gotta get off this bed," she said, standing up and walking to the other side of the room. "Damn Hunter," she added. "You must've had a hell of a night last night." He stared at her.

"What are you talking about?"

"Ah, that's better," she said, ignoring his question. "Who's the girl you've been seeing?"

"Her name's Trixie," he answered.

"What does she look like?"

"Blond hair, blue eyes," Hunter replied. "Cute," he added. He frowned then. "She looked exactly like the woman from the tryouts," he added.

"Which one?"

Hunter explained what had happened after the first round of eliminations, after he'd faced the homeless wretch in that tiny room. The woman who'd looked like Trixie's twin. When he finished, Sukri just stared at him for a long moment.

"What?" he asked.

"You're talking about the woman who tried to seduce us," Sukri stated. Hunter nodded.

"Yeah, that's right."

Sukri stared at him a moment longer, then crossed her arms over her chest.

"How did you meet her?"

Hunter explained his meeting with Ekrin, and how Trixie had been tasked with showing him the town, and his apartment. When he was done, Sukri paused, then sat down on the bed next to him again, shaking her head slowly.

"Holy shit," she muttered. She turned to look at him. "You do realize what she is, don't you?"

"Uh, no."

"Hunter," Sukri stated, putting a hand on his arm. "Your girlfriend's a prostitute."

Hunter stared at her blankly.

"That woman at the test," Sukri pressed. "She was a prostitute too."

"Ha ha," Hunter replied. "Very funny Sukri." But Sukri shook her head.

"I'm dead serious," she retorted. "All of the higher-end hookers in the city look like that. Exactly like that."

"That doesn't make any sense," Hunter protested. "Trixie's not a hooker! Why would Ekrin send a hooker to help me find my apartment?"

Sukri regarded him silently for a long moment, then sighed. "You're right," she mumbled. "It doesn't make much sense, does it?"

"No, it doesn't," Hunter agreed.

"Sorry," she mumbled.

"Hey, no problem," Hunter reassured her. "You're just looking out for me, I get it."

"That's what friends do," she agreed, giving him a smile. Then she turned, looking down at the bed, the sheet covering it bunched up at the end. She ran a hand over it, then laid back, turning so that she was laying lengthwise. She shuffled over, leaving an empty spot next to her, and patting it with her hand. "Come on, take a load off, Crispy."

"Like, lay down?" he asked.

"I've been standing and sitting the whole damn day," she replied. "I'm gonna let the blood outta my legs." She patted the bed again. "Come on," she pressed. "It feels weird with you sitting over me like that. Like you're my dad putting me to sleep."

"All right," Hunter agreed. He laid down next to her, feeling a little awkward. She laughed.

"Look at you, all nervous," she observed. "You shy, Crispy?"

"Only around pretty girls," he quipped, smiling back. She arched an eyebrow.

"All right," she murmured. "You got *some* game." She rolled onto her side, looking at him. "How're you holding up, anyway?"

"What do you mean?"

"Well let's see," she began. "You're stranded on a strange world forever, no chance of ever going back home. You're living in a rotten slum with a bunch of people that hate you and are afraid of you." She grinned then. "And your apartment sucks. I mean it *really* sucks."

"Tell me about it," he agreed, breaking out into a grin.

"So?" she pressed. "Answer the question."

"I'm…" he began, then sighed. The truth was, he didn't know how he was doing. He hadn't really had much time to think about it. His days had been spent with Sukri and the rest of the gang, and his nights with Trixie. He hadn't had much time to himself. To reflect. "I don't know," he confessed.

"Sorry Hunter," she murmured, putting a hand on his arm. "I can't imagine what it would be like, being you."

"What, being black?" he quipped. But she didn't smile.

"Being lost," she countered.

He said nothing, but swallowed noisily, turning away from her and staring up at the ceiling. She was right…he *was* lost. And Sukri, Kris, Gammon, and of course Trixie were the only people he had in this new world. Hell, if it hadn't been for Sukri, he'd never have had a chance at finding his mom.

"Thanks for everything, Sukri," he said, turning back to her. She smiled, saying nothing, looking back at him silently with those blue, slightly slanted eyes. He found himself staring back, once again surprised at how striking her eyes were. Again, he found his gaze drawn to her lips, so much fuller than Trixie's thin, pale lips. They were slightly parted, and whether due to a sudden burst of affection for her, or her closeness, he had the sudden urge to kiss them.

"Whatcha thinking?" she inquired.

"Nothing you'd wanna know," he replied with a smirk. She arched an eyebrow.

"You sure 'bout that?"

"Not really," he admitted. She raised both eyebrows then, and rolled onto her back, stretching her arms over her head and yawning. He stole a glance at her body; she was curvy in all the right places, unlike Trixie's slim, more angular shape. Sukri was more…feminine. He raised his gaze to her eyes as she finished her stretch, rolling back onto her side and looking back at him. She put a warm hand on his arm again, then slid it down until it rested on his upper thigh.

"Let's see if I can figure it out," she murmured, leaning in close, her lips inches from his now. He felt her hand slide sideways on his upper thigh, toward his groin…and felt himself growing to meet that hand, sliding under it. Part of him wanted to pull away, to stand up and leave the room. But he was intoxicated by her…her eyes, her scent. Her closeness. He stayed where he was, feeling her hand on him, the gentle pressure promising a…

Then she pulled away, sitting up.

"What...?" he began.

"Wow," Sukri said, running a hand through her hair. "Okay, I think I need to stop there." She took a deep breath in, then let it out. "Have I made my point?"

"What point?" he asked, sitting up and hastily hiding the bulge in his pants. She glanced at it, then at him.

"Objects absorb emotions, right?" she said. Hunter nodded. She patted the bed with one hand. "I'll give you one guess what emotion your bed's absorbed."

Hunter stared down at the bed, then blanched.

"Yeah," Sukri stated. "Your bed is horny as hell." She backed away from him, getting off the bed and standing up. "And if I don't get off of it now, we're *going* to have sex."

Hunter stared at her, then got off the bed too, staring at it.

"You're saying that my bed is making me...uh, us...horny?" She nodded.

"Sorry to say," she replied with a wry smirk. "Not that I don't like you, Hunter. But I barely know you."

"Why did you..." he began, remembering how she'd touched him.

"I wanted to prove my point," she answered. "Touching your happy place wasn't part of the plan, but I underestimated how goddamn powerful that bed is." She shook her head. "Must've had a hell of a night last night, huh?"

"Tell me about it," Hunter muttered. That explained why he wasn't able to stop Trixie from having her way with him last night, when he'd thought she was someone else. The bed had affected him just as much as Thorius's crystal sphere, controlling his emotions. "Jesus," he murmured, shaking his head.

"Hunter," Sukri said, breaking him from his reverie. "I'm sorry to say this, but your girlfriend really is a whore."

"Come on," Hunter retorted. "How can you say that?"

"Every girl from the higher-end brothels looks the same," Sukri explained. "They're raised in the brothels, absorbing all the...emotions stored in the rooms. I'm talking a shit-ton of lust, hundreds of years' worth of it, stored in those buildings." She sighed. "The girls raised there worship at a different altar than everyone else. An altar in the brothel, one that turns them into friggin' nymphomaniacs."

"I don't get it."

"Well," Sukri began, "…it's hard to explain to someone who hasn't grown up here. I mean, it's like you don't even know how the world works."

"Then teach me."

"I'll try," she replied. "But I need to get away from that fucking bed. Let's go for a walk."

They did just that, Sukri leading him out of the apartment and down the stairs to the docks below. The sun was close to setting, light splaying across the water below. Hunter realized that he didn't feel aroused at all anymore. He glanced at Sukri; she was attractive, and did have pretty eyes, but he no longer found her irresistible.

"Okay," Sukri stated. "Here goes. So, every generation, there's a few people who are just absolutely amazing at whatever their job is. Geniuses who're better than everyone else, right?"

"Right," Hunter agreed. Like Einstein.

"Eventually these people die," she continued. "And the kingdom mummifies them, then keeps their bones."

"Why would they do that?"

"Well, you know how stone absorbs emotions better than wood?" she replied. Hunter nodded; Thorius had said as much. "Bones are like stone," she explained. "They absorb everything about a person, because they live with that person for their whole life, obviously."

"Makes sense."

"So here you have it…everything about a person, down to their personality, their appearance, *everything*…is stored in their bones after they die. Especially the skull, since it was so close to the brain. And anyone who goes near those bones will start to absorb that shit."

"So you're telling me that if I went near someone's bones," Hunter stated, "…I'd start absorbing everything about them?"

"Right," Sukri confirmed. "If you did it for long enough, anyway. You'd start looking a little more like them, acting like them…you'd even start *thinking* like them."

"Jesus."

"Every profession in Tykus has a bunch of these geniuses from different generations, their bodies mummified and their bones stored where apprentices can be exposed to them. After years of exposure, these apprentices almost *become* those geniuses." She paused. "That way, these geniuses throughout history are never lost.

144

They live on through each generation, continuing their work for the kingdom."

Hunter said nothing, trying to take it all in. The idea that someone could almost *become* someone else just by being near their bones for long enough...

"Well, the same thing is used in the sex industry," Sukri continued. "The sexiest, most insatiable women...their bones are preserved, and placed in altars in the brothels. Or sometimes even under the prostitutes' beds. So they're exposed to that all day long."

"Holy shit."

"That's not all," Sukri stated. "See, the prostitutes become insatiable, but they also *exude* that sex drive, and give it – at least temporarily – to anyone they're near for long enough."

"So anyone that's around them gets turned on," Hunter deduced. She snorted.

"Not just turned on, Crispy. Horny as *hell*." She smirked. "Like, can't help yourself horny." She gestured back the way they'd come. "What do you think would've happened if I hadn't gotten off that bed on time?"

Hunter said nothing, knowing exactly what would've happened. The same thing that'd happened when he hadn't realized it was Trixie.

"I'm telling you," Sukri insisted, putting a hand on his shoulder. "Your girlfriend's a prostitute. I'm not saying she doesn't like you...they like *everybody*. Remember, they're insatiable. And I can guarantee you she's never met someone who didn't like her, at least eventually." She sighed. "If you spend enough time with them, you're going to have sex with them. Doesn't matter who you are, or if you're a girl, or a boy, or don't even like girls."

"I don't know..." Hunter mumbled. He couldn't imagine Trixie as a prostitute, selling herself like that. She was too sweet, too kind and thoughtful.

"What did you think of her when you first met her?" Sukri asked.

Hunter turned away from her, staring at the docks as he walked.

"I wasn't impressed," he admitted. He'd thought she was dumb, and pretty, but not *that* pretty. A stupid snap-judgement, or so he'd thought.

"Not until you were near her for a while, huh?" Sukri pressed. He glanced at her, then nodded, feeling a sinking sensation in the pit of his stomach. The idea that everything he'd felt for her – the affection, the attraction, the lust – had been her manipulating him, just as Thorius's sphere had done, was monumentally depressing. He felt Sukri's hand squeeze his shoulder, and glanced up at her.

"Sorry Hunter," she apologized. "I hate to be the one to shit on your joy."

"I can't believe it," he muttered.

"Hey, if it makes you feel better, we can go back to your place and lay on your bed," she offered with a grin. "Not gonna lie, I was damn tempted to let that play out earlier."

"Ditto," Hunter confessed. The way he'd felt about Sukri then, the sudden, overwhelming attraction, was proof enough that she was right about the bed. And maybe even about Trixie. Now that he was walking with Sukri, he had no such feelings at all. If Trixie herself was the source of that emotion, then being near her would be the same as being near his bed…to similar effect.

"I'd better get going," Sukri said, flashing him another smile. "Don't let anyone near your bed," she added. "Especially Kris."

"I'll do my best," he replied. Sukri stopped, then leaned in and gave him a hug.

"Take care of yourself, Crispy."

"You too," he replied. "And thanks."

She pulled away, waving at him and walking back toward her apartment on the other end of town. He watched her go, then sighed, standing where he was. He could go back home…*had* to go back home, eventually…and that meant dealing with Trixie. If he went anywhere near his bed – or her – he wouldn't be able to control himself. They would end up in bed together for another marathon session. And while he would most certainly enjoy that, the better part of him resented not being in control.

The question was, why did Ekrin hire a prostitute to show him around? Why would Ekrin want him to fall for Trixie?

He sighed again, staring across the water at Lowtown in the distance. He *had* to go home. There was no place else for him to go, unless he tried staying with Sukri. And he didn't very much feel like sleeping on their couch. He had to face Trixie, and turn her away. Avoiding the issue wouldn't solve anything.

He took a deep breath in, then began the short walk back to his apartment.

CHAPTER 11

The Duke of Wexford's carriage moved steadily down the King's Road, the vast wasteland of the Deadlands extending off into the distance to meet the tree line of the Fringe. The road ran parallel to the forest for a few kilometers, then pulled away, turning left to cut through the barren landscape. It would only be a few more kilometers before they reached Tykus now.

Dominus stretched his back, sore from being in the carriage for the last few hours. He used to be able to make these trips without feeling any discomfort at all. Time was destroying his body; he considered it a gift that it hadn't taken his mind. At seventy-five, he'd reached an age that few were lucky enough to experience. Each day now was a gift, one he dared not take for granted.

Suddenly the carriage slowed, then stopped. Dominus frowned, feeling Axio's gaze upon him. He ignored the boy, looking out of his window at the road ahead. There were soldiers there, standing at the edges of the road on either side. They weren't his personal soldiers either…they wore the uniform of the Acropolis's Royal Guard. One of these soldiers approached Dominus's carriage, only to be intercepted by Dominus's personal guards. After a brief conversation, one of these guards stepped up to the window, bowing before Dominus.

"My liege," he greeted. "There's been a complication."

Dominus just stared at the man, who swallowed nervously.

"There's been an attack on the Deadlands military base," he informed. "And on the soldiers guarding the Gate." He hesitated. "It was the Ironclad, your Grace."

"When?" Dominus inquired calmly.

"Last night."

"What is the damage?" he pressed.

"Still being assessed," the guard answered. "Moderate casualties, but very little damage to infrastructure."

"How large was the attacking force?"

"Huge," the guard replied. "The survivors had never seen so many of the things in one place before." He paused. "I'm surprised anyone survived." He wiped sweat from his forehead. "Survivors say the things seemed to be looking for something."

Dominus frowned, lowering his gaze to his lap for a moment, then turning back to the guard.

"Is the King's Road secure?" he asked. The guard nodded.

"It is, my Duke."

"Then continue," Dominus ordered.

The carriage continued forward moments later, passing a long line of Royal guards. Dominus ignored them, feeling Axio's eyes upon him. He turned to the boy.

"Speak," he stated.

"I'm surprised your Grace," Axio admitted. "The Ironclad haven't attacked us in years, much less a full-scale assault."

"True," Dominus agreed.

"Why would they do so now?"

"The answer requires deduction," Dominus answered. "The Ironclad have targeted a military base and a single post on a road remote from that base."

"By the Gate," Axio added.

"The Ironclad were apparently looking for something," Dominus continued. "Or perhaps someone." He considered the possibilities. "There are no vital artifacts, Ossae, or personnel in that base. Certainly not vital to the kingdom, nor valuable to the Ironclad. And the forces they deployed should have been able to destroy the base entirely…yet they did not."

Axio said nothing, to his credit. The boy really did know how – and when – to listen. The when was perhaps even more important than the how.

"The Gate post was not attacked randomly," Dominus continued. "It's too far away from the base, and there are other posts closer to the base. So we have two assumptions we can make: the Ironclad are looking for something, and that something is related to the Gate."

Again, Axio remained silent.

"The Ironclad have patrolled the Gate since they appeared twenty-three years ago," Dominus stated. "No Originals have come through in that time frame. This leads me to believe that an Original came through recently, and that Tykus took the Original in, likely after a battle with the patrolling Ironclad."

"I left Tykus only a few days ago, my liege," Axio countered. "I did not hear of an Original coming through the Gate."

"Then we have our timeframe," Dominus replied. "There are only two places the Ironclad would suspect an Original would go: the base, or the kingdom itself. If the Original was in the base, we have lost them. If they are in the kingdom, then we must prepare for another assault."

Axio stared at Dominus for a long moment.

"An assault, your Grace? On Tykus?"

"Correct," Dominus confirmed.

"But…"

"The Ironclad have greater numbers than we estimated," Dominus interrupted. "They value the Original highly enough to risk an army to find her. Or him," he added.

"But why would the Ironclad want an Original?" Axio pressed.

Dominus sighed, turning away from the boy and staring out of the window, at the barren landscape of the Deadlands. A man-made desert, the ashes of a war that had torn Tykus apart. All because of one damn woman.

"That," Dominus replied at last, "…is an excellent question."

* * *

Hunter swung his legs over the side of his bed, rubbing the sleep out of his eyes. Then he yawned, squinting against the bright light coming through his bedroom window. He stood up, glancing down at the bed, seeing an all-too-familiar woman lying on her side there, half-covered by a thin sheet.

Damn.

She'd come for him the night before, maybe an hour after Sukri had left. He'd tried to resist her, tried to send her away, but she'd leaned in to hug him, and then they'd started kissing. One thing had

149

led to another…and another, and another. They hadn't actually slept until early the next morning…and he was paying for it now.

He yawned, thankful that she was still asleep. Despite everything, half of him wanted to wake her up, to go at it again. Even knowing that it was Trixie's influence twisting his mind wasn't enough…he wanted her, and wanted her badly. She was like an itch that wouldn't go away, no matter how many times he scratched it. And yet it felt so good each time.

He pulled on his uniform silently, grabbing his medallion, then exiting his apartment, leaving Trixie there. He went downstairs, making his way to the community center.

You have to cut it off tonight, he told himself, weaving between apartments. He reached the community center within minutes, enjoying the usual reception from the rest of the townsfolk. He ignored them, walking into the building. To his relief, he didn't see Sukri anywhere…or Gammon or Kris, for that matter. It looked to be almost noon, so they were probably already waiting at the guild. He grabbed some grub, eating quickly, then took the long walk to the Guild of Seekers. As predicted, Sukri and the gang were standing before the double-doors to the guild, along with Donahue, Lucus, and the other candidates. Sukri smirked at him as he approached.

"Couldn't do it, could you," she greeted. Hunter grimaced.

"You were right," he admitted.

"Of course I was," Sukri agreed.

"Right about what?" Gammon asked.

"Never mind," Hunter grumbled, giving Sukri a look. Mercifully, she said nothing, and Gammon, being ever the polite giant, didn't press the issue.

"Hey man," Kris greeted, clapping him on the shoulder. "Hope you did better than me last night."

"Doubt it."

The doors opened, and Master Thorius himself appeared.

"Come," he ordered. He led them into the building and through the hallway to their customary room, and each candidate split up, going with their respective trainers. As before, Thorius stayed in the room with Hunter. The man eyed Hunter with that unnervingly unreadable expression he always had.

"Come closer," he ordered. Hunter obeyed, stepping up until he was only a foot from the man. Thorius put a hand on Hunter's shoulder, closing his eyes. Then he opened his eyes, raising an eyebrow.

"You've been consorting with interesting company," he stated. Hunter grimaced.

"So I've learned," he admitted.

"Stop," Thorius ordered. Hunter grimaced.

"I tried," he replied, shaking his head. "I couldn't stop myself."

"You'll have to," Thorius retorted, "…if you want to become a Seeker." He let go of Hunter's shoulder. "I told you yesterday that you needed to train your willpower, so that you could resist the effects of transmitted emotions."

"How?"

"You must be aware of the emotions around you," Thorius answered. "To do that, you have to be aware of what is you and what is not."

"What is me?"

"You need to be very aware of who *you* are," Thorius explained. "Without that, you'll never realize that others are attempting to change you." He reached in his pocket, retrieving a familiar crystal sphere. "Take this."

Hunter hesitated, then did as he was told.

"Pay attention to who you are now," Thorius continued. "To how you feel about me. Try to hold on to that," he added. "When you feel your emotions shifting away from that center, recognize the shift, and try to center yourself again."

Hunter nodded, feeling suddenly uneasy. He glanced at the crystal, then at Thorius. Then he closed his eyes, trying to focus on what he was feeling. Nervous, certainly. Not angry though, at least not yet. Maybe a little irritated, though. Thorius had jumped right in to this test, without really preparing him for it. Kind of a dick move. If he'd been a better teacher, he would've actually, you know, *prepared* Hunter first.

Hunter opened his eyes, seeing Thorius eyeing him critically. Waiting for him to crack, no doubt. The guy probably got a hard-on watching students fail these tests over and over, proving his superiority over them. And beating the crap out of them when they inevitably attacked.

Wouldn't mind that job, Hunter mused.

Hunter waited, and still Thorius just stared at him.

"We gonna do this all day?" Hunter muttered. Thorius said nothing. Didn't even bother to answer.

Prick.

Hunter gripped the sphere tightly, its surface slick against his sweaty palm. Another minute passed, and still Thorius just stood there.

"Come on man," Hunter protested. "Haven't we done this long enough?"

Still nothing.

"Jesus," Hunter grumbled, glaring at the man. Thorius stared back impassively, looking smug, as usual. Hunter had the sudden urge to wipe that smug look off his face. Maybe the asshole wouldn't get so lucky this time, and Hunter would get a good hit in. Knock the bastard right on his self-righteous ass.

Hunter glanced at the sphere, staring at it.

Pay attention to who you are, he thought.

He closed his eyes, remembering how he'd felt earlier. Mostly calm, neutral toward Thorius. Maybe a little intimidated.

That's before he started acting like a dick, he told himself. *Refusing to talk to you, ignoring your questions.*

He opened his eyes, staring at the sphere. Then he looked past it, at Thorius. He felt a spike of irritation, a sudden desire to chuck the sphere as hard as he could, right at the asshole's face. He imagined himself smashing the man's face in with it, beating him over and over until his face was a bloody mess. The image made him feel almost giddy, and he gripped the sphere tighter, imagining how good it would feel to give in.

"I can't," he blurted out, dropping the sphere and stepping backward. Thorius darted forward, snatching the sphere out of the air with shocking speed and placing it back in his pocket. Hunter backed away from the man, his heart pounding in his chest.

"Well done," Thorius declared, nodding at Hunter. "You lasted far longer than I expected."

"Jesus," Hunter muttered, his back striking the wall behind him. He pressed himself against it, feeling the rage dissipate quickly, replaced by a sudden exhaustion. "Holy crap that thing is powerful."

"It is," Thorius agreed, patting his pocket. "Trust me, I know."

"How do you do it?" Hunter asked. "I wanted to bash your skull in with that thing," he added. "No offense."

"None taken," Thorius replied. "It isn't easy," he added. "It takes a lot of practice. There's an old Seeker saying: 'emotion is temporary, action is forever.' Acting on your impulses will rarely benefit you. Developing a strong foundation of *self*, of a core being that is undeniably *you*, is the key." He sighed. "But first, we must create a better you."

"A better me?"

"That is the purpose of your medallion," Thorius explained. "Come," he added. "Let's go for a walk."

With that, Thorius led Hunter out of the Guild of Seekers and across the bridge over the moat, to the courtyard beyond. They crossed the courtyard quickly, heading into the streets of Lowtown. The streets were crowded, likely due to the noon lunch break, and they would have had trouble making their way forward if it hadn't been for Hunter's disagreeable appearance.

"What do you notice about these people?" Thorius asked, gesturing at the crowd around them.

"They're assholes," Hunter replied. Thorius smirked.

"Perhaps to you," he conceded. "Can you tell me why?"

"They think I'm contagious," Hunter answered. "That they'll turn brown like me."

"And what do you think about that?" Thorius pressed. Hunter shrugged, remembering Trixie's subtle tan…and how her eyes had started to turn green when she'd been around him for too long.

"I think they're a bunch of racists."

"Hmm," Thorius murmured. "You think they hate you because of the color of your skin?"

"Don't they?"

"No," Thorius replied. He pulled out the crystalline orb from his pocket, holding it out at Hunter. Hunter took a step away from it reflexively.

"What are you doing?" he demanded. Thorius put the sphere back in his pocket.

"Why did you back away?" he inquired.

"Because I don't like having my emotions messed with," Hunter answered. "And I'd prefer not to murder anyone today, thank you."

"You want to stay yourself," Thorius translated.

"Right," Hunter agreed.

"Isn't that all these people want?" Thorius inquired, gesturing at the people around them – giving them wide berth, as usual.

"Well yeah, but that's different."

"Oh really?" Thorius pressed, raising his eyebrows. "Tell me, what makes you *you*?"

"My personality," Hunter replied. "My memories, my thoughts…"

"And your appearance, correct?" Thorius stated. Hunter paused, then nodded grudgingly. "What if you woke up tomorrow and looked like someone else? How would that make you feel?"

"Not great."

"What if you knew that, just by being close to someone, you might start to lose who you were?" Thorius pressed. "Your appearance, your personality, your thoughts?"

"Well yeah, but that doesn't really happen like that, does it?" Hunter countered. "I mean, sure they might get a little tan, but that's it."

"Not true," Thorius retorted. "Emotions aren't the only thing that objects – including people – absorb and transmit. Personality, appearance, skills…all of these qualities are transmittable. Even memories," he added.

"I find that hard to believe."

"I'm quite serious," Thorius insisted. "Every aspect of who you are is 'contagious,' as you put it. It is exactly the same as the process that changes emotions, only slower. The more powerful the trait, the more rapidly it will be absorbed by another. Proximity and duration of exposure determine the extent of change."

"You're saying I could change people's *personalities*?"

"And they can change yours," Thorius added. "And everything else about you."

Hunter stared at the people around him. Suddenly it didn't seem so insulting that they chose to stay away from him. He turned to Thorius.

"Why aren't *you* afraid of me?" he asked.

"Traits are absorbed more quickly in those whom those traits are weak," Thorius explained. "People with weak wills are more easily influenced by those with strong wills. Conversely, people with strong wills – such as myself – have less to fear. We're far more likely to change others than be changed ourselves."

"What about me?" Hunter pressed. He'd been around Trixie a lot recently, and Sukri, Gammon, and Kris. Had *they* changed him? He felt the same as he always did, but would he really know if he was different?

"You have a strong will," Thorius reassured him. "That is, in part, why you were chosen as a candidate for the guild."

"So I haven't changed?" Hunter pressed.

"Regrettably, no."

"Ha ha," Hunter grumbled. "So you're saying that anyone can change anyone else…just by being close to them for long enough?"

"Correct…depending on their will."

"Wow," Hunter muttered. "Damn."

"So you see," Thorius continued, "…these people don't hate you because of your skin. They don't hate you at all. They just don't want to lose who *they* are. And everything about them…their skin color, hair color, eye color, customs, beliefs…defines who they are. 'Mixing' with you, or anyone else who is greatly different from them, would threaten their very identity."

They rounded a corner, reaching the church plaza. Thorius stopped in the middle of the plaza, watching as people filed into the massive building. He kept well clear of the crowd, and people kept well clear of them.

"Look at these people," Thorius said, gesturing at the line. "What do you see?"

Hunter did so. The people were all tall, thin, with blond hair and blue eyes. They could all have been part of the same lily-white 1950's family. It was like the Brady Bunch's big family reunion.

"They're all the same," he observed.

"They are one people," Thorius explained. "United by a shared ancestry, shared appearance, shared customs. They don't fear each other because they're one race."

"I get it," Hunter conceded.

"Imagine if your family were the same," Thorius continued. "And a stranger – looking differently than you, talking differently, with strange customs – came to live with you. If you let him, that stranger would forever change you. He would, by mixing with you, make you different than your family. You would no longer belong. And if you were to then stay near your family, they too would begin to change, until everything that made you *you* – and everything that made your family what it is – was destroyed."

Hunter said nothing, watching the line of people. Then he turned to Thorius.

"I get it," he repeated. "I don't like it, but I get it."

"Look down," Thorius ordered. Hunter did so, seeing the large rectangular stone blocks that made up the floor of the plaza. "What do you see?"

"Stone," Hunter answered.

"And what does stone do?" Thorius pressed. Hunter blinked.

155

"It stores emotions," he answered. Thorius raised an eyebrow. "And?"

"And other traits," Hunter added.

"These stone slabs were placed here purposefully," Thorius explained, gesturing at the ground. "Every time a particularly devout citizen dies, they're buried here, beneath one of these gravestones."

"These are graves?" Hunter blurted out, taking a step back.

"They are," Thorius confirmed. "And the bones of the devout lay directly below, exuding the traits of those who died. The gravestone absorbs these traits, and transmits them up to the people near the church."

"Making everyone more devout?" Hunter asked. Thorius nodded.

"In this way, the devout are rewarded with a prestigious grave, and the populace benefit from the desirable traits of the deceased." He gestured at the church. "The *most* devout have their bones added to the altar, where worshippers will benefit."

"Making sure everyone drinks the Kool-Aid," Hunter concluded. "Got it."

"The what?"

"Never mind," Hunter muttered. "So if I stand here long enough, I'll start believing this sh…tuff?" Thorius frowned.

"You seem skeptical of our religion," he observed. "Why?"

"You worship some guy named Tykus," Hunter replied with a shrug. "I don't believe anyone is worthy of worship."

"That may be true," Thorius reasoned. "But are some men worth emulating?"

"Yeah, sure."

"And that is what our religion is truly about," Thorius explained. "We worship Tykus, yes…because He was a model human being, of superior intellect, will, and wisdom. If more people emulate Him, they will benefit from it by elevating themselves. The kingdom itself benefits from a populace of superior intellect and wisdom, does it not?"

"Alright, I'll give you that one."

"To worship is to revere, to recognize the superior qualities that make something worthy of admiration and adulation. Tykus is worthy of this."

"Still seems like a cult to me," Hunter retorted.

"You have a strong will," Thorius replied. "You naturally resist things that are not you." He turned away from the church, beginning the walk back to the Guild of Seekers. "Come," he urged. "I want to show you one more thing."

They made their way back to the guild, and Thorius led Hunter to their usual meeting room. The Master Trainer gestured at Hunter's medallion.

"This is made of obsidian," he stated. "Can you guess its function?"

Hunter frowned, grabbing the medallion and turning it over in his hands. Then he closed his eyes, taking stock of how he was feeling. A little tired, but otherwise neutral. He waited, but felt nothing else, and opened his eyes, shaking his head.

"I can't tell."

"There are no significant emotions in it," Thorius informed him. "But there is a great deal else."

"Like what?"

Thorius burst forward suddenly, shoving Hunter backward. Or at least he tried to; Hunter stepped to the side just in time, shoving Thorius's shoulder. The man fell into a backward somersault, rising to his feet in one smooth motion.

Hunter stared at Thorius, then at his own hands. He hadn't even had time to think about what to do, yet he'd reacted instantly to Thorius's attack.

"How the…"

"The medallion," Thorius interjected calmly, "…transmits skills." He smiled. "Skills we Seekers find valuable, such as self-defense."

"You mean I learned that from a rock?" Hunter asked. Thorius smirked.

"A carefully produced piece of obsidian," he countered, "…exposed to experienced Seekers over long periods of time. Engineered with the singular purpose of making you," he added, pointing at Hunter's chest. "…more like them."

Hunter glanced down at the medallion resting on his chest, then back up at Thorius.

"So you're saying if I wear this, I'll end up as good as them?" he asked. Thorius shook his head.

"Not quite," he replied. "Skills – and every other absorbable trait – can never be as powerful as their original source." He gestured at the medallion. "Something is lost every time their skills are transferred. Your medallion holds less skill than the Seekers who made them, and you in turn will hold less than the medallion. Anyone exposed to you will absorb even less. The original source of the trait is always the most powerful."

"Oh," Hunter replied. He touched the medallion. "That's why you want us to carry these things with us all the time," he realized. "To maximize our exposure."

"That's right," Thorius agreed. "And why you can't wear it when others are close by, such as the prostitute you've been enjoying."

Hunter felt his cheeks flush, and was thankful for his dark skin. "I didn't know," he protested. "Ekrin had her show me around town, and one thing led to another…"

"I understand your innocence," Thorius reassured. "And your handler was doing what he thought was right, ensuring that you would remain…occupied at night, so as not to get in too much trouble."

"What do you mean?"

"The kingdom has had trouble with Originals in the past," Thorius explained. Or rather, with one particular Original. Ensuring that you were…well taken care of served the purpose of endearing you to the kingdom. Tykus hardly wants another Civil War."

"I heard about that," Hunter said. "Some Original came fifty years ago, starting the war?" Thorius nodded.

"A woman much like you," he confirmed. "With dark skin, and a strong will."

"She was black?" Hunter asked.

"Brown," Thorius corrected. Hunter frowned, staring at the Master Trainer for a long moment.

"What was her name?" he pressed. Thorius hesitated.

"That's an interesting question," he replied. "Why do you ask?"

"Just curious," Hunter said. Thorius sighed.

"Her name," he answered, "…was Neesha."

CHAPTER 12

The Lord Duke Dominus's carriage stopped in front of the massive portcullis of Tykus, the only way through the great wall surrounding the city. One of the two guards at the gate walked up to the side of the carriage, peering inside. Of course the guard knew that it was Dominus's carriage, by virtue of its unique appearance, and by the literal army of soldiers that had accompanied him. But the guard was still obligated to check. Dominus had designed the wall, and the system of securing it, himself, at the king's request. One guard would verify the identity of anyone requesting entrance, while the other guard stayed behind in case of an ambush. More guards were hidden above, within the wall, peering through narrow slits. Archers could attack through these slits, killing potential intruders. And even if someone managed to fool the outer guardsmen, there was still the inner portcullis to protect the city, with a large number of soldiers occupying the relatively narrow tunnel in-between, able to surround and destroy the enemy.

Not a single intruder had gotten by the system since its construction.

The guard saw Dominus, then bowed deeply.

"My Duke," he greeted. He gestured at the other guard, and moments later the portcullis began to rise. Nearly a meter thick, the gate was wrought of steel, and utterly impenetrable. When it finished opening, the carriage moved forward again, entering the tunnel beyond. The inner portcullis opened soon afterward,

159

Dominus's carriage – and his army of soldiers – passing through into the street beyond.

"Will the coronation be today?" Axio inquired. Dominus nodded.

"Tykus must be reborn in our newest king," he declared.

Axio hesitated, then cleared his throat.

"Will anything of you be left?" he asked. Dominus sighed.

"When the process is complete," he replied, "...very little of the man who lived before will remain. He will be, for all intents and purposes, Tykus himself."

They stopped before the grand stairway to the Acropolis, and the driver detached the horses from the carriage, pulling them to one side. Dominus's guards swarmed around the carriage then; there were small posts on the sides, and the guards grabbed these, heaving the carriage up off of the ground. More guards removed the wheels, and then began the long journey up the massive staircase, carrying the carriage above the stairs. His guards would replace each other as they tired, carrying the carriage all the way up to the inner wall surrounding the Acropolis. Dominus of course could not have made it up the stairway himself; it'd been nearly a decade since he'd made this trip on his own legs.

How time had betrayed him, decay rotting his body slowly, from the inside! His lifeblood barely flowed through his arteries; it was only a matter of time before it stopped altogether. Every bit of flesh on his feet that died, that turned black and withered away, was a reminder of the inexorable march of time.

Of his impending doom.

"I think I understand how the king serves," Axio stated. Dominus regarded the boy silently. Axio was staring off into the distance, a troubled look on his face.

"I suspect you do," Dominus agreed.

"How long does it take?" Axio pressed.

"It varies," he answered. "In the relatively weak-willed, very little time. In the strong, it takes longer. But in the end, all are converted."

Axio fell silent then, and the carriage continued up the stairway. It was a long time before it reached the inner wall surrounding the Acropolis. Every bit as robust as the outer wall, it protected the aristocracy not only from intruders, but from the populace itself. A keen reminder of the Civil War, and the terrible power that the people could wield when the illusion of powerlessness was shattered.

The carriage stopped before yet another portcullis at the top of the stairs. Again guards came to verify Dominus's identity, and again the portcullis opened, revealing a tunnel identical to the first. The guards re-attached the wheels, and a second set of horses were brought from the tunnel and attached to the carriage. They moved forward, undergoing the mandatory secondary checks, and then passed through the second portcullis…and into the courtyard beyond.

The large courtyard stood between the inner wall and the Acropolis, surrounding it completely. Its gardens were far different than those at Wexford, a spartan number of ornamental trees and bushes forced into twisted shapes by the royal gardeners. Dominus far preferred his own gardens, with its much larger variety of wild plants. A novice would assume the Acropolis's gardens to be superior, ignorant of the far greater effort Dominus had employed to force such diverse species into a reluctant co-existence.

Much as he had done within himself.

He stared at a few of the gardeners tending to the courtyard, watching them kneel as the carriage passed. All of them of royal blood, steeped in the essence of their ancestors. Blond-haired, blue-eyed, with skin as pale as the fairest cloud. Each a fine representation of their great race, the descendants of Tykus.

"When we enter the Acropolis," Dominus stated, "…do not speak unless spoken to. You are not to reveal yourself as my heir."

"Yes my liege."

The carriage passed through the courtyard toward the massive double-doors of the Acropolis a quarter kilometer away. Dominus gazed at the various pools and fountains along the way, watching as nobles interrupted their leisure, kneeling as the carriage passed. Then he turned to the Acropolis ahead. It was truly massive, perhaps the largest single structure ever built by Man. A tremendous feat of engineering, both physically and in the attributes it had absorbed over the millennia. For countless generations had imprinted their wills onto the stones that made up the Acropolis, ensuring that future generations would absorb the fine qualities of their predecessors. Yet another wondrous system, impeccably designed. Self-sustaining.

Perfect.

Dominus sighed, watching as the fortress's doors drew closer. Perfection had its price, of course. The chaos of the world outside of Tykus's outer wall, the corruption of the Fringe and the forest beyond, was a constant threat to the order of the kingdom. The majority of nobles never left the Acropolis, and knew nothing of the danger to their way of life. Dominus's home, so far from the city, gave him a unique perspective. The forest surrounding Wexford reminded him of the omnipresent danger to his people, their way of life.

I am the beekeeper.

The carriage stopped before the double-doors, and the carriage doors opened, a guard helping Dominus down onto the street. Axio stepped down as well, and Dominus steeled himself, knowing that even with his cane, the short walk to the Hall of Tykus would bring him intense pain.

This was very likely the last time he would ever make this walk.

The huge double-doors opened before him, revealing an opulent hall beyond. A tiled marble floor with grout of solid gold, walls made of the same. The ceiling some fifty feet up, supported by massive stone pillars, each with intricate carvings on their surfaces, detailing the many battles Tykus had fought and won. Massive crystal chandeliers hung downward, their innumerable gemstones glittering in the light. And in the center of the hall, a huge fountain topped with a statue of Tykus himself, raising his hands to the heavens. The statue was so tall that its head nearly reached the ceiling, water shooting upward all around it, then arcing downward to a pool below. This pool, Dominus knew, drained to the main aquifer for the Acropolis, supplying the nobles with their potable water. Steeped in the essence of Tykus, drinking it exposed the nobles to his will, and to the wills of the other great men that had graced the kingdom.

A group of five men were standing before the statue, dressed in fine white, gold, and blue uniforms. All of them older, appearing so similar that it was difficult to tell them apart. The insignia on their uniforms betrayed their identities: his fellow dukes, second only to the king in station. In the king's temporary absence, the five dukes, along with Dominus, ruled the land.

"Good afternoon Dominus," one of the men greeted, a tall, thin man with long gray hair and a long beard, bowing slightly. It was Duke Ratheburg, second in power to Dominus himself. Dominus inclined his head.

"Ratheburg," he replied.

"I'm relieved that you arrived safely," Ratheburg stated, walking back toward the other dukes. Dominus followed, with Axio trailing behind. "I trust you received news of the attack?"

"I did."

"Dreadful," Ratheburg opined.

"What are the specifics?" Dominus inquired, following Ratheburg and the other four dukes as they made their way down the giant hall toward a stairway leading to an arched doorway. Ratheburg paused, glancing back at Axio. Dominus waved away the duke's obvious concern. "Axio is family," he reassured. "He may listen."

"Hundreds of Ironclad stormed the base, perhaps more," Ratheburg revealed. "They scaled the walls, eviscerating our perimeter defenses. A portion of their forces held off a counterattack while the majority swept the residences."

"They were looking for something," Dominus deduced. Ratheburg nodded.

"It appears so," he confirmed. "Casualties were rather mild for the scale of the attack, and the Ironclad left without incurring many losses. It appears they did not find what they were looking for."

"And what *were* they looking for?"

"That is unclear," Ratheburg admitted. "But I think I speak for all of us when I say we cannot tolerate their existence any longer." He shook his head. "It was one thing when the monstrosities kept to themselves, staying near the Fringe, or patrolling the Gate. It's quite another now."

They climbed the stairs to the arched doorway, and Dominus felt the familiar awful ache building in his calves. He resisted the urge to grimace.

"There is a new Original," Dominus guessed. Ratheburg hesitated, then nodded.

"So I hear," he confirmed. "A boy, unusually dark of complexion. The Office of Immigration is handling him."

"What do we know of him?" Dominus inquired, ascending the stairs and walking with Ratheburg and the other dukes through the large doorway. Beyond was another depressingly long hallway, with huge paintings on either wall depicting Tykus's various victories. He ignored the growing pain in his legs, wondering if he would make it all the way down the hallway without his legs giving out.

"He's mostly ignorant of his world's technology, regrettably," Ratheburg answered. "Though he did bring another of those 'guns' we'd confiscated from the other Originals. He was set up with an apartment in the Outskirts, as per the protocol you and King Tykus devised."

"Go on."

"He's quite enamored of the prostitute we set him up with, of course," Ratheburg continued. "We have him safely addicted...and sleep-deprived as a result," he added with a smirk. "Based on our preliminary findings, he's a hotheaded youth, sharp of tongue, distrustful of others, and incredulous regarding our ways."

"Hmm," Dominus murmured. "Is he a danger?"

"Not particularly," Ratheburg replied. "He's naïve and narrow-minded. Self-interested and without any sort of leadership skills."

"His occupation?"

"Quite convenient, in fact," Ratheburg answered. "He's an initiate in the Guild of Seekers."

Dominus stopped, turning to stare at Ratheburg, and the man stopped beside him.

"His will is that strong?" Dominus asked.

"I hear he's being taught by Thorius himself," Ratheburg confirmed. Dominus frowned, feeling suddenly irritated with the man. Ratheburg should have led with that information.

"I must speak with Thorius then," he decided. "What of the Original's affiliations?"

"The whore and a few others," Ratheburg answered. "Misfits, naturally...and also initiates, coincidentally."

They came to the end of the hallway, where there was a set of closed double doors. Standing before them was a tall man in his thirties, with short blond hair and blue eyes, and a short beard. Beside the man were two members of the Royal Guard. The man bowed as Dominus and the others approached.

"Your Graces," he greeted, nodding at the other dukes. He turned to Dominus. "Father," he added.

"Conlan," Dominus replied, stopping before his son. He eyed Conlan critically, noting his own likeness in the man. A few years in the Acropolis should have softened those features, molded them into a figure more resembling the other nobles here. Conlan's will was strong, but not *that* strong. Or so Dominus had assumed.

"I received word that you wanted me to accompany you?" Conlan asked.

164

"Yes," Dominus confirmed. "Your presence is requested for the transition."

"Shall we then?" Duke Ratheburg prompted, gesturing at the doors. The guards opened them, and Dominus stepped through...onto a large balcony overlooking a large inner courtyard. Thousands of people stood below, the crowd hushing as Dominus made his way to the edge of the balcony. The Acropolis's walls enclosed the courtyard, stone gargoyles gazing down at the gathered people atop the roof.

Dominus strode to the edge of the balcony, resting his cane against the stone railing and staring down at the people below. He felt their eyes upon him...and the presence of the other dukes standing behind him, as well as Conlan and Axio. Duke Ratheburg walked up beside him, smiling broadly.

"Good afternoon, Lords of Tykus," Ratheburg greeted the crowd, his voice booming across the courtyard. The crowd applauded, and Ratheburg held up his hands for silence. "We are gathered here today in remembrance of our king, of the passing of the vessel that held him."

The crowd hushed.

"For over half a century our king served his people," Ratheburg continued. "He began his life as Varka, heir to the throne of Tykus, a man destined to continue his father's great sacrifice." He paused, gazing over the crowd. "He ended it as King Tykus, founder of this great city!"

The crowd applauded again, and this time Ratheburg let them, waiting as it died off slowly. Then he lowered his gaze.

"Sadly, he never sired an heir," he continued solemnly. "But Tykus the Legend, in his infinite wisdom, foresaw this occasion, and decreed that in such an event, He would still have the occasion to live on. To guide His people generation after generation, for all eternity."

He gestured at Dominus then, a smile on his lips.

"It is the wisdom of Tykus that brings us our newest vessel for our great king," he stated. "That in the absence of an heir, the Duke of Wexford shall ascend to the throne." He paused then, raising his arms to the sides. "It is with great pleasure then," he declared, "...that I introduce to you your future king: Dominus, Duke of Wexford!"

The crowd burst out into applause again, and Dominus smiled back at Ratheburg, turning to gaze out at the crowd of nobles.

165

Ratheburg waited for the applause to die down, then addressed the crowd once more.

"After his father's untimely death during the Civil War," he stated, "...Duke Dominus fought back against the dark forces that threatened to destroy this great kingdom. He used his superior strategic mind to help end the war once and for all, spearheading the evisceration and expulsion of the terrorists that dared rise against us. He drove out their leader, the great brown bitch who imagined herself a queen, a Legend," he added, his voice dripping with disdain.

The crowd booed, and Ratheburg smirked.

"But Duke Dominus was not done," he continued. "After driving the terrorists out, King Tykus ordered the destruction of their corrupted city, which Duke Dominus executed, smashing it to bits. Then he tore the very soil from the ground, tossing it into the sea, so that no citizen standing upon it would be tainted against our great kingdom."

Ratheburg lowered his arms.

"Lastly, he oversaw the creation of the great wall protecting our city," he continued. "And since its erection, not a single immigrant, nor animal, nor dark creature from the Fringe has entered our great nation without our consent!"

The crowd roared, and Ratheburg grinned, raising one fist in the air triumphantly. At length, the crowd quieted, and Ratheburg lowered his arm, turning to face Dominus.

"Now, after a lifetime of impeccable service," he continued, "...what more perfect end to one's career than to let oneself become the vessel of our great king." Ratheburg put a hand on Dominus's shoulder, then turned to face the other dukes, one of which handed Ratheburg a crown. It was made entirely of bone – the bones of one of Tykus's sons – with jewels embedded within.

Ratheburg paused, then handed Dominus the crown.

"So it is that we," he declared, "...the dukes of the great kingdom of Tykus, crown the Duke of Wexford king of our people!"

The crowd applauded yet again, and Dominus held the crown in his hands, lifting it above his head for all to see. The applause died out, and Dominus lowered the crown, his gaze sweeping across the crowd.

"Thank you," he stated, his voice echoing off of the courtyard walls. "I am, and have always been, a humble servant of my people."

He paused, looking down at the crown.

"It has been a great honor serving my country," he continued, gazing at the crowd once more. "There is no more awesome responsibility than to ensure that this great nation, and its people, endure the passage of time. For it is time, and the insidious corruption of the outsider, that are constant threats to our way of life. Only through constant vigilance can we maintain our borders and defend that which makes us...*us*."

He lifted his gaze to the crowd.

"It has been my life's work to defend us from the dilution of our culture, of our bloodlines, and our traditions by those who do not share them," he stated. "It has been my pleasure and my privilege," he added, "...to be your Duke of Wexford."

The crowd applauded, and Dominus let them, waiting until they were done to continue.

"Duke Ratheburg is correct," Dominus stated. "It is Tykus's will that the Duke of Wexford ascend the throne in the absence of a direct heir." He sighed, lowering his gaze. "That is why I cannot accept this crown."

There was a collective gasp from the crowd, and Dominus heard Ratheburg take a sharp breath in. He felt Ratheburg's eyes on him, but ignored the man, keeping his eyes on the assembled nobles.

"I cannot accept this crown," Dominus declared, "...because I am no longer the Duke of Wexford."

"No longer...?" Ratheburg hissed in his ear. "What are you saying?"

"I've chosen my heir to replace me as Duke of Wexford," Dominus revealed. He turned then, facing Axio and Conlon, who were standing behind the assembled dukes. "In fact, he is standing here with us today."

"Dominus..." Ratheburg began, but Dominus cut him off.

"The successor to the late king," he declared, "...and the rightful wearer of this crown, is my son Conlan, Duke of Wexford!"

Chapter 13

Hunter stared at Master Thorius in disbelief, hardly believing his ears.

"What was her name again?" Hunter asked.

"Neesha," Thorius repeated. "The Outsider's name was Neesha."

Hunter stared at Thorius a moment longer, then lowered his gaze, feeling numb. Disconnected. As if he were suddenly a spectator in his own life.

"I need to sit down," he muttered, swaying a little. He felt Thorius's hands on his shoulders, felt himself being lowered to sit on the floor.

"What's wrong?" Thorius pressed, kneeling before Hunter, his hands still on Hunter's shoulders. Hunter glanced up at him.

"You're sure it was Neesha?" he asked. Thorius nodded. "And she was…brown," he continued. Another nod.

Jesus.

"Who is she to you?" Thorius inquired, his eyes boring into Hunter's. Hunter took a deep breath in.

"She's my mom," he confessed.

"Your *what?*"

"My mom," Hunter repeated. "She…went through the Gate, uh, seven years ago, almost eight. I came here to find her."

Thorius dropped his hands from Hunter's shoulders, sitting down on the floor beside him and eyeing Hunter with an unreadable expression.

"I see."

"But you said she came here fifty years ago," Hunter protested. "That doesn't make any sense."

"There is a...temporal anomaly with Originals passing through the Gate," Thorius explained. "Time seems to flow differently between our worlds." He stood then, offering Hunter a hand. Hunter took it, and was hauled to his feet. "In fact, it is a near-universal finding on Originals, that the timing between arrivals is much longer here than on the original world."

"So you're saying she *could've* been my mom," Hunter pressed. Thorius hesitated, then nodded.

"Yes."

Hunter turned away from Thorius, staring at nothing in particular.

She was here.

He felt a sudden giddy sensation. She'd made it across the Gate, made it alive. And she'd been *here*, in Tykus, in this very city!

Then he had a terrible thought, and he turned back to Thorius.

"What happened to her?" he asked, feeling a chill run through him. He immediately regretted asking, terrified of the answer.

"No one knows," Thorius admitted. "She was driven out at the end of the Civil War, past the Fringe. It's unlikely she survived, and even if she did, she's almost certainly died of old age by now."

"Oh," Hunter mumbled, his heart sinking. Thorius was right, of course; it'd been fifty years here since she'd arrived, and she'd been in her late thirties when she'd disappeared. Even if she happened to still be alive, she'd be nearly ninety by now. He felt as if the wind had been knocked out of him.

I was too late.

"I'm sorry, Hunter," Thorius apologized, putting a hand on his shoulder. Hunter glanced at him, then lowered his gaze, moisture blurring his vision. He blinked it away, gritting his teeth, saying nothing. Thorius sighed. "I think that's enough for today," he stated. "You should go home and get some...rest." He paused. "I do have an artifact that has absorbed a considerable amount of positive emotion, if you want to borrow it."

"No thanks," Hunter muttered. He sighed, then got to his feet. "Thanks for telling me," he added. Thorius inclined his head.

"I'll see you tomorrow."

Hunter left him then, walking out of the room and through the hallway to the foyer. He exited the Guild of Seekers, making his way back to the Outskirts. His stomach growled, but he hardly felt like eating, and walked to his apartment instead. He climbed the three stories to his apartment, closing the door behind him and flopping on his bed.

I missed her, he thought, covering his eyes with his hands.

If only he'd gone up to the attic earlier, gone to find her a few years ago. She might've still been alive then, or at least young enough to have had a *chance* at still being alive. But now it was too late. Even if she was alive, she was probably too old and demented to remember who he was.

Once again, he'd come here for nothing. And now he'd joined the Seekers for nothing.

He sighed, pulling the bedsheet over his head and rolling onto his side. All he wanted to do now was sleep, to escape into his dreams. To escape from this hell he'd fallen into.

There was a knock at the door.

Hunter groaned, rolling over onto his other side, hoping whoever it was would just go the hell away. But moments later, another knock came. He yanked the sheets off, lugging himself out of bed and walking to the door, opening it up.

It was Trixie.

She smiled at him, and when he didn't smile back, she frowned, stepping inside the apartment and closing the door. She reached up, putting her hands on his cheeks.

"What's wrong baby?" she asked. He lowered his gaze, feeling moisture brim in his eyes again. She lifted his chin up, leaning in and kissing him on the lips. He smelled her faint perfume, felt the softness of her mouth on his, and enjoyed a familiar rush of pleasure. It cut through his despair like a scalpel, dulling it almost instantly. He had a sudden, mad desire to drown himself in that feeling, that animal pleasure that she promised simply by being close to him.

You need to stop, he remembered Thorius telling him.

Hunter parted his lips, kissing her back passionately, feeling her arms wrap around him, her tongue snaking into his mouth. He moaned, pulling her back toward the bed, then sitting down on it. She straddled him, shoving him onto his back on the bed, then pulling off her shirt. She grabbed his hands, placing them over her breasts, her flesh hot against his palms.

Fuck that, Hunter thought, feeling himself growing as she laid atop him, her mouth on his. Her hand went to his groin, cupping it gently, and he felt his despair shrinking, replaced by lust for her. For this extraordinary creature, this perfect being who had such power over him.

It was glorious.

She lifted her hips from his, grabbing his pants and pulling them off. Then she smiled at him, pulling her head away, then making a slow, sensual crawl backward, kissing his neck, then his chest, then belly. She paused then, her perfect blue eyes on his, then crawled backward a bit more, lowering her head again.

God I need this.

Hunter closed his eyes, resting his head against his pillow, taking a sharp breath in as she got to work.

* * *

Dominus leaned on his cane, watching as his son Conlan paced before him, running a hand through his short blond hair. After the coronation ceremony, they'd left the dukes and Axio behind, descending to the basement of the Acropolis, to a room known as the Hall of Tykus. It was surprisingly small, the room, particularly in contrast to the grand halls he'd walked through earlier, before the ceremony. The floor was a thick, smooth block of perfectly transparent crystal, within which countless human skulls had been embedded. The walls were unpolished gray stone, and yet more bones had been embedded within them. Four columns fashioned of stone and more bones rose from the floor to the ceiling, and in the center of the Hall was a long table with seven chairs...one for the king, and one for each duke. The ceiling was made of another sheet of solid transparent crystal, with yet more skulls staring down at them with their empty eye-sockets.

The bones of their ancient ancestors, their wills preserved for eternity in a crystalline tomb.

"This isn't fair," Conlan protested, stopping his pacing and turning to face him. "You can't do this!"

"Do what?" Dominus inquired calmly. Conlan snorted.

171

"You know damn well what you did," he retorted angrily. "That was a nice trick, signing that contract giving me the Duchy right when the king died."

"It wasn't a trick, son," Dominus countered.

"It damn well was, and you know it!" Conlan retorted, jabbing a finger at Dominus's chest. "You 'gave up' the Duchy just to get it back again when I became king!"

"It was the sensible thing to do," Dominus insisted.

"Sensible?" Conlan spat. "*Sensible?*"

Dominus sighed, limping up to one of the chairs at the table and sitting down. His legs ached even from standing for too long. He looked up at his son. His only son.

"I'm dying, Conlan."

Conlan stared at him for a long moment, then crossed his arms over his chest.

"Bullshit."

"Come here," Dominus urged. Conlan hesitated, then obeyed, walking up to him. "Help me take off my boot," he added, pointing to his right boot. Conlan helped him pull it off, and he took off his sock as well, exposing his foot. His blackened stump of a big toe, the mottled instep. His pinky toe, the small black spot having expanded to cover the entire tip. The rot was spreading quickly, his flesh dying as its lifeblood was cut off.

Conlan's head jerked back, and he stood, taking a sharp breath in, staring at the foot in horror.

"It's spreading quickly," Dominus explained. "I can barely walk more than a few dozen meters without terrible pain. The doctors want to amputate my legs," he added. "Both of them."

Conlan just stared, swallowing visibly. Then he shook his head.

"I'm sorry, father," he mumbled. "I didn't know."

"I kept it from you," Dominus confessed. He put his cane on the tablet, pulling his sock and boot back on.

"Why?"

Dominus sighed.

"I've always been your father, Conlan," he answered. "The patriarch. I've never been comfortable with…vulnerability."

Conlan just stared back at him, looking shaken. Dominus could hardly blame the boy. The man, rather. He'd never had a *real* conversation with his son before. Certainly never expressed regret, or any other emotion betraying weakness or failure. Their relationship had always been…difficult.

172

"I'm dying son," he repeated, gazing at his son. "The kingdom needs stability. I gave you the kingship because I did not want to become king only to die soon after." He paused. "And I didn't want you forced into the kingship without me present to guide you."

"How much time do you have?" Conlan asked.

"I don't know," Dominus admitted. "If they cut off my legs, perhaps a year or two. I get pains in my chest when I walk too far," he added. "They say the lifeblood is being cut off from my heart, and that the rot will blacken it as it has blackened my feet."

Conlan lowered his gaze.

"We're both going to die," he muttered.

Dominus sighed, lowering his eyes to the tabletop. Wrought of human bones cemented together, it was a morbid thing, but filled with power. With the will of the ancients. Had his will been weaker, he would have feared their influence.

"That is our sacrifice," Dominus said. "To give ourselves to our great nation."

"That is *my* sacrifice," Conlan countered bitterly, looking up at him. "What are you sacrificing?" he added. "At least you'll die *you*."

"I've spent my life in service to this kingdom," Dominus retorted.

"And you'll get to watch me die," Conlan shot back. "You'll still be alive while I fade away, while Tykus kills me slowly, eating away at my soul!"

Dominus just looked at him, saying nothing. There was nothing to say, after all. His son was correct.

Conlan resumed his pacing, his boots *clopping* on the crystalline floor.

"This is your duty," Dominus reminded him. "It is the greatest honor a man can have, to give himself to Tykus."

"Is it an honor?" Conlan retorted. "Is it an honor to be forced to *become* someone else?"

"It is," Dominus insisted.

"What about me?" Conlan pressed. "What about *my* soul? Don't I matter?"

"Of course you do."

"Then let *me* be king," Conlan stated, stopping his pacing. "I have ideas, you know. I have merit. Why does it have to be Tykus, year after year, generation after generation?"

"Conlan…" Dominus began, but Conlan cut him off.

"Do I have nothing to offer my kingdom?" he pressed.

173

Dominus sighed, glancing around the room, at the countless generations of men buried within it. Thousands of souls that had given their lives to their kingdom, giving still even in death, providing their essence to any who drew near.

"You have much to offer," he said at last, turning back to his son. "But Tykus has more."

"How do you know that?" Conlan shot back. "How do you know I wouldn't be a great king?"

"Do you doubt the power of Tykus?" Dominus inquired, his tone suddenly cool. Conlan stared at him, then started to say something, stopping himself. He began pacing again.

"Just because I'm not the great and almighty Tykus doesn't mean I can't do great things," he reasoned. He gestured at Dominus. "Haven't *you* accomplished great things?" he pressed. "Why can't I be like you?"

Dominus grimaced, biting his tongue. His son, despite his considerable intelligence and will, was not his match. Not even close. Conlan was too fiery, too temperamental. He lacked a strategic mind, reacting instead of acting. Even now, he reacted. And he lacked the most important quality of all: the wisdom to understand his limitations, and the discipline to transcend them.

"You have many gifts Conlan," Dominus stated at last. "But you are not a Legend."

Conlan stopped pacing, crossing his arms over his chest.

"How can you be sure?" he countered. He gestured at the room around him. "I've been here for years, and yet I'm not like the others," he reasoned. "My will is stronger than theirs."

"It is," Dominus agreed.

"Then how do you know I'm not a Legend?" Conlan pressed.

"Because I met a Legend once," Dominus answered. Conlan frowned.

"Who?"

Dominus sighed, rubbing his face wearily.

"The Original," he replied.

"The…" Conlan began, then snorted. "That bitch?"

"Do not swallow the propaganda they feed you whole," Dominus chided. "Treat it like food. You must chew on it, digest it. Process it. Only then should you incorporate it into your being."

"You're saying that bitch was a Legend?" Conlan pressed incredulously. "The dukes…"

"The dukes refused to recognize her because she was a woman," Dominus interjected. "And because she was the enemy. But I guarantee you, my son, she was most definitely a Legend."

"But…"

"And I can assure you," Dominus continued, "…until you meet a Legend, you have no idea the power that they wield." He shook his head. "Strong as you are, you are *not* a Legend…and you never will be. And neither will I."

Conlan said nothing, lowering his gaze to the floor.

"What is done is done, my son," Dominus stated gently. "You will be king. You *must* be king."

"It isn't fair," Conlan insisted.

"You're right," Dominus agreed. "It isn't. You've been asked to give the ultimate sacrifice for your people. For your country." He grabbed his cane from the tabletop then, standing and walking up to his son, putting a hand on the man's shoulder. "You must rise above your selfish desires," he added. He gestured at the Hall of Tykus, at the countless bones ensconced within. "One day, your bones will be here, along with all the others who've given their lives to Tykus."

Conlan swallowed visibly, his jawline rippling.

"I'll be here for you," Dominus murmured, raising his hand to Conlan's cheek. "Every step of the way. And I promise I won't leave until it is done."

* * *

Dominus walked alone through the hallways of the Acropolis, the butt of his cane ringing sharply on the granite floor as he went. It was a distressingly long journey to his chambers on the second floor of the fortress, one that required multiple stops for rest. As duke, he had earned the luxury of residing within the Acropolis itself. The lower nobles lived within the walls surrounding the Acropolis, but in a building separate from the massive fortress. A luxurious estate, it still paled in comparison to the Acropolis's magnificent suites. Securing a suite within the Acropolis was a great honor, bestowed only upon the most loyal and powerful of the aristocrats. His suite had been passed down from generation to generation since the founding of the kingdom.

Centuries of service to Tykus. An unbroken chain of excellence.

He sighed, rounding a corner, seeing the door to his room fifty meters away. He stopped for a moment, leaning on his cane, his legs aching terribly. He'd had to stop frequently during the walk…had insisted on making it alone so that no one would see him struggle. Weakness was not befitting the Duke of Wexford.

Nor in his son.

He grimaced, continuing forward. Conlan's reticence was expected, of course. Understandable even. But it was pointless for the man to resist his destiny. Tykus's will would begin its work on him, the Ossae slowly transforming him. Conlan's resistance would fade, and Tykus would be reborn within him.

Still, Dominus knew that he had to stay within the Acropolis. Conlan would not go quietly. Dominus had to ensure that the transformation was completed.

He stopped again, his legs cramping terribly, and waited for them to recover. He also had to get in contact with his Seeker if he was going to retrieve that shipment from the carriage the Ironclad had attacked. So much to do, and so little time to do it.

He heard footsteps approaching behind him, and stopped, turning to glance back down the hallway. A guard was striding quickly toward him.

"Your Grace," the guard called out, catching up to him and bowing deeply.

"What is it?"

"I bring a message from Master Trainer Thorius of the Guild of Seekers," the guard answered. "He requests an audience with you."

Dominus sighed. He *had* wanted to speak with the Seeker, but now was not the time.

"I'll arrange a meeting for tomorrow," Dominus replied. The guard hesitated. "What?" Dominus pressed, feeling irritated.

"He says it's urgent, my Duke," the guard pressed. "He was quite insistent."

Dominus sighed. Thorius was a man of considerable restraint, and not one to alarm easily. If the Seeker claimed a matter was urgent, it most certainly was.

"Very well," he stated.

CHAPTER 14

Hunter felt Trixie shift on the bed beside him, rolling away from him, her warm buttocks pressing against his hip. He sighed, staring up at the ceiling, feeling exhausted. They'd gone at it all night, as usual, until they'd been too tired to keep their eyes open. Days of getting too little sleep were starting to take their toll on him. Still, he was grateful that she'd come last night, thankful for the distraction.

Hunter glanced at the back of her head, at the gentle scoop of her lower back, and had the sudden urge to wake her. He resisted, knowing that she needed her sleep. She had a long day of work ahead of her, no doubt. He turned to stare up at the ceiling, not wanting to think about what that entailed.

Trixie stirred again, rolling onto her other side, her arm flopping over his chest, her cheek resting on his shoulder. She opened her eyes, squinting at him.

"Hey," she mumbled, yawning and rubbing her eyes. "Morning."

"Morning."

She sat up, looking out of the window, then at the rectangular beam of light passing through it to strike the floor.

"It's late," she realized, crawling over him to get out of bed. She walked to the windowsill, glancing at the sundial there. "I have to get going."

"What time is it?" he asked, taking a moment to appreciate her nude form. The sunlight danced through her long golden hair, making it seem like it was glowing.

"Eleven," she answered, turning around to smile at him. "I'll be back this afternoon," she added. "To take you to Ekrin."

"Okay."

She got dressed then, leaning over to kiss him, then waving goodbye. He watched her go, then sighed, rolling onto his back and staring at the ceiling again. Part of him felt guilty about seeing her again, knowing what she was...and knowing that she was manipulating him. He hated the idea that he was being controlled, that his feelings weren't *his* when he was around her. But then he thought about how amazing it'd felt, being with her. How utterly intoxicating it had been.

He felt his groin stirring, felt it waking up.

Get off the fucking bed.

He sighed, rolling off the bed and walking across the room, glancing at the Seeker medallion he'd placed in the corner. He hesitated, then turned away from it, staring at his bed. At the messy sheets strewn across it. He felt his desire fading, seeping out of him slowly. Part of him was sad to feel it go, and he had the sudden urge to lay back in bed, to experience that wonderful feeling again.

Don't.

He turned back to the medallion in the corner, staring at it. He still had time to catch a quick brunch at the community center, then head to the Guild of Seekers. But then he remembered what Thorius had told him yesterday, and his heart sank, a crushing depression coming over him.

What's the point, he thought. *Mom's dead.*

There *was* no point, really. No point to him becoming a Seeker, no point to him being in this god-forsaken world at all. No one wanted him here, not really. No one wanted him corrupting their perfect little lives.

He turned away from the medallion, feeling antsy. Sukri and the others would come looking for him if he didn't show up soon, just as Gammon had yesterday. Hunter had no desire to face them. No desire to talk to anyone at all. But if he stayed here, they'd find him...and force him to come with them to the guild.

Hunter sighed, glancing at his initiate uniform, then at the clothes Trixie had bought him when they'd gone shopping. He hesitated, then grabbed the latter, pulling them on. Then he opened the door, walking out of the apartment. He locked the door, then went downstairs, walking outside. The sun was warm on his skin, the air thick with the smell of the lake below. His stomach grumbled, but he ignored it, resisting the urge to go to the community center and heading toward Lowtown instead. It wasn't long before he reached the church plaza, crowded as usual. It seemed like there were parishioners going in and out of the church constantly, people stopping by whenever they could to worship at the altar of Tykus. He was suddenly curious, having the urge to go inside to see what all the fuss was about. But given the startled looks people gave as he walked near them – treating him as if he had the plague, as usual – he decided against it.

He continued onward past the church plaza, walking down the now-familiar roads that weaved between the buildings of Lowtown. He passed various shops, then saw a building with a tempting sign: a mug of beer. He stopped before it, staring at the sign.

If anyone here could use a beer right now, it was him.

He opened the front door, walking into the bar. It was rather poorly lit, as bars typically were, no doubt to help the beer goggles out a bit. A few men were sitting at the bar, along with one woman. Hunter walked up to the bar, waving down the bartender.

"Hey," he greeted. The bartender – of course looking like everyone else in the damn city – turned, then glared at him.

"What do *you* want?" he asked. The other men at the bar turned to stare at Hunter.

"A beer would be nice," Hunter replied, ignoring the man's tone. The bartender grabbed a beer, setting it down none-too-gently on the bar top.

"Five pounds," the bartender stated. Hunter grabbed the beer, then reached into his pocket. It was empty, he realized; he'd left his money in his Seeker uniform.

"Damn," he muttered. "Sorry, I grabbed the wrong pants. I'll be back." He pushed the beer back toward the bartender, who glanced at the other patrons, shoving it back at Hunter.

"Just take it," he insisted.

"Thanks."

Hunter sat down on the stool in front of the bar, taking a swig of his beer. Then he realized the bartender was eyeballing him.

"I'm gonna have to ask you to drink that outside," the man said.

"What?"

"I'm asking you to drink that outside," the bartender repeated. Hunter frowned, glancing at the other patrons. They were eyeballing him too.

"There a problem here?" Hunter pressed, feeling irritated. He'd had enough of people looking at him like this. Like he was some kind of second-class citizen.

"You got your beer," the bartender replied, pointing toward the door. "Now get out."

"Why?" Hunter pressed. "I'm not doing anything wrong."

"I'm not going to ask you again," the bartender warned. One of the men at the bar – a tall, rather muscular man – stood up from his stool, swaggering toward Hunter.

"The gentleman asked you to leave," he growled, crossing his arms over his chest. "I suggest you leave."

"I'll leave in a minute," Hunter shot back, his irritation turning to anger. He'd put up with this racist crap for long enough, had just stood there and taken it for days now. Being a victim instead of standing up for himself.

Mom wouldn't have taken this shit.

He took another swig of his beer, staying right where he was.

"You either leave on your legs," the big man stated, looming closer, "…or you can leave on your back."

Hunter took another swig of his beer.

"You been practicing that line all day?" he inquired.

"Kurt's right," another man piped in. "Come on man," he added. "Bartender asked you nicely."

"Oh, yeah?" Hunter shot back. "So being a racist is fine if you're 'nice' about it?" He took another swig, glaring at the man.

"You got five seconds to get your ass outta that stool," the big guy – Kurt, apparently – warned, stepping right up to Hunter and glaring down at him. Hunter ignored him, taking a long swig of his beer, almost finishing it. Then he glanced at the bottom, swirling the little bit of liquid that remained.

"Hold on, still got some left," he said.

"That's it," Kurt growled. He grabbed the bottle, tearing it out of Hunter's hand and setting it on the bar. Then he pulled Hunter up off the stool by the front of his shirt, shoving him toward the door. Hunter shoved the guy right back.

"Keep your hands off me," he growled.

"Just go," Kurt muttered. "It's not worth it, trust me."

"That a threat?"

"We don't want trouble," Kurt insisted. "You got a free beer man. Just be thankful for that and go home."

"Or what?" Hunter shot back. "You gonna beat the crap out of me?"

"Just go buddy."

"Make me," Hunter spat.

Kurt sighed, then grabbed Hunter's shoulders, pushing him toward the door. Hunter leaned in, digging his heels into the floor and shoving the guy back. Kurt grabbed Hunter's arm, twisting it.

Or at least he tried to.

Hunter reacted automatically, turning his back to the guy and jerking Kurt forward with his twisted arm. At the same time, he executed a back-kick, his heel slamming into the guy's chest.

Kurt flew backward, slamming into the bar, toppling over a barstool. Then he slid to the floor on his buttocks, grasping at his chest, his eyes wide.

"Surprise, asshole," Hunter quipped. "You mess with me, you mess with the Seek…"

Hands reached around from behind him, pinning his arms behind his back. Hunter struggled, trying to pull away, but another guy got up from his barstool, walking up to him and punching him square in the belly. Hunter grunted, doubling over in pain.

"The gentleman asked nicely," the guy stated calmly. He wound up, slamming his fist into Hunter's abdomen a second time.

That hurt.

Hunter gasped, the air blasting out of his lungs. His legs gave out, and he slumped to the ground, but the man holding him from behind hauled him upward, forcing him to stand.

"You're a real smartass, kid," the guy who'd punched him observed. He wound up again, socking Hunter right in the nose. Stars exploded in Hunter's vision, pain lancing between his eyes. His legs buckled again, and this time the man holding him let go. Hunter fell onto his back, his head bouncing off the wooden floor. A wave of nausea came over him, bile welling up in his mouth.

Hunter felt hands under his armpits, felt himself being dragged backward. His butt struck the threshold at the door, then slid across the hard stone street. They tossed him in the middle of the street, giving him a kick in the stomach before leaving him there, curled in the fetal position.

He puked, vomit spilling onto the street.

The pain in his belly subsided slowly, and he straightened out, rolling onto his back. Blood poured down the back of his throat and out of his nostrils, and he gagged, spitting blood and clots onto the street.

Shit.

He laid there, staring up at the blue sky, the sun hot on his skin. He waited for the nausea to dissipate, and eventually it did. Then he rolled onto his belly, trying to push himself up onto his hands and knees.

Mistake.

Another wave of nausea struck him, and he puked again, bile and maroon clots pouring out of his mouth. He groaned, closing his eyes and gritting his teeth, staying perfectly still until the nausea passed again. Then he slowly – very slowly – rolled onto his side. He stared across the street, seeing people staring back at him in the distance by the shops a few blocks down.

He heard footsteps from behind, and stiffened. He rolled onto his back again, feeling more nausea as he did so, and squinted up at the sky. A shadow loomed over him, a figure silhouetted against the noon sun.

"Don't touch me," Hunter mumbled, "…or you'll turn black."

The shadowy figure knelt down, reaching out with one hand.

"Get up," a familiar voice said, gripping the front of Hunter's shirt and pulling him up to his feet. Hunter gagged, nearly vomiting again, then swaying a little. His head was pounding, his nose throbbing. He turned to the man standing before him, feeling his heart sink.

It was Thorius.

"Hey," Hunter mumbled, lowering his gaze. His shirt was covered in blood, along with chunks of vomit. He was pretty sure he looked exactly like he felt: like shit.

"Come on," Thorius replied, grabbing Hunter's upper arm and pulling him down the street with him. Hunter obeyed, walking alongside the Seeker, his eyes downcast.

"Little late," he muttered. "Could've used your help back there."

"I saw that."

"You were there?" Hunter asked. "Why didn't you help me?"

Thorius glanced sidelong at him.

"The guild protects initiates that *aren't* assholes."

"Well good then," Hunter muttered. "Because I'm not an initiate anymore."

"Is that so," Thorius replied coolly.

"That's right."

"Well I disagree," Thorius countered.

"Well I don't give a damn," Hunter retorted. "You can't force me to be in your little club." Thorius's expression didn't change.

"I seem to remember you signing a contract," he replied calmly. "One where you agreed that once you were an initiate, you would abide by our charter."

"Yeah, well I can't agree to something I couldn't read," Hunter retorted.

"You signed it," Thorius reminded him. "And it's legally binding. So you're an initiate until I say you're not…or until you're dead." He raised an eyebrow at Hunter. "Which way out would you prefer?"

Hunter stared at Thorius for a moment, then lowered his gaze, following alongside the Seeker silently. He had no doubt that the man would make good on his unspoken threat…and that he would be perfectly capable of accomplishing the task.

"I expect you to be on time from now on," Thorius stated. Hunter hesitated, then nodded.

"Yes Master Thorius."

They went back to Hunter's apartment to get his uniform, after which Thorius led him through Lowtown, eventually reaching the Guild of Seekers. They walked into the foyer, going down the hallway to the usual meeting room. Everyone was there…Sukri, Gammon, Kris, and the other five initiates. Thorius stopped before them, gesturing for Hunter to join the group. Hunter did so, standing next to Sukri, who glanced at him, arching one eyebrow. He ignored her.

"Now that everyone is here," Thorius stated, "…we can begin." His gaze swept over the group, ending on Hunter. "It is time for the first of the Trials." He turned his gaze on the other initiates. "To become Seekers, you must successfully complete three Trials. Each of the Trials involves demonstrating skills that are critical to being a successful Seeker."

Another Seeker entered the room then, handing Thorius a roll of paper. Thorius unrolled the paper, glancing at it, then turning it around to display it. Drawn on it was a picture of a small chest, like a treasure chest.

"This," Thorius declared, "…is your objective." He gestured at the picture. "A small chest, likely within a carriage near the Fringe.

Inside is a single bone." He handed the paper to one of the other initiates. "Pass it around. Your mission is to retrieve this artifact. You will keep the bone within the chest at all times during transport."

The paper was passed to Sukri, who passed it to Hunter. Hunter stared at the picture of the chest; below that was a sketch of a small, curved bone resembling a rib. And below that, a drawing of the carriage. Then he passed the paper back to Thorius.

"For this Trial, you will be split into two teams," Thorius continued. "Each team will compete to see who can retrieve the artifact first, and return it to the guild. The members of the winning team will be exempt from disqualification for this Trial." He paused, gazing at the initiates. "The losing team must choose two of its weakest members for disqualification."

Thorius gestured at the initiates to his right.

"You five will be one team," he declared. Then he turned to the other initiates...which just so happened to be Sukri, Gammon, Kris, and Hunter. "...and you four will be the other. Seeing as you have one fewer member, your team will have an hour's head start on the other team."

"Yes Master Thorius," Sukri stated.

"You will have access to a variety of rations and other gear for the Trial," Thorius declared. "We will provide a single pack for each of you to put these in. It is up to you to choose what to bring, and how much. You will also be provided with a map showing the general location of the carriage containing the artifact. Any questions?"

Gammon raised his hand, and Thorius nodded at him.

"When do we start, Master Thorius?" he asked. Thorius smiled.

"You begin," he answered, "...right now."

CHAPTER 15

Hunter strode through the open gate of the outer wall of Tykus, Sukri, Gammon, and Kris at his side. The vast, barren landscape of the Deadlands greeted them, the King's Road rising above the land in the distance. Hunter glanced back, seeing the gate closing behind them. Within moments, it shut, sealing them off from the city.

"Come on," Kris said, striding forward. "We gotta get ahead if we're gonna beat the other team."

The others strode after Kris, and Hunter did as well, the pack Thorius had given him weighing rather heavily on his back. He'd filled it with rations and various other things like rope and bandages, as well as a hunting knife. Thorius had given each of them a large hammer, much like the one Alasar and the other soldiers had used on the Ironclad the day he'd come through the Gate. Hunter's was considerably smaller than Alasar's had been, but still formidably heavy. He'd strapped it onto his pack to spare his arms the constant weight.

"We need a plan, guys," Gammon said, carrying his pack and hammer with ease. Sukri pulled out the map Thorius had given them.

"We need to avoid the Gate," she said, "...and the southwest part of the Deadlands. Thorius said there's a chance Ironclad could still be roaming around there."

"Agreed," Kris stated. "If we run into one of those things, we're screwed."

"If we *do* run into one, we drop our stuff and run," Sukri advised. Hunter shook his head at her.

"We're not gonna be able to outrun one, if that's what you're thinking," he countered. "They're friggin' *fast*...believe me."

"Ah, right," Gammon piped in. "You've fought one before."

"I have," Hunter confirmed. "And if we run into one, believe me...we're dead."

Sukri eyed Hunter, slowing down to walk at his side.

"Looks like you already ran into one today," she observed. "What the hell happened to you anyway?"

"I fell down the stairs," Hunter grumbled. Sukri arched one eyebrow.

"Who pushed you?"

"I...might have run my mouth off a little," he admitted with a rueful smile. "Guess I got what I deserved."

"I figured as much," Sukri replied. "Thorius save your ass?"

"Not really," Hunter answered. "He kinda let me get the shit kicked out of me."

"Sorry Crispy," she said, putting a hand on his shoulder. She hesitated. "You alright?" He sighed, giving her a weak smile.

"I will be," he lied.

She nodded, saying nothing more...and for that, Hunter was grateful. As much as he liked Kris and Gammon, he didn't feel comfortable being vulnerable in front of the guys. He'd tell Sukri the full story the next time they were alone. And not anywhere near his bed, preferably.

They continued forward, aiming to the left of the King's Road. Thorius had forbid them from taking the King's Road on the way there; apparently braving the influence of the Deadlands – and the Fringe – was part of the Trial. If they returned corrupted by its influence, they would fail their test, and be disqualified. Hunter didn't really care if *he* passed anymore, but he didn't want to hurt his friends' chances of becoming Seekers. He had to do this for them. He owed them that much, after everything they'd done for him.

The packed earth sloped downward, the weight on Hunter's back forcing him forward. The sun was still high in the sky, its hot rays beating down on him. Sweat began trickling down his forehead, stinging his eyes.

"Anyone else think this mission is bullshit?" Sukri asked suddenly, glancing at the others. Kris frowned.

"What do you mean?" he inquired. "It's one of the Trials."

"Yeah," Sukri replied. "But we're not exactly well-trained, you know. Going out into the Deadlands is bad enough, but the Fringe? Even fully trained Seekers have died there."

"Gee, thanks for cheering me up," Kris grumbled. "Always a ray of sunshine, Sukri."

"I'm just saying," Sukri shot back. "I don't think we're ready for this."

"Maybe that's the point," Gammon piped in, rubbing his chin thoughtfully. "Maybe the real test is just surviving this mission."

"No," Kris retorted. "The *real* test is beating the other team to finding that artifact. And I suggest we concentrate on doing that instead of being all gloom and doom."

"Yeah, well," Sukri muttered. "I don't like that they took our medallions before we left." Thorius had insisted they all hand in their Seeker medallions, except for Hunter, of course. He'd left his in the apartment.

"If we die, they wouldn't want to lose them in the Fringe," Gammon reasoned. Kris threw up his arms.

"Enough with us dying already!" he complained.

"Fine," Sukri agreed. "We still need a plan."

"What are you thinking?" Gammon asked.

"Well, we have an hour on the other team," Sukri reasoned. "So if we can make good time, we should get to the Fringe first. We'll want to get there before nightfall."

"Right," Gammon agreed. "The Ironclad come out mostly at night."

"I say we go to the Fringe, find the carriage, and get out before sundown," Sukri proposed. "Then we can veer southwest toward the military base."

"But Thorius said to avoid the southwest Deadlands," Kris reminded her.

"True," she conceded. "But the only route up the King's Road near the Fringe is there. If we can get up the King's Road on the way back, we should be safe."

"Master Thorius said we can't use the King's Road," Kris reminded her.

"On the way *to* the Fringe," Sukri countered. Kris hesitated, then nodded grudgingly.

"That's actually a pretty good idea," he admitted.

"I like it," Gammon agreed.

"What if we don't find the artifact today?" Hunter argued. "Or it gets too late?"

"Well," Sukri replied, "…we'd have to go back to the military base or to the King's Road, then wait 'till morning to try again."

"Yeah, but then the other team might get to it first," Kris protested. Sukri gave him a look.

"They can't win if they die."

"I agree with Sukri," Gammon stated, picking up his pace. "Come on," he urged. "We need to hurry if we want to get to the Fringe on time."

Hunter and the others walked faster to keep pace with the big guy, and within a few minutes the land leveled off, making it a bit easier on their knees. Hunter fell into a bit of a trance, finding himself counting his steps to a hundred, then going back to zero and counting again. It wasn't long before his legs started to burn with the exertion. He grit his teeth, pushing himself to keep up with the others. If no one else was going to complain, he sure as hell wasn't. They went on like this for what seemed like an eternity, no one talking, each of them concentrating on the task at hand. After a while, Hunter glanced up at the King's Road to their right, realizing it was splitting into two roads ahead.

"What's that?" he asked, pointing to the split.

"The King's Road splits into two roads," Sukri explained. "The right one goes to the military base, and the left one goes into the forest."

"*Into* the forest?" Hunter pressed. "I thought no one went into the forest except the Seekers."

"The King's Road goes all the way to Wexford," Sukri said, "…and to a few other lands owned by the kingdom. The only people who go into the forest without taking the road are Seekers…or sometimes the military, but only in large numbers."

"Is that where the Ironclad come from?" Hunter asked. "The forest?" Sukri nodded.

"Along with a whole bunch of other monsters," she added. "The Ironclad are the most dangerous, though…at least that we know of."

"Are there any cities other than Tykus?"

"Sure," Sukri answered. "There are a few other kingdoms, but they're pretty far away. My great-grandparents were from New Vinland, a kingdom far south of here. They came to Tykus back when they allowed immigrants in."

She fell silent then, and Hunter got back to focusing on keeping up with Gammon. Despite being significantly overweight, the guy was in impressive shape, marching at a formidable pace. The fact that his legs were so long certainly didn't hurt. They passed the split, veering leftward with the King's Road, following it closely. In the distance, Hunter saw a dark line breaking the seemingly infinite bleakness of the Barrens. A dark *green* line.

"Is that the forest?" he asked.

"That's the Fringe," Sukri corrected. Hunter frowned.

"What's the difference?"

"The Fringe is more dangerous than the deeper forest," she explained. "At least as far as absorbing emotions goes. The deep forest is more dangerous in every other way."

"I don't get it," Hunter admitted.

"The Fringe hates humans," Sukri stated. "Particularly humans from Tykus. So when we're there, we have to be very careful."

"Why's that?"

"We'll absorb that emotion," she answered. "And might start hating each other." She glanced at Kris, then smirked. "More so than we already do."

"So if we start feeling like that, we have to resist it," Gammon said.

"Easy for you to say, big guy," Kris piped in. "You don't absorb emotions."

"He doesn't?" Hunter asked. Gammon shrugged.

"I do, but not well," he clarified. "Some people are like that."

"Yeah, well you and I certainly do," Sukri countered, nudging Hunter. Hunter smiled, remembering their…encounter back in his apartment.

"Don't let us kill each other," Hunter told Gammon.

"I'll try," Gammon agreed.

They continued toward the tree line in the distance, everyone struggling to keep up with Gammon. It was difficult to estimate how far away the forest was, but it looked to be a few miles at least. They fell into a comfortable silence, everyone focusing on putting one foot in front of the other. Hunter found himself daydreaming about home, back when Mom had still been around. She'd loved taking them on hikes through the woods, and had been in incredible shape, making Hunter and his dad look like weaklings in comparison. She would've been able to keep up with Gammon easily. Hell, she probably would've left the big guy in the dust.

Hunter sighed then, pushing the thought out of his head. Thinking about his mom just made him depressed. He focused on the forest ahead, growing steadily bigger now. From here, he could see that there was a steep incline at the forest's edge, the packed earth leading up sharply to the forest floor.

"We're almost there," Sukri said, glancing down at the map, then peering at the tree line ahead. "We're too far east," she added. "We need to go about a half-kilometer to the right." She veered rightward, toward the huge wooden pillars supporting the King's Road. "We have to pass under," she explained. Hunter followed, as did the others. They passed below the road, and Hunter couldn't help but remember the last time he'd done so…when the Ironclad had attacked him.

If he hadn't shot that thing, or if he'd missed…

"We're looking for a few boulders at the tree line," Sukri said. "We should enter the Fringe there."

"Got it," Kris replied. "We're making pretty good time, huh?" he added, grinning at her. "We're gonna kick that other team's ass!"

"I didn't see them behind us," Gammon agreed. "We *are* making good time."

"There it is," Sukri stated, pointing ahead. There were three boulders near the forest's edge, resting on the packed dirt of the Deadlands. A slight dirt incline led to the forest beyond. "Ok, remember what I said earlier," she added. "If you feel any anger or even irritation with each other, it's the Fringe."

"Right," Hunter muttered, remembering how pissed at Thorius he'd gotten, even when he'd known that it was that damn crystal sphere that had been making him feel that way. Knowing hadn't helped at all then…he'd still ended up wanting to smash the guy's face in. What chance did he really have at resisting the forest's influence?

"If you stay near me," Gammon said, "…you'll absorb my emotions. That might lessen the effect of the Fringe on you."

"How you feeling, big guy?" Kris asked. "You can have some of my rations if you want," he added with a grin. Gammon chuckled, rubbing his belly.

"This could work out for me," he quipped.

"Alright, let's do this," Sukri piped in, reaching the boulders. She sprinted up the incline, reaching the forest floor above. Gammon went next, followed by Kris and Hunter. They stood on the forest floor, a bed of stubby grass and fallen leaves and twigs, with the dirt path winding between the trees ahead. All of them turned to Sukri.

"Now what?" Kris asked. Sukri studied the map.

"The carriage followed this path," she said, gesturing ahead. "So it should be somewhere along it. This says it's probably a few kilometers in."

"That far?" Gammon inquired, looking worried. "That's a long time to be exposed to the Fringe."

"Wait," Hunter interjected. "Isn't the Fringe just at the border of the Deadlands?"

"Yes, but it extends a few kilometers into the forest," Gammon explained. "Everyone stay close to me." Kris grinned, walking up beside Gammon and wrapping an arm around the big guy's waist, leaning his head against Gammon's beefy arm.

"Aw big guy," he quipped. "I could use some cuddling, you know."

"Is that what you tell all the girls you bring home?" Sukri inquired, walking up to Gammon's other side. "Get 'em in bed and let all that stored-up sexual tension just seep into them?"

"Hey, whatever works," Kris retorted. "Tell me you haven't done it."

"I don't *need* to," she retorted with a smirk. "All I gotta do is bat my eyes and the guys come running."

"That's true," Gammon agreed. "It's really impressive actually."

"How about you, Hunter?" Kris asked. "You got the ladies knocking on your door?"

"Just one," Hunter replied. Kris scoffed.

"Good looking guy like you?" he pressed. "Come on, you could have a line out the door!" He glanced at Gammon. "Am I right?"

"He's right," Gammon agreed.

"Aw, come on now," Sukri piped in. "Hunter's a one-woman man, alright? Nothing wrong with that."

"Also right," Gammon opined. But Kris shook his head.

"That's a load of crap," he retorted. Sukri arched an eyebrow at him.

"Oh yeah?" she replied. "And why is that?"

"You stay with a woman for more than a year or two, and *bam*...the sex dries up," Kris explained. "You ask and ask, but she's always got a reason why she won't. Then you start looking at other girls, wondering what it'd be like being with them...remembering what it was like to actually be *wanted*. To be the object of someone's desire. Your girl doesn't think not wanting to have sex really matters, and you feel more and more unwanted, and then you start arguing all the time. Pretty soon the only reason you're still in the relationship is because you're emotionally dependent on each other…not because you actually enjoy being together."

"Wow. That's not bitter at all," Sukri grumbled.

"Tell me I'm wrong," Kris pressed, then glanced up at Gammon. "I'm right, aren't I big guy?"

"That has been my experience," Gammon admitted.

"Maybe that's because all you guys ever think about is sex," Sukri countered. "There's more to a relationship then that, you know."

"Ah *ha*," Kris exclaimed. "That's what they tell you! That you're just a sex-crazed maniac. They completely ignore the fact that when you got together, you were at it all the time! You *wanted* each other."

"I'm not ignoring that," Sukri countered. "That's how it's supposed to be…at the *beginning*."

"Granted," Kris conceded. "But isn't it important to keep things going?" He threw up his hands. "Look, I'm not asking for having it every day, I mean just *sometimes*, that's all. Enough so I don't feel neglected." He gestured at one of the plants on the ground. "You know what happens when you don't water a plant, right?"

"It goes limp," Gammon offered. Sukri rolled her eyes.

"Hey, I'm not arguing with you," she retorted. "I like sex as much as anyone. I'm just saying that constantly nagging us for it doesn't exactly make us *want* it."

"Yeah, well I'm just saying that after a few years, it's all the same," Kris stated. "No matter how great it started, I end up resenting the hell out of a girl because she friggin' neglects me." He grinned. "So when that happens, I do what any self-respecting man would do: I leave their unappreciating asses and find someone who *doesn't* neglect me."

"I didn't realize you waited that long," Sukri shot back. "Or maybe it just doesn't take that long for girls to figure you out."

"What is that supposed to mean?" Kris demanded.

"You're not exactly the type of guy a girl takes home," Sukri explained. "It's not like you cook for them or do thoughtful things. You just have sex with them until they bore you."

"Sometimes that's all they want," Kris retorted.

"Uh huh," she grumbled. "Face it Kris, you're just an insecure man-whore."

"Oh *really.*"

"Yup," Sukri replied. "You find a girl, make her think you're the greatest thing ever, and when she finally starts to realize you're not perfect, you kick her out and find someone else."

"Wow," Kris muttered. "Bitch."

"Am I right?" Sukri inquired, eying Gammon. The big guy frowned.

"I'm not touching that one."

"Really?" Kris exclaimed, turning on him. "You're not going to defend me?"

"I'm not defending anyone," Gammon replied. "We have a job to do."

"Well there's a cop-out if I've ever heard one," Kris grumbled. He turned to Sukri. "You got anything else to say?"

"Not really," Sukri replied.

"No," Kris insisted. "I really want to hear it. Come on," he added. "Give it to me straight, I can take it."

"Apparently not," Sukri retorted.

"Guys," Hunter interjected, feeling rather annoyed at their bickering. But they ignored him.

"Okay then," Kris said. "My turn. You know what *your* problem is, Sukri?" he continued, jabbing a finger at her. "You always have to be in charge, taking control of everything and everyone."

"Ooo," Sukri shot back. "Stop, it hurts so bad."

"And you know why?" Kris continued. "Because you can't trust anyone but yourself. Ever wonder why no guy ever stays with you for very long?"

"I'm sure you're going to tell me."

"Because you control them too," Kris replied. "Suffocating them with your nagging and your plans until they're desperate to get away from you." He sneered at her. "You pretend to be this cool, laid-back chick to draw them in, and they love it. But when they find out who you *really* are, they all run the fuck away."

"Okay, that's enough," Gammon interjected.

"And each time, there you are," Kris pressed, "…crying your eyes out, asking us what went wrong. You have no *clue*, Sukri. If guys knew what you were really like, they wouldn't go near you with a ten-foot pole."

"Oh yeah, asshole?" Sukri shot back. "Then why did *you* try to get with me that time?" Kris snorted.

"That was before I knew what a bitchy shrew you were."

193

"That was a *year* ago," she retorted. "You're so full of shit, Kris. Just like always. Your fragile little ego just can't take someone not wanting to be with you."

"Enough!" Gammon shouted.

Both of them turned to the big guy, clearly startled. Gammon glared at Sukri, then at Kris.

"You do realize what's going on, don't you?" he pressed. "The forest is influencing you. Making you angry."

"Bullshit," Kris retorted. "I'm angry because of what she *said.*"

"You both were getting along fine until we came to the forest," Gammon pointed out.

"Yeah, well that's because she hadn't started running her big mouth yet," Kris retorted. "We were all trying to keep up with your goddamn death march."

"The forest is influencing you both," Gammon insisted. "Try to stay focused."

"Uh, kinda hard to stay focused with this asshole running *his* mouth," Sukri muttered. Kris shot her a venomous look.

"Keep it up and I'll shut yours."

"Both of you be silent," Gammon ordered. "Or I'm going to knock you out and carry you." And by the look he gave them, it was quite clear that he wasn't joking. The big guy glanced back at Hunter, who'd been trailing the three. "You okay?" he asked. Hunter glared at Kris and Sukri.

"You're all annoying the hell out of me," he admitted. "But I'm alright for now." And it was true; knowing that the forest was affecting him – and seeing it affect Sukri and Kris – did help a little. He wanted them all to shut the hell up already, but he didn't want them dead. Yet.

"Hold up," Sukri said, stopping suddenly. Gammon gave her a look, and she held up one hand. "Whoa there, don't knock me out just yet," she added hastily. "Look."

Gammon did so, as did Hunter and Kris. There, on the narrow dirt path ahead, was a man leaning against a large tree trunk. Sukri grabbed her hammer from her pack, as did Kris and Gammon. Hunter glanced at them, then did the same, holding his weapon in both hands. It felt unfamiliar, its heft uncomfortable. The man leaning against the tree watched them approach, hardly seeming concerned.

194

"Afternoon," Gammon greeted, striding toward the man, holding his weapon easily in one hand. He stopped ten feet away. "I'm Gammon, and these are my friends."

The man stared at them, his arms crossed over his chest. Hunter walked up beside Gammon, Sukri and Kris at his side. From here, Hunter saw that the stranger was dressed rather oddly. He wore a suit of dark brown leather armor, countless bones embedded in the fabric...and the face of a human skull at his chest. He wore no gloves, but his wrists were covered with ivory bracelets, numerous metallic and ivory rings on his fingers. A long, narrow sword was sheathed at his left hip, and some sort of mace on his right.

"Who're you?" Sukri asked. The stranger turned his head slightly to look at her, glancing at her weapon, then her feet. Finally, his eyes went to hers. Still, he said nothing.

"We don't want any trouble," Gammon warned.

"Then you shouldn't have come here," the stranger replied. To Hunter's surprise, the stranger's voice was feminine, if somewhat deep. Indeed, the stranger's face was as well...a bit narrow, with high cheekbones and large green eyes. But his...or rather, *her*...light brown hair was so short she was nearly bald.

"That a threat?" Kris shot back, shifting his grip on his hammer. The stranger's eyes settled on him.

"Everything here seems like a threat," she replied coolly. She gestured for them to pass. "To people like you."

Kris glared at her, clearly still eager to pick a fight. But the stranger said nothing more, her arms still crossed over her chest. Gammon strode forward past her, as did Sukri. Kris and Hunter followed, and Hunter glanced at the stranger as he passed. She was rather pretty up close, in a strange sort of way. But there was something...off about her.

Her eyes followed him as he passed, not so much as blinking.

They continued onward down the trail, putting their weapons back on their packs. Sukri checked her map again, scanning it briefly. Luckily, she and Kris seemed less pissy than before, so Gammon didn't have to knock anyone out. For the moment, at least.

"Should only be a half-kilometer 'till we reach the carriage," Sukri notified them. "Based on the survivors' estimates."

"Then it's grab and go," Kris stated eagerly. "We're gonna win this Trial easily!"

"Always obsessed with scoring," Sukri muttered, but she too looked pleased. Thankfully Kris let the comment go. Gammon, for his part, quickened his pace, forcing everyone to keep up with him again. Hunter supposed it was just as well...the less time they spent in the Fringe, the better.

The dirt road curved to the right, and then they saw it: a carriage by the side of the road, tipped over on its side, maybe a hundred feet away.

"Bingo," Hunter exclaimed. Everyone turned to give him funny looks.

"Huh?" Kris asked. Hunter grimaced.

"Figure of speech."

"I'll search the carriage," Sukri stated, placing her map in her pack. "You guys stand watch."

"Yes master," Kris grumbled.

They walked up to the carriage, and Sukri hopped up onto it, pulling the side-door up to swing it open. She peered inside, then lowered herself into it, vanishing from sight. Gammon turned away from the carriage, peering off into the woods. The big guy retrieved his hammer from his pack, holding it in one hand. Kris hastily did the same, and Hunter followed suit. He peered at the carriage, noting trails of maroon that had dripped down the side door. The window had been smashed...and that wasn't all. Two of the wheels were broken, the front wall crumpled inward. Whatever had attacked the carriage must've been incredibly strong...and it very well could be nearby still. Watching them.

"I got a bad feeling about this," Kris muttered, scanning the forest. Hunter nodded, doing the same. He saw only an endless expanse of trees and bushes, their branches swaying slightly in a warm breeze. Something was bothering him though, something he couldn't put his finger on. He peered through the forest, shifting his weight from one foot to the other, the leather grip of his hammer feeling slick in his sweaty hands. Then he realized what was wrong.

There was no sound.

No birds, no insects, no *nothing*. Just the rustling of the wind through the leaves.

"Come on Sukri," Kris called out. "Hurry it up in there."

There was no reply.

"Sukri?" Kris pressed, glancing back at the carriage. Hunter did the same, a trickle of fear running through him. What if something had been waiting inside the carriage? What if it had gotten Sukri?

"I'm going after her," Kris decided. He set down his hammer, climbing up on top of the carriage. Hunter swallowed in a suddenly dry throat. What if whatever was inside the carriage was waiting for them, ready to take them out one-by-one as they went to check on each other?

"Kris," he warned.

And then the carriage door burst open.

"Shit!" Kris exclaimed, backing away to the edge of the carriage and nearly falling off. Sukri's head poked through the carriage doorway.

"It's not here," she declared, shaking her head. She boosted herself up onto the side of the carriage, then hopped down to the ground. Kris stared at her incredulously.

"What do you mean it's not here?" he demanded.

"Go check for yourself," she offered. "It's not inside the carriage."

"You gotta be kidding me," Kris grumbled, kneeling down and peering into the carriage. "Shit."

"Come on," Sukri urged, starting a slow walk around the carriage. "Maybe it fell out somewhere."

"Or maybe it's not here," Kris retorted, standing up and shaking his head. "Shit!"

"Maybe you could actually, you know, *help*?" Sukri grumbled. Hunter hesitated, then joined her, scanning the surrounding vegetation. He didn't see anything…just pieces of wood that had been broken off the carriage, scattered on the forest floor. And a whole lot of dried blood.

"Come on guys," Hunter urged. "We'll have a lot more to worry about than your arguments if we don't hurry up."

"That's for sure," Kris grumbled, hopping down from the carriage. "This place freaks me out."

"It's the area," Gammon spoke up, still standing guard, scanning the forest. "When the people in the carriage died here, their fear imprinted into everything around them."

"Or maybe it's because of all the goddamn blood," Kris shot back. "And the fact that we're in the goddamn Fringe."

"It's not *here* guys," Sukri interjected, shaking her head in frustration. "We've searched all around the carriage."

197

"Maybe it fell into the woods," Hunter reasoned. "We should expand our search area."

"Good idea," Gammon agreed. "The farther you guys get from the scene of the murders, the better off you'll be."

They did just that, fanning out in all directions, scanning the forest floor for an ornate chest, or its morbid contents. There was a thick layer of forest litter on the ground obscuring things...and the fact that it was getting darker by the minute certainly didn't help.

"There's nothing here guys," Kris called out, clearly frustrated. Hunter had to agree with him. The chest couldn't have been thrown far from the carriage, and he'd already checked a good thirty feet from it. Which meant that someone must have taken it...or that it was never on the carriage to begin with.

"I've got nothing either," Hunter admitted. "You got anything Sukri?"

"Think I would've kept it to myself if I had?" she shot back. Hunter had to smile at that.

"Yeah, stupid question," he replied. He glanced back, seeing Gammon still near the carriage, scanning the forest methodically. The big guy had been right, as usual. Now that Hunter was farther from the carriage, the fear he'd been feeling had faded away. The land really *had* been affecting him...and he hadn't had a clue it was happening. If it hadn't been for Gammon, Sukri and Kris would've killed each other by now...and Hunter would've freaked out and ran.

I have to get better at this, he thought. He hated the thought that his emotions could be manipulated so easily. First Trixie, now this. Hell, who knows how often he'd been manipulated since he'd gotten to this bizarre world, his emotions being controlled while he remained utterly oblivious? The thought was sobering...and reaffirmed the importance of becoming a Seeker. Thorius obviously knew how to control his emotions and to sense when they were being manipulated. The Master Trainer had offered to teach Hunter those skills, and since Hunter was going to be here for the rest of his life, he'd be far better off learning them.

"This is pointless," Kris grumbled. "I'm fifty feet away and I haven't found shit." He stopped, shaking his head. "It's not here, guys."

"He's right," Sukri agreed. "For once."

Hunter sighed, turning around and walking back toward the carriage.

"What now?" he asked.

"It's getting dark," Sukri replied, glancing at the sky. Her jawline rippled. "We need to get back before it's too late."

"Agreed," Gammon said.

"Great," Kris muttered. "So what, we just come back empty handed? You know what that means, right?"

"If it's not here, it's not here," Sukri retorted. "Would you rather be dead?"

"Alright, fine," Kris grumbled. "You volunteering to be disqualified then?"

"Knock it off," Gammon interjected. "We got here first, and we didn't find it."

"Damn right," Sukri agreed. "The other team probably won't find it either…and since they haven't even made it to the carriage yet, if they *try* to find it tonight, they won't make it back alive."

"Granted," Kris conceded grudgingly.

"So that means we've still got the advantage," Sukri reasoned. "Either the artifact is somewhere around here, or it's gone for good. And if that's the case, the other team won't find it, and we'll both return to the guild empty-handed."

"What then?" Kris pressed. Sukri shrugged.

"I don't know, but if we prove we made it to the carriage first, they might say we still won."

"That's a big if," Kris countered. "I don't know about you guys, but I'm not ready to lose my one chance at becoming a Seeker on a maybe."

"Then we'll come back tomorrow," Gammon decided. "We can start early, and still beat the other team, assuming they've given up for the night and gone back too."

"Or we can stay here and die," Sukri added. "We need to move it."

She began walking back toward the dirt path, and Gammon followed, catching up with her easily. Kris sighed, trudging after them, as did Hunter. They stepped back on the narrow path, taking it back toward the Deadlands. Kris kicked a pebble.

"This is such bullshit," he groused. "We got to the carriage first. It's not our fault the thing wasn't there."

"The mission was to retrieve the artifact, not find the carriage," Sukri countered. Kris glared at her.

"Thanks for the pearl of wisdom, oh wise and fearless leader."

"You know, you don't have to be such a dick," Sukri retorted. "I don't know what's gotten into you lately."

"Don't blame me," Kris grumbled. "It's the forest, remember?"

"Yeah, well the forest wants me to kick your ass," Sukri shot back. "And I'm starting to agree with it."

"Remember what I said about knocking you guys out?" Gammon interjected.

"Yeah yeah," Kris grumbled. "Actually, I'd prefer that. At least then I wouldn't have to listen to her…"

A massive shape burst out of the bushes to their right, slamming into Kris, sending him flying headlong onto the forest floor.

"Shit!" Sukri swore, stumbling backward, fumbling for her hammer. "Guys!"

A huge, black *thing* stood there on the path, blocking their way. A massive creature over seven feet tall, covered in thick, armored plates. Two pairs of arms hung from its sides, its four hands clenched into fists. It turned toward them, black eyes glaring down at them.

Holy…!

Hunter backpedaled, reaching behind himself for his hammer, but he couldn't reach it. He shrugged off his pack, reaching for his hammer with trembling hands. The Ironclad shoved Sukri backward with one hand, then stomped toward the fallen Kris, still lying dazed on the ground. It reached down for him, grabbing him by the wrist and picking him right up off the ground. Kris cried out, his feet dangling over a foot above the forest floor.

"Kris!" Sukri cried, rushing forward and swinging her hammer at the thing's back. It bounced right off, nearly throwing Sukri off her feet.

"Help!" Kris shouted, kicking at the thing's chest frantically. His boots bounced off its armor harmlessly. "Guys!"

Gammon rushed forward, swinging his hammer in a wide arc. It struck the Ironclad in the middle of its back, shoving it forward. The beast grunted, catching itself, then turning around, swinging one armored fist at Gammon's chest. The blow knocked Gammon backward, and the big guy fell onto his butt on the dirt path, his hammer falling from his hands.

The Ironclad turned back to Kris, still suspended in the air. It grabbed Kris's arm with another hand, squeezing so hard it made Kris howl.

"Kris!" Sukri shouted, swinging her hammer again. But the Ironclad stepped *into* her swing, grabbing the shaft of her hammer. It yanked backward, tossing the hammer – and Sukri – through the air with ease. She landed on the forest floor with a *thump*, her hammer falling from her hands.

Hunter glanced at her, then at the Ironclad, gripping his hammer in both hands. He stared at the massive thing, remembering how Alasar's soldiers had been brutalized, highly trained men being slaughtered one-by-one. He hesitated, his heart hammering in his chest.

"Help!" Kris yelled. The Ironclad turned back to him, squeezing Kris's arm so hard it was turning purple. It let go of Kris's wrist then, grabbing his elbow with the other hand. It snarled, then jerked its hands, snapping Kris's upper arm like a twig. The horrible sound echoed like a gunshot through the forest.

Kris *shrieked.*

"Guys!" Sukri screamed, grabbing her hammer and sprinting toward the Ironclad. Gammon pushed himself up from the ground, grabbing his own hammer and rushing the thing. The Ironclad ignored them, glaring at Kris, suspended by his broken arm. Jagged bone stuck out of his flesh, marrow dripping from the ends.

Then the creature gripped Kris's arm on either side of the break, and tore his arm off.

Kris howled, staring wide-eyed at his severed limb. Blood sprayed from the stump in rapid pulses, splattering on the forest floor. The Ironclad tossed Kris's arm aside, then turned to the fast-approaching Sukri just as she swung her hammer in a tight arc, striking the back of its knee. Its leg buckled, and it dropped Kris, landing on its knees.

"Get Kris!" she shouted at Hunter.

Hunter complied, running up to his fallen comrade. Kris was lying on his back on the forest floor, staring wide-eyed at his bleeding stump, his face as pale as death. Sweat beaded up on his forehead, trickling down the side of his face.

"I got you," Hunter said, looking down at the wound. It was still spurting blood, the sharp end of Kris's arm bone jutting out of the rust-colored muscle. Hunter grimaced, putting his fingers into the bleeder and pressing down hard. He glanced back at the Ironclad, watching as it rose to its feet. Sukri swung her hammer again, but the monster caught the hammer in mid-swing, tearing it out of her hands. It turned the hammer around, swinging it right back at

Sukri's head…just as Gammon's hammer slammed into the back of its skull.

The Ironclad stumbled to the side, its hammer missing Sukri's head by mere inches. It caught itself, then dropped the hammer, facing Gammon. Gammon stood before the monstrosity, nearly as tall as it was, clutching his hammer with both hands.

"Kill that asshole!" Sukri shouted.

The Ironclad swung one huge fist, punching Gammon in the belly. Gammon grunted, taking a step back, then swung his hammer at the thing's head. It burst forward into the swing, ramming Gammon with its shoulder and shoving the big guy backward. Gammon stumbled, then caught himself, slamming the butt of his hammer's handle into the Ironclad's forehead. It took the blow without flinching, gripping the handle and ripping the hammer out of Gammon's hands, tossing it to the side. Then it reached out with all four hands, gripping Gammon's shoulders with one pair, and his forearms with the other.

Hunter heard Kris groan, and looked down, seeing blood pouring from between his fingers. Kris's eyes fluttered, his breath coming in short gasps, his skin slick with sweat. Hunter swore, pressing harder on Kris's stump, being careful not to cut himself on the sharp bone-end.

"Guys," he called out. "Guys!"

Gammon grunted as the Ironclad pulled on his arms, yanking them to the sides. He grit his teeth, his muscles going taut as he struggled against the creature's powerful grip. Then he jerked his head forward, slamming his forehead into its face.

His head bounced back, and he stared at the Ironclad, looking dazed.

The Ironclad headbutted Gammon back, slamming its armored forehead into Gammon's nose. Gammon's head snapped backward, and the Ironclad headbutted him again, blood gushing down Gammon's nose and mouth.

"Hunter, help!" Sukri cried, picking up her hammer and swinging it wildly. It struck the back of the creature's knee, causing it to buckle. The Ironclad fell, landing on its back, and Gammon fell on top of it, looking stunned.

Hunter glanced down at Kris. Blood was merely trickling from his wound now. His face was as white as a sheet, his eyes staring upward, his mouth slightly open. He was barely breathing, a gurgling sound coming from his throat.

Shit.

"Hunter!" Sukri shouted, grabbing Gammon's arm and yanking backward, trying to pull the big guy off the Ironclad. Gammon slid halfway off, clutching at his face with his free hand.

Hunter cursed, grabbing his hammer and standing up, rushing toward them. He skidded to a stop before the Ironclad, swinging his hammer like an axe, aiming for the thing's grotesque face. But it intercepted the blow, blocking the strike with two of its armored forearms. The hammer bounced off, the ricochet tearing the handle from Hunter's hands. He stumbled forward, then felt the thing's hand wrap around his ankle. It jerked his leg forward, and Hunter lost his balance, falling onto his back on the packed earth. The air exploded from his lungs, the back of his head bouncing off the ground.

The Ironclad let go of Hunter's leg, shoving Gammon off itself and rising to its feet. It turned to Sukri, who let go of Gammon's arm...just as the thing punched her square in the face.

Sukri dropped like a stone.

The Ironclad glanced back at Hunter, then grabbed Sukri by one ankle, lifting her upward until she was dangling upside-down above the ground. It gripped her lower leg with another hand, and her thigh with another.

And snapped her lower leg in half.

Sukri let out a blood-curdling scream, her leg bent at an impossible angle. Gammon roared, pushing himself off the ground and rushing the beast, throwing himself at the Ironclad. He slammed into it, shoving it to the side. It dropped Sukri, somehow managing to keep its balance, then shoved Gammon backward. The big guy planted his feet, then kicked the thing in the chest, knocking it backward again.

"Hunter!" he bellowed.

Hunter grimaced, scrambling to his feet, finding his hammer lying on the ground. He snatched it up, then ran at the Ironclad, swinging wildly at its back. The hammer struck true, but again it bounced off the thing's thick armor, barely moving it. Hunter wound up to swing again, but the Ironclad smacked the hammer out of his hands.

Then it reached out with one massive hand, its fingers wrapping around his neck.

Hunter grabbed at its hand, trying desperately to pry its fingers from his throat. But its grip was impossibly strong. It lifted him upward, staring at him with those horrible black eyes, its mouth twisted into a snarl. The blood rushed to Hunter's head, a pressure so intense that he felt it would explode. He tried to take a breath in, but no air came.

He gasped, clutching at its hand, feeling the world start to fade around him.

Gammon roared, grabbing his hammer. He rushed the Ironclad, smashing the hammer into the side of the creature's head. It lurched to the side, turning to face Gammon, lashing out with two fists. Gammon dodged the blow, then came in again, smashing the thing square in the face.

Hunter felt the fingers clutching his throat open, and he fell to the ground. He landed on his back, grunting with the impact.

Gammon went in a third time, but the Ironclad ripped the hammer out of his hands, tossing it far into the woods. It grabbed the front of Gammon's shirt, tossing him onto the ground. Gammon rolled, stopping right next to Sukri.

"Run!" she cried. "Get out of here Gammon!"

Gammon grunted, pushing himself to his feet. He glanced at Kris, then at Hunter.

"Come on!" he shouted, scooping Sukri up and sprinting down the path, back the way they'd come. Hunter scrambled to his feet, sprinting after them.

Something shoved him from behind, sending him careening into the packed dirt of the path.

Hunter gasped, pushing himself up onto his hands and knees. He felt hands grip the back of his arms, felt himself rising up above the ground. He kicked his legs uselessly, crying out as the Ironclad's grip tightened, sending pins-and-needles down his arms. The creature turned him around to face it, pulling him forward until his face was inches from its all-black eyes. He could feel its breath hissing through its narrow mouth, the odor making him gag.

"Hey," a voice behind the Ironclad called out.

The beast twisted around, looking over its shoulder. Hunter spotted someone standing on the path a dozen feet away. A woman wearing a dark brown leather suit, her hair so short she was practically bald. It was, Hunter realized, the woman they'd met earlier. She glanced at Hunter, her green eyes locking on his for a moment, then turned to the Ironclad. She crossed her arms over her chest.

"Drop the boy," she ordered.

The Ironclad turned its head to stare at her for a moment, then pivoted to face her, holding Hunter to the side with one hand. Then it stomped toward her, swinging one huge fist at her head.

She grabbed the mace at her right hip, ducking down and to the side, whipping the mace in a tight arc at the Ironclad's leg – all in one smooth motion. Her mace smashed into the thing's right knee, forcing its leg to lock. It toppled over, dropping Hunter as it fell face-first into the dirt path.

Hunter rolled away from the thing, scrambling to his feet.

The stranger was already standing again, facing the Ironclad, who rose to its feet, limping slightly. The armor at its right knee had crumpled, red fluid oozing from the flesh beneath.

"Run along," the stranger ordered, waving the thing away with one hand. Hunter realized that her mace was back at her right hip. The Ironclad gave a deep growl, then grabbed a hammer from the ground. It picked up another, then strode toward the stranger slowly, eyeing her warily.

She just stood there.

The Ironclad burst forward suddenly, swinging both hammers with terrible speed, right at the stranger's head. She stepped backward, avoiding the blows by mere inches, her hand going to her mace at her hip. She whipped her hand outward, her mace whirling through the air, the end smashing into the thing's knee.

Again.

The Ironclad's knee *crunched,* bending backward with the blow. It roared, falling forward onto its hands and knees, the hammers dropping from its hands. The stranger strode forward, putting a boot on the back of its head and shoving its face into the dirt. Then she walked on its back, hopping to the ground on the other side and bending over to retrieve her mace. She secured it to her right hip, turning to face the Ironclad.

It grunted, rising upward, standing on its good leg. Then it spun around, facing the stranger once again. She crossed her arms over her chest, staring at it with those green eyes.

"Go," she ordered, "...or die."

The massive creature stared at her, then turned its head, its black eyes boring into Hunter. It tilted its grotesque head backward then, its narrow mouth gaping open.

A deep wailing sound came from its throat, ending sharply. The creature paused, then made the sound again. It echoed through the forest, so loud that Hunter had to cover his ears.

The Ironclad returned its gaze to Hunter, looking at him for a long, uncomfortable moment, its beady eyes glittering in the fading sun.

Then it charged at the stranger, hopping on its good leg toward her.

The stranger dodged to the side just as the thing was upon her, unsheathing her longsword and swinging it at the thing's injured knee in one smooth motion. The blade went right through the shattered limb, severing it in one blow. The Ironclad roared, falling onto its belly with a *thump*. She sheathed her sword, grabbing her mace and leaping into the air toward its head. She *slammed* the mace into the back of the Ironclad's skull with enormous force, its armor denting inward under the blow. Then she brought the mace up again, striking downward in the exact same spot, the back of the creature's head crumpling inward. She unsheathed her sword, thrusting it straight down into the creature's skull. The black blade buried itself into the Ironclad's brain, the monster's limbs spasming once, then again.

Then it lay still, a pool of blood forming around its severed leg.

The stranger yanked her sword from the thing's corpse, sheathing it, then turning to face Hunter. She crossed her arms over her chest.

"Told you you shouldn't have come here," she muttered.

CHAPTER 16

Dominus leaned back in his chair, glancing down the long table in the center of the Hall of Tykus. The other dukes sat in their chairs along the sides, Dominus's son Conlan seated at the head, in the king's chair. Conlan was king in name only, at least until his transformation was complete. For only Tykus could command the dukes, and by extension, the kingdom.

Dominus slipped his right boot off under the table, tapping the ball of his foot against the cool crystalline floor. He grimaced at the gnawing pain in his toes; they'd been aching since this morning, a constant pins-and-needles sensation torturing them.

"Our next issue is that of the Ironclads," Duke Ratheburg stated. "Dominus, you requested a thorough review of the recent attack. I took the liberty of mobilizing the Royal Guard to secure the military base and collect evidence. We've questioned the survivors, of course, and are continuing to do so."

"What have you found?" Dominus inquired.

"Your initial suspicion was correct," Ratheburg replied. "The Ironclad were indeed searching for something. Or rather, some*one*."

"The Original, I presume," Dominus guessed. Ratheburg's eyebrows rose.

"Correct," he confirmed. "How did you know?"

"The Ironclad have been patrolling the Gate for two decades now," Dominus explained. "This is the first time an Original has come through in that time period."

"Yes, well," Ratheburg said. "One of the surviving soldiers was attacked by a group of Ironclad on the King's Road near the city." He hesitated then. "He gave a rather...odd report."

"How so?" Dominus asked, feeling irritated with Ratheburg. It was a pointless game, this withholding of information for dramatic effect. He glanced at Axio, standing at one corner of the room. Now Dominus's officially recognized heir, the boy needed to be present for nearly all of Dominus's meetings. He would test the boy later, to see how observant Axio was.

"He claimed that there was a particular Ironclad that attacked him," Ratheburg stated. "A rather unusual variant. One we've never encountered before."

"Go on," another duke prompted.

"Apparently this beast was a full third of a meter taller than the typical Ironclad," Ratheburg continued. "And possessed of a glowing blue mane composed of some gelatin-like material enclosed in a translucent membrane."

Dominus frowned, lowering his gaze to the tabletop. A new variant of Ironclad was of significant concern, at least potentially.

"Even more curious was the fact that this same soldier was posted at the Gate when the Original arrived," Ratheburg added. "And in fact was instrumental in saving the boy...from an Ironclad of the same variant, with a glowing mane."

"Does anyone else corroborate this story?" another duke inquired.

"Several soldiers admit to seeing the maned beast during the attack on the Original," Ratheburg confirmed. "It was killed with great difficulty, I hear...and might have killed everyone at the post single-handedly if it hadn't been for the Original's weapon...the gun." He sighed. "We only have the word of the one soldier for the second spotting."

"I'd like to study the corpse of the one they killed," Dominus stated. Ratheburg grimaced.

"Unfortunately that is impossible," he countered. "The soldiers never retrieved the body."

"Why not?"

"Apparently the corpse wasn't there when they went to retrieve it," Ratheburg answered. "Perhaps there was a hidden Ironclad that spirited the corpse away."

"This begs the question, of what to do with the Original," another duke, a man named Mezgar, stated. "If we keep him in the

208

city, the Ironclad may attempt to attack." His expression turned grave. "We've clearly underestimated their numbers," he added. "And they scaled the walls of the military base easily. What if they attempted to attack the city?"

"The walls they scaled were seven meters high," another duke replied dismissively. "Ours are nearly twenty. I doubt the beasts would have much success."

"They could have taken out that entire military base," Duke Mezgar pressed. He was a famously cautious man by nature...and the man responsible for maintaining the city's inner defenses, particularly those of the Acropolis.

"Their numbers are a concern," Dominus agreed. He himself had been responsible for designing the outer defenses – the wall and the King's Road. "The Original appears more trouble than he's worth."

"But they want him for a reason," Ratheburg pressed. "The question is: why?"

"The boy has taken up with the Seekers," Dominus replied. "I spoke with Master Thorius myself yesterday. The boy is strong-willed, but not particularly gifted otherwise. And as you yourself said," he added, "...he knows little of his world's technology. He's not much use to us."

"But what use is he to the Ironclad?" Ratheburg pressed. "That is the question."

"He's of no use to them if he's dead," Dominus replied. "Seeing as he's an initiate in the Guild of Seekers, there's a good possibility he won't survive." A possibility that was far more likely after his...discussion with Thorius earlier.

"Perhaps so," Mezgar admitted.

"And how would the Ironclad respond?" Ratheburg pressed. Dominus shrugged.

"No worse than if we kept him in Tykus," Dominus ventured. "In any case, we can't afford to think defensively," he added. "The Ironclad have attacked us. We must not let that go unpunished."

"I agree," Ratheburg replied. "We cannot tolerate their existence any longer."

"What do you propose?" Mezgar asked Dominus.

"I've already commissioned the Guild of Seekers to find where the Ironclad live," Dominus answered. "High Seeker Zeno put his best men on it yesterday." He turned to Ratheburg. "We've lived with this menace for long enough. I agree with you…we need to end them once and for all."

"But how do you know they even live in one place?" Mezgar pressed.

"They're organized," Dominus explained. "Hierarchal. All hierarchies in nature have a leader, and a territory they call their own."

"It's a sound idea," Ratheburg opined.

"Indeed," another duke agreed.

Conlan leaned forward, propping his elbows on the table. Dominus glanced at him, then shook his head ever-so-slightly. The law stated that a king in transition could not speak during these meetings…not until his transformation was complete. No single man could rule Tykus except the incarnation of Tykus himself. In the interim, the dukes ruled.

Conlan's eyes met Dominus's, and his jawline rippled. But he said nothing.

"I propose we fund the Seekers generously," Ratheburg proposed. "Perhaps we can also have these Seekers contaminate the Ironclad's land with artifacts promoting insanity?"

"Paranoia would be a useful emotion against them," another duke offered. "Stone from the asylum would work. It would turn them against each other."

"Wouldn't that represent a danger to the Seeker transporting it?" Ratheburg inquired. "We can hardly afford to have mad Seekers running about."

"Seekers specialize in transporting dangerous wills," Dominus replied. "This would be routine for them." He stood then, signaling the end of the meeting. "I'll draft a comprehensive strategy," he declared. "The Seekers will deploy tomorrow."

* * *

Sukri cried out as Gammon sprinted through the woods, following the narrow dirt path back toward the Deadlands. Pain shot up her left shin with each step Gammon took, the ends of her broken bones grinding against each other. She grit her teeth, sweat trickling down her forehead.

She heard a mournful wailing behind them, and then another, the terrible sound echoing through the woods. She glanced over

Gammon's shoulder, hoping beyond hope to see Hunter following behind them.

"We gotta get Hunter!" she urged.

Gammon ignored her, weaving through the forest as fast as he could. She'd never imagined that the big guy could move so fast. "Gammon," she pressed, then cried out again as a particularly sharp pain lanced through her leg. "Ah, shit!" she swore, holding her breath. "Damn it!"

"Sorry," Gammon apologized. But he didn't slow down. She looked ahead, seeing the edge of the forest in the distance, the barren expanse of the Deadlands beyond. Then she reached down, gripping her broken leg, trying to stabilize it. But it was no use…each step Gammon took sent agony through it. She moaned, closing her eyes and burying her face in his shoulder.

An image of Kris came to her then. Lying there on the ground, his eyes staring lifelessly upward.

"Hold on," Gammon warned. She opened her eyes, seeing the path ahead take a slight dip into the Deadlands. Gammon reached the end of the path, his boots *thumping* on the hard, packed earth. Each vibration sent more jolts of pain through Sukri.

"Oh god fucking dammit!" Sukri swore, crying out again. "Slow down, slow down!"

"In a minute," Gammon promised. He pressed onward, his breaths coming in short gasps now, his skin slick with sweat. She could feel the heat radiating from him, his heart hammering in his chest. She looked over his shoulder, seeing the Fringe shrink steadily behind them. The Ironclad was nowhere to be seen. It hadn't followed them…and she knew the terrible reason why.

Hunter.

"We have to get Hunter," she urged, looking up at Gammon. "He might still be alive!"

"He's gone Sukri," Gammon retorted, veering left until he was running almost parallel to the tree line. "They're both gone."

"You don't know that," Sukri pressed. But Gammon said nothing more. He was starting to slow down, she realized. At this rate, he'd kill himself before they ever reached the city. "Stop," she ordered.

Gammon continued running.

"Gammon, stop!" Sukri repeated. "We're far enough away now…you need to rest."

211

Gammon hesitated, then slowed down to a walk, being careful not to jostle her leg too much. Still, the pain was extraordinary, worse than anything she had ever felt. She cried out again, clutching at her shattered limb.

"Hold on," Gammon said, stopping suddenly, then lowering her gently to the ground. Even that sent agony through her leg, and she laid there on the dirt, doubled over in pain. Gammon took off his backpack, rummaging through it and pulling out a long, sheathed dagger and some rope. "This is going to hurt," he warned.

"What are you doing?" she demanded, staring at him warily. He reached for her leg, pressing the dagger against the side of it, then wrapped the rope around her leg and the dagger, forming a crude splint. He tied it off, the rope uncomfortably tight around her leg. Then he picked her up carefully, continuing forward. It still hurt with each step he took, but it was a little more manageable now.

"Thanks," Sukri mumbled, resting her head against the big guy's shoulder. She closed her eyes, another image of Kris's lifeless body coming to her. She grit her teeth.

I'm sorry Kris.

"It's getting late," Gammon observed. "The closest shelter is the military base."

"Ok," she mumbled.

"You all right?" he asked, glancing down at her. She shook her head.

"No."

Gammon continued forward, saying nothing for a long moment. Then he sighed.

"I couldn't save them," he muttered.

"I know."

"I tried," Gammon pressed. Sukri glanced up at him, seeing the moisture in the big man's eyes. He was staring off into space, his lips pulled into a thin line.

"I know you did," she replied, patting his broad chest with one hand. He *had* tried, standing toe-to-toe with the Ironclad while the rest of them had been thrown around like ragdolls. If it hadn't been for Gammon, *all* of them would be dead.

Sukri sighed, turning to gaze at the Deadlands ahead. The sun touched the horizon in the distance, sending a splash of red-purple across the scattered clouds high above. She lowered her gaze, remembering the last moments she'd spent with Kris. How she'd hated him, wanted to tear into him.

And how awful was it, that in that brief moment before the Ironclad had attacked, she'd wanted him dead.

CHAPTER 17

Hunter glanced down at the corpse of the Ironclad, half-expecting it to rise up from the ground and attack him. But it laid there in a pool of its own blood, the back of its skull a sunken mess. He glanced up at the strange woman who'd killed it. Who had single-handedly taken on the massive beast, defeating it in a matter of seconds.

"Who are you?" he asked. She stared back at him with those green eyes, her arms still folded across her chest.

"Vi," she answered.

"Like the letter 'V'?"

"Right," she replied. Then she glanced down at Kris's body on the side of the path, shaking her head. "What are you morons doing out here anyway?"

"We're not morons," Hunter retorted. Vi arched one eyebrow, and Hunter glared at her. "We were sent here," he explained. "We're initiates of the Guild of Seekers."

"Oh really," Vi grumbled. She strode up to Hunter then, reaching out and grabbing the front of his shirt. She yanked him toward her. She was as tall as he was, and surprisingly strong, her arms far more muscular than his. She peered at him, her face inches from his, and he pulled away from her...or tried to. Her grip was like iron.

"What are you..." he began.

She shoved him backward then, lowering her arms to her sides.

"You *are* an initiate," she muttered. "What are they doing sending babies like you out to the Fringe?"

"Babies?"

"You're fresh from the picking," Vi explained. "You've barely got their stink on you." She frowned, pulling him in again. "Thorius chose you," she realized. "My my, aren't *you* special."

"How did you know?" Hunter asked. Vi smirked.

"You have Thorius's stink on you too."

Hunter just stared at her.

"You don't know shit, do you?" she inquired. Hunter started to reply, but she held up one hand. "That was rhetorical."

"Who *are* you?" Hunter asked.

"Already answered that."

"I mean, *what* are you?" he pressed. "Are you with the guild?" She clearly knew about it, and about Thorius.

"I was."

Hunter glanced down at the fallen Ironclad, then back at Vi.

"Thanks for saving me," he offered.

"Yeah, well you'd better get going," Vi replied. "That sound it made was it calling its friends to come join in." She waved him away with one hand. "Run off while you still can."

"Wait," Hunter urged, glancing over her shoulder. He could barely see the tipped-over carriage in the distance. "We were supposed to get something from that carriage."

Vi turned to glance at the carriage, then eyed him with an expression he couldn't read.

"Thorius sent you," she replied, pointing to the carriage, "...to get that?"

"There's supposed to be a chest inside," Hunter explained. "With a bone or something."

Vi just stared at him.

"What?" Hunter asked.

"Thorius sent you to retrieve that Ossae," she stated. Hunter paused, then nodded. "Really," she added.

"Yeah, that's our Trial."

"Oh my," she murmured, shaking her head. "All right then."

"What is it?"

"The guild must be slipping," she replied. "Sending untrained initiates to the Fringe is a suicide mission, especially in Ironclad territory."

"We would've made it if the chest had been there," Hunter protested. "We would've been in and out before that thing ever found us."

"Uh huh."

"We would've," he insisted. She ignored him, turning around and walking down the path toward the carriage.

"Run along," she called out over her shoulder. "You don't want to be here when that thing's friends arrive."

Hunter glanced up at the sky, seeing red-purple clouds high above. The sun was setting...and pretty soon it'd be dark. There was no way he'd get back to the city in time, if he could even find it without Sukri's help.

"Wait," he called out, rushing to walk beside her. "I can't go home now. It's too late, and I don't know how to get back."

"Should've planned better," Vi shot back.

"I didn't have the map," Hunter countered.

"Should've memorized it."

"Didn't think I'd need to," he said. She glanced sidelong at him. "This change your mind?"

"Yeah, watching one of my friends get murdered changed my goddamn mind," Hunter retorted. Then he sighed. "Sorry, I'm just...I've been through a lot today, and I could really use your help."

"That's for sure."

"Look," Hunter pressed, feeling exasperated. "What was the point of saving me from that thing if you're just going to leave me to die out here anyway?"

Vi didn't respond, striding over the path with an eerie fluidity, her boots hardly making a sound on the dirt.

"I need a place to stay for the night," he continued. "Can I stick with you until the morning?"

Vi stopped suddenly, turning to stare at him silently for a long moment.

"Something's wrong with you," she accused. Hunter blinked.

"Excuse me?"

"You're...simple," she explained, cocking her head to the side and putting a hand on her chin.

"Gee, thanks," he muttered.

"Your aura," she clarified. "The wills you've absorbed in your lifetime. You barely have any."

"I'm not from around here," he admitted. "I'm an Original."

216

She stared at him for a long moment, her green eyes unblinking. Hunter felt increasingly uncomfortable under her gaze. There was something... *off* about her, about the way she held herself. Or maybe the way she looked. He couldn't quite place it.

She turned suddenly, continuing down the path. He hurried to catch up with her, and they walked around the fallen carriage, continuing past it.

"Will you help me?" he asked.

"When did you go through the Gate?"

"A couple days ago."

"And the Seekers sent you out here," she muttered, shaking her head. "Who'd you piss off?"

"No one," Hunter answered. Vi arched one eyebrow, and he grimaced, remembering the barfight. "Well, no one important." He hesitated. "Will you help me?" he repeated. She hesitated, then sighed.

"Fine. Come with me. Don't annoy me or I'll leave you out to die."

"Thanks," Hunter replied. "I owe you one."

"Two actually," she corrected.

Vi veered off the path then, traipsing through the woods, weaving between the tall trees and wide bushes. She moved quickly and gracefully, and Hunter was forced to follow her from behind, quickening his pace to keep up. This gave him an unfettered view of her back; her brown leather uniform clung tightly to her tall frame, and despite her height, she was not lacking in femininity. She had somewhat broad shoulders, and a defined, muscular back, tapering down to thick, powerful-looking legs...and a butt to match. She was clearly in phenomenal shape, and judging on how quickly and effortlessly she'd killed that Ironclad, an experienced fighter.

"Where are we going?" Hunter inquired.

"My place," Vi answered.

"Where's that?"

"Wait and see," Vi replied.

A deep wailing sound echoed through the air, and Hunter stiffened, glancing around. It was similar to the sound the Ironclad had made earlier, before Vi had killed it. He sprinted up to her side, glancing over his shoulder.

"Is that more of them?" he asked.

"Definitely."

"Will they attack us?" he pressed.

"If they find us."

"Can you take on more than one at a time?"

"Wouldn't be the first time," she answered. "They usually run away when they see me."

"Wait, *they* run from *you*?" Hunter exclaimed. Vi nodded.

"If they're smart," she confirmed. "Not sure why that one was stupid enough to stay and fight."

She veered to the right, toward a steep, rocky slope leading to a valley some fifty feet below. Without so much as a pause, she sprinted right down it, stepping from rock to rock as if she were running downstairs. Within moments, she was at the bottom; she glanced back up at Hunter, gesturing for him to follow.

"Oookaaay," he grumbled, pausing at the top. He took a tentative step down, aiming for a large, stable-looking rock. It carried his weight without rolling, and he paused there, searching for another.

"Any time now," Vi called out.

"I'm not a goddamn mountain goat," he muttered under his breath, taking another step down, then another. After an embarrassingly long period of time, he reached the bottom. Vi had already resumed walking, and was a good hundred feet away, forcing Hunter to run to catch up with her. Thankfully she didn't make any more snide comments. They continued forward, the red-purple sky darkening steadily until the first of the stars were visible in the sky. Hunter thought he heard the sound of water in the distance.

"How far away are we?" he asked.

"You're an impatient one, aren't you," Vi observed.

"Just wondering," Hunter countered. "It's getting dark. I thought the forest was more dangerous then."

"Do I look worried?"

"No," Hunter admitted. And it was true; she might as well have been taking a stroll in the park. He sighed, walking alongside her in silence. The sound of rushing water grew loud as they went, and before long he saw a narrow stream to their right, its dark waters flowing around large rocks in the riverbed. The stream was moving in the same direction they were, the water gurgling pleasantly. Vi followed it silently, her pace as brutal and consistent as Gammon's had been. Hunter pictured the big guy, wondering how he and Sukri were doing...and if they were even still alive. If so, they'd make it to the city and tell Thorius what'd happened. Chances were they'd assume Hunter was dead. Hell, they probably wouldn't even send a search party to find him.

The stream veered to the left, and Vi followed it, Hunter trailing behind now. His legs were starting to burn, and it took a considerable amount of effort to keep up with her. If she noticed, she certainly didn't slow her pace. After a few minutes, the sound of gushing water grew louder; Hunter spotted a clearing ahead, the trees ending abruptly. Beyond that, the forest floor terminated in a steep drop-off. Vi took them to the edge of it, then stopped. Hunter stopped beside her, looking past the edge of the cliff.

His breath caught in his throat.

The cliff gave way in a sheer vertical drop to a large canyon several hundred feet deep, and as wide around as several football stadiums. The stream flowed off the cliffside, forming a small waterfall that cascaded all the way down to a large lake below. Countless other streams surrounding the crater formed waterfalls all the way around, the sound of rushing water near deafening now. And there, in the center of the lake far below, was a small island. A house stood in the middle of it, a narrow wooden bridge connecting the island to the shore of the lake at the perimeter of the canyon.

"There it is," Vi declared, gesturing at the house. "Home sweet home."

"Uh," Hunter said, looking around. "How do we get there?"

"We jump," Vi replied. Hunter stared at her, then looked back down into the canyon. It was at least a three-hundred-foot drop to the lake below...and there was no telling how deep it was.

"You're kidding, right?" he asked. Vi smirked.

"Just seeing if you'd do it."

"Wow," Hunter grumbled. "No offense, but you're kind of a dick."

"Unfortunately that's something I'll never have," Vi replied. She slapped him on the back, hard enough that he stumbled forward, nearly falling over the edge of the cliff. He swore, backpedaling quickly, and shot her a murderous glare.

"Jesus, you could've killed me!" he exclaimed.

"Sure could've," she replied, still smirking. "Follow me," she added, turning leftward to follow the cliffside. Hunter grit his teeth, swallowing his anger and following behind her.

"You're a piece of work, you know that?" he grumbled.

"You have *no* idea."

Vi continued along the edge, striding within a few feet of it without fear or hesitation. Hunter kept farther from the edge, having always had a healthy fear of heights. Or at least heights significant enough to kill him. Eventually they came to a narrow path that dipped downward gradually into the canyon, corkscrewing along its outer wall for as far as the eye could see. Vi took the path downward, not even bothering to see if Hunter was following. Hunter hesitated, glancing at the path warily. It was maybe four feet wide, the canyon wall rising upward to the left, and the sheer drop to the lake below to his right.

"Okay then," he muttered to himself. "This couldn't possibly go wrong."

"Try not to die," Vi said over her shoulder.

"I'll do my best," he grumbled.

"You're definitely going to die then."

"Ha ha," he muttered, stepping carefully onto the path. He hugged the wall to his left, keeping as far from the edge as possible.

Don't look down, he thought, his heart thumping in his chest. He wondered what would happen if he panicked…if he had a panic attack halfway down. Or if he got dizzy, or his foot slipped.

"Stop freaking out," Vi said.

"I'm not freaking out," he lied.

"Uh huh."

"I respect things that can kill me," he explained.

"You should respect me then," Vi quipped. She slowed down, turning to look at him. "Stay right behind me," she ordered. "You'll feel better."

"Not if you're going to shove me off," he retorted. But he obeyed, walking right behind her. To his surprise, he felt his trepidation slowly fade. They continued down the spiraling path, and after a few minutes he felt no fear at all, even if he glanced over the edge.

Huh.

They continued down the path, gradually descending into the canyon, until at long last they reached the bottom. The lake was surrounded by a crescent-shaped rocky shore only fifty feet wide; Vi strode toward the wooden bridge in the distance, the one leading to the island in the center of the lake, Hunter following behind. He glanced up at the path they'd taken, at the sheer cliff walls surrounding the canyon on all sides. He wondered why the canyon hadn't filled entirely with water. After all, there didn't appear to be a river or stream draining the lake, and with the countless waterfalls feeding the lake, the canyon should've been filled by now. He asked Vi about it.

"There's an underground river out of the lake," she explained, reaching the bridge, which was only wide enough to allow them to cross single-file. They did so, Vi taking the lead. Eventually they reached the rocky island on the other side, the house standing before them. Hunter studied it; it was one story tall, and made of rough stone blocks cemented together. The roof was made of what appeared to be curved clay tiles. There was, he discovered, a second, smaller island adjacent to the first, with a small wooden bridge spanning the gap. There was a smaller building there, squat and perfectly square. Vi walked up to the larger building, retrieving a key from her pocket to unlock the door.

"This is your place, huh?" he asked. "It's nice."

"There's one bed," she replied, turning to face him. "And I'm sleeping in it."

"Uh, okay."

"And you're not," she added. "Seeing as I'm not a whore."

"What?" he replied. "I never said…"

"I know you like your whores," she interrupted. "It's all over you."

Hunter grimaced, shaking his head. He felt his cheeks burning, and was glad that she wouldn't be able to see it.

"I didn't know she was a whore, okay?" he retorted. "I was set up."

"Mmm hmm," Vi replied, smirking at him. "They really fucked with you, didn't they? You probably thought she was just *super* into you. Like you were some sort of irresistible sex god."

"How was I supposed to know?"

"So they went from turning you into a sex addict to throwing you into Ironclad territory in the Fringe," she continued. "Quite the fall from grace. You know, you might just be interesting enough to keep around."

"Well now you're making me feel all warm and gushy inside," he grumbled.

"Good," she replied. "You're gonna need that warmth. You're sleeping outside."

Hunter stared at her.

"What? You're kidding, right?"

"Nope."

221

"Why?" he pressed. "I promise I won't try anything," he added hastily.

"If you did, I'd do a lot more than break your nose," Vi replied.

"You're really going to make me sleep outside?" he pressed, putting a hand to his nose. It still smarted.

"Trust me," she replied. "If you think that whore screwed with your head, spend a night in my house."

Hunter considered that for a moment, then sighed.

"Do I at least get a blanket or a pillow or something?"

"You got one in your pack?" she asked. He shook his head. "Then nope."

With that, she walked in the door, and shut it behind her. He heard the *click* as the lock was engaged.

Well then, he thought, turning around. He walked up to a relatively flat part of the island, sitting down. It was hard grey stone, hardly the type of surface he'd want to sleep on.

He heard the door open behind him, and Vi's head popped out.

"Get off my property kid," she ordered, pointing at the bridge. "You sleep on the shore."

Hunter sighed, rising to his feet and crossing the bridge until he was at the shore again. He looked around, managing to find a spot where some leaves had fallen, along with some dirt from the forest floor far above. He swept these into a pile with his hands, then took off his backpack, removing everything hard from it. Then he laid down on his back, using his backpack as a pillow. He stared up at the night sky, countless stars twinkling against the infinite blackness. Three crescent moons hung there, the smallest of which still appeared larger than the moon back home. It was a poignant reminder of where he was. On a world far from home...a world he had no hope of ever leaving.

Where was this place? And how had the Gate – whatever it was – gotten him here? Who made the Gate in the first place, and why? No one on Earth had such technology, after all. Not humans, at least. Was it alien technology? An advanced species from another galaxy?

Hunter sighed, rolled onto his side. He hadn't even considered any of this...hadn't had time to, with Trixie dominating his nights. Now that he was away from her, it was obvious that she'd become an obsession for him. Like a drug...no, *better* than a drug. With her around, there hadn't been time for reflection, for any thoughts other than sex.

He felt a sudden chill, staring off at Vi's house in the distance.

Maybe that had been Ekrin's plan for him all along. Like Vi had said, he'd been turned into an addict, with Trixie as his drug. No wonder why Thorius had wanted him to ditch her.

He sighed again, curling into the fetal position, a cool breeze ruffling his hair. Whoever had made that Gate, and wherever this world was, he was stuck in it for good. There was no going home, that much was clear...and his mother was almost certainly dead. He thought of Sukri, Gammon, and Kris then, an image of Kris's body lying lifelessly on the ground flashing in his mind's eye. Of that horrible sound as the Ironclad had snapped Sukri's leg in two. He felt a crushing sadness come over him, knowing that there was a very real possibility that she was dead too...and Gammon. It'd been close to sundown by the time they'd managed to escape. If there were more Ironclad patrolling the area...

He forced the thought out of his mind, taking a deep breath in, then letting it out.

His friends were almost certainly dead, and there was nothing he could do to change that. He'd been powerless to save them. And if today had taught him anything, it was that if he didn't start figuring out how to make it in this world, he clearly wasn't going to last for very long.

CHAPTER 18

Dominus sat on the edge of his bed in his spacious suite in the Acropolis, facing the doctor he'd called upon only a half-hour ago. The doctor knelt before him, pulling the boot off of his right foot. Dominus barely felt the boot slip off; his foot was numb, but that gnawing pain was ever-present, as if he'd plunged his foot into ice-cold water.

"Let's see what we're dealing with here," the doctor said, pulling off Dominus's sock. He stared at Dominus's foot, trying unsuccessfully to hide a grimace.

The rot had spread, his pinky toe now completely black, as were most of the other toes. The instep of his foot was pale and mottled, a beefy redness spreading from the deep ulcer on the side of his ankle.

He didn't need a doctor to know that it was dying.

The doctor put two fingers on Dominus's instep, then on his inner ankle, just behind the bone. He shook his head, then tapped Dominus's instep with one finger.

"Do you feel that?" he asked.

"No."

The doctor reached behind Dominus's knee, digging his fingers in the crease there. Then he apologized, putting two fingers near Dominus's groin. That done, he stood, sighing heavily.

"The foot is dying," he declared apologetically. "You've no pulse in either vessel there, and only a faint pulse behind the knee.

You've still got blood flowing through the groin, which is promising."

"You want to amputate," Dominus stated flatly. The doctor nodded reluctantly.

"The foot will have to come off," he admitted. "Your ulcer is infected, and I'm afraid the pus will go to the bone. Once it's there, it will not leave."

"Not just the toes?" Dominus pressed. The doctor shook his head.

"It's only a matter of time before your whole foot rots," he explained. "If there is any blood flowing to it, it isn't much…and it won't last."

Dominus stared at his foot in disgust, at the gangrene slowly consuming his flesh. He had no doubt that the doctor was correct, that his foot would not last much longer. But it would impair him significantly to undergo major surgery now, to endure a painful recovery, potentially complicated by an infection from the procedure itself. Not to mention learning to walk without a foot, or with some ghastly prosthesis. This was too momentous a time to be distracted by such things; his son's transition must be ensured, as well as Axio's.

"Remove the toes," he declared, looking up at the doctor. "The gangrene only."

"But your Grace…" the doctor began.

"Cut off the rot when it comes," Dominus interrupted. "Preserve that which remains for as long as possible."

The doctor hesitated, then nodded.

"I'll assemble my team," he declared, bowing and leaving the suite. The door closed behind him.

Dominus sighed, staring at his foot, remembering how it used to look. Pink, warm, full of life and vigor. It had been with him, a part of him, for his entire life, since he was pushed out into this world. And now it was dying, and if he didn't remove it, it would kill him too. The infection had to be contained, or it would spread.

As with the kingdom, he thought darkly. He'd spent his first years as duke removing the infected limb that had been the uprising peasants, the immigrants who'd been welcomed into the city generations earlier, then sought to claim the kingdom for their own. Breeding like rabbits, then demanding they be considered equals without ever earning such a distinction.

They had been the infection, the foreign invader that had burrowed into the kingdom's flesh, making it rot. And Dominus had cut off that great limb from the city, destroying a large portion of Tykus to rid the kingdom of them.

There was a knock on the door.

Dominus sighed again, slipping on his sock, then his boot.

"Come in," Dominus called out. The door opened, and Axio stepped through, bowing before him.

"Your Grace," he greeted. "You called for me?"

"Yes," Dominus confirmed. "I wanted to know what you thought of the meeting in the Hall of Tykus earlier. Speak your mind freely...do not fear that your words will reach the other dukes."

"Yes your Grace," Axio replied. He hesitated, but only for a moment. "I felt that it was overly long."

"Go on."

"The other dukes do not speak as you do," Axio continued. "They take many words to say very little...particularly Duke Ratheburg."

Dominus smiled, pleased at this.

"Those who speak volumes often have the least to say," he stated. "But be careful not to think better of those who speak little. Being spartan of speech is often a sign of having nothing to say rather than being possessed of great wisdom."

"Yes your Grace."

"Words are like gems," Dominus explained. "The rarer they are, the more valuable they are perceived to be."

"I agree your Grace."

"Judge a man by the content of what he says," Dominus continued. "If he says nothing, you must reserve judgement until he does speak. As for you, listen carefully, speak little. Formulate your plans within your mind first, then consider how much to reveal to others."

"Yes your Grace."

"If you speak everything you think," Dominus continued, "...you'll have no secrets, and therefore no power." He shifted his weight on the bed, grimacing at the continued pain in his right foot. "What is your opinion of the substance of the meeting?"

"I fail to see how killing the leader of the Ironclad would significantly impact them," Axio admitted. "Won't another just appear in its place?"

"Can you imagine what would happen if the Ossae of Tykus were destroyed?" Dominus replied. Axio's eyes widened. "Tykus would never again return through the body of the king...his wisdom would be lost. The kingdom would never recover."

"Such a thing is impossible," Axio protested, clearly disturbed by the idea.

"Nothing is impossible," Dominus retorted. "Don't be blinded by the things you cherish. Consider the worst and plan to prevent it. That is your role as Duke of Wexford," he added. "You are the last defense of the kingdom, the preserver of our way of life, our culture, our great race."

"Yes your Grace."

"I am the beekeeper of our people," Dominus stated. "And my hive is the city of Tykus. *That* is why I tend to my bees, Axio. It is a constant reminder of my role."

"Now I understand, your Grace," Axio murmured. "That is why you live outside of the kingdom." Dominus nodded, smiling at the boy.

"Indeed."

"I have another question," Axio stated.

"Go on."

"The Original," Axio began. "Why not just kill him?"

"Ah yes," Dominus murmured. "He is clearly dangerous, isn't he? Strong willed, with distasteful qualities that could spread to the populace."

"He is dark, like the bitch Neesha," Axio agreed. "And the Ironclad want him."

"He is," Dominus replied. "And they do."

"Why not kill him then?" Axio pressed.

"That is one possible solution," Dominus admitted. "Tell me...what did I tell you about people?"

"That they are tools, your Grace."

"Correct," Dominus replied. "Is a knife not a tool for a butcher?"

"It is."

"Would a butcher destroy a knife merely because it was very sharp?" Dominus pressed. "Even though he may cut himself?" Axio shook his head.

"No your Grace."

"We do not destroy a tool merely because the tool is dangerous," Dominus explained. "But like the butcher, we must

227

wield it with great care. The Original is a tool like any other man," he continued. "And we must be prepared to use him as such."

"For what purpose, your Grace?"

"That is yet to be determined," Dominus confessed. "Suffice it to say that if the Original survives the mission I set him on, then he will have proven himself a useful addition to the Seekers." Dominus had made excellent use of another protégé of the guild, after all…and a far more dangerous one at that.

"I see."

"It was King Tykus who asked me to develop the immigration system for the Originals," Dominus revealed, "…after the Civil War. The other dukes wanted to destroy any new Originals. I convinced them to *manage* the Originals. Place them in the Outskirts where they cannot infect the aristocracy. Convert them to loyal citizens through the use of Temple Stones. Attach them to a prostitute. Sleep-deprive them."

"For what purpose?" Axio inquired.

"An addict lives for his drug," Dominus explained. "The drug consumes his thoughts, allowing nothing else." He smiled. "Sex, like any other pleasure, can be a drug."

"Most ingenious, your Grace."

"Which is why you must never engage in such things," Dominus continued. "As duke, you must never allow yourself to become addicted to any pleasure. Your role is too vital to allow for such distractions."

"Yes your Grace."

"Very well then," Dominus stated, suddenly tired of their conversation. "Leave me now. I will call for you again soon."

Axio bowed, then left. Dominus watched the boy go, noting a slight limp as the boy walked…in his right leg, of course. He smiled, relieved at Axio's progress. The boy was changing, however slowly. His will was strong, and the metamorphosis would take some time…but that was preferable. It would be useless if the boy were too malleable.

He lowered his gaze then, looking at his right foot, hidden within his boot. One would never suspect the rot that existed below the surface, beneath that fine clothing. As with the kingdom, unfortunately; there was rot there, hidden within the fine walls of the city, and of the Acropolis itself.

Cut off the rot when it comes, he thought, recalling the lame queen bee he'd crushed the life out of, so that the hive might produce another. *Preserve that which remains for as long as possible.*

* * *

"Hey."

Hunter groaned, rolling onto his back and opening his eyes, squinting against the bright sunlight. He blinked, seeing a shadow looming over him, silhouetted by the sun.

"Get up," a voice said. It took Hunter a moment to recognize the voice.

"Oh, hey," he mumbled, sitting up and rubbing the sleep out of his eyes. He saw Vi standing above him, dressed as usual in her brown leather uniform, her sword and mace at her hips...and a bow in her hand. He stood up, grimacing at how sore and stiff his back was. He was surprised he'd even managed to fall asleep, given how uncomfortable the bed of leaves and dirt had been. He'd never have imagined that he'd pine for his stiff cot back in the Outskirts. "Morning," he grumbled.

"Hungry?" she asked. Hunter nodded, his stomach growling in agreement. "Go get some food then," she said, handing him the bow. He stared at it, then at her.

"Excuse me?"

"Kill something," she clarified, "...then eat it."

"I don't know how to use a bow," he protested. Sure, he'd shot a few arrows with his parents in an indoor archery class once or twice, but that'd been years ago...back when his mother had been around.

"What *do* you know?" she shot back. Hunter glared at her.

"Physics," he replied. "Chemistry."

"Huh?"

"It's complicated." he grumbled. "You wouldn't understand."

"Hunger is simple," Vi retorted. "Learn to hunt or starve."

Hunter sighed, and Vi handed him a quiver filled with arrows. He slung it over his shoulder.

"Come on," she prompted, pointing to a small tree standing near the canyon wall. "Hit that from here."

Hunter hesitated, then nocked the arrow on the bowstring, trying to remember what he'd learned as a kid. Vi immediately grabbed the arrow from his hands, showing him how to do it properly. She made him put his index and middle fingers on the string above the shaft of the arrow, his ring finger below.

"You're left-eye dominant," she told him. "Put your right foot forward." He frowned, doing so.

"How did you…"

"Draw the bowstring back," she interrupted. "Keep your other arm straight. No," she added, lifting his elbow up until it was at 90 degrees to his flank. "Elbow up. Keep your legs planted," she ordered. "Toes pointing to the side. Good."

Hunter aimed, then glanced at Vi.

"Eyes on the target," she scolded. "Now let go with your fingers only. Don't move your arm."

He complied, and the arrow whizzed through the air, hitting the canyon wall to the left of the tree trunk.

"Try again," she ordered.

He did so, removing another arrow from the quiver awkwardly. She showed him how do to it right, then watched as he nocked the arrow. Again she corrected him. He drew it back, then aimed, letting the string go. The arrow struck the tree near the base of the trunk.

"Too low," she stated. "Hit it at your chest level. Raise your straight arm."

He tried again, with more corrections as he went. He shot the arrow, and it went higher, but to the right of the trunk.

"Your feet aim," Vi instructed. "Keep them parallel. Your hips aim next, keep them lined up with your target. Your straight arm aims last, keep your shoulders lined up with the target."

"Got it," he muttered.

"Then prove it."

He sighed, lining his feet up, then his hips, then his shoulders as instructed. He drew back, then fired the arrow…and it struck dead center, right at chest level. He turned to Vi and smirked.

"Boom," he declared. Vi rolled her eyes, grabbing the bow from his hands and three arrows from his quiver. She strode up to the long bridge, walking all the way across it until she was standing next to the house…and a few hundred feet away from the tree.

"What are you…" he began.

She strung and shot an arrow in one fluid motion, then shot the other two before the first had even finished flying over the lake. There were three *thumps,* and Hunter turned to look at the tree. His eyes widened, his jaw going slack.

All three arrows were embedded in the tree…each having split the one before it…and his own arrow.

"Holy shit," he blurted out, staring at the arrows, then turning back to her. She walked back across the bridge, handing him the bow again.

"Boom," she quipped, smirking at him.

"How the hell?" he began, then stopped, shaking his head. "Damn."

"Come on buttercup," she said, slapping him on the butt, hard enough to make him stumble. "Impress me."

He sighed, turning to face the tree again, then shooting another arrow, then another. Some hit the trunk, some didn't. Each time, Vi made some corrections. To his relief, she kept the trash-talking to a minimum, and when he depleted his quiver, she had him retrieve the arrows and start over again. After what seemed like hours, she had him stop…which was just as well. His fingertips were on fire, the bowstring having given him painful blisters.

"That's enough," she declared. "At this rate you'll starve to death."

"That might be preferable," he grumbled, shaking his hand out.

"Grow some callouses," she ordered. "And a pair of these," she added, reaching down and grabbing him between the legs. He jumped back, feeling the blood rush to his cheeks.

"Hey, that's not cool," he protested.

"Thought you liked girls grabbing you there," she countered.

"Just whores," he shot back. "Maybe I *should've* liked it," he quipped. Vi rolled her eyes.

"Come on," she prompted, grabbing the bow and quiver from him and walking toward the path spiraling up the canyon. "I'll get us breakfast."

* * *

Hunter sat cross-legged on the ground before the small campfire Vi had helped prepare, tearing the meat from the roasted wing of a large bird Vi had shot down earlier. It'd taken a single shot, of course…and she'd knocked it clean out of the air in mid-flight. She'd asked him to make the fire, and he'd started to try. It hadn't taken her long to realize he had no idea what he was doing. To her credit, she'd shown him how to do it, but made him do the work. Eventually he'd gotten the fire going. It'd felt surprisingly good for such a small accomplishment. He wanted to try again, to see if he could do it by himself.

"Thanks for breakfast," he offered. Vi was sitting across from him, biting into her own wing. "And for saving me yesterday."

"Mmm hmm."

"I guess I'd better get going back soon," he ventured, taking another bite. The meat was a little gamey, like chicken but fattier, but he ate it greedily. He was famished after all, not having had a real meal since lunch the day before. "How do I get back to the Deadlands?"

"You don't," Vi replied.

"What?"

She looked up from her meal, staring at him with those big green eyes. Again, he got the sense that there was something *off* about her, something exotic that he just couldn't place.

"You shouldn't go back now," she explained.

"Why not?"

"You're too new," she answered. "Too easy to manipulate. You soak up emotions like a sponge." She tore off another piece of meat, chewing vigorously. "If you go back now, they'll either trap you with that whore or get you killed."

"I'm done with her," he countered. Vi snorted.

"Yeah right," she shot back. "Five minutes near her and you'll do anything she wants." She made a ring out of her thumb and forefinger, then inserted her other index finger through it. "Over and over and…"

"Okay, okay," Hunter interjected. "I get it."

"You won't stand a chance kid," Vi declared. "You talk a good game, but you're weak."

"Weak?"

"Well let's see," she began. "You're a teenager…young, dumb, and full of cum."

"Wow."

"And you're a sponge for emotions, unfortunately," she added. "That's not your fault, of course…it's just bad luck."

"What do you mean?"

"That's right," she remembered. "You have no idea." She sighed then, staring into the fire. Then she looked back up at him. "This world is different than yours."

"Kinda gathered that."

"According to the histories, when people first came here through the Gate, they didn't understand how the world worked either," she explained. "They started absorbing each other's traits without realizing it, and even started absorbing the traits of plants and animals around them."

She bit off another piece of meat, chewing it slowly.

"When people started changing – visibly changing their appearance to look like the world around them – at first they thought it was a disease. Thought the people who were changing were infected somehow."

"Makes sense."

"After a few generations, they started figuring out how things worked," Vi continued. "We still don't know the mechanism, but we do know that traits – your appearance, personality, skills, and so forth – are transmissible and absorbable. Supposedly a few people in the past could even absorb memories, but we haven't seen anyone with that power in over a century."

"Thorius mentioned something like that," Hunter agreed. Vi snorted.

"Don't listen to Thorius," she replied. "Listen to me." She leaned forward. "Some people absorb certain traits really well, and others poorly," she continued. "You absorb emotions easily, but you have a strong personality. And you don't absorb appearances very well."

"How can you tell?"

"Because you've spent a day with me," she replied. Hunter frowned.

"What's that supposed to mean?"

"I'm…strong-willed," she explained. "I'm strong *everything*. When you walked near me on the path down the canyon, you stopped freaking out…you absorbed my emotional state. My calm. But you look as ugly now as you did yesterday."

"You're a real sweet-talker," he grumbled.

"You still suck at archery," she continued, "…so you don't absorb skills very quickly," she continued. "Get it?"

"Yeah."

"I still can't tell how well you absorb other traits," she continued. "But we'll figure that out soon enough."

"Wait," he said. "So you're taking me in?"

"Afraid so," she confirmed. "You're either dead or an addict if I don't. Not that spending a lifetime of having mind-blowing sex is that bad a fate."

"Gotta agree with you there," he admitted. As much as he'd hated not being in control, being with Trixie had been the most incredible experience of his life.

"See, I just can't stand the thought of you having that much fun," Vi continued with a grin. "Besides, Thorius *was* right about one thing...you've got potential."

"Aw, thanks."

"But the last thing you need is to get sucked in to being one of them," she added darkly.

"Why's that?" he asked. "Weren't you a Seeker?"

"I was," she confirmed. "I was the best goddamn Seeker they ever had, too," she added. But she said it matter-of-factly, without a trace of pride.

"What happened?"

"I didn't have testicles," she answered with a smirk. "And I was too...non-traditional, even for them. Couldn't wrap their little brains around me."

"I don't get it."

"Well, first of all, I didn't give a rat's ass about the guild," she explained. "Or their 'sacred mission.' And I was too strong for them to try and brainwash me with their medallions."

"Wait, what?"

"Those medallions they gave you," Vi explained. "Sure, you'll learn some skills wearing them, but they're mostly to brainwash you into being good little boys and girls."

"Shit," Hunter muttered.

"Didn't work, did it?" Vi asked. Hunter shrugged.

"I don't give a crap about the guild, if that's what you mean."

"Then it didn't," she confirmed. "Anyway, if that wasn't bad enough, I didn't fall into their narrow-minded concept of what people should be like either."

"What do you mean?" he pressed. Vi smirked, glancing down at his crotch. He frowned, closing his knees together.

"You think I'm into guys?" she inquired. He hesitated, studying her.

"Not really, now that you mention it."

"That really blew their little minds," she stated. "Should've seen my parents. They tried to hook me up with a male prostitute too,

234

hoping I'd be like you and absorb all that sexual energy and jump his bones. Turn me right around, they thought. Didn't work, of course…I was too strong. Ended up converting *him*."

"Huh," Hunter mumbled, trying to figure out what that meant.

"They had me hang out with all the girly girls," she continued, "…hoping I'd act more like them. Girls all turned into tomboys," she added. Then she smirked. "Converted them too. *That* was fun."

"Ah."

"Anyway, they threw me to the Seekers, desperate to get me the hell out of the city before I 'corrupted' everyone around me. The Seekers took me in, of course, but I was too strong for them too. They sent me on a few suicide missions, hoping to off me. Sound familiar?"

"Little bit."

"But I didn't die," she continued. "I passed the Trials, and they sent me out on all the missions they thought no one could accomplish. I kept accomplishing them. I did better than any of them, but did I ever get promoted?"

"Gonna guess no," Hunter ventured. She nodded.

"That's right. Can't have a free-thinking lesbian Seeker outshining the clean-cut boys' club," she added. "So eventually I got out and made my own way. Came here, started freelancing. Best thing I ever did."

"So you're still working?" he asked. She nodded.

"Still hunting down artifacts," she confirmed. "Got plenty of clients too," she added. "Not that any of them would ever admit to hiring me. It's against the law to hire non-guilded Seekers."

"So what were you doing out there yesterday?" Hunter pressed. "Another job?" She nodded.

"I was," she replied. "Lucky for you."

"Still can't believe that artifact wasn't in the carriage," Hunter said.

"Why am I not surprised," Vi grumbled. Hunter frowned.

"Why do you say that?"

"Think about it," she pressed. "Thorius sent all of you out into the Fringe without any training whatsoever, knowing damn well the Ironclad patrol this route."

"That was the Trial," Hunter protested. Vi gave him a withering look.

"That was a suicide mission," she corrected. "Thorius wanted you dead, kiddo…and trust me, the Seekers don't give a shit about the color of your skin. Which means someone in the Acropolis wanted you dead, and told Thorius to make that happen. And Thorius was willing to sacrifice three of his initiates to do it."

Hunter stared at her silently, swallowing in a suddenly dry throat.

"You can't go back to the city," Vi stated, her tone final. "And you can't go back to the Seekers. If you do, at best you'll go back to being that whore's boy-toy."

"And at worst?" he asked.

"At worst," she replied, "…you'll be dead."

CHAPTER 19

Sukri grimaced as the carriage they'd taken from the military base to Tykus reached the end of the King's Road, rolling across the uneven terrain of the Deadlands beyond. Somehow Gammon had carried her all the way to the military base the night before, and the doctors there had tended to her and Gammon's injuries. Amazingly, the big guy had suffered only bruises and a concussion. Sukri hadn't been so lucky, of course. Despite the cast that a nice doctor in the base had placed on her right leg the night before, any significant movement still hurt her.

The carriage continued onward toward the great wall surrounding Tykus, stopping before the gate.

"You okay?" Gammon asked. He was sitting beside her, a concerned look on his face.

"Just sore," she replied. She smiled then, patting him on the leg. "Thanks for everything, Gammon."

"You're welcome."

The two guards at the gate checked them over, and the portcullis rose, allowing the carriage into the tunnel beyond. They underwent a second screening, this time from a representative from the Guild of Seekers scanning them for foreign wills. Apparently they passed, because they were allowed through the inner gate. The carriage took them forward into Lowtown, moving slowly through the streets.

"I can't believe they're gone," Sukri muttered, staring out of the window. She closed her eyes, picturing the Ironclad breaking Kris's arm. Tearing it off.

"I know," Gammon replied, his tone hushed. She opened her eyes, glancing at him again; his eyes were downcast, his expression somber.

"What are we going to tell Thorius?" she asked. Gammon shrugged.

"The truth."

"They might not let us stay in the guild," she warned.

"It's not up to us."

"You're right, it isn't," she agreed, sighing heavily. "I hate this," she muttered. "Not being in control."

"I know."

"Kris was right, wasn't he," she continued, staring out of the window, watching the buildings go by. "About me."

"About some things," Gammon replied.

Sukri sighed again, spotting the courtyard of the Guild of Seekers ahead. Her stomach twisted into a knot, and she shifted her weight on her seat, wincing at a twinge in her injured leg.

"Let's get this over with," she muttered.

The carriage stopped before the short wooden bridge going over the moat surrounding the guild, and Gammon got out first, pulling out a wheelchair from the trunk, then coming around to Sukri's side and helping her down from the carriage. She sat in the wheelchair, and Gammon got behind it to push her.

"No," she blurted out. "No thanks," she added more gently. "I can do it." Gammon let go, and Sukri wheeled herself across the bridge and up to the double-doors. Gammon knocked, and moments later the doors opened, a Seeker they didn't recognize standing beyond.

"Come," the Seeker prompted, turning about and leading them in. Sukri glanced up at Gammon, then wheeled through, turning down the usual hallway to the room they always met in. As it was nearly noon, the other five initiates were already there. Lucus and Donahue smiled at them, the other initiates just staring at them, saying nothing.

This is going well, she thought.

Moments later, Master Thorius himself strode into the room, followed by two other Seekers.

"Good afternoon," he greeted.

"Good afternoon Master Thorius," everyone droned.

"I see that two of our initiates have returned," Thorius stated, glancing at Gammon and Sukri. "Where are the others?"

"Dead," Gammon answered. Thorius frowned, glancing at Sukri, who just nodded, then lowered her gaze.

"I see," Thorius murmured. "I'm sorry to hear that."

"We didn't retrieve the artifact," Gammon continued. "We made it to the carriage, but it wasn't there, and it wasn't anywhere near it."

"And how did your teammates die?" Thorius pressed.

"An Ironclad ambushed us," Gammon answered. "He killed Kris, and broke Sukri's leg," he added, gesturing at Sukri. "We fought the Ironclad, but it was too strong. We fled, but Hunter didn't make it."

"He was killed?" Thorius asked.

"I didn't see it," Gammon stated. "The last thing I saw was the Ironclad picking Hunter up." He shook his head. "There's no way Hunter could've survived."

"Agreed," Thorius replied, sighing heavily. "That is unfortunate." He glanced at the other five initiates, then turned back to Gammon and Sukri. "Seeing as your team failed to retrieve the artifact, I have no choice but to disqualify two of its members from becoming Seekers."

Sukri and Gammon lowered their gazes to the floor.

"However, as two of your members have already disqualified themselves," Thorius continued, "...you two will remain as initiates of the guild."

Sukri glanced up at Thorius, and Gammon bowed at the man.

"Thank you Master Thorius," Gammon stated.

"Wait," Sukri protested, gesturing at the other five initiates. "What about them?" Thorius raised an eyebrow at her.

"What about them?" he inquired.

"Did *they* retrieve the artifact?" she pressed. "It wasn't even there...and we never saw them anywhere near the Fringe."

"They did not retrieve it," Thorius replied. Sukri stared at him incredulously.

"Then how come *we're* the losers?" she demanded. "At least *we* got to the Fringe, and to the carriage!"

"They never left the city," Thorius answered.

"*What?*"

239

"This was *your* Trial," Thorius explained. "Yours, Hunter's, and Kris's. I added the incentive of competition to give a sense of urgency to your task. Your team was the only one that left the city."

"You *lied* to us?" Sukri exclaimed, her voice rising in anger. "How could you…"

"Because I dictate the Trials," Thorius replied calmly. He arched an eyebrow at her. "Do you question my methods?"

Sukri glared at him, and was about to answer to the affirmative when she felt Gammon's hand on her shoulder. She glanced up at him, feeling his calmness seep into her. He was always doing that for her, saving her from herself.

"We're concerned that we were undertrained for the mission," Gammon replied evenly. Thorius turned to him.

"Yet here you are," he countered. "You survived the Ironclad and have passed your first Trial."

"Only because we ran," Gammon pointed out.

"When faced with a much more powerful opponent," Thorius stated, "…running is often the wisest strategy."

"You could have taught us how to defend ourselves first," Sukri pressed.

"I have been," Thorius retorted. "Through your medallions."

Gammon nodded, saying nothing more. Sukri knew that if his hand hadn't been on her shoulder, she would've had much more to say. But with the temporary gift of Gammon's preternatural calmness, she was able to hold her tongue.

"Any other concerns?" Thorius inquired. He waited a moment, then smiled. "Good. Now, seeing as I no longer have an initiate to train, I will be taking you," he stated, nodding at Sukri, "…as my pupil. Gammon, you will remain with your previous trainer."

"Yes Master Thorius," Gammon and Sukri replied.

"Very well then," Thorius declared. "Let's get to work."

* * *

The sun was at its zenith in the sky when Vi lead Hunter away from the dying fire they'd eaten their breakfast at, trudging through the woods until they'd reached the carriage – and the path – that Hunter had traveled to yesterday. She hadn't mentioned that this was where she was leading him, nor given a reason why. And Hunter hadn't asked more than once, having reluctantly accepted her silence. If she was going to tell him something, she'd tell it in her own time. Still, it was one thing to know that, and quite another to accept it. He couldn't help but be frustrated by her...although seeing as how they were at the Fringe again, his frustration could be due to the effect of the forest.

Vi walked right up to the carriage, stopping before it, and Hunter stopped at her side, waiting for her to say something. She turned to him, a rare smile curling her lips.

"You're learning," she observed.

"Alright," he stated, gesturing at the carriage and trying not to show his irritation. "I know you're going to tell me what we're doing here."

"You're blind," she stated. "I'm going to teach you how to see." Hunter blinked.

"Excuse me?"

"You have no sense of what's around you," Vi explained. "The traits that objects and people around you have absorbed and radiate. It makes you an easy target," she added. "You're affected by objects without even realizing it."

Hunter nodded grudgingly. He hadn't even realized Trixie's effect on him, or the power of Thorius's crystal sphere. He wouldn't have had a clue that the Fringe could make him angry and hate other people if Sukri hadn't warned him first.

"If you're aware of the properties of the things around you," Vi continued, "...you can learn to either manage their effects on you, or avoid getting close to objects with negative effects."

"Makes sense."

"How are you feeling now?" she asked.

"Irritated," he answered. "It's the forest, isn't it," he added. Vi nodded.

"The Fringe hates humans," she agreed.

"Why's that?"

"I'll tell you later," she promised. "Touch the carriage," she ordered. Hunter hesitated, then complied, walking up to the side of the carriage and touching one of the wheels. "Close your eyes...tell me how you're feeling."

Hunter did so, feeling the warm wood on his hand. He was still irritated, but he didn't feel much else. After a moment, his mind wandered, and he pictured the Ironclad that had attacked them, so close to where they were now. How it'd ambushed them, coming from nowhere and tossing them around like rag dolls. He felt a pang of fear at the thought, suddenly wondering if any more of the beasts were nearby. What if it attacked them again? What if it managed to kill Vi?

"Talk to me," Vi ordered.

"Sorry, I kinda spaced out," Hunter admitted.

"What do you feel?"

"Fear," he confessed. "I was remembering what happened yesterday."

"Okay," she replied. "Touch the metal rim and let me know if you feel anything else."

He did so, keeping his eyes closed. Sukri had jumped up onto the carriage before the Ironclad had attacked. He pictured her hopping onto the side of the carriage, opening the door and jumping down. It'd been empty...no bodies. Some blood on the seat cushions, and on the inside of the carriage door. He felt another pang of fear, much more powerful now.

Something bad was going to happen...and soon.

Hunter opened his eyes, jerking his hand away from the wheel. He glanced around the forest, his heart pounding in his chest.

"Well?" Vi pressed. He turned to her, realizing she was staring at him, her hands on her hips.

"We should get out of here," he replied, rubbing sweating palms on his pants. "The Ironclad might come back."

"You're freaking out."

"No I'm not," he retorted. "The..."

"You're panicking," Vi interrupted, putting a hand on his shoulder. He tried to pull away, but she moved with him. His heart slowed, the profound sense of doom slipping away gradually. He stared at her, then at the carriage.

"Shit," he mumbled.

"Now how do you feel?" she pressed.

"Better," he admitted. "You're doing that, aren't you?" She nodded.

"See how you keep reacting as if the emotions came from you instead of outside of you?"

"Yeah."

"We need to work on that," she stated. Hunter nodded, realizing she was right. He'd been manipulated again.

"How?" he asked.

"It's all about your mindset," she answered. "You're a reactionary person. You let things effect you, react, then think later."

Hunter lowered his gaze, remembering how he'd acted in the bar yesterday. How he'd gotten suspended after beating the crap out of Tyler at school.

"You don't have to act on every emotion you feel," Vi continued. "Emotions are temporary. They come and go. That's why they're absorbed so easily…emotions aren't permanent, they aren't like your personality, or your appearance."

"Okay."

"You need to learn to experience an emotion without acting on it," Vi continued. "That way you can sense emotions in objects and people without being manipulated by them."

"How do I do that?" he pressed.

"Same way as anything else," she answered. "Practice."

"Show me."

"Touch the carriage again," she ordered. He hesitated, then did so, taking a deep breath in and letting it out slowly. "Close your eyes," she added. "Now breath in through your nose, out through your mouth…slowly. Concentrate on how it feels."

He complied, feeling air come in through his nostrils, his chest expanding as his lungs filled with air. Then he let the breath go, feeling warm, moist air pass his lips.

"When you have a thought or a feeling," Vi continued, "…you'll stop focusing on your breathing. Don't get frustrated, just return to focusing on your breathing…how it feels. Let your thoughts and emotions be in the background."

Hunter continued breathing in and out. He felt a pang of trepidation, his concentration wavering. But he refocused on the air coming in through his nostrils, the feeling of his chest expanding. He let the breath out, feeling another pang of fear…but he refocused on his breathing again, taking another breath in.

The Ironclad called its friends, he thought. *They'll be here soon.*

He felt his heart start to race, and nearly opened his eyes. Instead, he tightened his grip on the wheel, gritting his teeth.

Breathe in, he thought, feeling the air coming through his nose. *Breathe out.*

He could feel the panic in the periphery of his mind, demanding to be let in. He felt its urgency, knew that if he didn't address it, something terrible would happen. He pictured himself riding in the carriage, felt it suddenly lurch to the side. Felt it topple over, throwing him sidelong into the carriage door below. Then pain shooting through his right shoulder, and terror gripping him.

He cried out, letting go of the wheel and stumbling backward. He felt hands on his shoulders, and spun around to see Vi standing before him.

"Calm down," she soothed.

The terror seeped out of him, a sense of profound calmness washing over him. He realized his whole body was rigid, and forced himself to relax.

"Thanks," he muttered. "This shit's hard."

"You did better," she replied approvingly. He nodded.

"The breathing helped a little," he admitted. "Until my mind started playing tricks on me."

"What do you mean?"

"I imagined being in the carriage when the Ironclad attacked," he replied. "Freaked myself out."

Vi frowned, staring at him with her exotic green eyes for a long moment. Then she pulled him away from the carriage.

"Come on," she prompted. "The guild is going to send Seekers to find your body. We shouldn't be here when they come." She began walking back the way they'd come, and he jogged to catch up with her, slowing to a walk at her side.

"How do you know that?"

"That's what I would do," she answered. "Whoever sent you here is going to want to make sure you're dead. We don't want them knowing you're still alive...not yet, anyway."

They trudged through the forest, leaving the carriage behind. Hunter stared at the forest floor as he walked, feeling daunted by how difficult it'd been to stay calm in the presence of the carriage. How Thorius and Vi were able to manage such powerful emotions was beyond him. He wondered if he'd ever be able to manage his...or if he'd just be a slave to them for the rest of his life. Especially his damn temper.

"Well aren't you optimistic," Vi stated suddenly, yanking him from his reverie. He blinked, glancing at her.

"Huh?"

"Time for your next lesson," she replied, ignoring his questioning look. "You can sense emotions in objects and people by figuring out how you feel after being close to them. If someone's anxious, you'll start feeling anxious. If they're depressed, you'll feel depressed."

"Okay."

"If they're angry at you, you'll get angry at them," she continued. "The same goes with objects that have absorbed emotions." She eyed him critically. "The problem is, *you* don't see objects as having feelings. You need to start treating inanimate things like people."

"It's hard for me," he countered. "I'm not from here."

"Everything hard becomes easier with practice," Vi replied. "Now, certain objects store traits much more easily than others...and transmit them easily as well. Generally speaking, the denser an object, the more it stores and transmits."

"Like stone," Hunter offered. Vi nodded.

"Be very careful around stone," she warned. "It can be extremely dangerous. Stone in Tykus isn't so dangerous...most of it has been engineered to transmit traits the kingdom finds useful to control the people."

"Like at the church?"

"Exactly," Vi agreed. "But out here, stone could have absorbed anything. And it isn't just emotion you need to worry about."

"What do you mean?"

"You have a strong personality...what we call 'will,'" she replied, "...so you don't need to worry about absorbing other personalities too much. But that isn't the case for most people. Most people are like sheep, bending to the will of others, desperate to fit in. The kingdom takes advantage of that, believe me."

"How so?"

"People are all too eager to be told what to do," Vi answered. "They swallow everything the ruling class tells them without digesting it, without really questioning it." She shook her head. "They deserve everything they get," she added. "Slaving away for nothing while the people in the Acropolis take almost everything, throwing them scraps every once and a while to keep them from revolting. It's the same old story in every kingdom. Believe me, I've been to more than a few."

They reached the steep, rocky decline they'd traversed last night, and Vi sprinted down it easily. Hunter made his way slowly as before, but this time she waited for him before resuming their walk.

"People are sheep," Vi continued. "Never forget that."

"At least you're not bitter," Hunter quipped.

"My point is," she replied, ignoring him, "...you don't have to worry about *absorbing* people's personalities too much, but you *do* have to realize that anyone with a weak will is going to absorb *your* personality."

"How do you mean?"

"They'll start acting like you," she explained. "Agreeing with your point of view. After a while, they'll start *thinking* like you."

"That's not creepy at all," he muttered.

"You can tell the emotions that something is radiating by how *you* feel around them," she continued. "And you can tell how strong someone's will is by how they change when they're around you."

"But if someone has a stronger will than me, I'd start being like them, right?" She nodded.

"And unless you're trained, you wouldn't even realize it was happening," she replied.

"Well shit," he grumbled. "How do I stop from changing people?"

"Stay away from them."

"Really?" he pressed. "There's no other way?"

"Nope."

"But I don't want to change other people like that," he protested. And he sure as hell didn't want *his* personality changed. He took a step away from Vi, eyeing her warily. Had *she* changed him? She'd said her personality was strong, after all. She must've noticed his trepidation.

"Don't worry," she assured him. "You're not going to change me."

"That's not what I'm worried about."

"Then don't get too close," she replied. She shoved him playfully then, smirking at him. "You'll be alright," she reassured. "We've both got strong personalities."

"Somehow I don't feel better," he grumbled. The idea that someone could change him…change who he *was*, was profoundly disturbing.

"This is the way the world works," she stated. "You don't have to like it, but you do have to live with it."

"Fair enough," he replied. "So now what?"

"We've talked about emotions and personality," Vi replied. "But there are many other types of traits that can be transmitted." She turned forward then, and so did Hunter. The forest was ending…and beyond, Hunter could see the canyon. She made her way up to the edge, turning to the left to reach the path spiraling downward. Hunter followed behind, feeling less trepidation than he had the first time.

"Like skills?" he asked.

"Exactly," Vi agreed. "Something that you," she added, "...are in desperate need of."

"Gee, thanks. You're so encouraging."

"Yeah, well," she replied. "You're going to have to learn to fight if you want to stand a chance against the Ironclad. Come on," she added. "We've got a lot of work to do."

CHAPTER 20

Seeker Draken strode up the gradual incline from the Deadlands to the Fringe, wiping sweat from his forehead. He glanced at Seeker Jarl, a middle-aged man with short blond hair and a trimmed goatee. They'd been walking side-by-side for the last few hours through the Deadlands in the hot afternoon sun. With packs and weapons, it was a demanding hike…even for a Seeker. He'd found himself enjoying the challenge, a welcome change from the routine of the guild. Being called back from active duty to train the newest batch of initiates wasn't exactly physically demanding. He'd much rather be fulfilling contracts for his clients, but when the guild called, he was duty-bound to answer.

"Hope this is quick," Jarl said as they entered the forest.

"Should be," Draken replied. "Carriage can't be more than a kilometer or two from here."

"Was it your initiate that died?" Jarl asked.

"Nah," Draken answered. "It was the party boy and the dark kid."

"Damn," Jarl muttered. "Were they any good?" Draken shrugged.

"Mediocre," he replied. "Dark kid had promise, but his attitude sucked. I knew the party boy wouldn't make the cut."

"Still don't get why Thorius sent brand-new initiates to the Fringe," Jarl muttered. "Like throwing your baby at a pack of wolves." He shook his head. "That's not a Trial, it's an execution."

"I don't disagree," Draken replied. "Thorius is no fool though," he added. "If you ask me, he *wanted* them dead."

"Yeah."

"I bet that's why we're out here," Draken continued. "Thorius didn't want to disqualify my initiate or the big guy, or he would've already done it."

"So he wanted the party boy or the dark kid dead," Jarl reasoned.

"My thought exactly," Draken agreed. "Party boy wasn't worth killing, but the dark kid...that's my bet."

"So we find the bodies and get out."

'Yeah," Draken confirmed. "Hopefully they're still around," he added.

"Think the Ironclad ate them?" Jarl asked. Draken shrugged.

"No clue," he admitted. "I just know they have a habit of stealing human corpses."

"They're just big bugs, right? What do bugs eat?"

"Couldn't tell you," Draken admitted. "Looks like we're getting close," he added, gesturing ahead. The narrow dirt path extended forward through the forest ahead, and in the distance he spotted something to one side of it. A carriage on its side. "You keep watch," Draken ordered. "I'll find the bodies."

Jarl nodded.

Draken strode forward slowly, scanning the forest carefully. It was deserted, the gentle hills of the surrounding terrain littered with a thick bed of fallen branches and leaves. The trees grew densely here, tangled vines hanging from them. He glanced back at Jarl, suppressing a flash of irritation at the man. It was the forest, he knew...it's anger, its *hatred*, was seeping into him. He ignored the emotion, concentrating on the task at hand.

He spotted something on the forest floor, a slight irregularity to the side of the road. He strode up to it, kneeling down.

It was an arm.

Draken studied it, feeling a twinge of fear. He noted the emotion, then disregarded it, knowing it was coming from the arm itself...and the surrounding soil. The arm was pale, torn off at the mid-humerus. Covered in bugs. It had to be party-boy's. The kid had been terrified right before he'd died, of course. That explained what Draken was feeling now.

He stood, spotting another, larger shape in the grass, and walked up to it. It was the rest of the body...and it *was* party-boy.

One down, one to go.

He continued toward the carriage, walking up to it, feeling that slight sense of fear weaken, then strengthen again as he drew near. He felt a spike of anger as well…whoever had attacked the carriage had been furious. Draken studied the carriage, surveying the damage. Then he started walking in a loose spiral, starting at the carriage and moving outward. The dark kid's body should be somewhere nearby, but it might be easy to miss in the hilly terrain, and with so much leaf litter. If he wanted to find it, he'd have to be methodical.

There was a rustling sound in the distance, followed by a muted *thump.*

Draken froze, turning toward the sound. He saw the carriage behind him, and the path winding back toward the Deadlands. Other than that, the forest was empty.

Where the hell is Jarl?

He reached back, grabbing the war hammer strapped to his pack and gripping it in both hands. Then he crouched down low, slowly stepping toward a large tree. He hid behind the trunk, scanning the forest carefully.

That idiot was supposed to keep watch!

He grit his teeth, shoving the thought aside. The forest's anger was getting to him again. Jarl was no fool; if he wasn't there, it meant that either he'd been forced to hide…or that he'd been compromised. Either way, it wasn't good.

Shit.

Draken strained his ears, continuing to scan the forest…but he heard – and saw – nothing.

And then his eyes fell to the forest floor.

He froze, his breath catching in his throat, his eyes on a spot not ten meters from where he stood. There was a mound of leaves there…and another a dozen meters beyond that. And beneath the mounds, a hint of black. As he watched, the mounds rose and fell slightly. Rhythmically.

Shit!

He gripped his hammer tightly, his palms slick on the metal shaft. There were two mounds visible between him and the path. Ironclad were excellent sprinters…he wouldn't be able to outrun them. That meant he had to kill them…and he couldn't count on Jarl. The man was probably already dead.

There was a *crunch* behind him.

Draken spun around, seeing a black mound rising from the ground not two meters from where he crouched, leaves cascading down from it. Two pairs of huge arms burst through the debris, sending leaves flying in all directions. Still the thing rose, a monstrosity over two meters tall, towering over him. Grotesque black eyes glared down at him silently.

Draken cursed, swinging his hammer in a wide arc toward the thing's head.

The Ironclad dodged backward, the hammer missing it by mere centimeters. It lunged forward then, grabbing at him with two of its hands as Draken overswung. He pivoted, spinning in a circle, using the momentum from the missed swing to power a second, barely avoiding the thing's grasp in the process. The hammer slammed into the thing's armored chest, bouncing off...but leaving a small crack there.

The Ironclad stumbled backward...but reached out with one hand, grabbing the shaft of his hammer as it recoiled. It yanked on it, pulling Draken forward and upward. He flew through the air, the hammer slipping out of his hands.

He struck the ground, somersaulting and springing to his feet, turning to face the beast. He unsheathed the longsword at his hip in one smooth motion, pointing its tip at the Ironclad...and scanning the ground for his hammer. He spotted it a few meters behind him and to his right.

The Ironclad charged at him with unnerving speed!

Draken sprinted toward his hammer just as the Ironclad reached him, sheathing his sword and reaching down to grab the hammer. The beast swung a fist at him, and he rolled under the blow, springing to his feet and swinging his hammer with both hands. It arced through the air, colliding with the thing's temple with a loud *crack*.

The Ironclad stumbled to the side, falling to its hands and knees.

Draken swung again, but the Ironclad raised two arms to block the blow, the hammer colliding with its forearms. It lunged forward then, grabbing the front of Draken's uniform with one pair of hands. Then it cocked a third fist back, slamming it into Draken's chest.

Air exploded from Draken's lungs, and he heard a loud *snap* as his breastbone caved in, pain lancing across his chest and through to his back.

He gasped, trying desperately to pull air into his lungs, but nothing came.

The Ironclad tossed him backward, and he felt himself falling, his back striking the ground. His vision blackened, the Ironclad's huge form looming over him. He tried to put his hammer between them, then realized he no longer had it. He reached for his longsword, starting to unsheathe it.

The Ironclad knelt down, batting his hand away. It tore the longsword from his scabbard, flinging it to the side. Then it stared down at him, its breath hot against his face. He finally managed to take a breath in, only to explode in a fit of coughing. Bloody sputum dribbled down his chin.

The Ironclad stood then, backing away from him.

"Fucker," he spat, coughing again. He crawled backward on his butt, spotting his hammer a meter to his left. He lunged for it, ignoring the sharp pain in his chest as he did so. To his surprise, the Ironclad allowed this; he grabbed the hammer with both hands, rising unsteadily to his feet and facing the thing. He coughed again, the stabbing pain in his chest as he did so nearly bringing him his knees. The Ironclad faced him silently, its four arms at its sides.

Then it turned away from him, walking back toward the carriage.

The hell?

He stared at its retreating form, then glanced downward. The mounds he'd noticed earlier were rising.

Shit.

He stared as two more Ironclad appeared, leaves streaming off of them. They faced him silently, unmoving. Then, as one, the three Ironclad knelt down on one knee, bowing their heads. He swallowed in a dry throat, gripping his hammer tightly, his heart pounding in his chest.

And then Draken saw it.

A huge Ironclad – over a third of a meter taller than the others – strode toward him, its feet *thumping* on the forest floor. A mane of pale blue ran from the top of its head like a mohawk, all the way down its back to a short, broad tail. It appeared to be made of a strange gel-like substance, covered by a thick, translucent membrane.

The bizarre creature strode up to him, its black eyes locked on his.

Draken took one step backward, then another, staring at the monstrosity. He glanced at the other Ironclad; they had risen from their kneeling position, but they did not move.

"What the hell are you?" he spat, falling into another fit of coughing. Agony shot through his chest, and he grimaced, nearly dropping his hammer. He stumbled backward as the thing approached, knowing that there was no point in fighting this thing. Even if he somehow managed to kill it, the other Ironclad would finish him off.

He was a dead man.

The thing stepped right up to him, stopping less than a meter away, staring down at him. Its mane glowed faintly, casting its grotesque face in a pale blue hue.

"WHERE," it growled, its voice deep and guttural, "...IS...ORIGINAL?"

Draken stared at the creature, his jaw dropping.

It can speak!

The Ironclad took a step forward, and Draken swung his hammer, aiming right for the thing's face. To his surprise, it didn't move, didn't even attempt to block the blow. His hammer slammed into the left side of its face, snapping its head back and to the side.

It stumbled backward a step, then caught its balance, turning its head to face him again. The left side of its face had crumpled inward slightly, its eye crushed and oozing clear fluid, blood trickling down its cheek. It reached out, grabbing Draken's shoulders with one pair of its hands. Its grip was like a vise, squeezing his shoulders so hard that he couldn't have moved them if he tried. Draken cried out, the hammer slipping out of his hands.

WHERE?" it growled.

"I don't know," Draken blurted out, his voice trembling. He coughed, pain lancing through his chest again. "You should know," he added. "One of you...*things* got him."

The creature stared at him silently, its remaining black eye glittering in the sunlight. Then it lifted him upward until its eye was level with his. Draken cried out, the pain in his chest almost unbearable. He stared into that horrible face, his breath catching in his throat.

Its crushed eye was re-expanding, its crumpled cheek reforming in front of his very eyes.

What the...

"WHY YOU HERE?" it growled.

Draken groaned as its grip on his shoulders tightened, pain shooting through his chest with each breath.

"He was an initiate in the guild," he gasped. "We were looking for him."

The creature lowered Draken to the ground, letting go of his shoulders.

"WHO IS THE…WOMAN," it growled, making a series of rapid gestures with one hand. One of the other Ironclad turned, making a mournful wailing sound.

"What?"

"WHO IS THE WOMAN," the creature repeated, pressing one finger into Draken's sternum. Draken screamed, jerking backward and clutching at his chest.

"I don't know what you're talking about!" he protested.

"SHE IS ONE…OF YOU," the thing stated. Draken shook his head, taking another step back as the thing strode toward him.

"I don't know of any woman," Draken insisted.

"SHE HAS…SKULL," it explained, gesturing at its own chest. Draken stared blankly at it. Then his eyes widened, realization dawning on him.

Vi!

"YOU KNOW HER?" the creature growled. Draken nodded.

"She's not one of us anymore," he stated. The Ironclad leaned in, grabbing Draken's shoulders again, then using a third hand to press its finger into his chest. He howled, struggling to free himself from the thing's iron grip, but it was pointless. It stared down at him with those terrible eyes, cast in the pale glow of its unholy mane.

"FIND HER."

* * *

"Stay here," Vi ordered.

Hunter sighed, stopping a few yards from her house on the small island in the middle of the canyon lake, watching as she unlocked her front door, then stepped inside. She closed the door behind her, and he only got a quick peek of what lay beyond…a single room, with a bed in the corner. And tons of stuff everywhere…knickknacks on shelves on the walls, a bookshelf filled to overflowing, countless weapons hanging on the walls. And on the bed, a whole lot of stuffed animals and what looked like children's dolls.

Okaaay, he thought to himself.

Moments later, Vi returned, exiting the house. She was carrying a longsword in one hand, still in its sheath, along with a belt.

"Here," she said, strapping the belt to his waist and setting the longsword at his left hip. "Now draw it."

He did so, grabbing the hilt and drawing it outward, like he'd seen in the movies. The blade came, but with some resistance. Vi stopped him.

"Not like that," she counseled. "Like this," she said, grabbing his hand and pulling at a different angle. Hunter nodded, trying again. This time, the blade came out much more easily. "Better," she stated. "We'll work on it. Now hold it in front of you."

Hunter did so, holding the blade in his right hand. It felt awkward, a little too heavy for his arm. She grabbed his left hand, bringing it to the hilt below his right hand.

"Two hands," she ordered. "It's a longsword, remember?"

"I thought that meant it had a longer blade," Hunter said.

"No, it means it has a longer hilt," Vi corrected. "Because it's supposed to be used with two hands."

"Gotcha," he replied. It *did* feel more natural now. He held it in front of him, tip pointed up and away.

"Longswords are good all-around weapons," Vi explained. "Good for slashing and thrusting. Here," she added, backing away and unsheathing her own longsword. "Do this." She thrust the point of her sword forward.

"Okay," he replied, mimicking her. She shook her head.

"No no," she corrected. "Use your hips and back leg to generate thrust. You're relying too much on your arms."

"Oh," Hunter mumbled. He tried again, this time twisting his hips and pushing off of his back leg. Vi grimaced.

"Damn that was terrible," she grumbled. "You've never held a sword in your life, have you."

"Uh, no," Hunter replied sheepishly.

"It shows," she quipped. "You could've used a bit more quality time with that Seeker medallion."

"I thought you said it would've brainwashed me," Hunter countered. She smirked.

"Might've been worth it," she replied. "You're terrible."

"Then teach me already," he shot back.

"The sword you're holding was owned by a famous warrior almost a century ago," she informed. "He'd used it for most of his life, and was buried with it when he died. I was hired to find it when I was still in the guild." She sheathed her sword. "It absorbed his skills over a lifetime, and his personality, which I can tell you was hardly one you'd want to be burdened with."

"What do you mean?" he asked, eyeing his sword warily.

"Don't worry about it," she reassured. "Your personality isn't much better."

"Anyone ever tell you you're an asshole?"

"*Oh* yeah."

"So it absorbed his skills," Hunter prompted. Vi nodded.

"And you're absorbing them right now," she continued. "If you spend enough time with it, you'll improve significantly...without even practicing."

"So why are we doing this?" he asked.

"Because," she answered. "You can learn skills through absorption, but keep in mind that you're only learning movement patterns...the specific motor actions needed to execute a movement you're thinking of doing. You're not learning experience, or strategy, or anything else...not well, anyway."

"Oh."

"If you actually *train* with the sword, you'll learn context and strategy. And having absorbed some skill, you'll practice better."

"What do you mean?"

"For beginners," she answered, "...practice is imperfect. They make mistakes from the beginning, and have to spend lots of time correcting them. They fall into bad habits, poor form...and they keep practicing, ingraining these mistakes."

Hunter nodded...made sense.

"By practicing while absorbing some skill," she continued, "...you'll perform each maneuver with the correct movement patterns. You'll be practicing and ingraining correctly from the beginning...and you'll never get into bad habits."

"Okay," he replied. It certainly explained how he was able to execute a perfect back-kick on that guy in the bar yesterday...and why he'd gotten his ass kicked afterward. He knew some moves, but not how and when to use them.

"So you've got your thrust," she stated, unsheathing her sword and thrusting it again. "And your slash," she added, swinging her sword slowly, so that the blade stopped a few inches from Hunter's neck. "The slash can be done at eight basic angles: up, down, left, right, and the diagonals."

She demonstrated each angle, stopping the blade before it struck him.

"Your longsword is double-edged," Vi continued. "You can cut with both sides...and both sides can cut you." She sheathed her sword, then reached forward, grabbing the middle of Hunter's blade with her bare hand.

"Whoa," he blurted out. "Careful!"

"The middle of your blade isn't sharpened," she reassured, tugging on his blade. She released it then, showing her palm to him. There were no marks, of course. "Here, try it."

He hesitated, then grabbed the blade where she had, albeit far more carefully. She was right...the blade was indeed dull there.

"Why?" he asked.

"Ever hear of half-swording?" she replied. He shook his head. She unsheathed her own sword, grabbing the hilt with one hand and the middle of the blade with her other, underhanded. She thrust it forward then, right at Hunter's chest. He jerked backward, staring at the point; she'd stopped it an inch from his chest.

"Jesus," he grumbled. "Stop doing that."

"Grabbing the blade gives you more thrusting power," Vi explained, lowering her blade. "Helps get you through tough armor. Try it," she prompted.

Hunter did so, gripping the blade gingerly.

"Grip it tight," she instructed. "Flatten your fingers, hold it so the edge isn't sitting in your palm. Now thrust."

He complied, thrusting as she'd shown him. It *did* feel more powerful this way. Still, he couldn't shake the thought that he might cut himself.

"Would this work against the Ironclad?" he asked. Their armor was pretty thick, after all. Vi shook her head.

"No," she replied. "Not unless you crack their armor first. For that you need something like that hammer you had no clue how to use...or a mace."

"Like you did."

"Right," she agreed. "Or a murder-strike."

"A what?"

She turned her sword around, gripping it by the blade with both hands as if it were the hilt. Then she swung it over her head, aiming

257

right for Hunter's head. The sword's cross-guard stopped a few inches from Hunter's scalp.

"You can use your sword like a hammer," she explained, sheathing her sword again. "If you hold the blade the right way – even the sharp part of it – you won't cut yourself."

Hunter stared at her dubiously. Vi gave him a look.

"This'll go faster if you trust me," she counseled.

"Sorry," he mumbled.

"Don't be," she replied. "Most people are full of crap and don't even know it. They have no idea what they're doing, but they think they do. Assume that's the case until they can prove otherwise."

"So you *want* me to doubt you?"

"Wouldn't have it any other way," she replied with a grin.

"You did kick that Ironclad's ass," he admitted. "That was pretty awesome. Thanks by the way."

"My pleasure."

"So you're better than the other Seekers?" he asked.

"Yep."

"Even Thorius?" he pressed. Vi gave him a sour look.

"Thorius is an academic," she replied. "He's competent, but nothing special...and it's been a long time since he's seen any action."

"You're that good," he pressed.

"Honey," Vi replied, slapping him on the shoulder. "I'm so good it's illegal." She smirked. "Literally."

Hunter smiled back, then remembered how the Ironclad had nearly killed him...and how it'd killed Kris, brutally tearing him apart. Vi had faced the thing without so much as blinking, and had taken it down in seconds.

"Teach me oh master," he begged, steepling his hands in front of him and bowing. She rolled her eyes.

"Spend some quality time with that sword," she replied. "Then the real fun begins."

* * *

Hunter sat cross-legged before the small campfire he'd made, staring into the flames as he chewed on some bird meat Vi had hunted for them. She'd told him that if she was going to do the hunting, he at least had to make the fire without help. He'd managed to do so, much to his surprise, and was rather proud of the accomplishment. In fact, he found himself looking forward to doing it again…and faster next time.

He felt Vi's eyes on him opposite the fire, and he glanced up, seeing her staring at him with those strange green eyes. She'd already finished her meal, apparently.

"What's up?" he asked.

"What's it like in your world?"

"You mean Earth?" he pressed. She nodded. "It's…" he began, then paused. How to explain it? "Well, it's nothing like here."

"Go on."

"Objects and people don't absorb or transmit emotions or personalities or anything," he continued. "There aren't any monsters either," he added. "And our technology is a lot more advanced."

She just sat there, staring at him, waiting for him to continue.

"We have lots of machines there," he continued. "Machines that fly…like a carriage, but with wings that can carry people all the way around the world. And carriages that work without horses."

"Really?"

"Yeah," Hunter confirmed. "And we have guns, and things called computers that…well, they…" He grimaced. "It's hard to explain."

"What's a gun?" she asked.

"It's a little weapon that shoots metal things called bullets," he answered. "So fast that they can go through people. I had one when I went through the Gate, and I used it on an Ironclad," he added. "Blew its face off with one shot."

"Wow," she murmured. "Bet they took it from you."

"Yeah."

"They'll try to reverse-engineer it, of course," she continued. "That'll give them an advantage over the Ironclad…and over the other kingdoms."

"Other kingdoms?" he asked. She nodded.

"There's a few of them," she explained. "They're all different. Tykus has the most powerful military, and is the most…human. They're the original city, the one created by the first humans, long before Tykus the Legend ever came here."

"Wait," Hunter protested. "I thought Tykus founded the city."

"No," Vi replied. "That's propaganda. The city was already here, but Tykus built the Acropolis on top of the existing structure…an ancient crypt. The original tunnels and chambers of the crypt are still there, below the Acropolis."

"Oh."

"Why'd you come here?" Vi asked. Hunter sighed, lowering his gaze to the flames.

"My mom," he admitted. "She was a...someone who studied old civilizations," he explained. "She and my dad found the Gate in a cave. She fell through trying to save someone else from being pulled into the Gate."

Vi nodded, continuing to stare at him. He sighed again.

"That was about eight years ago for me," he admitted. "My dad made up a story about how she died falling down the cave." He shook his head. "I spent most of my life believing she was dead. I found out the truth a few days ago, and confronted him. He confessed, and I went through the Gate to find her."

"Ah, I see."

"When I told Thorius," he continued, "...he said that time is different here, and that she'd come through almost fifty years ago."

Vi's eyebrows furrowed.

"Your mother came through fifty years ago?" she asked.

"Yeah," he confirmed. "Thorius said she was the one who started the Civil War."

Vi stared at him incredulously.

"What?" he asked.

"Your mother was the Original? *The* Original?"

"I guess."

Vi stood then, starting to pace in front of the fire. She stopped, turning to look down at him.

"It makes sense," she murmured.

"What does?"

She resumed pacing, her chin in one hand.

"Your...coloring," she answered. "And your will. You're very similar to her, you know. I should've recognized it sooner."

"What are you talking about?" he pressed.

"You're the son of a Legend, Hunter," Vi explained, stopping suddenly. "No wonder why they wanted to get rid of you...it all makes sense now."

"Not to me," he shot back.

"Hunter, you're the son of the woman who nearly destroyed Tykus," she explained. "She was a Legend...a true *Legend*, like

Tykus. She was the only human Legend known to exist in the last century."

"Really?" Hunter replied. "I don't know…she was pretty strong, but she was just my mom. She wasn't like…legendary or anything."

"Oh yes she was," Vi retorted. "Hunter, do you even know what a Legend is?"

"Kinda. Maybe."

"A Legend is extremely rare," Vi explained. "A person – or animal, or plant – that has a will so powerful that it can't be changed. No other will can dominate it. But it can dominate any will it encounters, given time. Your mother could make people think like her, act like her…could make them obey her just by being close to them for long enough. Even her enemies could be converted. Hell, just by *existing*, she could change an entire people to be like her, just like Tykus did."

"Really?"

"Really," Vi insisted. "That's why she was so dangerous. Just by being in the city, she started to change everyone in it to be like her instead of Tykus. If the kingdom hadn't forced her out, she would've singlehandedly ended their way of life. Their customs, their religion…everything." She shook her head. "They destroyed the old Outskirts, and even dug up the damn ground she'd walked on, dumping it into the ocean just to get rid of her influence. That's why we have the Deadlands."

Hunter stared at her silently, a chill running through him. It was just like Thorius had told him…why they didn't allow immigrants into the city.

"They didn't realize she was a Legend until it was almost too late," Vi continued.

"Wait," Hunter interjected. "They never said she was a Legend." Vi snorted, crossing her arms over her chest.

"They wouldn't," she replied. "She was a woman, remember? And she was the enemy. There's no way the kingdom would recognize another Original Legend like that. It would threaten their worship of Tykus."

"Oh."

"She was a hell of a woman," Vi continued. "From what I've experienced, she was a lot like you. Maybe that's why I decided to keep you."

"What do you mean, from what you've experienced?"

"I was hired to retrieve some artifacts of hers," Vi explained. "A while back, when I was still in the guild. I kept a few for myself." She paused, then started walking back toward her house. "Hold on," she added, walking past her house to the water's edge. She squatted, reaching into the water and pulling out a heavy-looking chest. She opened it, retrieving a necklace from it, then returning to Hunter to offer it to him.

"What's this?" he asked, taking it from her.

"Something your mother owned," she answered. "Go on, hold it up to your forehead," she added. Hunter gave her a questioning look, but she didn't elaborate further. He shrugged, holding the necklace to his forehead and closing his eyes.

And felt a sudden burst of anger.

He opened his eyes, nearly dropping the necklace, but Vi motioned for him to hold it up to his forehead again. He did so, bracing himself. He felt the anger again...not a violent anger, but a righteous one. As if he'd been wronged somehow.

"Keep going," Vi said.

He felt a sudden bitterness then, and a sadness. A loneliness and longing so profound that it made his heart ache. He pictured his father then, and himself when he was a just a kid. The longing intensified, until it all but overwhelmed him.

The necklace fell from his hands, and he opened his eyes, standing up and backing away from it. He stared at it silently, then looked up, seeing Vi eyeing him.

"Jesus," he muttered.

"You felt the power of it?" she asked. Hunter nodded. It'd been far more powerful than the crystalline orb Thorius had given him. More powerful even than Trixie's unique...gifts.

"It was hers," he murmured. "It was really hers."

"It was," Vi agreed.

"She was really here," he realized, another chill running through him. The thought that she'd been here, in this world...living in the very city he'd been in for the past few days...was overwhelming. He lowered his gaze, moisture coming unbidden to his eyes. He wiped them away quickly, taking a deep, shuddering breath in.

"I'm sorry Hunter," Vi murmured, kneeling down and putting a hand on his shoulder. He felt his sadness dissipate, replaced by a gentle somberness.

"She was really here," he repeated, shaking his head. Vi grabbed the necklace, returning it to the chest and placing the chest back in the water. She walked back to him then.

"I'll keep that for you," she offered. "You can borrow it if you need to feel her presence. But not for too long, or you'll absorb too much of her will."

Hunter nodded, feeling moisture blur his eyes again. He wiped them with one sleeve, feeling suddenly drained.

"Thanks Vi," he mumbled.

She smiled, sitting down across the fire from him once again. He could feel her eyes on him, but he didn't meet them. He stared into the dying flames of the fire instead, feeling its heat on his face, drying his tears.

"What am I going to do here?" he wondered. "I came to find my mom, and she's gone." He sighed heavily. "And now I can never go back home."

"Hunter," Vi began, hesitating for a moment. "Your mother may not be here, but a part of her is," she replied. "Like in that necklace," she added. "There are other artifacts with her inside of them...maybe even her Ossae." She smiled, getting up and sitting down beside him, putting a warm hand on his shoulder. "You can still have her...a part of her, anyway. In this world, the strong-willed carry on even after death," she continued. "And Legends...well, in a way, they live on forever."

CHAPTER 21

Conlan smiled as Dominus walked across the long hallway leading to the Royal Chambers, passing row after row of Royal guards that were forever stationed there. His son strode up to him, leaning in to embrace him.

"Good afternoon father," he greeted, pulling away. "How are you?"

"As well as can be expected," Dominus replied, eyeing Conlan critically. Dressed in the fine royal uniform of Tykus himself, resplendent with the amulet, rings, and crown the great king himself had once worn, his son certainly looked the part. He was early in the transition process, of course...no one would ever mistake his son for the one true king.

"Your leg is bothering you," Conlan noted.

"It always does."

"It's good to get out of that damn room," Conlan stated, gesturing at the huge set of double-doors at the end of the hallway. As a new king, he was forced to spend all but three hours a day in the Royal Chambers. Containing the Ossae of Tykus himself, and most of the one king's personal possessions, the Chambers were where Tykus's will was most potent...and where the transition would occur most efficiently.

"How is the transition going?" Dominus inquired.

"I question if it even is," Conlan answered. "To be honest, I don't feel any different than I did yesterday."

Dominus said nothing, eyeing Conlan. He seemed exuberant...confident. *Too* confident. Dominus felt a familiar irritation come over him.

"It's only been one day," he stated evenly.

"He's strong," Conlan admitted. "There's no doubt about it. But I think I'm almost as strong as he is."

Again, Dominus said nothing. Conlan smirked at him.

"You think I'm wrong," he observed. "You always give me that look when you think I'm wrong."

"Time will tell whether you are or aren't."

"You think I'll transition, don't you?" Conlan stated. "Well I'm not so sure. What if I don't?" he added, spreading his arms out wide. "Think about it!"

"Such a thing has never happened," Dominus retorted, feeling his irritation getting the best of him. "You underestimate His power."

"Maybe," Conlan replied, clearly unconvinced. "Like you said, time will tell."

"Indeed."

"So who's this boy you've taken under your wing?" Conlan inquired. "What's his name again, Axio?"

"He's your cousin," Dominus answered.

"The heir to the Duke of Wexford!" Conlan declared. He eyed his father. "You never were going to let me have the Duchy, were you."

"You are my only son," Dominus countered. "The Duchy would have been your birthright if the king had sired a son."

"Mmm hmm," Conlan replied. "You know what I think?"

Dominus didn't reply.

"I think the king could have had a dozen heirs and you still wouldn't let me succeed you," Conlan stated. "You never liked me very much, did you father?"

"I love you as my son," Dominus retorted.

"But you don't *like* me, do you?" he pressed. Dominus grimaced.

"You were a difficult child."

"Yes I was," Conlan agreed. "But only because I questioned everything. Questioned *you*, and I know how much you hate to be questioned."

"There's a difference between questioning and defiance," Dominus countered wearily.

265

"Isn't that what all old men call questioning?" Conlan pressed. "Defiance?" He shook his head. "I dared to question the holiness of Tykus, and you acted as if I murdered my own mother."

Dominus grimaced at that.

"Conlan…"

"What makes him so special?" Conlan interrupted. "Hmm? He was a Legend, granted. But my will is strong too…and there've been other Legends you know. Yet we keep bringing Tykus back. Why?"

"You know why."

"I've read a great deal about him," Conlan continued. "He was a radical, did you know that?"

Dominus grit his teeth, irritated at Conlan's smug attitude. He'd read more about Tykus than the boy could ever imagine…read more books than Conlan had read pages. It was the conceit of youth that, upon acquiring a parcel of the truth, they believed themselves masters of the universe, deriding their 'ignorant' elders.

"A man of superior will always prove himself in the end," Conlan stated. "I've spent a full night in the Royal Chambers, and yet I am still very much myself. This is unprecedented…no king has ever been able to withstand Tykus's will."

"And no king ever will," Dominus retorted.

"We shall see," Conlan replied with that irritating smirk of his. Dominus suppressed his annoyance, keeping his expression carefully neutral. Perhaps it was best to entertain Conlan's delusions, if only to make the transition smoother.

"I look forward to being proven wrong, son," he stated.

"I have a great many ideas for the kingdom," Conlan continued. "We're far too conservative father. Do you know that in the Kingdom of the Deep, they allow absorption of wild traits?" He raised his eyebrows. "They *encourage* it, father. Imagine, having the strength of a bull, or the speed of a…"

"Our humanity," Dominus interrupted, "…is our greatest strength."

"And our greatest weakness," Conlan countered. "I read the reports on the attack on the military base. Ten men killed by a single Ironclad! It's pathetic how weak we are."

"Yet we've created the most powerful kingdom in the world," Dominus reminded him. "We've built this enormous city, and driven out the Ironclad. What we lack in animal defenses, we more than make up for with our intellect."

"But why not have both?" Conlan pressed. "We would become the most powerful species in the world, father!"

"And lose our humanity," Dominus retorted. Conlan rolled his eyes, throwing up his hands.

"Humanity," he muttered. "What does it even mean? What is it worth, father? What is it *truly* worth?"

Dominus just stared at him.

"You cling to humanity as if it's some precious thing, something that must be preserved at all costs," Conlan continued. "It's nothing more than pathetic sentiment father."

"We've maintained our humanity for millennia," Dominus stated, feeling his irritation get the better of him. "The Originals are proof of that. Who are you to decide that, after thousands of years, we'll just give up everything we've worked for?"

Conlan smiled, putting a hand to his breast.

"I," he answered, "...am the king."

Dominus shook his head.

"Tykus is the king," he retorted. "You?" He gave Conlan a withering look. "You're just an empty cup waiting to be filled."

* * *

Hunter opened his eyes, squinting against the sunlight. He blinked, realizing that he was lying on his side on the canyon floor, on his makeshift bed of leaves and dirt. His hip was sore from having laid on it all night; Vi had once again insisted that he sleep outside while she slept in the comfort of her bed. With all those dolls and stuffed animals. Which was weird.

He grunted, pulling himself into a sitting position, finding the sword Vi had given him yesterday lying next to him in its sheath. She'd insisted he sleep with it, to better absorb its original owner's skills. He stood up, grabbing the sword and strapping it to his waist, glancing up at the sky. The sun was hovering just above the treetops high above, casting long shadows into the canyon. Vi's house was in the distance across the bridge...and the separate, smaller building to the right of it.

Hunter sighed, then walked up to the long bridge toward Vi's house, crossing it slowly. He reached the other side, then hesitated, glancing at the building to the right, sitting on its own little island. It was smaller than Vi's house, with no obvious way in. No door, no windows...nothing. He walked across the short bridge to it, circling the building slowly. There was a small moat surrounding it, maybe two feet wide, but with no bridge crossing it.

Strange, he thought.

He heard a door slam shut behind him, and flinched, spinning around.

"Looking for a way in?" he heard a feminine voice say. It was Vi, standing in front of her house. She wasn't dressed in her usual uniform; instead, she was wearing a tight white shirt that stopped far above her bellybutton, and short white shorts. She was surprisingly fit, but not in an overly masculine way. He realized he was staring, and looked away, feeling his cheeks flush.

"Morning," he mumbled.

"Never seen a woman in her underwear?" Vi inquired. He could *feel* her smirking at him. "What, did you and that whore do it in the dark? Or did you leave your clothes on?"

"Ha ha," he grumbled. "I was trying to be polite."

"Pfft," she shot back. "I don't give a crap if you look. Just don't be a creep…or I'll turn you into a woman."

"Noted."

She walked up to the edge of the island, then dove into the lake. Hunter watched her swim a ways underwater, then surface a few dozen feet from the shore.

"What are you doing?" he asked.

"Taking a bath," she answered. "You might want to join me," she added. "You stink."

"I'll pass," he replied. The water looked freezing.

"Suit yourself," she replied, dipping below the water again. Moments later, she resurfaced close to the shore, and pulled herself up, walking toward him. Her clothes clung to her rather scandalously, making it quite apparent that the water *was* cold. He turned away again, glancing at the smaller building.

"What's that?" he asked, pointing to it.

"Cipher room," she answered, walking up to his side. He glanced at her, taken aback by how strong she looked. Not only were her arms more muscular than his, her legs were remarkably powerful looking. She could easily overpower him if she wanted to. It was no wonder how she'd managed to break through the Ironclad's armor with her mace earlier, when even Gammon hadn't succeeded in doing so.

"What's a cipher room?" he pressed.

"A storehouse for artifacts," she replied. "The most powerful ones. When I bring them home, I need a place to put them where they won't screw with my other artifacts. So I built that."

"Why the moat?" he inquired. "And how do you get in?"

"It's a cipher room," she explained. "Partially filled with water on the inside, which is always flowing. And there's water flowing outside of it."

"Why?"

"Water absorbs traits," she explained. "If it's flowing, traits never have time to build up in the water, and never get to the stone beyond the water. It's carried away into the lake, and flows out through the underground river leaving the canyon. That leaves the building devoid of traits, relatively speaking."

"So the water insulates against the building absorbing the traits in the artifacts you store in it?"

"Right," she confirmed. "Otherwise a powerful artifact would influence the stone of the building, and then any other artifact I put in there would absorb the original artifact's essence and corrupt it."

"Huh," he muttered. "Pretty clever."

"The storehouse itself is made of neutral stone," she continued.

"What's that?"

"Stone that doesn't have any traits absorbed into it," she explained. "Soil and rocks at the surface have absorbed traits over time, but those much deeper down haven't. And rocks from volcanoes – from lava that comes from deep within the earth – are neutral as well."

"Okay."

"When I sense that the storehouse has absorbed too much despite the water," she continued, "…I knock it down and rebuild it with new neutral stone."

"So water insulates it so that takes a while?"

"Yep…but only if it's flowing." She ran a hand over her nearly bald head. Her hair had grown only slightly since they'd met, and was still so short it was barely visible. "Water is used in other ways as well."

"Like what?"

"If you take a powerful artifact and steep it in water for a while," she replied, "…the water will absorb its will, emotions…everything. Drink that water, and it'll get inside you, flowing through your blood…and get to every part of your body very quickly."

"So?"

269

"So what does transmission of traits depend on?" Hunter frowned, recalling what Thorius had taught him.

"Proximity and duration of exposure," he answered. Vi nodded.

"Drinking steeped water makes the stuff go *inside* of you," she explained. "You can't get any closer than that."

"What about the duration?"

"It depends," she answered. "But it usually doesn't last too long. But keep drinking that water over and over..." She paused. "You ate at the community center, right?"

"Where else was I gonna eat?"

"That water they served you?" she replied. "It was steeped in artifacts that promote apathy, blind loyalty. People drink it day in, day out...and live their lives working in the sewers, toiling away for shit wages and living in shit apartments. And yet they never speak up, never rebel."

"The kingdom does that?"

"Yep," she confirmed. "It's all about control. That's what governments do. They get in power, subdue the populace, leeching from them. They're the ultimate parasite, sucking wealth and power out of the lower classes. Once and a while they'll throw a few crumbs to the peasants to keep them satisfied. Because they know that if they don't, the peasants will rebel." She shook her head. "The water, and churches, and the artifacts all around the city...all that shit is just another way to keep the people in line. Keep them distracted and slaving away for nothing while the aristocrats lounge in luxury."

"Damn."

"And you know what the best part is?" she pressed. He shrugged. "The peasants are desperate to be like the wealthy...to be blond-haired, blue-eyed, tall, and pale. To be cultured and sophisticated. To wear expensive clothes. And you know what that water at the community center does?"

"What?"

"It keeps 'em a little brown," she answered. "Keeps every damn citizen in the Outskirts looking different, so they'll never get to be like the ones in power."

"That's messed up."

"That's life," she countered. "But most people don't even see it. I did because they couldn't control me...I was too strong. None of their shit worked on me."

She started walking back toward the house then.

270

"Enough talk," she declared. "I'm getting dressed…and then we're going to spar."

* * *

Hunter held his wooden sparring sword in both hands, facing Vi. She was holding her wooden sword in one hand at her side, looking as relaxed as always. She'd changed into her customary uniform, and they'd walked across the bridge to the shore of the lake.

"Thrust like I showed you last night," she ordered. Hunter couldn't help but grin.

"Might want to change the way you say…" he began.

"Shut up."

Hunter's jaw snapped shut, and he focused, thrusting the point of his sword at her, using his hips and his back leg as she'd instructed yesterday. To his surprise, the move came easily, almost naturally.

"Good," she stated, clearly pleased. "You're absorbing some skills…now we have something to work with." She gestured at him. "Do it again."

He did, and again the move came smoothly, the point of his sword aiming right at her solar plexus, the area below her breastbone. He smiled, having a hard time believing he'd had such difficulty with the move yesterday. It was so simple!

"All right," she stated. "Now practice the eight slashing angles I showed you yesterday."

Hunter did so, slashing upward, then downward, then left, then right, and then at each diagonal. Again, the moves came easily, as if he'd done them a hundred times before. Vi nodded.

"Not bad," she said. "Still need a lot more time with that sword before you're up to snuff though. You absorb skills at an above-average rate, but not exceptionally well."

"Can I get better at it?" he asked. Vi paused.

"For an Original, that's a complicated question," she answered. "But ultimately, you can't change the strength of your will. It just means you'll need to spend a lot more time with artifacts than I would."

"Oh, okay."

"Alright," she stated, "…let's spar." She gestured for him to come at her. "Hit me."

"Uh…"

"Come on," she prompted. "Don't be scared."

He hesitated, then made a half-hearted lunge at her. She moved quicker than he could see, batting his sword to the side and smacking him across the side of his thigh with the flat of her wooden blade. Hard.

"Ow!" he cried, stumbling back and rubbing his thigh. He glared at her. "What the hell?"

"You gonna fight or not?" she inquired. He grimaced, raising his sword again, then feinting another lunge. She didn't take the bait, just standing there with her sword down. "Come on little boy," she taunted. "Scared of a *girl?*"

He lunged forward, slashing at her neck. But she blocked the blow easily, thrusting the tip of her sword into his gut. He grunted, stumbling backward.

"Boy you suck," she mocked. He glared at her, readying his sword again.

"Bet you feel real good picking on someone who's never used a sword before," he shot back. She smirked at him.

"Actually yeah," she replied. "It *does* feel good, now that you mention it."

"You're an ass," he grumbled, feinting again. Again, she didn't fall for it.

"Do you have to project *everything* you do?" Vi inquired. "I mean, a girl likes a surprise every once and a while, you know."

He swatted at her sword, trying to bat it to the side, but she stepped back, lunging forward immediately afterward. Her sword jabbed into his belly again – in the exact same place it had earlier. He grimaced, batting it away with his sword.

"Too late," she taunted. "You're already dead."

"Ha ha," he shot back. "Feel free to start, you know, actually *teaching* me."

"I kinda like this more," she retorted. He took a deep breath in, then focused, circling around her. He feinted once, then again, and still she didn't fall for it, much to his irritation.

"Hold on," he muttered, pretending to limp. He reached down with one hand, grabbing a rock. Then he shot up, throwing the rock at her, then lunging forward with a thrusting attack at her chest.

She flicked her sword one-handed, smacking the back of his right hand…while catching the rock in her free hand. His sword was knocked out of his hands.

"Ooo, tricky," she taunted, tossing the rock at him. It struck him in the belly, again in the same spot she'd hit twice before. He glared at her, backpedaling quickly and rubbing the back of his hand.

"God *damn* it," he swore. "That hurt!"

"Aww," she pouted. "You want me to kiss it better?"

"You know what?" he retorted, reaching down to pick his sword up. "I'm done with this. If you're not going to bother teaching me, then I don't see the point."

She lunged forward suddenly, swinging her sword so quickly it was a blur. He felt his sword lurch out of his hand, then felt a sharp pain in his shin as she kicked him. His knee locked, his body tilting forward, and she charged in, kneeing him in the gut, then shoving him backward. He fell flat on his back, the air bursting from his lungs. He gasped, clutching at his belly.

"I am teaching you," she stated coolly. She leaned over, offering a hand. He ignored her, rolling onto his side, then onto all fours, picking himself up off the ground. He turned to face her, giving her a murderous glare.

"Oh really," he muttered.

"Yeah really," she retorted. "If you'd been paying attention, you would've realized that." She gestured at him to pick up his sword. He glared at her for a moment longer, then grabbed it reluctantly, holding it at his side. "Problem is, you were paying attention to what *you* were doing instead of what *I* was doing."

He stared at her.

"The first time you thrust at me, what did I do?" she asked. He blinked, trying to recall.

"You batted my sword to the side, then smacked me on the thigh."

"Now do it," she ordered, thrusting at him. She stopped an inch from his belly. He hesitated, then batted her sword to the side, following with a slash to her thigh. "And the second time you attacked?" she pressed.

"You blocked it and stabbed me," he answered, glowering at her.

"So do it," she ordered, slashing at his neck. Again she stopped the blow before it hit. He blocked her sword, then thrust at her belly, just as she had done to him...but he didn't stop the thrust. She dodged to the side easily, smirking at him. "Nice try," she added. "And the third time?"

"You dodged back and thrust at me," he answered grudgingly.

273

"You were trying to bat my sword away," she explained. "You weren't aiming for me, you were aiming for my sword. All I had to do was get out of range, then wait for you to open yourself up and gut you." She went to bat his sword away, and he hesitated, then stepped back out of range. Then he lunged forward, thrusting at her belly. Again, she dodged out of the way just in time. "See?"

"Yeah yeah," he grumbled. "You could've just done it this way from the beginning you know."

"Wrong," she retorted. "There's nothing gentle about fighting," she added. "You have to learn how to take hits. You get pissed when you get hurt, and then you make stupid mistakes." She gave him a disgusted look. "Or in your case, you act like a damn child, expecting me to spoon-feed you everything."

"Yeah, well maybe I'm not cut out for this shit," he retorted angrily. "Ever think of that?"

"Nope."

He blinked.

"What?"

"I don't think you're a hopeless cause," she replied, pointing her sword at him. "*You* do."

"That's bullshit."

"Is it?" she pressed. "I hit you because I wanted to see what happens when you fail. How you handle it. And you know what?" she added. "You *suck* at failing."

Hunter stared at her, feeling an ice-cold anger grow within him. He had the sudden urge to leave, to tell her to go fuck herself and head back to the city. He didn't need her, after all. He could go back to Tykus, go back to Trixie and the guild. He'd be perfectly happy there, having all the sex he could ever want, night after night. He didn't need this shit…and he didn't have to take it.

"Don't forget I can feel your emotions," Vi reminded him. "You lost your mother," she continued. "Trust me, I get it. You loved someone and they left you, and you're never going to make that mistake again."

"That doesn't…"

"You've given up on everyone and everything around you," Vi interjected. "Playing it casual and pretending you don't give a shit about anything. Problem is, you gave up on yourself too."

"That's not true," Hunter retorted.

"Oh yes it is," Vi shot back. "Take it from someone who's been there, kiddo. It took me *years* to get my own head out of my ass. To stop being pissed at the world. To take a goddamn chance. If you wanna give up on everyone else, fine. But don't give up on yourself."

Hunter just stared at her.

"You're angry, I get it," Vi stated. "You have every right to be. But quit losing your shit every time life gets hard," she instructed. "Emotion is temporary, action is forever. Don't let your temper control you, or you'll regret it."

Hunter grit his teeth, lowering his gaze.

"I've got news for you kiddo," she continued, lowering her sword. "The only way you're going to get better is by failing until you stop failing. Losers fail and quit. Winners fail and learn from it." She raised her sword again, pointing it at him. "Better get used to failing," she stated. "'Cause you're going to be doing a whole lot of it from here on out."

Chapter 22

"Try again."

Hunter sighed, pulling yet another arrow from his quiver, then nocking it on the bowstring and pulling back. He squinted, spotting the large bird perched on a branch some twenty feet from the ground, not forty feet from where he stood. Vi had taken him up the path to the forest above the canyon to hunt for food…and told him that it was high time *he* caught dinner for once. She'd been hunting for them for a couple of weeks now, after all…and she refused to do it anymore. She'd made it quite clear that if he didn't catch dinner, she'd let him starve to death.

He aimed, then released the bowstring, hearing the *twang* as it shot forward. The arrow whizzed through the air toward the bird…and missed it by a few inches. The bird leapt from its perch, flying away.

"Damn it," he swore, lowering the bow and shaking his head. Vi clapped him on the back.

"Try again," she stated for the umpteenth time.

He sighed again, searching the trees for another target. He spotted the same bird circling through the air, and waited. Eventually it came back down to the branch it'd been on before, settling there. He took a deep breath in, then let it out, pulling an arrow from his quiver and drawing his bowstring again. He aimed, then fired, the arrow speeding toward the bird.

It hit!

Hunter's eyes widened as the bird fell from the branch, landing on the ground with a *thump*. It flailed on the ground for a bit, its wings beating the forest floor, then went still. He turned to Vi, a huge smile on his face.

"I did it!" he exclaimed. Vi smirked.

"Took you long enough," she retorted. He glared at her.

"Really?" he grumbled. "You can't even give me *one* victory?" She chuckled.

"You done good kiddo," she admitted. "Now go get us dinner before some asshole animal steals it from us."

He complied, jogging up to the bird and kneeling before it. He grabbed the shaft of his arrow, stepping on the bird and yanking the arrow out. Then he grimaced, picking the bird up by one wing, holding it as far away from himself as he could.

"It's not going to peck you," she yelled. He ignored her, walking past her toward the spiraling path down to the canyon nearby. He strode down it, feeling good despite Vi's merciless heckling. He'd finally managed to kill something, after all. They'd been trying for over an hour. Frankly, he thought he'd never be able to do it.

"Time to make a fire," Vi stated. "I'll show you how to clean the corpse."

"Thanks."

"Thanks for dinner," she replied, walking behind him. "Not so scared of heights anymore I see."

He frowned, glancing over the edge of the narrow path. She was right, he realized; the sheer drop to the lake below no longer made him nervous, despite the fact that it would quite certainly murder his ass. He wondered if it was because he was getting used to it, or because Vi was near him. She had a calming influence on him, he'd realized, and it didn't take her touching him to do it. Just by being near him, he felt rather peaceful. He wondered if she felt that way all the time.

Eventually they reached the bottom of the canyon, and Vi led them back to the site of the campfire they'd been using for the past couple of weeks. Hunter got to work gathering branches and tinder, and it wasn't long before they were crouched before a merrily crackling fire. Vi showed him how to clean and dress the bird, forcing him to do most of the work, as was her way. After the meat cooked, they ate in silence. The food was pretty good, actually…and it tasted even better knowing that he'd done everything to prepare it. He ate in satisfied silence, until there was no meat left.

277

"You had a good day," Vi opined, finishing her meal and eyeing him from across the fire. He nodded.

"Yeah, I did," he admitted. Not at first, of course. They'd sparred for most of the morning and early afternoon, as they had for the last couple of weeks, Vi coming at him relentlessly. Over and over again she'd beaten him...he hadn't gotten a single hit on her despite hours of trying. He had fresh bruises all over his body from the ordeal, of course. She'd been right though; the pain of getting hit had proven an excellent teacher, despite how pissed off he'd gotten at her. And any time he'd lost his temper and lashed out at her, she'd easily defeated him...and made him pay dearly for his temper.

It'd been a pretty painful two weeks, actually. In fact, he hoped he never had to go through it again. But he'd learned a hell of a lot...mostly through paying attention to what *she* was doing.

At the end of each day's sparring lessons, she'd drilled attacks and counterattacks for a full hour, making him do them until he was utterly exhausted...and today had been no different.

"Alright," she declared, standing up. "I'm going to bed."

"Already?"

"Yep," she confirmed. "Sleep is good for the mind. You should go to bed too."

"All right."

"Night," she added.

"Night."

She walked toward her home, unlocking her front door and opening it.

"Hey Vi?" Hunter called out. She turned to look at him, her green eyes almost iridescent in the darkness.

"Yeah?"

"Thanks," he said. "For everything."

She smiled at him, then stepped through the doorway, closing and locking the door behind her. Hunter sighed, turning back to the fire. The sun had dipped well below the canyon walls, the first of the stars twinkling in the night sky. Three moons hung there, suspended in the cosmos. A nightly reminder of where he was...and where he was not.

"All right," he muttered, standing up. He walked across the long bridge to the shore, finding his usual resting place. He'd seen fit to add some more forest litter to his bedding, in hopes of waking up with less soreness in his back and hip. He unstrapped his sword from his waist, setting it aside, then laid down on his back, staring up at the steadily darkening sky. He wondered what Vi would have him do tomorrow; probably more sparring. He grabbed his sword, clutching it to his chest.

Gonna need all the help I can get.

With that, he closed his eyes. And it was no surprise – given yet another day filled to the brim with exertion – that within moments of doing so, he was fast asleep.

* * *

The next morning, Hunter awoke to the sound of birds chirping. He stirred, hearing the sharp calls echoing through the canyon, piercing through the eternal din of the waterfalls crashing into the lake. His sword was still laying across his chest; he'd been sleeping on his back the entire night. As a result, his hip felt better…but his back ached something terrible when he sat up.

What I wouldn't give to have a bed, he thought.

Hunter got to his feet, brushing leaves and dirt from his clothes, then strapped his sword to his hip. Its weight felt surprisingly comforting there…natural, even, as if it were a part of him. He drew the blade from its scabbard, sliding it effortlessly free. The blade glimmered in the sunlight.

He studied it, studying the small symbols etched down the length of the blade. The hilt appeared to be made of ivory, with leather straps wrapped tightly around it. He held it in both hands, giving it one swing, then another. The blade cut through the air, and the movement felt even better than it had yesterday. More natural. He practiced a thrust, snapping at the waist to add power to it.

Not bad, he thought.

He imagined Vi thrusting at him, and blocked the blow, countering with a quick slash, then a thrust of his own. He couldn't help but smile; as much as he'd hated Vi for all the drills she'd put him through, he could feel the difference they'd made. His moves were faster, more precise. And most importantly, they just felt *right*.

He tried a few more drills with his imaginary opponent, then sheathed his sword, walking across the bridge to the island. He spotted the campfire in front of the house, realizing that he'd left the bow and quiver full of arrows near it. Hunter grabbed these, eager to try his hand at some target practice. There was little doubt in his mind that Vi would force him to hunt again today; the more practice he got, the sooner he'd get to eat.

I should've slept with the bow, he thought, mentally kicking himself. He'd probably have been a much better shot yesterday if he'd done so for the last couple of weeks. Oh well…he was going to sleep with it tonight, that was for sure.

He turned back to the bridge, crossing it, then stopping some thirty feet away from one of the trees growing near the canyon wall. Pulling an arrow from the quiver, he set it on the bowstring, pulling back, then letting go. The arrow shot just to the left of the trunk.

Damn.

He looked down, making sure his feet were pointed perpendicular to his target. Then he lined up his hips and shoulders, drawing another arrow and trying again. This time, the arrow shot true, slamming into the trunk.

Yes!

He drew another arrow, making sure to check his body position before making another shot. This too slammed into the trunk, a few inches below the first arrow. He smiled.

"All right," he murmured. "Not bad Hunter. Not bad."

He tried again…and again, the arrow shot true.

"Well shit," he said, grinning from ear-to-ear. "I think I've got it."

Just then, he heard a *snap* behind him.

He whirled around, dropping the bow and reaching for his sword, pulling it free from its scabbard and holding it before him in one fluid motion. Then he relaxed – it was only Vi. She arched an eyebrow at him, ignoring the tip of his sword less than a foot from her face.

"Morning kid," she greeted, glancing at the tree trunk. "Not bad," she opined. He sheathed his sword, picking the bow up off the ground.

"Morning yourself," he grumbled back. "Did you have to sneak up on me like that?"

"Yep," she replied. "Nice reflexes, by the way. You're improving."

"Thanks," he replied. He must've gained the reflex from sleeping with his sword. He glanced down, seeing a rolled-up piece of paper in Vi's hand. "What's that?" he asked. "Didn't know you could read."

"Bet you can't," she retorted. He grimaced, realizing she'd gotten him on that one. He *couldn't* read, at least not whatever language they wrote here. Strange that they spoke the same language though. He supposed it was possible that English-speaking people would've gone through the Gate, given that it was in North America. But the Native Americans had been in North America first, far before the British had arrived. He would've expected them to have a much larger presence here. None of it made much sense…but there had to be an explanation.

"So what is it?" he pressed.

"A job," she answered. "A carrier pigeon dropped it off this morning," she explained. "It's from one of my usual clients."

"What's the job?"

"Can't tell you," she answered. "It's confidential."

"Aw, come on," he pressed.

"A Seeker doesn't talk about her clients," Vi shot back. He raised an eyebrow at her.

"Thought you weren't a Seeker."

"I'm not a member of the *Guild* of Seekers," she corrected. "I still collect artifacts and Ossae for clients…you know, the definition of a Seeker."

"Fine," he grumbled. "What are we doing today?"

"Well," she replied, looking him up and down. "I enjoyed kicking your ass so much yesterday I think we'll do it again."

"Great," he muttered. "Now my bruises are gonna have bruises."

"Come on," she stated, stuffing the paper in a pocket. She went back into the house, returning moments later with their practice swords. "Let's see what you've got," she added, tossing the sword to him. He caught it, holding it in both hands.

"Don't worry," he said. "I'll go easy on you."

"Uh huh."

He backed up a step, staying just out of her reach, then circled slowly, keeping his eyes on hers, as she'd taught him. People had a tendency to look at what they were going to try to hit before they swung…a "tell" that could give him the upper hand. And keeping his eyes on hers prevented *him* from making the same mistake.

She lunged forward suddenly, thrusting at his belly.

He reacted, weeks of drills kicking in. He stepped to the side, blocking her strike to the outside, then slashing at her neck. She hopped backward, his sword barely missing her.

"Good," she stated, then thrust again without warning. He lurched backward, barely blocking her blade in time.

"Nice..." he began, but she lunged forward a third time, thrusting the tip of her sword right into his belly. He grimaced, backing up and slapping her sword away.

"Never assume your opponent is done," Vi chided. "They're only done when they're dead."

"Got it," he grumbled, getting back into his fighting stance. Vi smiled.

"Good," she replied...and thrust at him again. He blocked it, slashing at her, but she blocked *his* attack, thrusting yet again. He stepped to the side, swatting her sword away and kicking at her knee. She stepped back just in time, slashing at his neck. He blocked it, thrusting at her belly...and missing as she dodged to the side, her blade stopping right at his neck.

"Damn it," he swore. Vi smiled.

"You're doing well," she reassured. "Much better than when you started. God, you were such a little bitch."

"Learned from the best," he retorted, holding his sword in front of him.

"You know, if you were half as good at fighting as you were at slinging insults, you might make a good swordsman," she replied. "I'm going to be harder on you now," she warned. "Try to keep up."

She came at him again, this time with a flurry of slashes and thrusts. Each time he managed to block one blow, another came. After a few attacks, she managed to stab him in the stomach. Again.

"Can you pick a different spot to stab me in?" he grumbled, backpedaling and rubbing his throbbing belly.

"Aww, sick of being murdered the same way every time?" she teased, flicking her wrist. Her sword went right between his legs, stopping just before hitting his tender bits. "There better?"

"Just because you like girls," he retorted, stepping back and batting her sword away, "...doesn't mean you get to turn me into one."

"But I'm so lonely," she mocked, batting his sword to the side and placing the tip of her sword back where it'd been. "You know how long it's been since I got some?"

"I know a girl who could help with that," he shot back, batting her sword away again and thrusting at her belly. She parried the blow easily. "Probably doesn't like girls though."

Vi slashed diagonally downward at his neck, and he stepped inside, blocking her strike and cutting down at *her* neck. She turned to the side, dodging the blow with not an inch to spare…and kicked him in the shin, making his knee lock. He grunted, his body leaning forward reflexively, and she rapped him on the top of the head with the pommel of her sword. Gently, of course…but hard enough to smart.

"Ow," he blurted, shoving her backward. He rubbed his head, glaring at her.

"Girls like her like *everyone*, remember?" Vi replied, giving him an amused look. "Even you, surprisingly."

"I'll have you know," he shot back, feigning a thrust, "…she wanted me the first day she saw me." Vi didn't react to the feint, of course. She attacked, a flurry of slashes that he somehow managed to block.

"She must be special," she replied.

"She was special all right," he agreed, circling around Vi. She smirked.

"That's not what I meant."

She attacked again, raining blow after blow on him, forcing him backward. Again he managed to block each attack, dodging the last one and slashing at her exposed flank. She blocked it, then flicked her sword, rapping the back of his hand. Hard.

"Damn it!" he cursed, dropping his sword. She thrust at him, the tip of her sword stopping right between his eyes.

"Defang the snake," she stated, lowering her sword slowly. "Remember that the hand is a great target. Try to get around your enemy's cross-guard."

"Gentle with the hand," he grumbled, picking up his sword. She arched an eyebrow at him.

"I'm sorry, did you have plans for it later?"

Hunter blushed, and she chuckled, stepping back from him.

"You're learning," she stated, eyeing him approvingly.

"Don't have much of a choice, do I?"

"Well at least you're not trying to quit every five minutes anymore," she added. "See what happens when you try?"

Hunter smiled grudgingly. Vi stepped forward, patting him on the shoulder, and he had to resist the urge to swat her hand away with his sword. She had a point…he felt *good* about his progress, in a way he'd never really felt at school. He'd never had a teacher as brutal as Vi, of course. She'd forced him to learn, or get the crap beaten out of him.

"I'm hungry," Vi declared suddenly, throwing her practice sword to the ground. "Grab that bow," she ordered, "…and fetch me some breakfast, slave."

"Hey, watch it," Hunter shot back. "Sensitive subject there." Vi frowned.

"Excuse me?"

"My ancestors were slaves," he explained. "It's a kind of a big deal back home."

"Ah, my apologies," she replied. She picked up the quiver, handing it to him. "Fetch me some breakfast, bitch."

Hunter took the quiver, slinging it over his shoulder.

"Yes mistress," he droned. She smirked at him, walking toward the wooden bridge leading to the shore.

"You wish," she replied, slinging an arm around his shoulders.

"Kinda," he admitted. "It's a shame you don't like dudes," he added. "You're a pretty awesome chick."

"So are you," Vi replied with a wink. "So are you." She gave him a squeeze. "Come on," she added. "We'll hunt something that doesn't fly. I need to teach you tracking."

CHAPTER 23

Sukri sat in her wheelchair in the usual meeting room in the Guild of Seekers, surrounded by the other initiates. Of the other five, two had failed out of the class during *their* team's first Trial over a week ago. That left Sukri, Gammon, Donahue, Lucus, and a woman named Yala. She was in her early thirties, slightly overweight, with short black hair. Sukri found her a bit strange, possessed of an impressive intellect, but sorely lacking in social skills. Even Lucus had a certain charm about him compared to Yala; he was the kind of boy Sukri's mom would have insisted she date.

It'd been a couple of weeks since Sukri and Gammon's first Trial, and Master Thorius had spent day after day trying to teach Sukri how to control her emotions. It was her greatest weakness, that she absorbed them so easily...but also, he'd told her, her greatest strength. She had no idea what he'd meant by that, and he hadn't clarified his statement when she'd asked.

As if summoned by her thoughts, Master Thorius strode into the room without warning, stopping before them all, his hands clasped behind his back. Sukri found herself sitting up a bit straighter in her wheelchair.

"Today," he declared, "...you will undergo your second Trial."

Sukri felt a chill run through her, and she glanced up at Gammon.

"This Trial," Thorius continued, "...will be one that requires a Seeker's most important skill: the ability to sense the influence of objects and people around them." His gaze fell to Sukri. "Without an understanding of the world around them, a Seeker cannot evaluate potential dangers outside of the city…and will fall prey to them without even realizing it."

Sukri lowered her gaze, remembering how she'd laid into Kris that day, minutes before he'd been murdered.

"You cannot resist the forces around you if you don't recognize their existence," Thorius continued. "For this Trial, your ability to navigate and manage a hazardous area will be tested."

Sukri glanced up at Gammon, who smiled back at her. As usual, the big guy seemed utterly at ease…and probably was. Not for the first time, she wished that she had his temperament. She played at being in control, but her emotions always got the better of her. Gammon really *was* in control…and he'd proven it during their trip through the Fringe, not to mention during the fight with the Ironclad.

"Seeker Thomas will bring you to the site of your second Trial," Thorius stated. He nodded at the group. "Good luck to you."

With that, he left, and Seeker Thomas, a squat old man with short gray hair, gestured for them to follow him out of the room. He led them through the hallway and into the foyer, then forward through another hallway, one she'd never been in before. This led to a steep ramp sloping downward at the end; Seeker Thomas brought them down it, bringing them to the basement of the guild. Sukri struggled to prevent her wheelchair from flying down the ramp; luckily Gammon had her back, holding onto her chair from behind. They were met with another long hallway, but this was markedly different than the ones upstairs. For one, it was made entirely of stone instead of the usual wooden floors and paper walls. The ceiling was roughly three meters high, with large wooden beams supporting it. With no windows, the hallway was quite dark, lit by flickering torches bolted to the walls. Seeker Thomas strode down the hallway to a door at the end, using a key to unlock it. Then he opened the door, gesturing for everyone to walk through. They did so, Sukri taking up the rear. Seeker Thomas closed the door behind them, leaving them in the room beyond while he remained in the hallway. Sukri's eyes widened as she took in her surroundings.

The room was *huge*.

Stone walls some eight meters tall rose upward, the ceiling high above hidden in darkness, the light from torches bolted to the wall barely sufficient to illuminate the room. There were glass cubes as tall as she was in three rows of three spaced evenly throughout the room. Each contained squat wooden boxes as big and tall as a small table within, and atop each box were various…things. One had a simple metallic lever in the center, while another held a glass beaker. The glass cubes were entirely enclosed, save for a single opening in the front. The size of that opening varied from cube to cube, allowing only one way to access the various items within.

Sukri heard a click – the sound of the door behind her being locked from the other end.

"Welcome to your second Trial," a voice boomed from overhead. Everyone looked up, seeing a series of rafters high above their heads…and Master Thorius standing there, looking down at them. "You have one objective: make it out of the room through that door."

He pointed, and Sukri looked, seeing a large door at the opposite end of the huge room.

"This room," he continued, "…has various contraptions. There are three locks on the door that must be unlocked, and three of these contraptions unlock them." His expression turned grim. "But beware…all of the other contraptions represent a danger to you. Choose wisely."

With that, Thorius stepped out of view, leaving the initiates alone in the huge room.

"Okay then," Lucus declared, looking around. "We need to find the right three contraptions. Question is, how do we know which ones are the right ones?"

"We should start with this one," Donahue declared, walking up to the cube closest to them. Everyone followed him, peering at the machine within. It was quite simple: a metal table with a single lever angled away from them.

"So we just pull the lever and that's it?" Lucus asked. Sukri glanced at Gammon, who shrugged. It seemed too simple.

"We have a one in three chance of being correct," Yala calculated.

"But how do we know which ones are the right ones?" Lucus asked. "We can't just choose them randomly."

"He's right," Yala agreed. "With five of us, and six potential wrong choices, there's a chance that we might all fail even if we choose indiscriminately."

"Hmm," Gammon murmured, rubbing his chin. He glanced at Sukri. "Any ideas?" She hesitated, then shook her head, remaining silent. Gammon gave her a strange look.

"I'm checking the other ones," Donahue stated, walking to the cube to the right of them. He studied it. "This one's got a metal plate inside it," he said. "With a beaker of water or something on top of it."

Sukri rolled her wheelchair over to Donahue's side. He was right; it looked like a glass beaker of water sitting on top of a plain metal plate, which was, in turn, resting on a large wooden box.

"Weird," Lucus stated. "What are we supposed to do with that?"

"Beats me," Donahue replied. He moved on to the glass cube to the far left, as did everyone else. Sukri lagged behind, glancing at the first cube they'd seen. She wheeled herself up to it, stopping before the opening and peering at the lever. She hesitated, then reached for the lever, touching it with her fingers.

Don't do it.

She pulled her hand back, feeling suddenly uneasy.

"What's wrong?" she heard Gammon ask from behind her. She nearly jumped, turning around to face him.

"Nothing," she replied. "I mean…" she glanced back at the lever. "Something about that thing gives me the creeps."

Gammon frowned, gently pushing her to the side, then bending his huge frame over to peer through the glass. He hesitated, then reached for the lever as she had, touching it. He kept his hand there for a long moment, then pulled it away.

"I don't feel anything," he admitted.

"You never do," Sukri retorted. "Not emotions, anyway. I mean, from other things."

"True," he agreed, stepping away. "But you do."

"Yeah," she admitted ruefully. "I'm a frickin' sponge."

"Guys, I think I found one," she heard Donahue call out.

She turned, realizing that the rest of the group had made their way down to the second row of cubes. She and Gammon followed, and Donahue hunched over, peering through the opening. Inside, there was a wooden box with an empty metal plate inside, identical to the one they'd seen earlier, but without the flask of water.

"I bet if we take the beaker from the other cube," Donahue stated excitedly, "…and put it here, it'll unlock one of the locks."

"Or maybe two of them," Lucus reasoned.

"There are three pairs of cubes that are similar," Donahue continued. "Each is an incomplete version of the other. Like this one," he added, moving to another cube further down. In it was a wooden desk with a single silver key laying atop it. "There's another cube with a keyhole," he explained.

"Makes sense," Lucus reasoned.

"But Master Thorius said there were only three contraptions that would unlock the door," Yala countered.

"And only one of each pair is actually a contraption," Donahue reasoned. "The others just hold what we need to activate the contraptions."

Yala considered this, then nodded grudgingly.

"Let's do it," Donahue stated, walking back to the cube with the beaker of clear liquid. "We'll take this to the other cube and set it on the metal plate."

He leaned over, reaching through the opening in the glass, and grabbed the beaker.

"All right," he declared, lifting it upward. "Now…"

The metal platform shot upward suddenly, slamming into the bottom of the beaker. The beaker shattered, glass flying everywhere, the liquid spilling all over Donahue's hands and the wooden desk below.

"Shit," he blurted out, jerking his hands out of the opening.

Smoke began to rise from the wooden desk.

"Shit!" Donahue shouted, backing away suddenly, rubbing his hands on his shirt. "Ah, dammit!"

"What?" Lucus asked.

Donahue screamed, doubling over in pain, his hands balled into fists. The skin on his hands was turning bright red, the fluid eating away at his flesh. Smoke rose from his sleeves and the front of his shirt, holes appearing in the cloth, growing rapidly. He lurched to the side, running toward the door they'd come through.

"Help!" he screamed. "Open the door!" He pounded on it with one fist, then cried out, clutching his hand. Blood poured from the rapidly deepening wounds on it, the skin almost gone in places.

"Open the door!" Sukri yelled, glancing up at the rafters. Thorius was nowhere to be seen. "He needs help!"

There was no answer.

"*Help!*" Donahue shouted, ramming his shoulder into the door over and over again. Then he cried out, pressing his back against the door and sliding down onto his butt in front of it. He stared at his hands in horror; the skin on his fingers had melted away, exposing pearly white bone at his fingertips. "Oh god," he cried, scrambling to his feet and ramming his shoulder into the door again. "Oh god oh please god *help me*!"

Lucus stepped forward to help, but Yala stopped him.

"Stay away from him," Yala warned. "You don't want to get that stuff on you." Lucus turned on her.

"We can't just stand here," he protested. "We have to help him!"

"If you touch him," Yala interjected coldly, "...you'll end up just like him."

Donahue rammed the door again, then stumbled backward, falling against one of the glass cubes. He slid down onto his butt, his face pale and slick with sweat, his breath coming in short gasps. The flesh on his fingers was peeling from the bone, and blood spurted from the base of each finger, the skin on his wrists sloughing off. Without warning, blood shot out of the arteries there, and everyone backed away from the spray.

"Oh shit," Lucus blurted out. He turned away from the horrible sight, stumbling a few feet, then vomiting.

Sukri turned away as well, burying her head in Gammon's belly. She heard Donahue scream, a soul-piercing howl that send chills down her spine. Images of Kris came to her, of the Ironclad snapping his arm in two. Of the thing ripping his arm off, blood spurting from the wound.

She felt Gammon's hands cover her ears, muffling Donahue's screams. But she could still hear them. There was no escaping them.

After what seemed like an eternity, his screams stopped.

Gammon let go of Sukri's ears, and she swallowed past a lump in her throat, steeling herself for what she was about to see. Then she turned around to face Donahue.

He was lying on the floor in a pool of his own blood, his eyes staring unblinkingly at the ceiling far above. His hands – or what was left of them – lay at his sides. Countless holes had been burned into his sleeves and his chest had a huge, bloody hole in it. She turned away, shaking her head at Gammon.

"I don't want to do this anymore," she whimpered. He sighed, leaning in and hugging her, his lips at her ear.

"Sorry Sukri," he murmured. "We don't have a choice."

She nodded, knowing he was right. There were only two ways out of here: through that door, or by joining Donahue.

"We need you," Gammon whispered. "*I* need you."

She sighed, pulling away from him. He'd been the one to save her when the Ironclad had nearly killed her. She had to return the favor…or at least try to.

"Okay," she replied.

"I can't believe they let him die," Lucus muttered, staring at Donahue's body. "I can't believe they just let him fucking die."

"He's gone," Sukri stated coldly. Everyone turned to her. "There's nothing we can do about that. But what we *can* do is save ourselves."

"What are you proposing?" Yala inquired.

"This is a puzzle," Sukri reasoned. "Donahue tried to solve it with logic and that failed. This isn't a test of reasoning…Master Thorius said it was a test of our ability to sense the forces around us."

"What forces?" Lucus pressed.

"Ones we can't see," Sukri replied. "The influences around us…that's what he said." She strode back to the first cube she'd seen, the one with the single lever. "When I reached in here, I felt something. It made me nervous."

"You're saying it's another trap," Lucus reasoned.

"Maybe," she replied. "We need to go to each of the cubes and see how we feel with each of them."

"You're saying the emotions around the cubes will give away which ones are safe?" Yala pressed.

"Right," Sukri confirmed. "Maybe this room has been used before, for other trials," she reasoned. "If so, then the cubes that are traps will have absorbed the negative emotions of the people who triggered them."

"And the ones that don't have those emotions are the safe ones," Yala concluded, giving a rare smile. "That's a good idea."

"I sense emotions really well," Sukri stated. "So I should be the one to test them." She went to the rightmost cube in the first row, leaning before the opening in the glass. Within was a bare metal box with another beaker of clear liquid sitting inside it. She hesitated, then put an arm through, holding her fingers close to the glass. She closed her eyes and waited.

Nothing happened.

She let go of a breath she hadn't realized she'd been holding, withdrawing her hand.

"This one's not bad," she declared.

She moved to the next one, which had another lever in it, this one colored red. She reached in again, touching the lever lightly with her fingertips.

Terror gripped her.

She jerked her hand away, backpedaling from the cube.

"That's bad," she warned.

She continued onward, testing each of the cubes – except for the one Donahue had triggered, of course – eventually coming to the end. Two of the cubes had made her feel relieved; the rest had instead scared the crap out of her...except for the first one, which had made her profoundly uneasy.

"These two are definitely good," she concluded.

"There are supposed to be three," Yala pointed out.

"I know," Sukri replied. "But I'm telling you what I felt, and that's what I felt."

"So we trigger those two," Lucus stated. "And then what?"

"Then we have to make a choice," Sukri answered. "I can check them again."

"With Donahue's trap and two good ones, we'd still have six cubes to choose from, and only one correct choice," Yala reasoned. "We could all die trying to find the last one."

"First thing's first," Sukri countered. She wheeled herself back to the cube with the beaker of liquid in it, and reached in again, holding her hand near it. Again, she felt nothing. She brushed her hand against the glass, half-expecting it to shatter...but it didn't. Relieved, she hesitated, taking a deep breath in.

Here goes...

She wrapped her fingers around the beaker, then lifted it upward, closing her eyes and turning her head away.

Nothing happened.

She opened her eyes, staring at the beaker. It was intact!

Sukri breathed a sigh of relief, pulling the beaker through the opening, then handing it to Gammon. She heard a *click* in the distance.

"The door," Lucus exclaimed. "Did you hear that?"

"Okay," Sukri stated, rubbing her sweaty palms on her pants. "Next one."

She wheeled herself over to the next safe cube, stopping before the opening in the glass. It was the one Donahue had mentioned earlier, with a wooden desk and a metal platform in the center of it.

Donahue had proposed they transfer the beaker he'd taken to it; he'd clearly chosen the wrong beaker.

"Get me the beaker," she told Gammon, who handed it to her. She held it carefully, being sure not to spill any of the liquid, then reached inside the cube's opening, setting it on the metal platform.

Click.

"It worked!" Lucus stated excitedly. Gammon smiled at Sukri, putting a hand on her shoulder.

"Good job, boss."

"Thanks," Sukri replied, smiling back at him. "Okay, there's one more," she added, looking around. "I'm going to test the rest of them again."

She got to work, repeating her initial scan. The results were identical...most of the cubes scared the shit out of her, while that first one made her very uneasy.

"I don't know," she admitted. "They're all not great."

"Which is best?" Gammon inquired. She paused, then wheeled herself to the first cube.

"This one makes me uneasy," she answered. "The rest are much worse."

"So that's the one," Lucus reasoned. Sukri hesitated.

"Maybe."

"It's the most logical choice," Yala piped in. Sukri gave her a sour look.

"Logic didn't work so well for Donahue."

"That was the wrong logic," Yala shot back. Sukri sighed, knowing she was right.

"I guess we have to try it," she muttered, wheeling herself up to the opening. Inside was the single lever, angled away from her. She hesitated, then reached in...and felt a hand on her shoulder. She twisted around, pulling her hand out. It was Gammon.

"I'll do it," he stated, pulling her wheelchair back.

"No, it's my responsibility," she countered.

"I'm doing it," he pressed.

"What if I'm wrong?" she countered. Gammon shrugged.

"Then you're wrong."

"I'm not watching you die," she insisted. "If I'm wrong, *I'll* pay for it."

"We need you," Gammon retorted gently. "You can sense emotions better than any of us. If you die, we're all going to die."

"Based on the odds," Yala interjected, "...he could be right."

"Gammon," Sukri began, but the big guy shook his head.

"I'm doing it," he stated firmly, walking up to the opening in the glass. He bent over, then reached in with one beefy hand. Sukri wheeled forward, grabbing his waist and pulling backward.

"No Gammon," she ordered. "Don't do it."

"Sorry boss," he replied.

"I'm not watching you die," she insisted. "I can't do it."

"You won't have to," he countered, wrapping his fingers around the lever. Sukri shook her head, panic gripping her.

"Stop it," she commanded. "Gammon, don't do it!" She pulled back on his waist again, but she might as well have been pulling a statue. "Gammon, what if I'm wrong? I can't watch one of my friends die again. I can't!"

Gammon turned to look at her, giving her a reassuring smile.

"I believe in you Sukri," he said.

And then he pulled the lever.

CHAPTER 24

Hunter jerked awake, his eyes snapping open. He took his sword and bow off his chest, setting them aside, then sitting up. It was still dark out, the canyon floor bathed in the soft glow of the stars and the triple moons high above. He frowned, looking around.

Could've sworn I heard something.

He waited, but the never-ending cacophony of waterfalls crashing into the lake was the only sound he heard. He laid back down, grabbing his sword and bow and clutching them to his chest again, closing his eyes.

Clunk.

His eyes snapped open, and he turned his head, spotting a rock rolling to a stop on the ground a few yards from where he lay, right next to the canyon wall. He stared at it for a moment, then glanced upward. All he saw was the long, spiraling path far above, and beyond that, a hint of treetops. He looked back down at the rock, staring at it.

The hell?

He sat up again, then stood, looking around. The lake was rippling, the force of the waterfalls feeding it causing its surface to churn constantly. The high walls of the canyon cast inky-black shadows over the shore, making it difficult to see. But as far as he could tell, the shore was deserted, save for himself.

"Vi?" he asked, wondering if she was trolling him. He reached down, strapping his sword to his waist, then slinging his bow and quiver onto his back.

Clunk.

Hunter spun around, seeing another rock bounce off the ground, rolling to a stop a few yards from him. He paused, realizing that he'd unsheathed his sword and was holding it before him. Looking upward, he saw the path again, over fifty feet above his head. He spotted movement in the periphery of his vision, and looked further up the path, spotting inky shadows silhouetted against the moonlit canyon walls. Shadows that moved down the spiraling path to the canyon floor.

He froze, staring at the shadows as they advanced. It was impossible to make out what they were in the darkness…and he wasn't about to wait for them to make it all the way down to find out. He turned toward Vi's house, making his way as quietly as possible to the bridge. He stepped onto it, glancing back to see the shadows reach the bottom of the path…and many more coming down the path behind them.

Shit.

Hunter broke into a run, his boots *clunking* on the wooden bridge. He glanced back again, seeing the shadows at the bottom of the path turn, moving forward.

Toward *him.*

He ran faster, now halfway across the bridge, eyeing Vi's house in the distance. Glancing back, he saw some of the figures reach the foot of the bridge. From here, he could make out a vaguely humanoid form. Two legs and two arms, and a head. No, not two arms.

Four arms.

"Shit!" he swore, sprinting as fast as he could now, his heart leaping into his chest. The creatures behind him began to run as well, moving with terrifying speed across the bridge toward him.

"Vi!" he shouted, pumping his legs hard, clearing the end of the bridge and sprinting toward her front door. "Vi!"

The things – the *Ironclad* – were halfway across the bridge now. And lots more of them were streaming down the spiraling path, spilling onto the canyon floor. All of them running toward the bridge.

"*Vi!*" he screamed, making it to her door. He pounded on it, trying to turn the doorknob. It was locked. "Open up!"

The Ironclad swarmed toward the end of the bridge behind him, reaching it and sprinting across the island toward him.

"Open *up!*" he screamed, reaching up to pound on the door again. It opened just as he swung, and he stumbled into the house, nearly hitting Vi in the head. She blocked the blow, glaring at him.

"What the hell are..." she began, and then glanced over his shoulder. Her eyes widened, and she yanked him inside, slamming the door shut and locking it by sliding a wooden crossbar.

"They're coming!" he panted, leaning over to try to catch his breath. "The Ironclad...lots of 'em."

"No shit," she shot back. She was dressed in the same white shirt and shorts he'd seen her in weeks ago. She stripped these off quickly, then grabbed her uniform, pulling it on. He turned away quickly, but not before he'd caught a glimpse of her. It hardly mattered, considering the circumstances.

"That door isn't going to hold them," Vi warned as she finished dressing. She grabbed her sword and mace, then her bow.

Bam!

As if on cue, the door rattled, but the thick wooden crossbar holding it shut held.

"Hunter," Vi said, grabbing the sides of his head and turning him to face her. Her expression was dead serious. "Do exactly what I say when I say it. Don't think...*do.*"

He nodded silently.

"If you don't, you're going to die."

He nodded again, feeling a prickly sensation crawl over his skin. He felt an acute awareness of his body and of his surroundings, as if everything were sharper, the colors more vibrant. Vi's eyes looked iridescent in the light cast by the single lantern on the wall, almost feral.

"Stay behind me," she ordered, putting herself between him and the door.

Bam!

Vi drew her mace from its holster on her hip, holding it in her left hand.

Bam!

The crossbar cracked, bending inward.

"Stay back," Vi stated. "When I say run, you *run.*"

Bam!

The crossbar shattered, the door bursting open. The massive, hulking form of an Ironclad shoved its way through the doorway, its black eyes glittering in the lantern light. A low growl issued from its throat, and it stared at Vi, its four hands clenched into fists. Its eyes flicked to Hunter, and it tilted its head back, emitting a mournful wailing sound.

Vi swung her mace into its knee with a loud *crunch*.

The beast's knee locked, its head jerking forward and downward…right as she swung her mace straight up. It smashed into the Ironclad's face, obliterating it.

The Ironclad fell backward through the doorway, and Vi spun around, back-kicking it in the chest as it dropped. It shot backward, slamming into two more Ironclad behind it, making them stumble backward.

"Run!" Vi shouted, bursting forward through the doorway. She made a sharp left, dodging the two Ironclad, and Hunter sprinted after her, ducking out of the way as one of the Ironclad reached for him. He felt its armored fingers brush against his shoulder, and jerked away, barely eluding its grasp. He glanced to his right, seeing more Ironclad sprinting across the bridge toward them.

Dozens of them.

Vi ran across the short bridge toward the smaller building – the storehouse – skidding to a halt in front of the narrow moat.

"Follow me!" she shouted – and jumped feet-first into the water.

Hunter glanced back, seeing Ironclad chasing after him, and jumped.

Ice-cold water engulfed him instantly, saturating his clothes. His throat spasmed as his head plunged below the surface, his breath locking in his throat. He opened his eyes, barely able to see Vi below him in the darkness. She was doing something with the wall in front of her; he maneuvered to one side, the weight of his clothes and gear pulling him quickly down beside her. She shoved against the wall, and a panel swung inward…it was a door, Hunter realized. She swam through it, and he followed after her, squeezing through the narrow opening. Beyond this, there was utter darkness. He felt Vi grab his arm, pulling him forward and upward. His lungs started to burn, and he resisted the urge to take a breath in, fear gripping him. He felt himself ascending through the inky blackness, his heart hammering in his chest. If he didn't get air soon…

He burst through the surface suddenly, feeling cool air on his face. He sucked air into his lungs greedily, feeling Vi's hand still on his arm. She slid her hand down to his, and pulled on it, placing it on something cold and hard under the water…a ledge of some kind. He grabbed on with both hands, grateful for the support. With his clothes and weapons weighing him down, he wouldn't have been able to tread water for very long.

He heard Vi grunt, then heard a *clanging* sound. Moments later, he felt a hand grip his, pulling upward. He kicked against the wall, sliding up out of the water onto what felt like a cold stone platform, an inch of water covering it. He shivered in the pitch blackness.

Suddenly, there was light.

Hunter squinted, finding himself on a submerged square stone platform surrounded by inky black water. Stone walls surrounded him, the roof two feet above his head. Vi was standing next to him, her hand on a glowing lantern hanging from a chain on the ceiling. In the center of the platform was a wooden box, and sitting upon it was a small object.

A bone.

Vi grabbed this, stuffing it into her cleavage, then turned to him.

"They'll break through soon," she warned. "We need to get across the bridge to get out."

"But there's dozens of them out there," Hunter protested, clutching his arms to his chest. He shivered, his teeth chattering.

"Didn't say it would be easy," she retorted. "When they break through, stay behind me, and don't let them get you."

Hunter nodded, and Vi snuffed out the lantern, throwing the room into darkness. Moments later, he heard a *thump*. Dust fell from the ceiling, making Hunter cough. There was another *thump*, and then another.

A crack appeared in the wall in front of him, faint light shining through.

Vi stepped in front of Hunter, another *thump* rattling the small building. The crack in the wall widened, hunks of stone falling into the water.

BAM!

A large black shoulder burst through the wall, chunks of stone spilling from the hole it created. More cracks appeared in the walls around them as other Ironclad smashed into the building.

"Go when I say go," Vi ordered.

The Ironclad yanked its shoulder from the wall, then slammed into it again, using its hands to pull hunks of stone out, widening the hole. Vi stepped to the edge of the platform, twisting her hips and swinging her mace *hard*. The Ironclad blocked the blow with two of its forearms, her mace bouncing off its armored plates. She spun in a circle, using the momentum from the ricochet and swinging her mace upward into the Ironclad's forearms this time, knocking them out of the way. She swung again without pause, striking the Ironclad's head. Then she sheathed her mace and unsheathed her longsword, gripping the middle of her blade and thrusting her sword right at the thing's head. The blade buried itself into the Ironclad's shattered face.

It dropped like a stone.

"Go!" she shouted, leaping through the hole. Hunter backed up to the rear edge of the platform, then ran forward, leaping after her. He barely cleared the moat beyond, sprinting after her as she ran toward the bridge.

Ironclad swarmed after them.

Vi reached the bridge, Hunter right behind her, their boots *thumping* rhythmically on the wooden planks. Hunter looked over his shoulder…just as the nearest Ironclad caught up with him. Its arms encircled him from behind, yanking him backward.

"Vi!" he screamed.

Vi spun around, her longsword flashing in the moonlight. It barely cleared the top of Hunter's head, the wind of its passage whipping over his scalp. He heard a grunt behind him, felt the arms holding him drop away.

"Go!" she shouted, shoving him past her.

They ran forward, Vi taking up the rear, almost halfway across the bridge now. He heard her curse, looked back to see another Ironclad rushing up to her. It swung a fist at her, and she blocked the blow with a swing of her mace, knocking its arm wide. Then she leapt at it, kicking outward with both of her legs and striking it in the chest. It stumbled backward, slamming into the Ironclad behind it. One of them fell off the bridge into the water, vanishing from sight.

Vi landed flat on her back on the bridge, somersaulting backward without skipping a beat. In one fluid motion, she pushed up into a handstand, twisting around 180 degrees and breaking into an all-out sprint after Hunter.

Hunter turned forward, then skidded to a stop, his eyes widening. There, at the far end of the bridge, were more Ironclad. Lots more. And the monsters were coming right for them.

Shit!

"Vi!" he cried. He felt her slam into him from behind, and barely kept his balance.

"Shit," she swore, glancing back. More Ironclad were coming from behind...too many to count.

They were trapped.

"What now?" he asked, turning to face her. Her jawline rippled, and she placed her mace back at her hip, putting a hand on his upper back. The Ironclad rushed toward them, closing in on them fast. Hunter knew with sudden, awful certainty that this was it.

He was going to die.

The nearest Ironclad sprinted toward them, twenty feet away now, and closing fast.

"Vi!" he shouted.

And then he felt her shove him...right off the bridge.

Hunter cried out, slamming face-first into the frigid water. He paddled furiously, bursting through the surface...and then felt something slam into his back, shoving him into the water again. He panicked, scrambling upward, kicking with his legs. He felt his boot strike something hard, and the weight on him vanished. He burst through the surface again, swimming forward as fast as he could.

"Asshole!" he heard a voice behind him cry.

He felt something grip his ankle, and he kicked again, but this time it didn't work. It pulled him backward...and then he felt a hand on his shoulder. He turned, ready to kick again, then stopped.

It was Vi!

"Follow me," she ordered, glaring at him, then paddling forward and to the left. He swam after her, but she was a much better swimmer, the distance between them rapidly increasing. He glanced back, seeing dozens of Ironclad standing on the bridge, and more along the shore, some of them wading up to their chests in the lake.

Tell me they can't fucking swim!

He focused, paddling faster, trying to keep pace with Vi. But he was too heavy, his waterlogged clothes and his weapons weighing him down. If the Ironclad decided to swim after him, they might catch him. There would be no way that Vi would be able to get to him in time...and without Vi, he wouldn't stand a chance.

"Come on!" he heard her shout.

He glanced back again, seeing the Ironclad in the water. To his relief, they hadn't moved...they were just standing there, staring at him.

They can't swim!

It made sense, of course. They were far too heavy with their armored bodies…they would sink to the bottom of the lake. But then again, the lake was entirely surrounded by sheer rock walls hundreds of feet high. Hunter and Vi couldn't just stay in the lake forever; they'd have to get out at some point. And the Ironclad would be waiting for them.

"Vi!" he shouted, swimming after her. She was almost to the canyon wall now, just to the right of a roaring waterfall. "Vi!"

She reached the wall, then stopped, turning to face him.

"Come on!" she shouted back.

He pushed himself, struggling to keep his head above water. But he was tiring fast, barely able to stay afloat. He gasped for air, his face plunging below the water. He collected himself, then kicked with his legs and swung his arms, pulling his head up out of the water. Taking another breath in, he did it again, only a few feet away from Vi now.

Come on…

He felt his hands touch cold rock, and scrambled for a handhold, finding one and pulling his head up out of the water again. He found a foothold in the rock wall, and dug the toes of his boot into it, keeping his head above the lake's surface.

"You okay?" Vi asked.

"Yeah," he replied. He paused, then shook his head. "No."

"Tiring out?" she pressed. He nodded. "Take a break," she ordered, glancing back across the lake. He followed her gaze, spotting something moving in the darkness by the shore. Something glowing a faint, pale blue.

His blood went cold.

It was a long blue line curved into an 'S' shape…a tall mane traveling down the spine of an Ironclad standing a full foot taller than the ones around it. The mane ended in a short, broad tail that swung side-to-side slowly in the darkness. The glow illuminated a monstrous black head, with inky eyes.

Eyes that were staring right at *him*.

"What the hell is that?" Vi blurted out, staring at the thing. Hunter shook his head.

"I don't know," he answered. "I saw one like it when I came through the Gate."

"Never seen one like that before," she muttered. Then she turned to face him. "Okay, you ready?" He frowned.

"Ready for what?"

"On my count," she replied, "Dive below the surface. I'll grab your arm. Whatever you do, don't let go."

"What..." he began.

"Three," she interjected. "Two. One!"

She took a deep breath in, then let go of the wall, vanishing below the surface. He barely had time to take a breath in before he felt her grab onto his arm, yanking him downward. His foot slipped off of the foothold, and he plunged into the water, surrounded by complete darkness. Vi's arm locked on his wrist, yanking downward...hard.

He felt a sudden pulling sensation, and before he knew it he was being thrust forward at unnerving speed, a powerful current carrying him. He tried not to panic, kicking his legs and swimming forward with his one free hand. Still out of breath from his swim earlier, his lungs were already burning again, the urge to take a breath in building up fast.

Hunter felt Vi's grip on his wrist tighten, squeezing it like a vise. He felt her tug him upward suddenly, felt her leg brush up against his side as she kicked. His lungs were on fire; he let out some air, gritting his teeth. His head was swimming now, his limbs starting to go numb.

Come on!

She yanked his wrist again, and he swam upward, the current pulling him forward. But she didn't move; his legs swung forward with the current, and try as he might, he couldn't swim against it. His lips trembled, then opened, water spilling into his mouth.

No!

He raked his free hand through the water, kicking his legs desperately, barely feeling his limbs now. A burst of bubbles exited his lips, and he felt the urge to breathe overtake him, that primal instinct overriding his will. Water sucked into his throat, coursing down his windpipe. He coughed reflexively, his eyes wide and unseeing, raking his limbs madly through the water. He took another breath in, gulping more water into his lungs, barely feeling them burn anymore.

Bright flashes of light burst before his eyes, his body utterly numb now. He took another breath in, feeling the world slip away.

And then nothingness claimed him.

CHAPTER 25

Sukri turned away as Gammon pulled the lever through the small opening in the glass cube, closing her eyes.

Click.

She hesitated, resisting the urge to open her eyes and look.

"Well you're not screaming," she ventured. "That's a good sign."

"You can open your eyes now," she heard Gammon say. She did so, turning to see him withdrawing his arm from the cube. The lever was angled toward them now...and Lucus was staring off into the distance, a huge smile on his face.

"The door!" he exclaimed. "It's open!"

Everyone turned to look. Lucus was right...the big door at the end of the room had swung inward, revealing a hallway beyond. And there, standing in the middle of that hallway, was Master Thorius.

"Yes!" Lucus nearly shouted. "Oh thank god," he added, practically sprinting to the door. Yala, Gammon, and Sukri followed behind, stopping before Master Thorius.

"Close the door behind you," Thorius ordered, nodding at Gammon. The big guy complied, and Thorius turned to face the rest of them. "Congratulations," he stated. "You've passed your second Trial."

Lucus grinned, and even Yala managed a smile. Sukri, however, did not.

"What about him?" she asked, gesturing at the door behind them. Thorius looked down at her.

"I assume you mean Donahue."

"You let him die in there," Sukri accused.

"Did I?" Thorius replied, his expression unchanged.

"We asked for help," she shot back. "He bled out on the floor like a stuck pig, and *you* let him." She glared at him. "You didn't tell us we could die in there!"

"I believe I mentioned that many of the contraptions presented a danger to you," Thorius countered.

"Yeah?" Sukri retorted. "Well that doesn't change the fact that you let him die. That's on *you*," she added, pointing a finger at him.

"If you recall," Thorius stated, "…the contract you signed mentioned the very real possibility of death or dismemberment during the application process. Or did you forget?"

Sukri stared at him, feeling cold anger course through her. She was about to reply when she felt Gammon's hand on her shoulder. She shrugged it off, knowing what Gammon was trying to do.

"Donahue acted brashly," Thorius continued, eyeing the other initiates. "He ignored my initial instructions regarding the purpose of the Trial, and paid for his carelessness with his life." He turned back to Sukri. "If you ever qualify to become a Seeker," he continued, "…you'll understand why our selection process is so rigorous."

"It's not right," she grumbled, feeling Gammon's hand on her shoulder again. She tried to shrug it off, but Gammon didn't let her. Anger seeped out of her, and she hated to see it go, wanting desperately to appease it, to lash out at Thorius.

"Agreed," Thorius replied, his eyes boring into hers. "You were the one who solved the puzzle and saved yourself and your friends," he continued. "Congratulations," he added. "Perhaps if you'd spoken up sooner instead of letting your guilt silence you, Donahue would still be alive."

* * *

"What an asshole," Sukri swore, wheeling herself into her apartment. "Stupid son of a bitch!"

"Sukri…" Gammon said from behind, closing the door to their apartment behind him. She felt his hand on her shoulder, and wheeled herself away from him, turning her wheelchair around to glare at him.

"Don't try to calm me down," she retorted. "I don't *need* to calm down!"

"I disagree," he replied with that irritatingly rational way he always had. She suddenly wanted to hit him. To lash out and hit him and make *him* angry.

"You think he's right, don't you," she accused. Gammon shook his head.

"I think Donahue didn't need to die to be disqualified," he replied. "Neither did Kris or Hunter."

"You're trying to placate me."

"True," he admitted. "But I think that's how initiates are disqualified."

She frowned.

"What?"

"Kris and Hunter died," Gammon reasoned. "So did Donahue. We never saw what happened to those other two initiates that were disqualified...but have you seen them around since?"

"What do you mean?"

"They're gone," Gammon explained. "They used to eat at the community center, but they don't anymore. I haven't seen them since they went through the first Trial."

"You think they're *dead*?" Sukri pressed. Gammon nodded.

"I think everyone that's disqualified is."

Sukri considered this, then realized that Gammon was right. Now that she thought about it, she hadn't seen those two initiates since they'd been disqualified either.

"Shit," she mumbled.

"It makes sense," Gammon reasoned. "No one knows what happens in the Trials...we didn't know before we went through them. The guild doesn't want its secrets coming out, so it kills off anyone who doesn't qualify."

Sukri said nothing. Couldn't say anything. It was all right there, plain as can be. In fact, she couldn't believe she hadn't seen it earlier.

"I still can't believe he had the gall to accuse *me* of killing Donahue," she pressed, feeling her anger return. Gammon sighed.

"That wasn't fair," he agreed. "Donahue tried to take charge and he didn't think things through." He hesitated, then walked up to Sukri, kneeling down and putting a hand on her knee. She glared at him suspiciously, feeling her anger start to fade.

306

"Why are you doing that?" she asked.

"Master Thorius did have a point," Gammon continued, giving her an apologetic look. "You're a leader Sukri," he added. "A good one. Taking control isn't always a bad thing."

"Oh god," she muttered, pulling his hand off her knee and wheeling herself away from him, aiming for the door to her bedroom. "You're going to bring *that* up again."

"Sukri…"

"I don't want to hear it," she shot back, wheeling herself into her room. She tried to turn around to shut the door, but Gammon was already in the doorway. "I *really* don't want to hear it," she added, glaring at him. "You can get out of my room now, by the way."

"You shouldn't ignore this," Gammon insisted, not budging.

"I'm not ignoring anything."

"Kris was wrong," Gammon pressed. Sukri felt grief rise up inside her, and swallowed it down, shaking her head and turning away from him.

"Stop."

"You can be in control and trust other people at the same time," Gammon continued, walking up to her and putting a hand on her shoulder from behind. She tried wheeling forward, but struck the bed. She cursed, pounding the armrest of her wheelchair with one fist.

"Don't touch me," she warned.

"I trusted you," he stated quietly.

She closed her eyes, feeling his calmness invading her, robbing her of her anger. She resisted it, hating the fact that he could take it from her. That *anyone* could control her like that. But it worked, as it always did, and she felt a calm melancholy come over her. She sighed, shaking her head, still turned away from him.

"You're sad," she muttered.

"Yes," he replied. "I am." There was a pause, and she felt his hand squeeze her shoulder. "I miss them too."

Moisture welled up in Sukri's eyes, and she wiped it away quickly.

"Yeah."

"Do you trust me?" Gammon pressed. Sukri sighed, sniffing loudly, and wiping her eyes again.

"Gammon," she replied. "I think you're the only person in this world I trust."

She felt his hand slip away from her shoulder, and saw him come to her left side. He knelt down, grabbing her behind the knees with one hand, and sliding his other hand behind the small of her back.

"What are you…" she began.

He lifted her out of the wheelchair, twisting to set her down gently on the bed, pulling the bedsheets up to her belly. Then he sat down on the edge of bed, looking down at her with those gentle eyes of his. She felt a sudden, powerful affection for him.

"Thanks," she mumbled.

"Thanks for saving my life," he countered with a smile.

"You saved mine first."

He paused, then leaned forward, kissing her on the forehead. Then he pulled away, standing up and walking toward the doorway.

"G'night Gammon," she called out to him. He stopped, turning around and smiling at her.

"Goodnight."

And then he was gone.

CHAPTER 26

"Good evening father," Conlan greeted, stepping out onto the balcony overlooking the inner courtyard of the Acropolis. The same courtyard within which he'd been announced as the successor to the previous king, where thousands had gathered to witness the newest vessel for their great leader. Dominus studied his son, leaning on his cane to take the weight off of his recently butchered foot. The doctor had done as Dominus had requested, of course, hacking off only the dead tissue, cutting into flesh until the blade had met bleeding skin, the telltale sign of life. Dominus had been told not to walk on it for a time, but after a few days he'd stopped heeding the doctor's advice. There was too much to do to lie in bed all day, and he wouldn't suffer the indignity of a wheelchair.

"Good evening," Dominus replied. "You wanted to see me?"

Conlan had called for him a half hour ago. Which, given their previous encounter, had surprised Dominus. They hadn't talked in over a week since. But Conlan hardly looked upset, smiling at him with that faint air of superiority he always had.

"Indeed," Conlan confirmed. "I was going stir-crazy staying in that room all day," he added. As the future king, Conlan was mandated by law to remain in the Royal Chambers – and therefore in the presence of Tykus's Ossae – for all but three hours of the day. "I will admit, Tykus's will is stronger than I imagined. It's been quite the battle, being exposed to him for so long. But as you can see, I'm still very much me."

"Indeed," Dominus stated, trying to keep the distaste out of his voice.

"I've been thinking a lot about our last conversation," Conlan admitted.

"What of it?" Dominus inquired, doing his best to keep his tone casual.

"Oh, don't patronize me," Conlan scolded. "We both know what you called me. A mere vessel for Tykus, a warm body waiting to be filled with the great king's essence."

"I was angry," Dominus apologized. "Forgive me."

"Oh, it's forgiven," Conlan replied. Then he wagged a finger. "Never forgotten, though. You see, I finally figured out why you detest me so much."

"I don't…"

"Please," Conlan interrupted, contempt dripping from his voice. "We argued constantly when I lived in Wexford, and you sent me to the Acropolis as soon as you possibly could to get rid of me."

"To have you absorb the essence of great men there," Dominus corrected. Conlan snorted.

"Bullshit father," he shot back. "I've no more absorbed their 'essence' than you have, and you knew I wouldn't." He shook his head, leaning against the railing. "You knew how strong my will was."

"You do have a strong will," Dominus conceded. "We both do. It isn't uncommon for strong-willed people to cohabitate poorly."

"True," Conlan admitted. "In theory. But now I know why you *really* got rid of me. Why you can't stand to be around me…and why you loathe to hug me, or even touch me."

Dominus took a deep breath in, letting it out slowly, feeling his irritation mounting.

"Do you now."

"Oh yes," Conlan insisted. "You see, it came to me all of a sudden, while I was pacing in my room. A flash of insight," he added with a smile. "I *did* hate you for what you said," he confessed. "But now all I feel for you is pity."

Dominus sighed, clenching his jaw. He stepped away from the railing, glaring at Conlan.

"If this is why you called for me," he stated, "…then I won't be answering that call from now on."

"Oh come now father," Conlan pressed. "I took your insult the day before in stride. Aren't you man enough to do the same?"

Dominus ignored him, walking toward the doorway to the interior of the Acropolis. He tried not to limp, but couldn't, and hated the fact that his son would see him vulnerable in this moment.

"I pity you father," Conlan called out after him. "You hid it from me for all these years, but now I know."

"I hid nothing," Dominus retorted.

"You can walk away from me," Conlan yelled as Dominus passed through the doorway. "But you can't walk away from the truth. You sent me away because you realized my will was stronger than yours…and you couldn't stand the thought that you might start to become like me!"

* * *

"Wake up!"

Hunter felt a sharp pain in his left cheek, his head jerking to the side. He groaned, his eyes fluttering open. He saw Vi kneeling over him, barely visible in the dim light of…wherever he was. He fell into a fit of coughing, water shooting out of his mouth. His lungs felt like they were on fire, burning with each breath.

"Sit up," Vi ordered, putting a hand behind his upper back and lifting him upright. His head swam with the movement, a wave of nausea coming over him. He closed his eyes, waiting for the sensation to pass, then opened them, looking around. They were in a small cave, it appeared, a single ray of pale light coming through a hole in the ceiling some eight feet up. To his left, he saw the cave floor give way to a small body of water, its black waters rippling in the faint light. The cave ended beyond, the ceiling sloping downward to meet the water, dipping beneath the surface. To his right, the cave continued onward, a narrow tunnel leading into darkness.

"What happened?" he asked, coughing again.

"You drowned," she answered. He blinked.

"I what?"

"You drowned," she repeated. "Freaked out right when we reached this place," she added. "I surfaced and grabbed the edge, but you didn't come up. I tried to pull you, but you freaked out." She shook her head at him. "Pulled you up after you went limp."

311

"Damn," he mumbled. He gave her a weak smile. "Thanks. I owe you one."

"Just one?"

"One more," he corrected. She smirked at him, ruffling his wet hair with one hand. Then she stood up, lending him a hand. He grabbed it, and she hauled him to his feet. Once again, he was taken aback by just how strong she was.

"Come on," she urged, walking down the tunnel toward the darkness. He followed behind, rubbing his chest and upper belly. They were terribly sore.

"Why does my chest hurt so much?" he asked.

"I had to push the water out of your lungs."

Hunter considered this, feeling a chill pass through him. Just how close had he come to dying? He could barely remember what'd happened. Hell, the last thing he remembered was them jumping off the bridge and swimming across the lake.

"Where we going?" he asked.

"This cave leads to the forest," Vi answered. "A few kilometers from the Fringe. If we'd taken the underground river, we'd have ended up a half-kilometer downstream, where the river goes above-ground again."

"And we both would've drowned," he grumbled. Vi glanced back at him with a smirk.

"Speak for yourself."

She vanished into the darkness, and he followed. He felt her grab his arm, pulling him to her side. They walked together, and even though Hunter could barely see, Vi strode forward without hesitation, weaving through the tunnel. Hunter allowed himself to be led, trusting that Vi knew what she was doing. After all, she'd never *not* known what she was doing, in his experience.

He felt a sharp pain in his chest as he walked, and rubbed it again. If it hadn't been for her, he would have died there. Would've drowned, floating downstream until his bloated body washed ashore. And that would have been that. The idea terrified him…that it was so easy for him to lose his life, the most precious gift of all. That it could have been taken from him just like that. He'd always assumed he was special, that the universe would somehow take care of him.

Now he knew he'd been fooling himself all along.

"Quit dragging your feet," Vi ordered, pulling him forward. He realized he'd slowed down a bit, and sped up to match her stride.

He saw a faint light ahead, another beam of moonlight piercing through the ceiling. It reminded him of the light that had shone through the crack in the cipher room wall when the Ironclad had slammed into it.

"What *was* that thing, anyway?" Hunter asked, remembering the bone Vi had retrieved from the cipher room.

"Gonna have to be more specific."

"That thing you got from the cipher room," he clarified.

"Just an artifact," she answered.

"Duh," he grumbled. "Why'd we have to go grab it?" he pressed. "We had a clear line through the Ironclad to jump in the lake instead of going to the storehouse."

"It was for a job," she explained. "I always come through for my clients. That's why I'm the best."

"What job?"

She didn't answer, continuing forward. A brighter light appeared in the distance, and as they moved forward he realized that it was the end of the tunnel. He spotted some trees silhouetted beyond, bathed in the pale light of this world's three moons.

"We could've died trying to get that thing," he pressed, annoyed by her silence. "You could at least tell me what it is."

"You saw it," Vi replied, sounding just as annoyed as he was. "You figure it out."

He thought back, trying to remember what it'd been. A bone, he recalled. A small, curved bone. It'd looked almost like a rib.

A *rib*.

He stopped dead in his tracks, staring at Vi as she continued down the tunnel. She stopped as well, glancing back at him.

"Come on," she urged. He stayed where he was, feeling a chill run down his spine. He'd seen that bone before, on the paper Thorius had given them for their first Trial. The bone they'd been tasked with retrieving.

"*You* took it," he blurted out. Vi just stared at him. He shook his head, taking a step backward. "I can't believe this."

"Hunter…"

"My friend died because of you!" he accused, jabbing a finger at her. "We spent all that time looking for that damn bone when *you* had it all along!"

"Just listen for a second," she insisted.

"That thing almost killed me!" he continued, glaring at her. "It broke Sukri's leg!"

"And I saved your ass, remember?" Vi shot back. "Now shut up and listen to me."

Hunter stared at her silently, his heart pounding in his chest.

"I was *hired* to get that Ossae," she stated, crossing her arms over her chest. "So I got it. And when I saw a bunch of kids strolling through the Fringe, how exactly was I supposed to know what you were doing there? Hmm?"

Hunter said nothing.

"I wasn't expecting Thorius to send a bunch of clueless initiates on a damn suicide mission," she continued. "There's a reason my employer hired *me* to do the job, you know." She pointed at her own chest. "I'm the best there is, kiddo."

"If that were true," Hunter retorted, "…my friend would still be alive."

"Bullshit," Vi shot back. "I didn't even know you were jumped until I heard you guys screaming. I was practically at the Deadlands then. I booked it all the way back, just in time to see that thing ready to murder you."

"And yet when I told you why we were there afterward, you didn't say a damn thing. You could have *told* me, you know." He pointed at her again. "My friends are either dead or disqualified because they didn't bring that thing back. And I probably will be too. Doesn't that mean anything to you?"

"It means," Vi replied icily, "…you were never meant to get it."

"Right," Hunter grumbled. "Sure."

"Think about it," she insisted. "Why would Thorius send you out to the Fringe to get this?" She pulled the bone from her shirt, holding it in front of her. "Something he knew I'd already been hired to get?"

"I don't know," he replied, throwing up his hands. "Tell me."

"Because they never *wanted* you to get it," she replied. "Thorius wanted you dead. Wanted *you* dead, not your friends. They were just collateral damage, kiddo." She stuffed the bone back down her shirt, walking up to him and poking him in the chest with one finger. "Your friend died because of *you*."

Hunter stared at her silently, swallowing past a sudden lump in his throat. She glared at him for a moment longer, then turned around abruptly, striding down the tunnel.

"You're an asshole," he snapped, staying right where he was.

"And you're an ingrate," she shot back.

"Well you know what? You won't have to bother with me any longer," Hunter called after her. "I'm done with you." Vi stopped, turning to face him. She put her hands on her hips.

"Oh *really*."

"Damn right," he replied. "I don't have to put up with your shit, you know. I can go back to Tykus and get laid every fucking night if I want to."

"Yeah, you go do that."

"I will," he growled. He turned away from her, walking in the other direction. Then he heard footsteps behind him, and turned just in time to see Vi run up and kick him in the hip. He fell onto his back, and Vi jumped on top of him, pressing his shoulders into the rocky ground with her hands. She leaned over until her face was inches from his, glaring down at him.

"Get off me!" he protested.

"I will *not* let you give up on me," she retorted.

"I'm not..."

"You are," she interjected. "I'm not your mother, kiddo."

"What the hell is that supposed to mean?"

"I'm not going to leave you."

"What?"

"I'm not going to leave you," she repeated. Hunter stared up at her, swallowing past a sudden lump in his throat. She held him down for a moment longer, then got up, looking down at him. "You expect everyone you love to leave you, so you either refuse to get close to anyone, or leave them before they can leave you."

He laid there, staring back at her. He felt his lower lip quivering, and grit his teeth, hating that she could see it.

"My parents gave up on me," Vi continued. "Couldn't stand that I liked girls. That I was different than everyone else. The two people in this world who I loved more than anything rejected me. And you know what that taught me?"

Hunter swallowed, not answering.

"That people were disposable," she answered. "That *I* was disposable. You think I ever wanted to get close to anyone after that?"

Hunter shook his head mutely.

"Damn right," she confirmed. "So I joined the Seekers. The only people I thought would accept me. Except they didn't either. So I set out on my own." She crossed her arms over her chest. "I had every reason to give up on you," she continued. "To let that

Ironclad kill you. To let you drown. But I didn't." She shook her head. "You want to push me away?" she asked. "Too fucking bad. You're stuck with me, Hunter. I'm not giving up on you, and you sure as hell aren't giving up on me."

She reached down then, offering a hand. Hunter hesitated, then grabbed it wordlessly, letting himself be hauled up onto his feet. She stared at him a moment longer, then turned around, walking away from him. He paused, then ran to catch up with her, slowing down to walk at her side. They reached the end of the cave, the tunnel opening up into dense forest. Hunter glanced back, seeing the cave entrance surrounded by a short cliff. To the left, he saw a large stream flowing away from them. He cleared his throat.

"So what now?" he asked.

"Now we go to Tykus," she answered. "That was the message I got this morning," she added. "My client asked to meet me in person."

"Why?"

"I don't know," she admitted. "This particular client only met me once, over a decade ago. They usually communicate by proxy."

"And what about me?" he pressed.

"What *about* you?"

"What do I do?" he pressed. "Just go back to my apartment and wait?"

"That's right," she answered. "I'll meet with my client, then meet up with you."

They walked in silence for a time then, dead leaves and twigs crunching underfoot. After a few minutes, Hunter turned to look at Vi.

"What?" she asked.

"It's not my fault my friend died," he stated. "You were wrong to say that."

"I know," she admitted. "You were pissing me off."

"Apology accepted," he grumbled, knowing that was as much as he was going to get from her. She smirked at him, throwing an arm around his shoulders. He hesitated, then put an arm around her waist, giving her a squeeze. "Thanks for not giving up on me," he offered. Vi squeezed him back.

"Ditto."

They walked together in silence then, trudging through the forest, heading slowly and steadily toward the Deadlands.

316

* * *

The vast emptiness of the Deadlands spread out before Hunter and Vi, extending as far as the eye could see in all directions. They'd been walking at Vi's brutal pace for hours now, having only stopped once while they were still in the forest, to get some water from the stream. The sun had long since risen above the horizon, its rays beating down on them mercilessly. Vi hardly seemed to mind, continuing forward with ease, but for Hunter it was an entirely different matter. Sweat trickled down his flanks, soaking his shirt. The weight of his sword – and the fact that it rubbed against the side of his leg when he walked – was becoming increasingly annoying.

"Can we take another break?" he asked, grimacing at the burning in his legs. His shins were particularly sore, the muscles there unaccustomed to the weight of his boots. Vi shook her head.

"Ironclad patrol the Deadlands," she replied. "I don't want to risk them circling back and looking for us here. The sooner we get into the city, the better."

"Can't you just kill them all?"

"Maybe," she answered. "But they might kill you in the process."

"I'll run away. I promise."

"Uh huh," she replied, smirking at him. "And they'll catch you and tear *your* arm off."

"Hey," he retorted, glaring at her. "Too soon."

"They run pretty fast," she reminded him. "Almost as fast as I do."

"You can outrun them?"

"Probably," she replied. "But you can't…and I sure as hell ain't carrying you."

"You know," he grumbled, "…just when I've decided you're a complete asshole, you say something nice and get me all confused." She chuckled, slapping him on the back.

"I'm a girl," she replied. "It's what we do." Hunter gave her a sour look.

"Maybe I should try dudes then," he muttered. She arched an eyebrow.

"Ever done it?"

"No," he replied. "Don't plan on it either."

317

"Aww, come on," she pressed, punching him on the shoulder. "You might like it."

"My dad," he panted, "...used to say that when I got old enough, either girls would become magical, boys would become magical, or both." He smirked then. "And then he'd add 'or neither, and that'd be a shame.'"

"And it was girls for you," Vi guessed. Hunter nodded.

"Can't help what you like."

"Ain't that the truth," she mused, shaking her head. "Life would've been a lot simpler if I liked dick."

"What I really like about you," Hunter stated, "...is your ladylike way of saying things. So cultured and proper."

"Says the guy who falls in love with a whore."

"I wasn't in *love* with her," he retorted. Vi grinned at him.

"But you loved what she did to you."

"Hell yeah," he agreed. "Not gonna lie...it was pretty awesome."

"Then go back to her," Vi replied. "You'll get your chance soon enough."

"Nah," he stated, shaking his head. "I don't like the idea of people manipulating me. Making me feel something just because they're there."

"I'm sure you affected her too," Vi countered. "Bet she was a bit more clever and sarcastic around you after spending a night."

Hunter considered this, then nodded grudgingly.

"She was, actually." He hadn't even noticed it at the time.

"Everyone affects everyone," Vi explained. "No way around it. Doesn't take absorbing their emotions to do it, either. It's human nature. We're all just a mixture of our own personalities and the people we meet."

"Yeah, well I like being in control of myself," he insisted.

"So do I," she agreed. "But that takes practice. You're a sponge for emotions, so it's going to be a lot harder for you than it was for me. Thank god you've got a strong personality."

They continued forward, and Hunter glanced to the left, seeing the huge wooden posts of the King's Road a hundred feet away. They'd been following it ever since they'd reached the Deadlands. He glanced at Vi, realizing that she'd pulled ahead of him, and couldn't help but look down at her posterior. She had powerful legs, far more muscular than his, and she seemed to take the brutal walk in stride. Literally.

318

"How'd you get so damn strong?" he asked, jogging to catch up with her.

"I work out," she replied. "Feeling inadequate?"

"Little bit."

"Good," she replied. "You *should* feel inadequate. Because, you know, you are."

"So you could really outrun an Ironclad?" he asked, ignoring her insult. She nodded.

"Very likely," she answered. Then she smirked. "Not that I've ever tried. Killing them just seems a whole lot easier."

"So you just work out all the time, and that's how you got so strong."

"Mostly," she replied, glancing at him sidelong. "I may have...tweaked things here and there." Hunter frowned.

"Tweaked?"

"I'm a Seeker," she explained. "I retrieve artifacts for my clients...powerful ones. That means I have to transport them back to the city. A little quality time with some good artifacts can do a lot. And I may have...significantly delayed returning the ones I *really* liked."

"Ah."

"Of course, the guild frowns upon that," she continued. "Technically there's a law against it. But I'm not part of the guild...and my clients are usually just grateful that I always perform." She patted her chest then, where she'd placed the Ossae earlier. "Like with this."

"What does it do?" Hunter inquired.

"Not sure," she admitted. "I kept it away from my other stuff just in case, at least till I could figure it out. That's why it was in the storehouse. But I still can't tell what it does."

"It's not human," he stated.

"Obviously," she agreed. "Never stopped me before."

"Hmm?"

"I've...dabbled in using wild artifacts and Ossae," she confessed. "That stays between you and me, of course."

"Understood," he replied. "Uh, what's a wild artifact?"

"Anything other than human," she explained. "It's highly illegal for anyone to knowingly expose themselves to wild artifacts," she added. "At least in Tykus."

"Why?"

"Because people who don't know what they're doing will lose their humanity," she answered. "They'll eventually turn into something else. And you know how nature feels about people," she added darkly.

"But *you've* done it?"

"A little," she admitted. "Nothing excessive, of course. Just enough to help me do my job."

"For example?" he pressed. She arched an eyebrow at him.

"Aren't *you* curious," she replied. "Maybe one day you'll figure it out on your own."

"Spoilsport."

"Anyway," she continued, "...I'm very careful to keep my humanity. You noticed all the shit I had in my house?" Hunter nodded, remembering the stuffed animals on her bed, the dolls, and things that looked like children's toys.

"I didn't want to say anything," he admitted. "I mean, I think it's cool that you still play with dolls and all, but *some* people might think that's a little weird."

"They're from my childhood," Vi explained, ignoring his baiting. "When I was...pure. Sleeping with them reinforces my humanity. My sense of self."

"Uh huh," he shot back, grinning at her. "Do you set up tea parties with yourself? Or do you bring women over and play dollies with them?"

"Hey, sore subject asshole."

"Oh," he mumbled. "Sorry."

"*Any*way," she continued, "...I keep my humanity, which means I'm allowed back in the city. Which means I can drop off artifacts to my clients. There's one kingdom a few hundred kilometers from here where the laws against wild artifacts are looser. Been there a few times," she added. "Strange place...creepy as shit."

The terrain angled upward, and Hunter struggled to keep pace with Vi, who strode up the incline as effortlessly as she did everything else.

"Hey," he called after her as she pulled further and further away. "Wait up!"

"Sorry kiddo," she shouted back, stopping to wait for him. "I keep forgetting how weak and pathetic you are."

"Yeah," he shot back, catching up to her. "Well I'm sorry if I haven't been hanging around mountain goats," he panted, "...absorbing their mountaineering skills."

320

"Sorry to burst your bubble," she retorted, "…but this," she added, gesturing at her lower half, "…is all me."

"Uh huh."

"That's why I'm better than those jokers at the Guild of Seekers," she explained, continuing forward, matching his pace. "I don't just hang around artifacts absorbing other people's skills."

"That's what the Seekers do?"

"Mostly," she confirmed. "That's their training. They get all their skills handed to them." She shook her head, a disgusted look on her face. "All their fighting skills end up being reflexes," she continued. "A knee-jerk reaction. They never really understand *why* they're doing what they're doing. They have no strategy."

"So you could beat Thorius?" he asked. What he wouldn't give to see *that* fight.

"Wow," she muttered, shooting him a glare. "I'm insulted you even asked that."

"So what do *you* do that makes you better?" he pressed.

"I practice every fucking day," she replied. "And I work constantly. Hell, I bet Thorius hasn't even wiped his ass as many times as I've been in fights."

"Thanks for the visual."

"Point is," she continued, "…I don't rely on other peoples' skills to survive. I use artifacts and Ossae to *learn* from them. I think of it as getting taught by the best instructors the world has ever seen. I spend time absorbing their skills, then use them to see how they work for me. If they don't, I discard them. If they do, I keep them and use them."

They reached the top of the hill, and the terrain leveled out again, giving them an unfettered view of what lay beyond. And what Hunter saw made his eyes widen. For there, hundreds of yards away, the great wall of Tykus towered above the landscape, the great city on the hill rising far above it.

"All right!" Hunter exclaimed, feeling a burst of energy come over him. He felt renewed vigor in his legs, and strode toward the gate in the distance eagerly. Not so eagerly that Vi couldn't easily match his pace, of course.

"Calm down kiddo," she warned. "They might not be so happy to see you, remember?"

He glanced at her, realizing she was right. If Thorius had sent him out into the Fringe to kill him, then it stood to reason that the guy would still want him dead. He slowed his pace, glancing at the city in the distance.

"Wait, am I going to be safe there?" he asked, feeling suddenly uneasy.

"I'll put in a word for you," Vi promised.

"What does that mean?"

"I'll be sure to have a little talk with Thorius when we get there," she explained.

Suddenly Hunter heard a shout from above.

He glanced up, seeing men standing at the edge of the King's Road, waving their arms and pointing behind Vi and Hunter. Hunter felt Vi grab his shoulder.

"Shit," she swore.

"What?"

"Run!" she ordered, bolting forward. Hunter broke out into a run after her, glancing back. In the distance, maybe a half-mile away, dozens of dark shapes were charging across the Deadlands toward them.

Fast.

He ran faster, struggling to catch up with Vi. But she was far too quick, the distance between them growing by the second. He pumped his legs as hard as he could, his calves starting to burn. He glanced back again, seeing the dark shapes gaining on them. There was no mistaking what was chasing after them.

Ironclad!

Arrows shot outward from the King's Road, flying into the group of Ironclad. But they had no effect, deflected by the Ironclads' armor. The creatures bounded forward with terrifying speed, now only a quarter mile away.

Hunter turned forward, seeing Vi over a hundred feet ahead…and the great wall of Tykus a few hundred feet away from her. She waved her arms wildly at the two guards posted before the gate.

"Open the gate!" she shouted. "Open the gate!"

She ran even faster, and Hunter struggled to keep up, his lungs burning and his legs on fire. Glancing back, he saw another volley of arrows fly into the Ironclad, again to no effect. They were closing in with terrifying speed, one Ironclad breaking away from the group and sprinting right toward him. It was only a few hundred feet from Hunter now.

"Open the fucking gate!" Vi screamed, sliding to a stop in front of the guards. They froze, spotting the Ironclad, then waved their arms madly at the wall. Moments later, the gate began to rise, dust falling from it. She turned to Hunter, who was still a hundred feet away. "Come on!" she shouted.

He struggled, his breath coming in short gasps, sweat pouring down his body. His legs felt like jelly, and it took everything he had to stay on his feet. Behind him, that single Ironclad sprinted at breakneck speed, closing the distance between them rapidly. It was only a few dozen feet away now…and the gate was still opening, rising as if in slow motion. He stumbled toward Vi and the guards, reaching them at last. Vi grabbed him, pulling him bodily toward the gate.

"Go!" she commanded.

The lone Ironclad ran right up to them, leaping at Vi. She spun around, her mace somehow already in hand, and swung it at the thing's grotesque head. It slammed into the Ironclad's temple just as it smashed into her, throwing her backward onto the dirt. She somersaulted backward, on her feet again before the Ironclad had even stopped sliding on its belly on the dirt, unconscious…or dead.

The other Ironclad charged toward the gate, a hundred feet away and closing fast.

"Go!" Vi repeated, turning back to the gate and running at it. She dropped to her back at the last second, sliding underneath the still-rising gate, barely clearing the spikes at the bottom of it. Hunter ducked through moments later, one of the spikes scraping his back painfully as he went. The two guards followed, screaming at the guards in the tunnel.

"Lower it! Lower the gate!"

Vi grabbed Hunter, pulling him all the way through the gate. Dozens of guards stood ready in the tunnel, their warhammers in their hands.

"Ready the trap!" another guard shouted.

And then the first of the Ironclad slid under the gate, its legs slamming into Hunter's. He fell right on top of it, the back of his head bouncing off its armored chest. He felt its powerful arms wrap around him, crushing the breath out of his lungs. He grabbed its armored fingers, trying desperately to pry them from him, but he might as well have tried moving a statue.

Vi walked right up to the thing, swinging her mace down in a vicious arc. It smashed into the creature's face with a sickening *crunch*, sinking inward. Hunter felt the arms around him spasm, then go limp. Vi grabbed his arm, hauling him bodily to his feet...just as more Ironclad spilled into the tunnel through the still-opening gate.

"Close *the fucking gate*!" a guard shouted.

"Not yet!" another cried. "The trap is ready!"

The guards scrambled back from the gate, and Vi pulled Hunter back with them. Hunter watched in horror as dozens of Ironclad swarmed into the tunnel, stopping to face the guards with their black, glittering eyes.

"Trap away!" a guard shouted.

Suddenly, a massive log swung down from the ceiling, suspended by huge chains. It cleared Hunter's head by a few feet, swinging right at the group of Ironclad. It plowed into them, launching them backward through the gate. They flew through the air like rag dolls, landing on the hard dirt of the Deadlands beyond.

"Emergency closure, *now!*" a guard yelled.

There was a loud *clunk*, and then the gate dropped with alarming speed, slamming shut with a deafening *boom*.

And with that, they were safe.

"You okay?" Hunter heard someone ask. He turned, seeing Vi looking at him. Her voice was muffled after the deafening boom, but he could still hear her. He nodded.

"Yeah, I think so," he answered.

"Let's not do that again," she stated. Hunter nodded, not even having the energy to smirk. He looked down at the motionless body of the Ironclad that had almost gotten him, imagining what it might have done to him if Vi hadn't acted so quickly...if he'd been hauled away. There would've been no saving him then. He shuddered, turning back to Vi, feeling sick to his stomach at the thought.

"You sure you're okay?" Vi pressed.

"I will be," Hunter replied. He gave her a weak smile. "Thanks for saving my life," he added. "Again."

CHAPTER 27

Dominus sat at his desk in his suite, eyeing Axio, who was standing before him. He'd asked for Axio, realizing it'd been far too long since he'd instructed the boy. Dominus's duties had made it difficult to spend time with his new heir…and he couldn't afford to neglect the future Duke of Wexford any longer. The rot slowly creeping up his leg was a constant reminder of his mortality; he could not assume that he would have much more time to groom the boy.

It promised to be a much smoother transition than his son was currently going through. For one, Axio's will was weaker than Conlan's, making him more susceptible to Dominus's will, but still powerful enough to resist the influence of the other dukes, who would undoubtedly attempt to take advantage of Axio as soon as he assumed the Duchy. Secondly, the boy was not nearly as obstinate and egotistical as Conlan, so the transition would be far less difficult…even if Dominus was not around to see it to its finish.

Dominus felt uneasy then, knowing that time was against him. He had to keep Axio at his side as much as possible from now on, so that he could bend the boy to his will, infusing his personality into the boy. It was as his own father had done to him, and his grandfather before that…an unbroken chain identical to that of the kings who carried Tykus's will. Well, *nearly* identical. He, nor any other Duke of Wexford, had ever been a Legend. He could not hope to fully dominate the boy, to turn Axio into himself. But enough of him would survive to ensure that his vision for the kingdom remained…so that the next Duke of Wexford would work tirelessly to maintain the greatness of their race. To ensure that their great people endured forever.

"Please, sit down," Dominus urged, gesturing for Axio to grab a seat. The boy did so, carrying it to the front of the desk and sitting down. "I wanted to speak to you about the Duchy."

Axio said nothing, waiting patiently for Dominus to continue. Dominus smiled inwardly, feeling suddenly wistful.

If only Conlan could have been like this, he thought. He *had* been, at least until he'd turned fourteen. That had been when his rebellious streak had reared its ugly head.

"The Duke of Wexford," he stated, "…has many duties. Chief among them are the preservation of our people."

"I understand, your Grace."

"But not just *our* people," Dominus continued. "We must also ensure the integrity of humanity itself."

"I don't understand."

"My first loyalty is to my people," Dominus explained. "To the kingdom…those that represent the ideal man, in the image of Tykus and the other great men – scholars, leaders, generals, philosophers – who have shown themselves to be pillars of intellect and virtue."

"Yes your Grace."

"Secondly, I must ensure the pacification and loyalty of the common folk," Dominus continued. "For they provide for the kingdom with their labor." He leaned back in his chair. "Recall the beehive, Axio."

"What of them?"

"I maintain the integrity of the hive," Dominus explained. "First by ensuring a strong queen, one that will give rise to all of the other bees within the hive. All of the same bloodline, their qualities a reflection of hers."

Axio nodded.

"Secondly, I ensure that the honey – the fruit of the labors of the lesser bees – is collected, not merely wasted by allowing the lesser bees to feed upon it. No, the honey must be stored, while leaving just enough for the hive to continue its labors."

"And what of the honey you store, your Grace?"

"That," Dominus replied, "…is the obvious question." He smiled. "I ensure the survival and integrity of the hive, and in return

I collect the fruits of the hive's labor. This is the role of any government."

"You're referring to taxes?"

"Not just taxes," Dominus corrected. "Tell me…what do most of the peasants do when they're paid?" Axio considered this for a moment.

"I don't know," he admitted.

"They spend it," Dominus answered. "Tell me…do they save what they've earned, to increase their wealth slowly?"

"No, your Grace?"

"Most often not," Dominus agreed. "They live for the moment, falling prey to their impulses. Then they bemoan their fates, cursing the wealthy for being 'luckier' than they are…when in fact it is their lack of wisdom that curses them. The wealthy understand the importance of investment…of deferring gratification for a much greater return in the future."

"As I've learned, your Grace."

"I'm sure you've been taught well in this regard," Dominus agreed. "But the peasants have weak wills in more ways than one, and cannot resist immediate gratification. Tell me…what would these peasants do if the Acropolis were destroyed? Would they create a government as sophisticated and just as that which we have created?"

"Of course not, your Grace."

"Indeed," Dominus agreed. "We know very well what happens when men of poor insight and character rise to lead. They form governments marked by corruption. Flagrant abuses of power. Disrespect for the rule of law. They become despots and dictators."

He leaned forward, propping his elbows on the table.

"Tell me Axio…is a son much like his father?"

"Undoubtedly so, your Grace."

"We say the apple doesn't fall far from the tree," Dominus agreed. "Men of superior character tend to produce men of superior character. Men of poor character – addicts, the melancholy, the stupid, the violent and brutish, those tortured by needless anxiety or delusions – tend to produce children in their image. Thus a man's heritage – his bloodline – most often dictates his destiny."

"As it did for you," Axio reasoned. Dominus nodded.

"We are blessed that these qualities are transferrable," he agreed. "That being in the company of greater men will elevate one's soul.

But in the same vein, being in the company of lesser men will *taint* one's soul. That," he added, "…is why the Acropolis must always remain isolated from the rest of the city. Why the nobles must never mingle with the poor."

"To allow such a thing would steer mankind to mediocrity," Axio stated.

"Precisely," Dominus replied, leaning back in his chair again. "Proper governments extract the goods of the common man's labor, concentrating them so that the leaders – the wealthy, the politicians – may redistribute them wisely for the good of the country. But one must be careful; give the common man too little reward for their labor, and they revolt."

"I understand, your Grace."

"The wealthy deserve the greatest reward, as they maintain the systems that generate wealth within the kingdom," Dominus continued. "Philosophers, politicians, scholars, businessmen – *they* provide the most good for the kingdom…they create and maintain it. The common man provides relatively little but the sweat of their labor, while benefiting from the gifts of wise leadership and a safe and stable government, and therefore deserves the smallest reward."

"Undoubtedly," Axio concurred.

"So, as I said," Dominus stated, "…my first loyalty as duke is to the Acropolis – to the ideal men who maintain the government. But I must also ensure the pacification of the common folk, so that they continue to provide their labor." He leaned forward, eyeing Axio critically. "My third duty is to humanity itself."

"How so, your Grace?"

Just then, Dominus heard a knock on the door. He grimaced, irritated at the interruption.

"Come in," he ordered.

The door opened, and a man appeared…one of the royal messengers. He bowed.

"My Duke," he greeted. "A visitor has arrived in Hightown, and is requesting your presence."

"A visitor?" Dominus pressed. The messenger hesitated, then nodded.

"They said you called for them," he clarified. "An urgent matter regarding an Ironclad attack on a convoy passing through the Fringe."

"Ah," Dominus stated, leaning back in his chair. "Prepare a carriage to Hightown," he ordered. The messenger bowed again, then left. Dominus sighed, turning to Axio. "More on this later," he stated, standing up with some difficulty. "I have business to attend to."

* * *

"Take care Hunter," Ekrin stated as Hunter stood from his chair, walking toward the exit. "And…it's good to have you back."

Hunter gave an obligatory smile, then left the small room, closing the door behind him. He navigated the hallways until he reached the inner gate in the large tunnel within the wall, waiting for it to open, then walking through. The long street between the two tall walls greeted him, and beyond that, the seemingly infinite stairway leading up to the Acropolis far above.

He sighed, trudging forward, feeling suddenly exhausted.

After he'd separated from Vi, he'd had a meeting with Ekrin. Or rather, an interrogation. First a Seeker had tested him for corruption…a test he must have passed, because the Seeker had left soon afterward. Ekrin had held him for over an hour, asking question after question about what had happened to him. From the journey to the Fringe to the battle with the Ironclad, to Vi rescuing him. Hunter had skipped the part about Vi training him, of course, but did mention that dozens of Ironclad had tried to kill them, and that they'd barely escaped, hiding in the woods for weeks before making the long journey back through the forest to return to the kingdom. It was a lie Vi had come up with during their trek through the Deadlands, so that they'd both tell the same story when they were asked. Once again, Vi had thought of everything.

Eventually, Ekrin had been satisfied, at least enough to let Hunter go. He'd even given Hunter another set of keys to his apartment, seeing as he'd lost them, probably during his swim in the lake around Vi's house. Now all Hunter wanted to do was go home and sleep.

He navigated the streets of Lowtown, passing the church and heading toward the Outskirts. It wasn't long before he reached his old neighborhood, walking across the docks toward his apartment. He'd planned to head straight there, but his stomach growled viciously at him, no doubt upset that he hadn't eaten since the night before. He turned toward the community center, bypassing the line in front of it in the usual fashion, then going inside. He scanned the tables for Sukri and Gammon, but they weren't there...it was already past noon. Ekrin had told him that Sukri and Gammon were still alive, for which he was immensely grateful. As vigorously as the man had interrogated Hunter, he still had a heart.

Hunter grabbed two plates heaping with food, then sat down, devouring his meal with unfettered glee. After the gamey, unseasoned bird-meat he'd eaten day after day at Vi's, the meal – glorified cafeteria food at best – was practically orgasmic.

That done, he exited the community center, walking back to his apartment. He climbed the three stories to the front door, unlocking it and stepping into his tiny room. It was, he found, exactly as he had left it...except that his Seeker medallion was missing. He sighed, flopping onto his back on the bed, marveling at how soft and comfortable it felt. Compared to his bed on Earth, it was a stiff cot...but it was a far cry better than a bed of leaves and dirt thrown over a frickin' boulder.

He sighed again, closing his eyes, feeling his meal starting to work on him. He always felt sleepy after a big meal, and after being woken up in the middle of the night yesterday, he was already exhausted. His mind started to wander, sleep pulling him into its otherworldly embrace.

There was a knock at the door.

Hunter groaned, slapping the bed with one hand, then pulling himself upright. There was another knock, and he sighed, standing up and walking to the door. He unlocked it, then opened it...and froze. There, standing before him, was Trixie.

"Hunter!" she cried, throwing her arms around him and hugging him tightly. He stumbled backward, then caught his balance. "You're alive!"

"Hey Trixie," he greeted, hesitating, then hugging her back. She pulled away, smiling radiantly at him. She was wearing her usual outfit, a tight black low-cut shirt and tight black shorts, her blond hair tied into a ponytail. She was attractive, sure, but hardly the gorgeous bombshell he remembered. Time away from her had helped him gain perspective, it seemed.

"I was so sad when I heard that you'd gone missing," she said, stepping into the room and closing the door behind her. "When Ekrin told me that you were alive..."

"It's good to see you too Trixie."

"Can you tell me what happened?" she asked, walking up to the bed and sitting down on it. She patted the bed beside her. "You can sit down if you want to."

Hunter glanced at the bed, hesitating. He knew exactly what would happen if he joined her there.

"I'll stand," he decided, forcing a smile.

"Oh, okay," she replied, smiling up at him. "Can you tell me what happened?"

"I uh," he began, not sure how to proceed. "I can't really talk about it," he confessed. "The Guild of Seekers doesn't let me talk about their secrets."

"Oh," she replied, frowning a little. But she perked up quickly. "That's okay," she added. "I'm just happy to see you."

"Yeah," he mumbled, scratching the back of his head. "Uh, well, I was actually going to take a nap when you knocked."

"Oh, I'm sorry," Trixie blurted out. "Did I wake you?"

"No, but I'm exhausted," he replied. "I just need to get some sleep."

"Okay," she replied, patting the bed again. "We can do that then."

He grimaced, feeling suddenly very awkward. Trixie clearly wanted to stay. And while the thought of her doing so was vaguely enticing – no doubt as a result of her will already starting to work its magic on him – he had no real desire to do anything with her. He was done being played around with. Done being manipulated by some politicians from afar.

"It's been a long day," he replied at last, giving her an apologetic look. "I kinda just want to be alone."

"Oh."

"Sorry," he mumbled. She stood up, giving him a smile.

"You don't have to be sorry," she replied. "I understand," she added, walking up to him. She gazed into his eyes, then leaned forward, wrapping her arms around him and squeezing him tight. "I'm glad you're okay," she murmured, her lips brushing against his ear. He hesitated, then hugged her back, his hands on the scoop of her lower back. She was very warm, and soft, and her faint, sweet perfume brought back memories. Memories of the time they'd spent together here.

He felt his groin stirring.

She held him, rubbing his back with one hand, then kissed him on the cheek. He felt a tingling sensation where her lips touched him, and when she pulled back, staring into his eyes, he felt his resolve wavering. Sure, she wasn't the sharpest tool in the shed…and she was a prostitute…but she was genuine. There was nothing manipulative about her *personality*, after all. It wasn't her fault that she had such an effect on him. Hell, she probably didn't even realize that she *was* having an effect on him. She probably thought he just really liked her.

And in a way, he did.

"I missed you," she murmured, staring into his eyes. She leaned in, pressing her lips against his other cheek, and he felt his groin grow, straining against the front of his pants and pressing into her lower belly. She stepped back, grabbing his hand and pulling him toward the bed.

"Trixie…" he began, but she sat down, pulling him down to sit beside her. She put a hand on his thigh, gazing at him with those perfect blue eyes.

"You can lie down if you want to," she offered. "I can help you relax."

"I'm too tired," Hunter protested. "I just need to sleep."

"Aww," she murmured, leaning in and kissing his cheek again. "You know I'm good at putting you to sleep."

Hunter grimaced, his groin uncomfortably full now. He found his gaze wandering downward, to her low-cut shirt, to the recesses of her cleavage.

It would *help me sleep*, he thought.

"Come on," she urged. "Lie down. You need to get some sleep."

He hesitated, turning away, staring at his feet. He *was* exhausted…and it was clear that Trixie wasn't going to leave. He didn't really have much of a choice if he wanted to get some sleep. Besides, after everything he'd been through – nearly being killed by the Ironclad, and almost drowning – he *deserved* a little something special for himself. Life was short, he knew now, and it could end in a blink of an eye. It would be downright stupid to turn down something good like this.

"Come on," she repeated, grabbing his shoulders and twisting him around. He let her, and she lowered him onto his back on the bed, sitting beside him. She put a hand on his chest, smiling down at him. "There you go," she murmured.

"I'll see you later?" he ventured, halfheartedly hoping she'd get the hint and leave.

"Of course," she replied, her hand trailing down to his belly. "I'll be right here when you wake up." Her hand stopped, resting on his lower belly. She frowned then, glancing down at his pants. "We can't have you sleeping in these," she stated disapprovingly. She unbuttoned his pants, then pulled them off, leaving him in his underwear. "There," she murmured, resting her hand on his naked belly. Her palm was warm, her touch sending a shiver down his spine.

"Trixie…" he mumbled.

She slid her hand down, her palm resting against his member. She stopped there, the gentle pressure making his breath catch in his throat.

You deserve this, he thought. *Just this once.*

"Relax," Trixie soothed, her hand sliding down, then up, caressing him. "I'm going to take care of you." She continued, patiently and gently massaging him through his underwear. His heart beat faster, his breath catching in his throat. She paused, then slipped her hand into his underwear, grabbing him and pulling him free from it. He stared down at her, watching as she leaned forward, pressing her lips against him. She kissed him once, then again, glancing up at him, her blue eyes twinkling.

Then she slowly took him into her mouth, her eyes locked on his.

He moaned, closing his eyes and resting his head back on his pillow. He felt her on him, going very slowly at first, then picking up speed, her mouth warm and wet…and amazing. She kept going, reaching a steady rhythm now, yet still slow and sensual, as was her way. He felt the unmistakable sensation of mounting pleasure; it grew, slowly and steadily, more powerful with every second.

Still she worked on him, keeping that same slow rhythm.

He groaned, feeling himself getting closer to the point of no return, his hips lifting off the mattress involuntarily.

You don't have to do this, he told himself. *You can still stop it.*

He opened his eyes, glancing down at her, seeing her blond bangs spilling across his belly. He reached down, placing his hands on the sides of her head. This only made her go faster, her mouth tightening suddenly around him.

Oh god.

He let go, feeling his pleasure peak, so powerful that he couldn't resist it anymore. She went faster and harder, bringing him well beyond the point of no return, far past any hope of resistance. He cried out, feeling pulse after pulse of ecstasy, coming one after another so quickly and uncontrollably that he couldn't hope to hold them back. Still she worked on him, until he was utterly drained, his body limp on his mattress. Sweat beaded up on his skin, trickling down his temples.

She released him then, climbing to his side and lying down next to him, draping an arm across his chest. He felt her lips on his cheek, and he turned to her, seeing her staring at him with her perfect blue eyes, a smile on her lips.

"Sweet dreams," she murmured.

And then, just as she'd predicted, he felt his eyelids grow heavy. He closed them, and within moments was fast asleep.

* * *

Hunter groaned, opening his eyes.

He was in his room, he realized. Sunlight streamed through his window, and he heard the sound of people talking outside of his building below. He rubbed his eyes, then rolled out of bed, sitting at the edge, feeling disoriented. It took him a moment to remember that he'd gone to sleep early that afternoon...or was it yesterday now? He wasn't sure how long he'd slept for, but judging by the angle of the sunbeam coming through the window, it was late morning now. That meant he'd slept almost an entire day.

He yawned, stretching his arms to the sides, then froze, remembering what had happened.

Shit.

He glanced back at the bed, half-expecting Trixie to be laying there, but she wasn't. She hadn't woken him at all throughout the night, not after she'd...helped him. True to her word, she'd let him sleep, which was the first time she'd foregone their usual marathon sessions. Once again, she'd been thoughtful and considerate...qualities that unfortunately made her even harder to resist.

Hunter sighed, rubbing his eyes again, then dropping his hands to his lap, staring at the floor. He closed his eyes, remembering how she'd smelled, how soft her skin had been. How it'd felt when she...

Get off the goddamn bed!

He stood up abruptly, walking as far away from his bed as he could and turning around to stare at it.

You're a fucking idiot, he told himself.

334

He'd fallen for Trixie's wiles yet again, giving in to her despite every intention not to. He'd promised himself he'd never be manipulated by her again, and yet here he was, back in the same old pattern.

"Damn it!" he swore, walking up and kicking the bed. He backed away quickly, then pulled his clothes on, strapping his sword to his waist and placing his bow and empty quiver on his back. He didn't want to leave them in his apartment, after all, and keeping them close would allow him to continue to absorb their power.

He left the apartment, going downstairs, then walking across the docks toward the community center.

Vi was right, he muttered to himself as he walked. *You're nothing but a goddamn addict.*

He sighed, kicking a pebble off the dock and into the water. People around him gave him dirty looks, keeping as far away from him as possible, but he didn't care. For the first time, he felt like he deserved it.

They made *you an addict,* he thought.

That was the worst part, of course. Some bureaucrat had planned this…and he'd fallen right into their trap. He grit his teeth, clenching his fists.

It's over, he swore. *I'm done.*

He glanced forward, seeing the community center ahead…and the usual line to get in. He strode right up to the front doors, taking perverse pleasure in the fact that everyone scrambled out of the way to avoid him.

Never again.

But even as he told himself this, he felt doubt creep into his mind. He thought of Trixie, of how good it'd felt to be with her. How good it'd felt to finally give in to her, to give in to temptation. It'd been ever more enticing because it'd been wrong. Because it was forbidden.

And he had the sinking suspicion that if she pressed him again, he'd probably give in. And it would feel, at least in that moment of surrender, utterly incredible.

Hunter made it through the double-doors, trudging up to fill a plate, then walking toward one of the empty tables. He felt a hand on his shoulder.

"Hunter?"

He turned around, seeing none other than Gammon standing there. The big man beamed down at him, giving him a big bear hug

335

that lifted him right off the ground. His feet dangled in midair, and he grunted, relieved when Gammon set him down.

"Gammon!" he cried, grinning back. "You're okay!"

"Yes I am," Gammon agreed. "Come on," he added, walking toward a different table. It was empty as well…except for someone sitting in a chair at the end of the table. Or rather, a wheelchair.

"Sukri!" Hunter cried, rushing up to her and bending over to give her a hug.

"Crispy?!" she exclaimed, hugging him back. He pulled back, and she grinned at him, punching him in the shoulder. "How the hell are you still alive?"

"I got lucky," he admitted. He sat down, telling the tale of his rescue. He left out most of the detail about Vi and her home, and their training, but relayed their harrowing escape from the Ironclad.

"Damn Crispy," Sukri said when he was done. "This chick sounds like a total badass."

"I felt pretty good about how I did against that Ironclad until just now," Gammon confessed.

"Aww, mad that you got shown up by a *girl*?" Sukri teased, punching Gammon in the arm. Hunter doubted the big guy even felt it.

"How's your leg?" Hunter asked. Sukri glowered at him.

"It sucks," she replied. "Wheeling myself around in this damn chair all the time. At least it doesn't hurt as much anymore." She grimaced. "Itches like hell though."

"So you're still in the guild?" Hunter pressed. Sukri glanced at Gammon, who nodded.

"So far," he confirmed.

"So everyone thinks I'm dead, huh?" Hunter mused. "Anyone come to the funeral?"

"Nope," Sukri replied. "There wasn't one. But really, we did miss you." Hunter smiled.

"I missed you guys too."

And it was true. Gammon and Sukri – and Kris – had been his first and only friends here, the people that had made him feel like he was part of something. They were all he had in this world, other than Vi of course.

"I'm guessing they're not expecting me back at the guild," Hunter ventured. Again, Sukri and Gammon exchanged glances. Sukri gave him an apologetic look.

"Sorry Crispy," she replied, putting a hand on his arm. "Master Thorius disqualified you. He had to disqualify two people from our team, remember?"

"I get it," Hunter reassured her. "I'm okay. Vi told me I can stick around with her. Besides, I won't go hungry," he added with a grin. "She's been teaching me how to hunt."

"I want to meet this chick again," Sukri said. "She sounds awesome."

"She *is* awesome," Hunter replied.

"We'd better get going," Gammon interjected. "It's almost noon." He stood up, getting behind Sukri's wheelchair, but Sukri turned around to glare at him.

"I got it," she grumbled. She turned to Hunter, putting a hand on his. "Let's hang out after," she proposed. "We can go for some drinks. You in?"

"Sure," Hunter replied.

"I'll make sure you get home safe," Gammon offered.

"Deal," Hunter agreed.

"Shit, we're gonna get *wasted*," Sukri exclaimed, grinning from ear to ear. She wheeled herself back from the table, then waved at Hunter. "See ya Crispy!"

Hunter waved back, watching the two as they made their way out of the community center. Then he turned his attention back to his plate, shoveling food in his mouth. He was starving, after all, having slept yesterday away. In fact, he planned on having a second plate after he was done with this one. He felt much better after having talked to his friends, his problem with Trixie seeming far less important than it had earlier. But he knew he was in trouble…that he was stuck. For the first time in his life, he had to admit that he couldn't fix this by himself. He needed help.

He sighed, remembering how he'd spoken with Sukri about Trixie earlier. She'd been incredibly understanding. Despite her glib exterior, she was awfully sweet. Maybe he would talk to her about it tonight.

CHAPTER 28

"Bring her in," Dominus ordered, gesturing at the guard standing by the door. He leaned back in his chair, drumming his fingertips on the desk before him. After taking his carriage to Hightown, he'd decided to use one of the lesser lords' offices for his meeting. A spacious room with relatively modest furniture, it paled in comparison to Dominus's suite in the Acropolis. But he couldn't very well meet his contact there; only the nobility was allowed in the Acropolis.

The guard left, leaving the door open. Moments later, a woman entered the room. She did not bow, or even salute, merely stopping a few feet from his desk. Dominus hid his disapproval, knowing full well she would not abide by the rules and customs of the kingdom, or offer any due respect for his office. That was, quite irritatingly, her way. If it had been anyone else, he would have had them hanged.

He regarded her silently for a moment, studying her. She had obviously engaged in some questionable activities, straying from the traits of her bloodline. Her eyes were a little too large, and almost iridescent. She was more muscular than a woman had any right to be, and moved with a catlike grace. All of these could be explained by exposure to legal, if questionable, artifacts.

But he knew better.

"Hey," she greeted, reaching into her shirt and pulling out a small white object. She placed it on the desk, then crossed her arms over her chest.

"Vi," Dominus replied. He glanced down at the object in front of him...a curved bone, appearing entirely unremarkable. No one would believe how much he'd paid for it...and if anyone of consequence found it in his possession, even he – second only in power to the king himself – would be put to death.

"I don't do this for free," she stated, staring down at him. He reached into his desk, tossing a bag filled with coins at her. She caught it, of course, shoving it down her shirt. He'd only met her once before, many years ago, but he'd remarked even then how strange her movements were. Too fast, too smooth. Effortless.

She was incredibly dangerous, this one. All of the guards in this office wouldn't stand a chance if she decided that they should die.

"You took too long," Dominus accused, finding himself putting a hand on his cane, which he'd rested against the chair beside him. She usually did. It was of course so she could leech traits out of the artifacts she procured. He had no doubt that she did this...and any other Seeker would be brutally punished for it. But again, she got away with it. Being two weeks late was excessive, however. Even for her.

"Something unexpected came up," Vi shot back. "You wouldn't believe this, but some idiot sent a few fresh initiates to the Fringe. Got one of them killed, too."

Dominus took a deep breath in, letting it out slowly. She had a way of getting under his skin, much the way his son did. They were perhaps the only two people that could do it. He decided not to try to hide his annoyance...she would see past the ruse anyway, and enjoy his failure.

"You saved the Original I hear," he stated.

"Sure did," she confirmed. "Nice kid. I like him." She smiled. "I think I'll keep him."

"How charitable of you."

"Saving him cost me," she added. "Few dozen Ironclad came to get some revenge. Destroyed my place."

"That should more than cover it," he countered, gesturing at where she'd stuffed the bag of coins.

"Suppose so," she agreed. "Got an apprentice out of it anyway."

His eyebrows rose involuntarily.

"You're teaching him?"

"Maybe," she replied, gazing down at him with those unnerving eyes. "Sure hate to invest all that effort just to have someone try to kill him," she added. "That would make me…extremely upset."

Dominus stared at her for a long, uncomfortable moment, then inclined his head slightly.

"Noted."

She smiled, uncrossing her arms.

"Anything else?" she inquired.

"I have another job for you," Dominus answered. "One that I hope you can complete in a more timely fashion."

"Go on."

"You are of course aware of the most recent attack at our gate," Dominus stated. "This makes three attacks this month. The other dukes and I have officially declared war on the Ironclad, as of today."

"And?"

"We hired the Guild of Seekers to send their best scouts past the Fringe to map out the Ironclad locations. In doing so, they believe they'd found their main base. In a cave to the south, past the Fringe. A new kind of Ironclad was seen entering that base recently. One larger than the rest, with a blue, glowing mane."

"Interesting," Vi murmured, leaning forward. That clearly got her attention.

"This new Ironclad has been spotted before," Dominus revealed. "One of our Seekers – a man named Jarl – witnessed it attacking a fellow Seeker in the Fringe." He frowned. "Jarl swore that the thing was capable of speaking." Among other things. If it was truly capable of what Jarl claimed…

"And you want me to kill it," Vi guessed.

"Correct," Dominus replied. "The Ironclad clearly defer to it. We strongly suspect that it is their leader.

"A coup d'état," Vi murmured. Dominus nodded.

"Your mission is to find it and kill it," he stated. "And most importantly, you must bring me its head. I'll be back in Wexford by then."

"Simple enough."

"Perhaps not," Dominus countered. "We only have intelligence regarding the outer portions of the base. We know nothing of the interior." He paused. "An all-out war with the Ironclad would result in heavy losses," he added. "The best strategy is to kill their leader, then take advantage of their inevitable confusion."

"Fine then," Vi agreed. "I'll do it."

"There is one condition," Dominus countered. Vi arched an eyebrow. "To receive payment for this job," he stated, "...you must bring your...new protégé along on the mission."

Vi stared at him silently for a long moment, then leaned back in her chair.

"You want him dead," she deduced. Dominus gave a small smile.

"If he should suffer such an unfortunate fate," he replied, "...I'd of course compensate you generously."

"That would be obscenely expensive," she warned. Dominus smirked back.

"How convenient," he replied, grabbing the rib on his desk and putting it in his pocket. "I happen to be obscenely rich."

* * *

"Here it is," Sukri declared, stopping her wheelchair before one of the bars in Lowtown. Gammon opened the door, gesturing for Sukri and Hunter to go in. Hunter hesitated, glancing at the sign. It looked distressingly familiar.

"Uh guys," he said, stepping back from the door. "I don't think we should go here."

"Why not?" Sukri retorted, giving him a look. "This is my favorite bar."

"I might have...run my mouth off a little the last time I was here."

"So?" Sukri pressed.

"...and got my ass kicked," Hunter admitted.

"Well no one's gonna mess with us," Sukri replied. "We're initiates."

"No one will mess with *you*," Hunter corrected.

"I'll protect you," Gammon offered. Hunter smiled, remembering how Gammon had stood up to the Ironclad. Some wasted dude in a bar wouldn't stand much of a chance.

"Not worried about *that*," Hunter explained. "I'd just rather not make a scene."

"Aw hell," Sukri replied with a shit-eating grin. "That's half the fun! Come on," she added, wheeling herself through the doorway. Hunter sighed, following her into the bar. It was moderately full, it still being late afternoon. Hunter looked around, relieved to see a different bartender this time. And the guys who'd beaten the crap out of him weren't there.

"Three starfuckers," Sukri ordered, wheeling herself up to the bar. Gammon helped her out of her wheelchair and onto one of the barstools. Hunter and Gammon sat on either side of her. The bartender nodded, and started mixing their drinks.

"Starfucker?" Hunter asked. Sukri grinned.

"My favorite drink," she explained. "Tastes like a girl, pounds like a guy."

"Umm…"

"Just try it," she urged. The bartender turned to set their glasses down, then froze, his eyes meeting Hunter's.

"What?" Hunter asked.

"You can't come in here," the bartender said. "You'll drive away my customers."

"Sorry," Hunter mumbled. He went to stand up, but Sukri put a hand on his arm, glaring at the bartender.

"We *are* your customers," she retorted. "Our money's as good as theirs," she added, gesturing at the few other men at the bar. The bartender sighed.

"Look," he replied, "…I'm just doing my job. My boss doesn't want anyone here that'll make customers…nervous." He pointed at Hunter. "He sits at the bar, I gotta throw out the damn stool. I gotta cleanse the bar."

"Tough shit," Sukri shot back. "This ain't Hightown. You deal with people from the Outskirts all the time."

"Not like him," the bartender countered.

"It's fine guys," Hunter interjected, standing up and stepping away from the bar. "I'll just go."

"You can have the shot," the bartender offered. Hunter nodded, grabbing it and chugging it. It was sweet…definitely a girly drink. But it was also pretty damn strong. It burned in his belly, and moments later, he felt an unmistakable stirring in his pants.

Well that's weird, he thought.

"This is bullshit," Sukri muttered, downing her own shot. Gammon didn't touch his – the guy didn't drink – so Sukri took his and drank it too.

"Well well," a voice from behind Hunter said. "Look who decided to come back."

Hunter turned, seeing a familiar group of guys entering the bar. The same guys who'd been there the first time he'd

342

come...including the big dude that'd beat the crap out of him. Kurt, if he remembered correctly.

"I was just leaving," Hunter said. Kurt sneered at him.

"Oh yeah," he agreed. "You're leaving all right. Same way you left the last time."

"Look, I'm sorry I acted like a jerk last time," Hunter apologized. "I was having a really bad day. I don't want any trouble," he added, trying to move past the guy. But Kurt blocked Hunter's way. Sukri turned around in her barstool, glaring at the men.

"Beat it assholes," she growled, grabbing her Seeker medallion and showing it to them. "Unless you want trouble."

"We got no problem with you," Kurt countered. "Just this guy."

"You mess with him," Sukri retorted, "...you mess with me." Kurt smirked at her...that is, until Gammon stood from his stool, rising to his full height. He loomed over the group of men, crossing his huge arms over his chest.

"And me," he pitched in.

The men stared up at Gammon, their faces paling. Gammon helped Sukri back into her wheelchair, then strode forward, putting an arm around Hunter's shoulders and escorting him out, Sukri following from behind.

"I'm not done with him," Kurt insisted, following them out of the bar. He put a hand to his waist, and Hunter glanced down, realizing the man had a sword at his hip. His cronies spilled out of the bar behind him.

"Come on," Gammon said, putting a hand on Sukri's shoulder. "We'll go to another bar." She glared at him, but visibly deflated.

"Fine," she muttered, wheeling herself away from the bar. Hunter turned to follow her, then heard the *shhhtck* of a sword being pulled from its scabbard behind him. He spun around, facing Kurt...and realized that his own sword was already in his hand. Kurt glared at him, his sword less than a foot from Hunter's.

"Better know how to use that boy," he growled. "Because I do."

Hunter gripped his sword tightly, feeling supremely annoyed. He suppressed the feeling, realizing it was almost certainly coming from being too close to Kurt.

Emotion is temporary, action is forever.

"Go have some drinks," Hunter replied calmly. "Have some fun. I'll buy you a round." Kurt paused, then lowered his blade, glancing back at his buddies.

343

"Come on Kurt," one of them said. "He's not worth it."

"Damn right," Kurt grumbled. He turned back toward the bar, and Hunter lowered his own sword, sliding it back into its scabbard...just as Kurt spun around, slashing at him with his sword!

Before Hunter knew it, his blade was in his hand again. He blocked Kurt's attack, then lunged forward reflexively for the counterattack. He pulled back sharply – just as the tip of his sword pressed into Kurt's upper belly.

He took a step back, lowering his sword, a chill running through him.

I almost killed him.

Kurt stumbled backward, looking down at his belly. A small red spot stained his shirt. He looked up at Hunter, gripping his sword so hard his knuckles turned white.

"I don't want to hurt you," Hunter warned.

"You fucking brown piece of shit!" Kurt shouted, rushing at Hunter and thrusting his sword at Hunter's chest. Compared to Vi's attacks, the lunge seemed slow and clumsy; Hunter parried the blow easily, slapping Kurt's blade away with his own. He kicked Kurt in the knee, forcing it to lock...and Kurt's upper body to jerk forward and downward. Hunter rapped the pommel of his sword on the back of the man's head. Not so hard as to kill him, but hard enough to be memorable.

Kurt dropped onto his hands and knees on the street.

"Don't even think about it," Gammon warned as Kurt's friends moved toward Hunter. The big man stood in front of them, his arms out wide.

They backed away hurriedly.

Kurt got to his feet, stumbling away from Hunter toward the bar, rejoining his friends. The barkeeper – who'd followed everyone out of the bar, no doubt to enjoy the show – raised both of his hands.

"We don't want any more trouble here," he said. Hunter sheathed his sword, sighing at the man.

"All we wanted was a drink," he muttered. He turned back to Sukri and Gammon, walking away from the bar. The two joined him, Gammon walking at his left side, and Sukri wheeling herself on his right.

"Damn Crispy," Sukri declared, gazing at him in wonderment. "I've never seen *anyone* move like that!"

"Yeah," Hunter mumbled.

"How did you learn to *do* that?" Sukri pressed. She looked up at Gammon. "Wasn't that awesome?"

"It *was* awesome," Gammon confirmed.

"I have a good teacher," Hunter explained, feeling rather awkward. He wasn't *that* good, after all…hell, every time he fought Vi, he felt like a klutzy toddler. But he was taken aback at just how bad Kurt had been.

"God damn," Sukri declared, "…but do I want to meet this chick. What's her name again?"

"Vi," Hunter answered.

"Can I meet her?" Sukri pressed. Hunter smiled.

"She's gonna meet up with me in a day or two, I think," he replied. "I'll ask if it's okay."

"Nice!" Sukri exclaimed, slapping Hunter on the back. They continued down the street then, until Gammon stopped suddenly. Everyone stopped with him.

"Where are we going?" he asked.

"Oh," Sukri replied, looking around. "I don't know. Maybe the Foaming Beard?"

"Okay," Gammon agreed. Hunter hesitated.

"I don't know guys," he muttered. "I think I'm gonna just go home." Sukri frowned at him.

"Aww, why?" she pressed.

"I don't want any more trouble," he explained. She pouted.

"But we were supposed to get some drinks."

"We did," Hunter countered. "And you had two."

"I understand," Gammon stated. "We'll walk you home."

Sukri sighed, but didn't protest any more. They walked back toward the Outskirts, then made their way back to Hunter's apartment, stopping before his building. Sukri and Gammon turned to face him, and he smiled.

"Sorry guys," he said. "But thanks for inviting me."

"Anytime Crispy," Sukri replied, pulling him down to give him a hug. "Next time we'll buy ahead of time, then party at our place."

"Sounds like a plan," Hunter agreed.

"What are you going to do for the rest of the night?" Gammon asked. Hunter shrugged, then felt a sinking sensation. He'd almost forgot; it was nearly sundown. The time when Trixie usually arrived. That shot he'd taken with Sukri and Gammon had been stronger than he thought. It *did* taste like a girl and pound like a guy…and it

345

meant that he was almost certainly not going to be able to resist Trixie's charms. He always got a bit frisky when he drank, for better or worse.

"Aww," Sukri said, "Huntie looks sad."

"Nah," Hunter muttered. "I just…" he paused, glancing at Sukri. "Can I talk to you for a sec?" he asked. "In private?"

"Sure," Sukri agreed. She glanced at Gammon, who glanced at Hunter, then at her, hesitating for some reason.

"I'll head home," he said at last. "See you later?"

"Of course," Sukri agreed.

Gammon stood there a moment longer, then left, walking down the docks away from Hunter's apartment. Sukri and Hunter watched him go, then turned to face each other.

"What's up?" Sukri asked. Hunter glanced around, feeling profoundly uncomfortable.

"It's, uh…private," he confessed. "Can we talk about it upstairs?"

"Sure Crispy," she agreed. He started up the stairs, then stopped, realizing that Sukri wouldn't be able to get up the stairs in her wheelchair.

"Need help?" he asked.

"Give me your arm," she replied. He did so, and she got out of the wheelchair, leaning on him. "Go slowly," she instructed. They did so, Sukri leaning on Hunter as they went up the stairs, one step at a time. Eventually they reached the top, and Hunter unlocked his door, stepping through. He closed the door behind them. "Bring me to the bed," she requested.

Hunter hesitated, then complied, walking her to the bed. She sat down, clearly glad to be off her feet.

"So what's up?" she asked.

Hunter hesitated, feeling his cheeks flush. He shoved his hands in his pockets grimacing at her.

"This is kinda embarrassing for me," he admitted. Sukri arched one eyebrow, unable to help herself from smiling.

"Ooo," she replied, rubbing her hands together. "Sounds juicy!"

"I have a problem," he confessed. "And I don't think I can solve it on my own."

"What do you need?"

"You remember that girl Trixie, right?" he asked.

"Who?"

"The…whore," Hunter clarified, grimacing again. Sukri nodded.

"Yeah, I remember."

"Well, she came to visit last night," Hunter explained. Sukri grinned at him, standing up on one leg and punching him in the shoulder, then sitting back down.

"You got lucky, huh?" she asked. "Nice Crispy!"

"Not really," Hunter countered glumly. "Thing is, I don't really *want* to be with her. But every time she comes…"

"You end up screwing her brains out?" Sukri guessed. Hunter sighed, nodding.

"And hating myself afterward," he finished.

"That *is* a problem," Sukri admitted.

"Tell me about it."

"So you need to get rid of this bitch," she stated.

"She's not a bitch," Hunter protested. Trixie didn't have any control over how she affected others, after all.

"Whatever," Sukri replied. "We'll get rid of her. You said she's coming tonight?"

"I'd bet on it."

"Not with you she's not," Sukri retorted with a sly grin. "Tell you what: I'll stay with you here until she comes, then tell her off."

"Thanks," he replied, feeling suddenly relieved. He smiled at her. "Thanks a lot Sukri. I appreciate it."

"Hey, what are friends for?" she replied. "Come on," she added, patting the spot on the bed beside her. He hesitated.

"Um," he began, staring at the bed. "That might not be such a good idea."

"What do you mean?"

"Remember what happened last time we were on this bed?" he asked. She paused, then shrugged.

"It's okay," she replied. "I'm supposed to be working on resisting emotional influences anyway," she added. "Master Thorius says I'm way too susceptible to emotions."

"Yeah," Hunter agreed. "Vi said the same thing about me."

"Well then we both have to work on it," Sukri stated, patting the bed next to her. "Come on, we'll practice together." Hunter hesitated.

"I don't know…"

"Just sit," Sukri insisted. "What's the worst that could happen?" Hunter raised one eyebrow at her.

"You know damn well what the worst that could happen is," he retorted. Sukri winked at him.

"Trust me," she replied. "It wouldn't be bad at all."

That got a smile out of him, and he sighed, giving in and sitting down on the bed next to her. She threw an arm around him, leaning her head on his shoulder.

"This should be interesting," she said. Hunter nodded, then had a sudden, terrible thought.

"Uh oh," he blurted out. Sukri frowned.

"What?"

"We're both drunk," he replied.

"Tipsy," Sukri corrected.

"And Trixie's coming over," he continued. "She like, *radiates* sex."

"So?"

"What if we...um...*both* get influenced by her?" he pressed. Sukri smirked.

"Well then," she replied. "She'd better be good."

CHAPTER 29

Hunter yawned, rolling over onto his side in bed and staring at the door to his tiny apartment. He froze, then twisted around, half-expecting Trixie to be in bed beside him. But he was alone, thank god. He relaxed, laying on his back and looking up at the ceiling. Sukri had stayed with him as promised, and they'd both had an awful time resisting the temptation his bed had exuded. Sukri had caved first, probably due to the two starfuckers she'd downed at the bar. He'd somehow managed to redirect her, and they'd sat on the bed for god-knows how long until it was *his* turn to crack. Sukri had been all-to-eager to oblige his advances, and they'd ended up making out at the edge of the bed. Sukri had just shoved Hunter down onto his back when there'd been a knock on the door, and Trixie had come in.

Sukri, being terribly cruel, just smiled at Trixie, told her "he's mine bitch," and went to town making out with him. Trixie hadn't even said a word, leaving the apartment. They'd both dissolved into laughter, forgetting for the moment what they'd been doing. It'd been just long enough to break the spell of lust the bed had provided, and they quickly got off it. Sukri had offered to stay, and it'd taken everything Hunter had to turn her down. He didn't want to take advantage of a friend...especially a drunk and artificially aroused friend.

And that had been that.

He sighed, picturing Trixie's expression when she'd seen him and Sukri. He felt like an ass now, knowing he'd hurt her feelings. After all, her feelings were almost certainly genuine, and she was just as much of a pawn as he was. It'd been a bit cruel, what he'd done to her…but his guilt paled in comparison to the relief of knowing that she wasn't going to come back. That he was finally free of that terrible cycle. Strange that he enjoyed his relationship with Sukri – and with Vi – far more than his relationship with Trixie, even though he'd never have sex with them. At least not with Vi, anyway.

Suddenly there was a knock at the door, and Hunter stiffened.

It better not be Trixie, he thought darkly.

The was another knock, and Hunter sighed, getting up and walking to the door. He wished there was a spyglass for him to look through, but no such luck. He hesitated, then opened the door.

"Hey kiddo," Vi greeted.

"Vi!" he exclaimed, backing up and gesturing for her to come in. She did so, glancing around the room.

"Wow," she muttered. "They gave you a shithole."

"Yeah, well at least I get to sleep on a bed," he retorted. She smirked at him, then walked up to the bed. Her eyebrows rose.

"Damn kid," she exclaimed. "Your bed *reeks* of hooker!"

"I took care of it," he informed her. "She's gone for good."

"Like hell she is," Vi retorted, backing away from the bed and wrinkling her nose. "She's gonna be in your mattress for years." She shook her head. "They went all out for you," she mused. She glanced at him, smirking as usual. "You're not going to be able to fold your sheets in a few months."

"You're gross," he retorted, feeling his cheeks flush. She grinned at him.

"Good news is," she stated, "…any girl you bring back here is *definitely* going to put out."

"Yeah, that's called rape," Hunter grumbled.

"See," Vi replied, tousling his hair. "That's why I like you…you're halfway decent."

"Something completely foreign to *you*," he retorted. But he smiled back. "It's good to see you," he added. "I kinda missed you."

"You won't after our next sparring session," she countered. "Let's go," she added, walking to the door. "We've got a job to do."

"What job?" he inquired, following her down the stairs and out onto the docks.

"I'll tell you in a bit," Vi promised.

"My friend Sukri wanted to meet you before we left," Hunter told her.

"No time," she replied. "My client wants this done as soon as possible."

"But..."

"I'll meet her later," Vi promised. "Come on."

Hunter hesitated, then nodded.

"Lead the way."

They left the Outskirts, traveling through Lowtown until they reached the long road leading to the inner gate. There was a carriage in the middle of the street, and a man standing beside it. He waved at them as they approached.

"Morning," the man greeted.

"Morning," Vi replied. The man opened the carriage door, and Vi stepped up and went inside. Hunter hesitated, then followed suit, entering the cabin. It was quite luxurious, with plush leather seats and rich golden wood. He sat down next to Vi; the man shut both doors, then hopped up to the driver's seat, snapping the reins. The carriage moved forward toward the inner gate, which opened slowly, allowing them into the tunnel beyond.

"Getting the five-star treatment, huh?" Hunter inquired. Vi stared at him blankly.

"What?"

"I'm just glad we're not going on foot this time," he clarified. "Much as I enjoyed your death march through the Deadlands."

The carriage stopped at the outer gate, waiting for it to open. At length it did, and the carriage moved forward again, exiting the tunnel. The Deadlands spread out before them, the King's Road rising above it in the distance.

"So what's this mission?" he inquired.

"We're going to take the King's Road past the Fringe," Vi answered. "Then we'll jump the King's Road and make our way through the forest on foot."

"Why?" Hunter pressed. "What's our destination?"

"Apparently the Seekers found the main Ironclad base," Vi replied. "My client wants me to go there and kill an Ironclad."

The carriage reached the King's Road, rolling onto the smooth stone slabs. Hunter raised an eyebrow.

"Just one?" he asked.

"Yep," she confirmed. "A new kind of Ironclad, apparently. One with a glowing blue mane made of gel or something…like the one we saw back at the lake. My client thinks it's their leader. All we need to do is bring back its head."

"Oh, that's it?" he quipped. "That easy, huh?"

"For me," Vi replied.

"Uh huh. Sure," he grumbled. But he couldn't really argue with her. She'd never failed to make good on her word, after all. He turned to stare out of the window at the passing terrain. From here, he could barely see a dark line on the horizon…a suggestion of the Fringe miles away. "So is this glowing Ironclad a different species or something?" he asked. "Did it mutate?"

"Animals and plants in the forest are always changing," Vi replied. "Think about it…they're constantly being exposed to the wills of other species. It's only a matter of time before new variations appear."

"That's why Tykus built the wall?" Hunter guessed.

"Pretty much," Vi agreed. "It was mostly to keep out immigrants."

"Why do they hate immigrants so much?"

"They don't," Vi replied. "They just want to keep their identity. That's why they didn't want me…I was different. I threatened their way of life. They wanted me out…they didn't give a shit if I lived somewhere else. They just didn't want me in the city."

"Because they're racist jerks," Hunter muttered.

"Call them what you want," Vi stated. "If we didn't separate ourselves, we'd all end up diluting each other's traits and customs, until we were all the same."

"You say that like it's a bad thing."

"You hate Tykus because they're all the same there," Vi countered. "Imagine a whole world like that." She shook her head. "There's something to be said for variety."

"Maybe."

"You wanna be like everyone else?" she inquired.

"Hell no."

"Neither do I," she agreed. "I like who I am. I *like* being different." She eyed him critically. "You said you had a people? Back home I mean?"

"Kinda," he admitted. "I'm half black, half white, so I have two."

"So they each have a unique identity, black people and white people?"

"Yeah, sure."

"What would happen if they were asked to give up that identity?" she pressed. "What if black people had to give up their customs, their culture, their identity…and so did white people? What if they all had to become the same?"

"Then we'd all be one people," Hunter answered. "We wouldn't have a reason to hate each other anymore."

"Think that'll ever happen?" Vi pressed.

Hunter considered this, then shook his head.

"Right," Vi agreed. "Glad to hear human nature sucks everywhere."

"So you agree with Tykus," Hunter stated. Vi gave him a look.

"God no," she retorted. "Just because I understand where they're coming from doesn't mean I have to agree with them."

The carriage reached a fork in the road, and the carriage turned left, continuing forward. The forest was clearly visible now in the distance.

"So we kill one of these new Ironclad and take it back home?" he asked.

"Yep."

"Why do they hate people so much?" he pressed. Vi shrugged.

"They're from the forest," she replied. "Anything near the Fringe hates humans."

"Are there any other monsters out there?"

"Plenty," Vi answered. "The Ironclad are the most dangerous ones near the Fringe. There are many others, but the most dangerous ones live in the forest near the Deep."

"The what?"

"The Deep," Vi repeated. "It's in the deep forest…far past the Fringe. Nobody knows much about it, because nobody sane ever goes there."

"Why not?"

"The Deep makes the Fringe look like your world," Vi answered. "The rules of the world are different there, much more powerful. Anything that goes in doesn't come out the same." She shook her head. "The few people that have come back from it…well, let's just say they weren't exactly human anymore."

"Have *you* ever been there?" Hunter pressed.

"Hell no," she replied. "Closest I've been is the Kingdom of the Deep," she added. "They're the closest to the Deep…and still kilometers away. Not even *they* are stupid enough to venture into the Deep, as much as they worship it."

She yawned then, stretching her arms over her head.

"Anyway," she continued, "…we're just going into the regular forest. We'll meet up with a few guides that know where the Ironclad base is."

"Then we just find a glowing Ironclad and decapitate it?"

"Well, there's something else I could do while we're there," Vi admitted. "Something my client would pay dearly for."

"What's that?"

"Don't worry about it," Vi answered. "You'll find out soon enough."

* * *

Sukri wheeled herself into the meeting room of the Guild of Seekers, Gammon walking at her side. They joined Yala and Lucus, who were waiting for Master Thorius's arrival. The two nodded at Sukri and Gammon, but no one said anything. For today, they knew, was their third and final Trial…the last hurdle before formally being accepted as apprentices of the Guild of Seekers.

Sukri sat there, waiting quietly with the others. The silence grew, more uncomfortable with each passing minute. She felt a knot in the pit of her stomach, knowing that whatever their Trial entailed, failure would almost certainly be fatal. No initiate who'd been disqualified had lived…except for Hunter, of course.

Master Thorius appeared, striding through the hallway and stopping before them. He eyed each initiate before speaking.

"Today," he declared, "…is a very special day for you all."

Two more Seekers walked into the room, stopping behind Thorius.

"Today," Thorius continued, "…is the day of your third and final Trial. For those of you who succeed, we offer a guarantee of membership in the Guild of Seekers. You will become apprentices, and the skills, knowledge, and secrets of the guild will be yours." He paused. "For those of you who fail…well, I trust you understand the consequences now."

Sukri glanced at Gammon, who put a hand on her shoulder. She felt a little better, her fear abating, but not completely. She brushed his hand off; her fear was bad enough, but knowing that Gammon was afraid – if only a little – was far worse.

"Come with me," Thorius ordered. He walked back into the hallway, everyone joining behind him, including the two other Seekers. They went back to the lobby, then forward through another hallway, turning this way and that until at last they reached a medium-sized room. It was unlike any Sukri had seen before, with a shallow copper basin on the floor, perhaps ten feet square. Master Thorius turned to them.

"Your third and final Trial begins now," he declared.

The two Seekers strode forward suddenly, circling around them to stand behind Lucus and Yala. They grabbed the two initiates, locking their arms behind their backs.

"Wait, what're you doing?" Lucus demanded, struggling against his Seeker. The Seeker yanked his arms backward roughly, and he cried out, freezing in place.

"For your third Trial," Thorius stated, reaching into his pockets and pulling out a dagger, "…you will demonstrate your loyalty to the Guild of Seekers." He handed the dagger to Gammon. Sukri frowned.

"By doing what?" she asked.

"By helping us disqualify your fellow initiates," Thorius answered, gesturing at Lucus and Yala. Sukri glanced at them, then at Thorius.

"What…"

"You will slit their throats," Thorius interjected calmly. "And watch them die."

The blood drained from Sukri's face, and she turned back to Yala and Lucus. Both of their eyes widened.

"*What?*" Yala blurted out. "We passed the other Trials," she protested. "You can't do this!"

"You didn't pass the Trials," Thorius countered. He gestured at Gammon. "Gammon won the first Trial, fighting valiantly against an Ironclad and surviving. Sukri won the second Trial. You two," he added, gesturing at Lucus and Yala, "…contributed nothing."

"*What?*" Lucus exclaimed. "We…"

"The Guild has chosen," Master Thorius interjected. He gestured at Gammon and Sukri. "You may proceed."

They both stayed where they were.

"Don't do it," Lucus urged. "Don't do this guys…it's just a test. You're not supposed to kill us!"

"That's right," Yala agreed. "That's the test."

"Proceed," Master Thorius repeated, his expression stony.

Sukri glanced up at Gammon, who stared back at her. She saw his Adam's apple rise and fall as he swallowed, saw him turn back to face Thorius.

"This is murder," he protested.

"Indeed," Thorius agreed. "And you would be sentenced to death if anyone found out about it."

"Then we can't do it," Sukri protested. Master Thorius turned to her.

"This is what binds you to the Guild," he explained. "You and every Seeker who has ever passed their Trials."

Gammon shook his head.

"This isn't right," he protested. "I won't do it." Thorius raised an eyebrow.

"If you fail to execute your responsibilities," he replied, "...then your colleagues will be freed, and offered the same conditions for entry into the guild...by killing you two."

"This is bullshit," Lucus blurted out. "Don't do it guys!"

"Indeed," Master Thorius stated. "He *would* want you to spare him. Are you so sure he'll return the favor?"

"You can't do this," Yala protested.

"Proceed," Master Thorius commanded, "...or your roles will be reversed."

"And what if we don't kill them," Sukri said, "...and they don't kill us?"

"Then none of you will become Seekers," Thorius answered.

"What does *that* mean?" Sukri pressed.

"Proceed," Thorius replied, his eyes hardening. "I will not ask again."

"Don't do it," Lucus insisted. "Guys, it's a trick! Remember the last Trial!"

Sukri glanced at Gammon, who stared back at her. She shook her head. This wasn't right...she couldn't kill someone in cold blood. It was murder...and she was not a murderer. Neither of them were.

Gammon hesitated, then put a hand on her shoulder. She felt a sudden calmness come over her, mixed with sad resignation. He withdrew his hand, turning to face Yala. He strode forward, stopping before the woman. Yala stared up at him, her eyes wide.

"Gammon, no," she pleaded, shaking her head. Tears welled up in her eyes. "Gammon, don't do this. I would never do this to you, you know that!"

"Don't do this Gammon," Sukri agreed. "This isn't right." But the big man ignored her, staring down at Yala, his expression flat. He gripped his dagger so hard that his knuckles turned white, then raised the blade, holding it before him. Yala stared at it, her eyes widening, her face turning deathly pale.

"Don't do it big guy," she begged, shaking her head, tears streaming down her cheeks. "Don't do it."

Gammon said nothing, staring down at her. Then he reached forward, grabbing her by the hair and forcing her head back, exposing her neck. He placed the edge of the dagger against her throat, holding it there. His jawline rippled, his lips trembling.

"No Gammon no," Yala pleaded. "No. Please god no. No!"

Gammon turned to Master Thorius, who nodded.

"Gammon, *no!*" Yala screamed.

He turned back to her, then slid the blade across her neck.

Her pale skin gaped open, blood spurting from the great vessels of her neck. The Seeker holding her let go, and Yala fell to her knees, grabbing her throat with both hands, blood spurting between her fingers and streaming down her arms. She made a horrible gurgling sound, dropping one hand to the copper pan below and crawling toward Thorius, blood pouring from her mouth.

Thorius stared down at her impassively.

Yala slipped, falling face-first onto the pan, then got on all fours. The pulsing at her neck grew weaker, and she stared down at the expanding pool of blood around her, her face terribly pale. Her eyes rolled up into her skull, and she collapsed.

Sukri stared at her in horror, her heart hammering in her chest. She watched as Yala's breathing slowed, then stopped. Watched her die lying in a pool of her own blood.

Fuck.

Gammon stared down at Yala, his face pale, his eyes moist. But he stood tall, raising his gaze to face Master Thorius.

"Well done," Thorius stated, nodding at Gammon. He turned to Sukri. "Your turn."

"No!" Lucus shouted, struggling mightily against his Seeker's grip. The Seeker held him easily. "Don't do it Sukri," he begged.

Sukri stared down at Yala's corpse, then realized that Gammon had extended the bloody dagger hilt-first toward her.

"You can do it," Gammon said. "You have to do it."

"You can't kill me," Lucus said. "You can't, it's not right!"

Sukri glanced up at Gammon, swallowing past a lump in her throat. The big guy – her gentle giant, a man who wouldn't hurt a fly – held the hilt of the dagger patiently, waiting. She shook her head at him ever-so-slightly, moisture blurring her vision.

I can't do this.

Gammon put his other hand on her shoulder, and she felt a terrible sadness come over her…and something else. A sudden, intense affection, and a profound protectiveness. A feeling so pure and complete that it made her want to cry. It was beautiful, this feeling. Something she'd been hiding for…

Sukri's eyes widened, and she jerked away from his touch.

"Gammon?" she blurted out. He sighed, grabbing her hand and turning it over, then placing the hilt of the dagger in her palm and closing her fingers around it.

"Do it."

She shook her head, her eyes blurring with moisture.

"I can't," she protested. "This isn't us."

"We can't be us anymore," Gammon countered. "We have to be Seekers."

She turned back to Lucus, who was still struggling, thrashing against his Seeker's grasp. The second Seeker came beside the first, grabbing Lucus's head and forcing it backward, exposing the boy's throat.

"No!" Lucus screamed. "No!"

Sukri took a deep, shuddering breath in, letting it out slowly. Then she put the knife in her lap, gripping the wheels of her wheelchair and rolling herself forward. The wheels hit the edge of the copper pan, and she pushed them hard, forcing the wheels up and over the lip of the pan. She went right up to Lucus, stopping before him.

We can't be us anymore.

"No Sukri," Lucus pleaded, tears dripping down his cheeks. A sob burst from his lips, and he began to cry. "Please. I have a daughter."

She grabbed her dagger, holding it in her right hand. The hilt felt slick against her palm, and she gripped it tightly, her heart thumping in her chest.

"I have a daughter," Lucus repeated, sobbing again. "Don't do this!"

Sukri stared at him silently, her lower lip quivering. She pictured him with his daughter, a young girl smiling up at her father.

He'll do it to you, she thought. *He'll kill you to save himself.*

She grit her teeth, staring down at the knife in her hand, at the gleaming metal of the lethal blade. Then she looked up, nodding at one of the Seekers. A chill ran through her, making the hair on her neck stand on end. It was fear...but not of killing.

In that moment, she was afraid of herself. Of what she was about to become.

"Bring him to his knees," she ordered, surprised at the coldness of her voice. The Seekers obliged, kicking Lucus in the back of the knees, then shoving him downward. They yanked his head back again, and he shrieked, struggling valiantly. But it was no use.

Sukri swallowed past a lump in her throat, then raised her dagger to Lucus's exposed neck, pressing the edge of the blade against his pale skin. She stared at the pulse there, suddenly terrified at how easy it would be to kill him. One simple act, and his life – his memories, his love for his daughter, his very *being* – would fade away forever.

I can't be me *anymore.*

She turned to glance at Gammon, who gave her a sad smile, nodding once.

She closed her eyes, then cried out, yanking the dagger across Lucus's throat as hard as she could.

There was a horrible gurgling scream, and then she felt hot wetness on her hand, trickling down her arm. Something struck her in the chest, and she flinched backward, opening her eyes and looking down.

Her uniform was red with blood.

She dropped the dagger and grabbed her wheels, pulling back on them frantically, her right hand slipping, coated with Lucus's blood. Another spray of hot blood struck her, and she gasped, wheeling herself away quickly. The wheels caught on the lip of the copper pan, and her wheelchair tipped backward. She cried out, feeling herself falling...and then Gammon grabbed her wheelchair, catching it in mid-fall.

He lifted the wheelchair up off of the ground, setting it well clear of Lucus. Sukri stared at her bloody hand and uniform, then turned her eyes to Lucus. Her brain screamed at her not to. To look away.

But she couldn't.

The Seekers held Lucus's arms back, keeping him on his knees. His head was tilted backward at an unnatural angle, the muscles of his neck severed. Blood spurted from his arteries, gurgling sounds coming from his severed windpipe. His eyes were wide with terror, his lips open in a silent scream.

Slowly, agonizingly, the spurting weakened, Lucus's lifeblood draining from him. Sukri watched as it gradually stopped, watched as his life was finally snuffed out. Her heart pounded in her chest, her breath coming in short gasps.

Oh god oh god…

The Seekers let go of Lucus's arms, and he fell forward onto his face with a dull *thump*, never to move again.

Oh god what have I done…

Sukri looked down at her hand, at the hand that'd killed him. The hand coated in his blood. The hand that had murdered an innocent man. Someone's husband. Someone's *dad*.

She stared at that hand, then at the dagger lying on the ground. She had the sudden, mad urge to grab it and cut off her hand. To sever the limb that had done this terrible thing, so that it would no longer be a part of her. She glanced up at Gammon, at her gentle giant, a man who wouldn't hurt a fly. At his big hand, spattered with the blood of an innocent woman.

What have we become?

"Well done," she heard Thorius say.

She turned to him, staring at him numbly. He smiled down at her.

"Congratulations on passing your third and final Trial," he declared. "You are now eligible to become apprentices of the Guild of Seekers…members for life."

He gestured at the Seekers, who grabbed two black bags from the corner of the room, then slid the corpses into them. The Seekers dragged the bodies out of the room. Then Thorius turned to face Gammon and Sukri again.

"Your apprenticeship…your *real* training," he stated, "…begins tomorrow."

CHAPTER 30

Dominus limped down the long hallway toward the Royal Chambers, the *clang, clang* of his cane striking the granite floor echoing off of the walls. He passed row after row of Royal guards as he went, feeling their eyes following him They did not move, did not bow; they lived only for the king. Having spent years absorbing advanced combat skills from the most skilled warriors in the Kingdom's millennia of existence, they were extraordinarily dangerous. Few men in the kingdom could stand against them. A single guard had been known to kill over a dozen armed, skilled opponents single-handedly.

Dominus ignored them, continuing forward. His foot ached terribly, the pain having grown steadily worse over the last few hours. He grimaced, picturing his foot as he'd seen it that morning. The once pale flesh at the site of the amputation had turned bright red, yellow-white fluid oozing from the wound. This despite having finally retrieved the wild Ossae from Vi. A rib from a skarlnex, a small lizard with the ability to heal rapidly, he'd slept with it last night in hopes of absorbing that ability. When he'd woken, he'd half-expected to find his foot having healed somewhat.

How quickly reality had dashed his hopes.

Maybe I need more time, he thought. Some abilities took prolonged exposure to absorb, after all. But he had to be careful; prolonged exposure could result in unpleasant side effects. *Visible* side effects.

At long last, he reached the huge double-doors to the Royal Chambers. The single guard standing before it eyed him stonily, carrying a large hollow scepter in one hand. The guard turned, placing the end of his scepter into a small hole in one of the doors. He placed his mouth on the other end of the hollow scepter, speaking into it.

"The Duke of Wexford is here to see you," he stated.

Moments later, there was a loud *thunk*, followed by a grating sound. Then the doors opened outward, revealing a large room beyond: the Royal Chambers, where Tykus himself had slept for nearly a third of his lifetime. His essence was powerful here; even Dominus, with his formidable will, could feel it.

Dominus strode through the double-doors and into the room beyond.

It was surprisingly small, the king's bedchamber, no more than seven meters squared, the ceiling a mere four meters high. It was by design, of course. The smaller the room, the closer every inch of it had been to the source…to Tykus. The furniture was made mostly of stone, a huge chandelier hanging above a large bed at the far end of the room. The chandelier was beyond ornate, thousands of crystals glittering in the light cast by lanterns bolted to the walls. The bed was more ornate still, its frame made of pure platinum, the densest of metals. The mattress was supported from below by a single large rectangular slab of transparent crystal. Crystal that contained the most valuable single artifact in the Acropolis…indeed, in the entire world.

And there, at the other end of the room, as far from the bed as possible, Conlan was pacing. He was dressed in a simple white, gold, and blue robe, the colors of the kingdom.

"You called for me?" Dominus inquired. Conlan stopped pacing, glancing up at him as if noticing him for the first time.

"Hello father," he greeted. He frowned, as if trying to remember what Dominus had asked. "I did," he replied at last. "Yes."

Dominus just stood there, leaning on his cane and staring at his son.

"It's annoying," Conlan muttered, reaching up to grab the sides of his head. "He's always here, like he's trying to burrow through my skull." He lowered his hands. "I'm fighting him – I am," he added. "It's just exhausting, you know?"

"I can only imagine," Dominus replied. Conlan grimaced.

"You must be enjoying this," he grumbled. "You *are* enjoying this, aren't you father?"

"No," Dominus answered. And to his surprise, he meant it. As egotistical as his son could be, watching him suffer...watching him struggle for his life, for his very *soul*...was difficult. Far more so than he'd expected it to be.

"Yes, well," Conlan muttered. "I'm strong. I'm still myself."

"You are," Dominus agreed. Still, he could already see some subtle changes. Conlan's hair was a shade lighter, a bright golden hue. His skin was paler, his chin stronger. And he could swear that Conlan was a little taller. The Ossae were imposing themselves on him, slowly but surely. The transformation had already begun.

"No one has ever resisted him for this long," Conlan continued, still pacing. "When I'm done proving my strength, when I've proven that Tykus can't have me..."

He trailed off, stopping in mid-stride, staring off at nothing. Then he blinked, turning to Dominus.

"What was I saying?"

"When you've proven that Tykus can't have you," Dominus prompted. Conlan nodded.

"I'll be king, father. *I'll* be king. I've spent a great deal of time thinking about the policies I'll enact. How I'll restructure the kingdom." He shook his head. "Things have been stagnant for too long, father," he added. "It's time for change."

"Perhaps so," Dominus stated noncommittally.

"We *have* to change," Conlan insisted. "Other governments have. Look at the Kingdom of the Deep," he continued. "They're not afraid of using wild artifacts. Of making people better, stronger, faster." He shook his head. "What happens when everyone is doing that but us? We'll be left behind!"

"No," Dominus retorted, putting a hand on Conlan's shoulder. "When everyone else does that, we won't fall behind. *They* will. And we'll be the last ones standing. The only kingdom left that will keep humanity alive."

* * *

Hunter shifted his weight in his seat, his left butt cheek numb after hours of sitting. Vi, who hadn't said much of anything since their last conversation, was staring out the window. The Deadlands had long since given way to the forest, the trees on either side of

363

the King's Road standing some thirty feet away. Far enough, Hunter imagined, to avoid corrupting the carriage…and the people within.

"We're getting close," Vi stated suddenly.

"Hmm?"

"To the jump point," Vi clarified. "Another half kilometer and we should be there."

"Then what?"

"We go through the forest on foot," Vi answered. "And meet up with our guides."

"Guides?"

"Seekers my client hired," Vi explained.

"Wait, I thought hiring you was illegal," Hunter pressed. She'd been the one to tell him that it was against the law to hire non-guilded Seekers, after all. "Wouldn't the guild refuse to work with you?"

"My client can be very persuasive."

It wasn't long before the carriage slowed, then stopped, just as Vi had predicted. The driver hopped down from his seat, opening Vi and Hunter's doors. Vi hopped out, and Hunter joined her, stepping onto the King's Road. He watched as the driver and Vi walked to the rightmost edge of the road. There was a ladder there; the driver retrieved it, lowering it over the edge, hooking the end on some grooves in the side of the King's Road. Vi swung over, climbing down the ladder.

"Come on kid," she prompted.

Hunter waited for her to climb down a bit, then stepped up to the edge, peering over. It was a twenty-foot drop to the ground below. He was suddenly reminded of his profound respect for heights, and hesitated. He saw Vi glance up at him as she climbed down; she rolled her eyes at him.

Hope I fall right on you, he grumbled to himself.

He crouched down, turning his back to the forest, then clung onto the side of the road, lowering one foot, then the other onto the rungs of the ladder. Then he grabbed the ladder with his hands, one at a time. Once he was actually *on* the ladder, it wasn't so bad. He made his way down, reaching the bottom and standing beside Vi. Moments later, the ladder rose as the driver hauled it back up onto the road again, leaving them stranded in the forest.

Vi nudged him, then began walking perpendicular to the road at her usual brisk pace, weaving between the trees. Hunter sighed, jogging up to her side and struggling to match her pace.

"What now?" he asked.

"My client hired quite a few Seekers to find the main Ironclad base," she answered. "Seems like after the attacks on Tykus, the kingdom isn't satisfied with just defending themselves against the Ironclad. Now they want to destroy them."

"What's that got to do with us?"

"Maybe nothing, maybe everything," Vi replied. "We're supposed to meet up with a couple Seekers that found the base," she explained. "They'll provide the intel we need to complete our mission."

"To bring back that thing's head."

"Right," Vi confirmed. "And by killing the Ironclad leader, I'll have helped the kingdom to significantly weaken the Ironclad, and the military will do the rest."

Hunter shook his head at her.

"Do you *ever* doubt yourself?" he asked. Vi arched one eyebrow.

"Now why would I do that?"

"Ass," he grumbled.

"I'm serious," Vi insisted. "Why would I doubt myself?"

"Because you're human," Hunter replied. "Everyone doubts themselves sometimes."

"Not me," she retorted. "Everything I do, I believe I can do. I know I can do it because I've accomplished everything I've put my mind to."

"Well lucky you," he grumbled.

"Bullshit," she replied. "Luck has nothing to do with it. Confidence is *learned*, kiddo. Real confidence, that is. Success breeds success. If you never try, you'll never get good at getting good."

Hunter said nothing, following along beside her. He felt the urge to contradict her, but he had nothing to say...not really. After all, he'd accomplished very little in his life. Vi was stronger, faster, smarter, more observant, and better at just about everything compared to him. He didn't know shit, and she did.

Which, as much as he hated to admit it, meant that she was probably right.

"Work hard, Hunter," Vi stated, putting a hand on his shoulder. "Nothing worthwhile is given to you. If you don't earn something, it ain't worth shit."

Hunter nodded, and Vi fell silent, walking at her customary quick pace. Hunter focused on matching her stride, his boots crunching on the twigs and fallen leaves on the forest floor. After a few minutes, Vi turned to him.

"From now on, no talking unless I say so."

He nodded, and they continued for what seemed like hours. He fell into a sort of trance, his mind wandering aimlessly. Eventually he heard running water in the distance. He glanced at Vi.

"What's…" he began, but Vi lifted a finger to her lips, glaring at him. His mouth snapped shut.

Pay attention, he scolded himself. *Stop being an idiot.*

He followed her silently, weaving through the trees for what seemed like over a mile, the sound of running water growing steadily louder ahead. Vi veered toward the sound, and after a few more minutes he spotted a break in the forest. It was a large stream, he realized, maybe thirty feet wide and rather shallow. As they got closer, he saw that the water was moving to the right, in the opposite direction they'd taken the carriage. The water looked to be about waist-deep, and moving rapidly downstream.

Vi turned left as she approached the shore, walking perpendicular to it. Hunter followed close behind, concentrating on keeping up with her. His endurance was improving, he realized. Whether from daily practice, or from absorbing a little of her stamina, he wasn't sure.

"We're close," she murmured. "Shut up," she added when he was about to reply. He grimaced, shaking his head and smiling ruefully. She'd said not to talk unless she said so, not if she decided to talk to him. He *did* need to pay attention better.

After a quarter mile or so, Hunter noticed that the grass underfoot had changed, now jet-black. It crunched underfoot, as if he were stepping on broken glass. He glanced at Vi questioningly.

"Must be from the Ironclad," she guessed. "The grass absorbed their will."

They continued forward, and it wasn't long before Hunter spotted two men in the distance, standing by the stream. As Vi led him closer, he saw that they were dressed in simple gray leather armor, warhammers strapped to their backs, swords at their hips. One was very tall, and bald, with a slight dent on the right of his skull. He was quite muscular, with a light brown goatee and strong eyebrows. He walked forward to meet them, nodding at Vi.

"Morning," he greeted. His voice was gruff and coarse, and hardly inviting. Vi stopped before him, crossing her arms over her chest. "Vi, I presume." He glanced at Hunter. "Who's this?"

"My apprentice," she answered. She nodded at Hunter. "Go on, don't be rude. That's my job."

"I'm Hunter," he greeted, extending a hand. The man stared at it, but didn't move to shake it.

"Traven," the man replied. He gestured at the guy next to him, a shorter, stocky man with short brown hair and a smooth-shaven face. "This is Edgar."

"Hi," Hunter greeted, waving at him like an idiot.

"Let's get to the forest," Traven said, turning away from the stream and walking toward the trees. "Don't want to stay out in the open too long." Everyone followed the man into the woods, and they walked a few hundred feet before stopping.

"So you're the best the guild could come up with," Vi observed, smirking at the two. "Times must be tough." Traven glared at her.

"We're the ones who found the main Ironclad base," he retorted. "Plenty of 'better' Seekers died trying. We didn't."

"Lucky you," Vi replied.

"Careful us," Traven corrected. "This place is crawling with Ironclad," he added.

"Don't see any," Vi observed.

"They live underground," Edgar piped in. "Like the fucking bugs they are, burrowing tunnels." He gestured behind him. "Main entrance is south of here, at the mouth of a cave on the southwest of a large hill near this stream. That's where they come in and out of."

"Lots of 'em," Traven added darkly. "We're talking hundreds of the damn things, if not more."

"And the new Ironclad?" Vi asked. "The one with the glowing mane?"

"The big one?" Traven inquired. "We saw it go in through the main entrance a few days ago. It hasn't come out since."

"We assume it's still in there," Edgar added.

"Saw it kill a few Seekers," Traven stated darkly. "The ones dumb enough to hang out too close to the entrance."

"A Seeker can usually go toe-to-toe with an Ironclad," Edgar added. "But this one wiped the floor with several at once. He's huge, and he's smart. A lot smarter than the others."

"So what's our way in?" Vi inquired.

"The main entrance is a no-go," Traven answered. "There's a side entrance further north, but it's heavily guarded. The only way in is through a back entrance to the southeast, near the stream."

"Go on."

"The water table is pretty high here," Edgar piped in. "The back entrance is an underground stream that flows into the main stream," he added, gesturing at the stream they'd walked away from. "We assume they use it as a water source, because we haven't seen them drinking from the main stream.

"The back entrance is guarded," Traven added. "By three Ironclad. They take rotating eight-hour shifts."

"How do we know the back entrance connects with the main tunnels?" Vi asked.

"We've seen some Ironclad with distinct scars go in," Edgar answered. "Then come out the main entrance."

"And you're assuming this is the main Ironclad base?" she pressed. Edgar nodded.

"There's a few more caves nearby," he replied. "But not as much foot traffic in and out. Plus, that big Ironclad – the glowing one – it must be their leader. All the other Ironclad defer to it. We've even heard it speaking, giving orders."

"So it does talk," Vi stated, clearly surprised. Traven nodded.

"Sometimes," he confirmed. "Mostly they communicate using some sort of sign language."

"Tell me about the back entrance."

"There's a short waterfall there," Traven explained. "Flows out into the stream. From what we can tell from a distance, there's a tunnel that angles upward into the hill. We can't tell much more than that."

"So we'll be going in blind," Vi grumbled. "Wonderful."

"We figure if we kill the three guards posted there at the beginning of their shift, we'll have eight hours to get in, do what we need to do, and get out."

"Should be plenty of time," Vi agreed.

"We'll guard the entrance," Edgar stated. "And kill any Ironclad that might wander by and see that the sentries aren't there."

"You sure you're up to that?" Vi inquired, arching an eyebrow. Edgar crossed his arms over his barrel chest.

"I've killed a few," he replied. "We both have."

"When you get what you came for," Traven continued, "...you'll come out the rear entrance and go back to the King's

Road. The carriage will be there, and will drop the ladder. You climb up, hop in the carriage, and that's that."

"Simple enough," Vi replied. "When does the next Ironclad shift start?"

"In a half hour," Edgar answered.

"Well then," Vi replied, turning to Hunter. "We'd best get to work."

CHAPTER 31

Sukri allowed Gammon to push her wheelchair through the streets of Lowtown toward the docks of the Outskirts in the distance, her eyes on her lap. Neither of them had said anything since they'd left the Guild of Seekers a few minutes ago. Since the Trial.

She stared down at her lap, at her hands resting there. She'd been allowed to bathe after the Trial, scrubbing Lucus's blood from her hands. She clenched and unclenched them; though she could feel them, could move them, they felt as if they weren't attached to her. As if they were someone else's.

Sukri heard Gammon clear his throat behind her, and lifted her gaze, realizing they'd made it to the ramp leading up to the docks of the Outskirts. The smell of the man-made river flowing below the miniature city reached her nostrils, immediately familiar and comforting. It was the smell of home. Gammon brought them up the ramp, and Sukri couldn't help but picture the big man standing over Yala, his dagger to her throat. The look on his face when he'd murdered her in cold blood. Gammon, her gentle giant, a man who wouldn't hurt a fly.

She closed her eyes, taking a deep breath in, then letting it out slowly. She felt her chest rise, felt the weight of the Seeker medallion resting there. She opened her eyes to stare at it, wondering why they'd been ordered to wear it…and what it was doing to them.

What it was doing to *her*.

They made their way through the Outskirts, eventually arriving at their apartment. Luckily it was on the first floor; Gammon stopped her wheelchair before the front door, opening it, then wheeling her inside. She saw the familiar living room with its U-shaped couch, and half-expected to see Kris sitting on it. But of course he wasn't. The room was empty.

"Do you want to sit on the couch?" Gammon asked, breaking the silence. Sukri shook her head.

"I just want to go to sleep," she muttered.

Gammon complied, wheeling her into her bedroom, stopping the wheelchair before her small bed. He put a hand on her upper arm then.

"Let me help you," he said. Sukri shied away from his hand, shaking her head. Gammon pulled his hand back. "What's wrong?" he asked. Sukri glared at him.

"What's wrong?" she retorted incredulously. "Are you really asking me that?"

Gammon just stared at her, a wounded expression on his face. But she didn't care.

"You murdered Yala," she accused. "I murdered Lucus. In cold blood. And you're asking me what's *wrong?*"

"Sukri…"

"And you didn't even hesitate!" Sukri continued, jabbing a finger at him. "You just slit her fucking throat!"

"I had to," Gammon protested.

"Did you?"

"I did," he insisted. "If I didn't do it, you wouldn't have. We both would have died."

"Oh yeah?" she retorted. "How do you know that? Yala and Lucus might have let us live, you know. Or didn't it occur to you that they might not be goddamn murderers?" she added.

"You heard what Master Thorius said," Gammon countered gently. Sukri glared at him, suddenly pissed that he was still so calm. That even after everything that had happened, he was still as unflappable as ever. That was the old Gammon, the Gammon she knew. "Even if they spared us, we would all have been disqualified," he explained. "You know what happens to initiates that are disqualified."

Sukri said nothing, knowing he was right.

"I couldn't do nothing," Gammon continued. He lowered his gaze. "If I didn't kill Yala, you would have died."

"So would've you," Sukri countered. Gammon glanced up at her, then shrugged.

"I could have lived with that," he replied. "But not with you dying." He sighed. "I did it to save you, Sukri."

Sukri stared at him silently, remembering how he'd touched her before handing her his dagger…and the feelings he'd revealed to her then.

"You're in love with me," she realized. Gammon stared at her silently for a long moment, then nodded.

"I am."

"How long?" she asked. Gammon sighed.

"Since the moment I laid eyes on you."

Sukri lowered her gaze to her lap, processing this. Then she looked back up at him.

"You hid it from me all this time," she realized. "I'm like a sponge for emotions, and yet you managed to hide it."

"I only touched you when I had it under control," he explained.

"Gammon, we've known each other for *years*," she protested. Gammon shrugged again, saying nothing. "Why didn't you tell me?" she pressed.

"I knew you didn't feel the same."

Sukri said nothing. It was true, after all. She loved him as a friend, there was no doubt about that. But as a lover? She'd never even considered it.

"I had to protect you," Gammon explained.

"Is that why you became a Seeker?" she asked. Gammon frowned at her.

"What?"

"Kris said you never wanted to be a Seeker," Sukri explained. "He was right, wasn't he?"

Gammon hesitated, then nodded.

"He was."

"So you joined the Seekers because of me," she said. Gammon nodded again. Sukri shook her head slowly. "Great Gammon," she muttered. "Just great."

"If I hadn't," Gammon replied, "…that Ironclad would've killed you."

"Yeah, well maybe that would've been for the best," Sukri muttered.

"No," Gammon insisted. "Sukri, you always wanted this. To become a Seeker."

"Yeah, well that was before they made me murder people," she retorted. She gestured at him. "And now I've turned *you* into a murderer," she added. "How am I supposed to live with that, Gammon?"

"You didn't make me do anything," he countered. "I made my own decisions."

"You did it for *me*."

Gammon said nothing.

"You were the only one of us who liked working in the sewers," Sukri stated. "You could've worked there the rest of your life and been happy."

"That's true," he admitted.

"Why?" Sukri pressed. "That was the shittiest job in the city," she added. "Literally." He shrugged.

"I didn't mind it," he replied. "I got to spend time with you guys. I didn't need anything more than that."

Sukri swallowed, knowing the unspoken truth. He hadn't needed anything more, but *she* had. Or at least she'd thought so at the time. What she wouldn't do to have her old life back, to have Kris and her gentle giant with her, laughing and going out for drinks. Hanging out and enjoying each other's company. Carefree again.

But she'd never been happy with what she'd had. She'd never appreciated it. No, she'd always dreamed of something better. Of being someone other than who she was. Of being a part of something greater.

Of being a Seeker.

And now she wanted nothing more than to just be herself again. But it was too late for that. There was no going back now. And now, because of her, Gammon had given up his happy life. He'd done something he never would've done if it hadn't been for her. She hadn't just ruined her own life, she'd ruined Gammon's.

"I wish we'd never done this," she muttered bitterly. "I wish we'd never tried to become Seekers."

"Don't say that," Gammon snapped, his tone suddenly sharp. Sukri flinched, staring at him wordlessly. He'd never talked to her like that. Never talked to *anyone* like that. "It's an honor to be accepted into the guild," he continued. "Many people tried to do what we did," he added. "They failed, and we didn't."

373

She just stared at him, feeling numb. In that moment, she hardly recognized him. She glanced down at the Seeker medallion resting on his chest, feeling the weight of her own medallion on hers. She had the sudden urge to take it off. To throw it as far away as possible.

What is it doing to us?

Gammon's shoulders slumped, and he reached out, touching her shoulder. She felt a familiar calmness come over her, settling her mind. But there was something new there, a sadness. A sense of resignation that had never been there before.

"I'm sorry," he murmured.

She felt a sudden affection for him then, and pulled away from his touch.

"What's wrong?" he asked.

"When you touch me, I feel…" she replied, trying to find the right words. "I feel love for you. But it isn't my feeling, it's yours."

"I can't help the way I feel," Gammon stated.

"Neither can I," she countered. "That's the problem, Gammon. Sometimes I can't tell which feelings are mine and which aren't."

"I'm not touching you now," he reasoned. "How do you feel about me now?"

Sukri hesitated, focusing inward. She *did* feel affection toward him. That was nothing new; she loved him as a friend, her gentle giant. But she'd never thought of him as a lover. And right now, she didn't want to contemplate such a thing.

"I just want to go to bed," she muttered. Gammon sighed, lowering his gaze. Then he offered a hand.

"Let me help you into bed."

"It's okay," she replied. "I can do it myself."

"All right," Gammon stated. He hesitated, then gave her a weak smile. "See you later?"

"Yeah."

He stood there for a moment longer, then left her room, closing the door behind him. Sukri lifted herself from her wheelchair, transferring over to her bed. She laid down, pulling the covers over her, then turned onto her side, closing her eyes.

And then she wept.

CHAPTER 32

Dominus leaned against the balcony railing, watching as Conlan paced before him. The sun overhead hid behind a few clouds, casting a shadow over the inner courtyard. He studied Conlan silently, noting how disheveled he looked...far worse than before. His son appeared as if he hadn't bathed in days, or shaved for that matter. He was more agitated as well, his pacing more frantic.

"I can *feel* him," Conlan complained, continuing to pace. "Even out here. He shouldn't *be* here," he added. "This is supposed to be my break!"

Dominus said nothing, putting most of his weight on his left foot. His right foot hurt even more than before. When he'd looked at it this morning, he'd been dismayed to find black spots forming further up on his instep, the rot spreading despite sleeping with his Ossae that night. It was either worthless, or his disease was too advanced to be slowed, much less stopped. He suspected the latter; the redness had spread from the edges of his wound to the entire foot, and even the ankle, tendrils of infection crawling slowly up his leg. He'd woken to soaked sheets this morning, evidence of having broken a fever last night. He'd hoped for more time...*needed* more time.

And now Vi – and that strange Ironclad's remarkable ability to regenerate – were his only chance at getting it.

Conlan stopped pacing suddenly, turning to Dominus.

"Do you know what it's like?" he asked. Before Dominus could answer, Conlan tapped his own temple with one finger. "He's in *here*," he stated. "Wherever I go now, he's here. I can feel him

375

father," he added, tapping his head viciously. "Eating away at my brain."

"Conlan…" Dominus began.

"You have no idea how powerful he is," Conlan interrupted, resuming his pacing. "I thought I could fight him. I thought I was strong. I *am* strong," he added. "But he's so much stronger, father."

"He is," Dominus agreed. There was no "I told you so" in his tone, no pleasure in being proven right. As much as he disliked his son, he still loved him. Watching him suffer like this – dying slowly but surely, losing himself to Tykus – was torture for both of them.

"I need to get out of here," Conlan muttered. "I need to clear my head. I can't think in this place."

"What place?" Dominus inquired, if only to keep Conlan talking.

"This damn fortress," Conlan answered.

"This is normal," Dominus stated calmly. "Every king goes through it."

"It's not normal for *me*," Conlan retorted. "You don't know what it's like," he continued, shaking his head. "It should've been *you* going through this, not me."

"You know why I didn't do this," Dominus stated wearily. Conlan sneered.

"Right," he muttered. "For the 'stability of the kingdom,'" he added snidely. "You're so full of shit father."

"Watch your tongue," Dominus shot back automatically, his tone cold.

"Or what?" Conlan shot back. "You don't scare me anymore, father. I'm the king."

"Not yet you're not."

"But I will be," Conlan retorted. "And when I am…" He trailed off then, staring into space. Then he turned to Dominus again. "Will I even remember this?" he asked. "Will I remember anything about me?"

Dominus grimaced, lowering his gaze.

"Will I?" Conlan pressed, taking a step toward him. "Or is everything I know going to die along with me?"

"Son…"

"Is any part of me going to be left?"

Dominus sighed, shaking his head. Conlan had entered the next phase of the transformation. He knew now that he would not survive, would not live to see whatever grand plans he'd concocted put into action. He had no hope now, only despair. This was the most dangerous part of the transformation…when would-be kings considered the unthinkable.

Suicide.

"I don't know," he admitted, raising his eyes to meet Conlan's.

"I thought you knew *everything*," Conlan retorted, glaring at him. Dominus sighed. Conlan's tone, once able to irritate him to no end, only made him feel sorry for the boy now.

"I know you're angry at me, but you know you would've had to go through this anyway, when I passed," Dominus reminded him gently.

Conlan said nothing, resuming his pacing. Dominus pushed off of the railing, intercepting Conlan. He hesitated, then put a hand on his son's shoulder. He felt a sudden affection for the boy, something he hadn't experienced in well over a decade.

"I wanted to be here for you," Dominus confessed. "I didn't want you to have to do this alone."

Conlan stopped, turning to stare at his father. His eyes were moist, his expression desperate. In that moment, he reminded Dominus of when he'd been just a boy…vulnerable, scared. Desperate for his father to tell him that everything was going to be okay. Dominus had been so hopeful then, that his son would grow up to be more like him. To have someone who would understand him implicitly, as only family could.

Conlan stepped in, leaning his head against Dominus's chest. Dominus hesitated, then wrapped his arms around his son, taking a deep breath in, then letting it out. As much as Dominus hated to admit it, his son *was* dying. Tykus was taking over, minute by minute, day by day. The man who was his son would slowly fade away, evicted from his own mind. His essence – his very soul – would be no more.

And for the good of the kingdom, Dominus had to watch his son die, piece by piece, until there was nothing left.

"I'll be here for you," Dominus murmured, embracing his son for the first time since he'd left Wexford…since he'd been a rebellious teenager, rejecting his father's wisdom, filled with foolish notions of his own.

"Don't leave me," Conlan pleaded.

"I won't," Dominus promised. "I'll be with you son. To the very end."

Hunter, Vi, and the two Seekers strode slowly and quietly through the woods near the shore of the stream to their right, their eyes on a large hill ahead. The hill dropped off in a cliff twenty feet high facing the stream, and on its face was the mouth of a cave. A stream of water gushed out of the cave in a waterfall only two feet high, falling to a short, narrow stream that joined the larger stream after a few dozen feet. Vi stopped, hiding behind a tree, and the Seekers did the same. Hunter followed suit, peering through the forest at the hill. He spotted three large, black creatures there, facing away from the mouth of the cave. He felt a chill run down his spine.

Ironclad.

Traven and Edgar glanced at Vi, who studied the three beasts carefully. They were, to Hunter's surprise, armed with warhammers, and each of them carried two huge shields in their lower pair of hands. They wore no armor, of course, seeing as they were already covered in the natural equivalent to platemail. Vi studied them for a moment longer, then turned to Traven and Edgar.

"You stay here," she ordered. "I'll take care of them."

"Are you crazy?" Traven retorted. "You can't take on three armed Ironclad by yourself!" But Vi ignored him, striding forward, going from one tree to the next, hiding for a moment, then continuing forward. Hunter smirked at Traven.

"Watch," he counseled, "...and learn."

Vi stopped behind a tree a few dozen feet from the nearest Ironclad, whose back was turned to her. She withdrew her mace, waiting. The other Ironclad turned to look at something past the stream, and that's when she made her move, bolting from behind cover and sprinting toward the nearest Ironclad. She leapt into the air, swinging her mace at the back of its head. The mace struck the creature's skull, snapping its head forward and sending it stumbling to the ground. Before its head could even bounce off the dirt, she'd put the mace back at her hip, withdrawing her longsword and driving its tip right into the back of its shattered skull, impaling it.

The second-nearest Ironclad turned, spotting her...just as she closed the gap between them. She flipped her sword around, grabbing it by the blade with both hands and swinging the hilt at the thing's face. The cross-guard smashed into its left eye, dropping the beast like a stone. She flipped the sword around again, grabbing the hilt with both hands and thrusting the point of her blade through its shattered eye socket.

The third – and last – Ironclad turned to face her, raising its shields and warhammer. She sprinted at it, reaching down to toss dirt at its face. It raised one shield to block the dirt, swinging its warhammer at her. But she dodged the blow easily, sliding underneath the shield it'd raised and swinging her mace into its knee. The beast's leg buckled, and it fell onto its knee as Vi continued past it, sliding to a stop, then turning around and running up its back, raising her mace and chopping downward at the back of its head.

The beast fell to the dirt, Vi's sword impaling its skull from behind moments later.

She withdrew her sword, sheathing it in one fluid motion. Then she strode casually back toward Edgar and Traven. The two Seekers stared at her silently, their mouths agape. Vi smirked at them.

"All right boys," she stated. "Class is over. Any questions?"

They just stared at her, then at the bodies of the Ironclad. It hadn't even been a minute since she'd left to kill them.

"God *damn*," Edgar breathed.

"Come on Hunter," Vi prompted, nodding at the cave entrance. She started walking back toward it, and Hunter followed behind her. She glanced back at Traven and Edgar, flashing them a grin. "Stay here and look pretty, boys," she added. "We'll be back."

* * *

Icy water soaked into Hunter's boots as he stepped into the stream pouring from the mouth of the cave, his feet going numb almost instantly. He grimaced, wading into the ice-cold water. It wasn't long before it reached up to his knees, drenching his pants. He trudged forward, his eyes on Vi's back as they waded up to the cave entrance. The current was powerful here, enough so that he had to struggle to stop himself from being swept off his feet...a feat made even more difficult by the fact that the rocks underfoot were dangerously slippery.

Vi reached the short waterfall at the mouth of the cave, climbing up onto the leftmost ledge, where the flow of water was the weakest. Then she extended a hand to Hunter. He waded up to the ledge, grabbing her wrist. She pried his hand loose with her other hand, grabbing his elbow.

"Grab my elbow too," she ordered. He did so, and she hauled him up the ledge to the mouth of the cave easily. She let go then, continuing forward into the cave itself. Hunter followed close behind, cleaving to the leftmost wall. The flow was slower there, the water shallower than in the middle of the cave. The cave narrowed slightly as they made their way forward, forming a long tunnel. They passed beyond the beams of sunlight streaming into it, engulfed by relative darkness. It took a moment for Hunter's eyes to adjust; he peered ahead, seeing the tunnel curving upward and to the right. He couldn't hear anything over the roar of water gushing through the tunnel. The rocks underfoot, covered with an inch or two of water, made the going treacherous. One slip would send him right onto his butt, and potentially into the deeper part of the stream. He had no doubt that the powerful current would carry him right out of the tunnel.

He steadied himself with one hand on the wall of the cave, stepping carefully forward. Vi, as usual, moved much more quickly and surely than he. She might as well have been taking a stroll on a sidewalk.

When I grow up, he thought, watching her move, *I want to be like her.*

They followed the tunnel as it curved rightward and upward, growing steadily darker and steeper as they went. It was just as well that there was a narrow ledge above the water at the leftmost wall ahead; without it, he doubted they would've been able to continue. They stepped onto it, clinging to the rock wall as they crab-walked up the incline. Eventually it became so dark that Hunter could barely see at all.

"I can't see," he whispered. "Do you have a light?"

"I can see," Vi whispered back, turning to face him. He swore her eyes glowed a little in the darkness, like a cat's. "No lights. We don't want to draw attention to ourselves."

"Yeah, you're right," he muttered. "Guess I'll die from falling instead."

"I'll guide you," she countered. She paused then. "Anyone ever tell you you're a pussy?"

"Says the only person here who has one," Hunter shot back.

"Now I've got two," she replied. And even though he couldn't really see her, he was sure she was grinning.

They kept going, Hunter crab-walking one step at a time, ensuring that there was a wide enough ledge to support him as he went. After a few minutes of this, he could swear he saw light ahead. Vi slowed, then stopped, and he barely made out the silhouette of the back of her head.

"Lantern ahead," she whispered. "No talking from now on unless I say so." She turned to face him, her eyes iridescent in the faint light. "You speak, you die."

Hunter nodded once, swallowing in a dry throat. He suddenly wished she'd left him with Traven and Edgar, doing this mission herself. After all, he was probably just slowing her down. Not that he could do anything about it now.

They crept forward silently, the ledge underfoot growing wider as they went, until they didn't need to crab-walk anymore. The stream took a sharp right turn into a waterfall that fell from a hole in the rightmost wall a few feet up, while the tunnel continued forward, the floor mercifully dry. Hunter let out a breath he hadn't realized he'd been holding as they left the stream behind. Ahead, he saw a lone lantern bolted to the wall, the flame within flickering slightly, casting a warm orange glow through the tunnel. There were no Ironclad to be seen, to his immense relief.

"Weird," Vi whispered, her voice nearly inaudible with the roar of the waterfall. Hunter looked at her questioningly. She pointed at the tunnel ahead. "These walls aren't natural," she explained. Hunter studied the walls, realizing she was right; the walls were made of irregular stone blocks that had been mortared together. This was an artificial tunnel, built into the hill. He stepped forward, feeling something crunch underfoot. Looking down, he saw a few bones lying on the tunnel floor.

Human bones.

"Don't do that again," Vi whispered, glancing down at his foot. He lifted it from the bones – a rib cage – and stepped carefully around it. She continued forward then, one step at a time, her eyes on the tunnel ahead. It curved to the right, still rising in a steady incline. They passed the lantern, and Hunter spotted another one further ahead. The lanterns were crude compared to those in Tykus, but only slightly so. There was no way the Ironclad could have made them, simple beasts that they were; people must have built these tunnels before the Ironclad had arrived. More bones littered the floor, and they stepped around them carefully.

Onward and upward the tunnel went, until at last it ended abruptly, opening up into a small cavern. Unlike the tunnel, this appeared natural, with rough stone walls. Several more tunnels branched out from the cavern, appearing man-made, like the tunnel they were in. Vi stopped suddenly, and Hunter stopped behind her, peering over her shoulder. His blood went cold; there, standing in the small cavern, were two Ironclad. Unlike the ones outside, these were not armed. One of them raised a hand, moving its fingers rapidly in some sort of sign language. The other nodded, turning down one of the other tunnels and vanishing from sight.

The remaining Ironclad stood there, facing away from Hunter and Vi.

Vi tapped Hunter on the shoulder, then pointed down. She pointed at herself then, and then at the Ironclad. Hunter nodded.

She bolted into the cavern suddenly, making a mad dash toward the Ironclad, her boots barely making any noise on the rocky floor. It was only by the time she was a few feet away that it heard her, turning around.

And by then, it was too late.

She whipped her mace right into its face as it turned its head, knocking it off its feet and onto its back. Its head struck the floor, bouncing off…just as her mace smashed into its face again, sinking into it with a sickening *crunch*.

Vi gestured for Hunter to come forward.

He walked quickly into the cavern, trying to move as quietly as possible. She grabbed one of the Ironclad's arms, and motioned for him to grab the other. They pulled it back into the tunnel they'd entered through, until they reached the stream. Hunter helped Vi shove the thing into the water, and watched as it slid downstream, vanishing down the tunnel beyond. Vi nodded at him, then walked back up the tunnel to the cavern, Hunter following close behind. To his relief, the cavern was empty, the other Ironclad nowhere to be found. There were two other tunnels, one to the left, and one straight ahead. The other Ironclad had gone down the tunnel to the left; Vi glanced down each, then pointed to the leftmost tunnel.

"We go that way," she whispered. "If I tell you to run," she added, "…get back to the stream and take it down to the exit." Hunter nodded, his guts squirming at the thought of the mission going horribly wrong. She strode toward the leftmost tunnel, and he followed close behind, their footsteps making not a sound. The tunnel had lanterns bolted to it, and again the passage appeared man-made, rising upward and curving slightly to the left. Vi slowed, inching forward silently, putting a hand up for him to stop. He did so, resting one palm on the cool stone wall.

Then he felt a crawling sensation on the back of his hand, and drew it back sharply, shaking it. Something small fell off, landing on the ground and crawling quickly away. Hunter peered at it; it was black, barely visible against the dark floor. An insect, he realized.

A small black beetle.

He stared at it, then noticed more of them crawling along the floor…and the walls. Dozens of them. He glanced down at his boots seeing a few climbing up his ankles. He grimaced, swatting them away, then stepping on one of them. But when he lifted his foot, the beetle scurried away, unharmed.

He glanced up, realizing that Vi was a few yards ahead, creeping forward, her hand on her mace. He rejoined her, staying a few feet behind. The tunnel ended ahead, opening up into another cavern. No, it was a room, Hunter realized; the walls were made of mortared stone, more lanterns bolted to them. It was perhaps eight feet by twenty feet, with an arched ceiling ten feet high. There was a single gate at the other end, made of vertical metal bars…and an Ironclad stood before it, facing away from them. It grabbed a large keychain from its hip, inserting one of the keys and turning it in the lock with a *click*.

Then it paused, glancing backward.

Vi pulled Hunter behind cover just in time, and he pressed himself against the tunnel wall, his heart pounding in his chest. He felt a tickling sensation on his scalp, and resisted the urge to swat at the beetles he knew were crawling in his hair. He waited, hearing a creaking sound as the gate opened.

Vi burst forward, sprinting toward the gate!

Hunter scrambled to catch up with her, making a mad dash behind her. The Ironclad stepped through the open gate and into the room beyond, closing the gate behind it. Vi reached the gate just in time, jamming her mace between the gate and the wall to stop it from closing all the way. Using the mace as a lever, she pried the door open, then ducked low as the Ironclad swung at her, cracking it in the knee with her mace. It fell forward, and she grabbed one of its arms, yanking it backward through the gate. With two more swings of her mace, she bashed the back of its skull in.

Then, as before, she had Hunter help her drag the corpse all the way back out of the room, down the curved hallway into the first chamber, then back to the stream. They dumped the body, then retraced their steps, arriving back in the room with the now-open gate. Hunter peered beyond the gate, spotting a much larger room…deserted, thank god. Vi stepped through the gate, Hunter following close behind. The room he found himself in was at least thirty feet square, with large stone columns supporting a high, arched ceiling. There was furniture here, a large rectangular table with oversized wooden chairs surrounding it. Paintings hung from the walls…some of wild landscapes, others portraits of people. He studied one of them; it looked like a portrait of a family, a quaint house in the background.

Hunter noticed Vi studying the room – staring at the columns supporting the ceiling. He glanced at them; there were symbols carved on them, symbols that looked vaguely familiar, though he couldn't place where he'd seen them. She shook her head slowly.

"This doesn't make sense," she whispered. He glanced at her questioningly. "These letters," she explained. "It's the same language we use in Tykus."

She stared at the symbols for a moment longer, then turned in a slow circle, taking in the room. There were two closed doors leading out of it. She walked up to one of them, pushing it open slowly and peeking through. She pulled back quickly, shutting it and shaking her head.

"Other door," she mouthed, walking up to it. She cracked it open slowly, peering through. Then she nodded, opening the door all the way and gesturing for Hunter to follow. They stepped through into a long, narrow hallway, a single door at the other end. Vi strode silently down the hallway, Hunter following her. They'd nearly reached the door when he heard a creaking sound behind them.

Vi stopped, glancing back. She shoved Hunter to the side, his back striking the wall. He stared at the door they'd come through, goosebumps rising on his arms.

Thump, thump.

Vi stepped between Hunter and the door, drawing her mace from her hip. The door opened slowly, two black armored hands gripping the edge. Vi shoved Hunter back just as the Ironclad stepped through, its black eyes glittering in the torchlight.

It froze.

Vi burst forward, swinging her mace at the thing's head, but it jerked backward, slamming the door shut. Her mace smashed into the wood, splintering it with a terrible *crack*. She cursed, grabbing the door handle and yanking back on it, but it didn't budge. An ear-piercing wail came from beyond the door, echoing through the tunnel.

"*Shit!*" Vi swore.

Hunter heard a creaking sound behind him, and turned…just in time to see an Ironclad burst through the door. It lunged at him with terrifying speed, and he jerked backward, unsheathing his sword in one smooth motion, slashing at the thing. But the blade was too long for the narrow hallway; it struck the wall to his left, bouncing off. The force of the impact jerked the hilt right out of his hands, his sword dropping with a clatter to the floor.

"Vi!" he shouted, reaching down and grabbing his sword…just as the creature grabbed him.

He heard Vi curse, heard a loud *crunch* behind him. The Ironclad wrapped its arms around Hunter, lifting him bodily off the floor and crushing him against its armored chest. It hauled him back toward the door it'd come through, squeezing him so hard he could barely breathe. He gasped, sheathing his sword and grabbing at the thing's hands, trying to pry them off him.

The Ironclad pulled him through the doorway, kicking the door closed. He saw more Ironclad swarming toward the door on either side, barricading it with their massive bodies. The Ironclad holding him tightened its grip, forcing the air from his lungs. He struggled futilely, trying frantically to squirm out of its grasp, to take a breath in. His head began to swim sickeningly, his vision blackening.

Hunter heard Vi's muffled shouting, saw more Ironclad swarming around him as he was pulled backward, his boots scraping against the floor. Another loud wailing sound echoed off the walls.

And then his vision faded, and darkness claimed him.

CHAPTER 33

The Royal Guard watched as Dominus limped down the long hallway, stopping at last before the door to the Royal Chamber. Conlan had requested he visit again in a few hours after their conversation on the balcony earlier. It'd been the first time in years that he'd seen his son so vulnerable. That they'd talked – *really* talked – without devolving into yet another argument. Afterward, a weight he hadn't realized he'd been holding lifted off of his shoulders, and he'd felt a sense of peace that had surprised him.

He smiled at the memory, not caring if the guards saw it. Let them wonder why an old man was smiling to himself.

He leaned on his cane, nodding at the guard standing before him, who placed his hollow scepter in the small hole in the door to the Royal Chamber, announcing Dominus's arrival. Moments later, the door opened, revealing Conlan standing on the other side, clad in his royal robes. He smiled at Dominus, seeming relieved to see his father. Dominus smiled back.

"Come in, come in," Conlan urged. Dominus complied, stepping into the room. The guard closed the door behind them. "Thank you for coming," Conlan added.

"How are you?" Dominus inquired. Conlan paused, staring off into space for a moment. Then he refocused on Dominus.

"I'm sorry?"

"How are you," Dominus repeated.

"I'll be better once this transformation is complete," Conlan answered crisply. "As much as I trust the dukes are maintaining the kingdom in my absence, you and I both know what can happen when men are given my power, even temporarily."

Dominus stared at Conlan, taken aback.

"Present company excluded, of course," Conlan added with a wry smile, slapping Dominus on the shoulder. "The Dukes of Wexford have ever been my staunchest allies."

"Indeed," Dominus murmured. He paused. "So you're doing well, Conlan?"

"Hmm?"

"Conlan," Dominus repeated, feeling a knot in the pit of his stomach. The transformation couldn't possibly be complete yet. He hadn't said goodbye to Conlan…hadn't had a chance to talk one last time.

"Yes?" Conlan pressed.

"You're doing well?" he repeated. Conlan shook his head, his shoulders slumping. He began to pace.

There he is, Dominus thought, feeling relieved.

"As well as a dying man can," Conlan muttered. "Tell me father, am I a fool to fear my own death?"

"It is not foolish to fear death," Dominus stated.

"Yes, it's the unknown, isn't it?" Conlan mused. "The great unknown, a future shared by all. Death. Nothingness." He shook his head. "Now I die so that this…" He gestured at himself in disgust. "…tyrant can live." He continued pacing. "You know what happens if I walk out of this room, hmm? If I leave before my mandatory break?"

Dominus held his tongue.

"I've tried it," Conlan confessed. "They pull me back in, my guards. Grab me and pull me right back in. So here I am, a prisoner awaiting his death sentence."

"Conlan…"

"Can you imagine a worse death, father?" Conlan inquired. "A more hideous way to die? To watch your very soul be torn bit by bit from your body?" He shook his head. "I had a *life*, father. I had a future. So many things I wanted to do, so many things I *could* have done. But thanks to you, I never got that chance."

"I didn't make the rules," Dominus protested.

"Bullshit!" Conlan retorted angrily. "These *rules* are all you care about and you know it!"

387

"That's not true," Dominus protested. "I care about you."

"Not as much as you care about Tykus," Conlan retorted. He sneered at Dominus. "Try to deny it."

Dominus said nothing. *Could* say nothing.

"My life is worthless because of Tykus," Conlan continued. "The man died thousands of years ago, yet we keep bringing him back. Reliving the glory days, when a true Legend ascended to the throne." He shook his head. "And what, pray tell, is so damn important about a goddamn Legend?"

"You know the answer to that," Dominus replied. "His will preserves the human race."

"Just because a man can bend another man to his will, that makes him important?" Conlan inquired. "A man's importance is in proportion to his ability to influence others? So what of everyone else…the millions born since who have weak wills? Do their lives mean nothing?"

"Of course not," Dominus replied. "They all play a role."

"Ah yes," Conlan muttered. "I remember your lectures well father. Every man has a role." He sneered. "You and your damn bees. People aren't insects, father!"

"You think I don't know that?"

"You treat them like they are," Conlan retorted. "You're treating me like one," he added. "Placing me in my role. Sucking all the meaning out of my life. Killing your own goddamn son."

"You're not just a role to me," Dominus argued. "You're my son."

"Then why did you let this happen?" Conlan demanded. "Why didn't you give me a chance?"

"I didn't have a choice," Dominus protested. Conlan snorted.

"You *chose* to cede the crown to me," he shot back. "You *chose* to make that inane suck-up your heir. What's his name?"

"Axio."

"And you could have given him the crown instead," Conlan argued. "You could've made him your heir before the king died, and he would've taken the throne, and I would've taken the Duchy. But you didn't do that, father. You didn't *want* to do that."

Dominus just stared at Conlan, unable to reply. He was right, after all.

"You didn't want me to be the duke," Conlan accused, jabbing a finger at Dominus's chest. "You did everything you could to prevent that. You *killed* me to prevent that."

"I gave you a great honor," Dominus retorted. "To be the embodiment of the king!"

"To become a dead man," Conlan sneered. "You're all living in the past, resurrecting old men with old ideas. This whole government is sick. It's *wrong*. A bunch of old men clinging to their glory days, terrified of change."

"Of losing our humanity," Dominus corrected. "You fear the loss of your identity," he added. "Why can't we fear the loss of ours?"

"I'm afraid of losing my *soul*," Conlan argued. "You're afraid of losing the color of your skin…your hair, your blue eyes."

"You know why…"

"You cling to this one image of Man," Conlan interrupted, "…this pinnacle of creation. It's bullshit, father. We're not meant to stay the same. We're supposed to adapt, evolve…improve."

"You *are* improving," Dominus stated coldly. Conlan grimaced.

"And you're clinging to the old ways," he shot back. "Saying they're better because they're comfortable. The future is unknown and frightening, isn't it father?"

"The future *is* known," Dominus countered. "We create it," he added. "We're creating it right now."

"Times change father," Conlan argued. "And we need to change with them. Everyone else outside of this damn kingdom will."

"So you would have us destroy everything we've created?" Dominus asked. "After millennia of safeguarding the very essence of humanity – an Original who was a Legend, purely human – you'd have us just throw it all away?" He threw up his arms. "For what?"

"For a chance at making humanity *better*," Conlan answered. "The Kingdom of the Deep is doing it," he added. Dominus rolled his eyes.

"Oh come on," he retorted. "Don't even mention those…*freaks*." He glared at Conlan. "Is that what you want? To turn men into animals? We can all become savages and lose everything that makes us *us*?"

"Not everything," Conlan countered.

"You're a fool," Dominus spat. "You think you know everything, but you know nothing."

Conlan smirked.

"Do I now father?" he stated. "I'd beg to differ. I think you'll find I know a great deal." He strode toward Dominus, stopping less than a meter away and clasping his hands behind his back. "I know what you've been up to…dallying in forbidden artifacts."

Dominus blinked, taking a step back.

"I know that *you*," Conlan continued, stepping forward again and jabbing a finger into Dominus's chest, "…have quite the collection now." He sneered. "Tell me father…have you started experimenting with wild artifacts yet?"

Dominus swallowed in a dry throat, a chill running through him. Conlan's smile broadened, and he nodded to himself.

"I knew it," he gloated. "The great Duke of Wexford, nobly sacrificing his son to preserve the kingdom, to save humanity…all the while corrupting his own." He shook his head. "How does it feel to be a hypocrite, father?"

Dominus said nothing, knowing that to admit what he'd done would be suicide. He couldn't imagine that Conlan would betray him, but in his current state of mind…

"How could such a thing happen?" Conlan mused, resuming his pacing. "I mean, how could the purest of men, the very Duke of Wexford, be led so astray?"

"These are baseless lies," Dominus growled. Conlan stopped pacing, rolling his eyes.

"Oh please father," he retorted. "Don't be stupid." He smirked again, in that maddening way he had. "I bet you don't even realize why you're doing it," he guessed. "You have no idea, do you?"

"I don't know what you're…"

"Bullshit!" Conlan snapped. "You started 'corrupting' yourself because of me, father."

"What?"

"I told you," Conlan stated. "My will is ever-so-slightly stronger than yours. You started dabbling in forbidden artifacts right before you sent me away, didn't you?" he guessed. "You started to realize my effect on you, and you threw me out of Wexford to save yourself from becoming more like me."

"Nonsense."

"Is it?" Conlan pressed. He gave Dominus a broad smile. "Take heart father. Even after I'm gone, you'll always have a part of me," he added, walking up to Dominus and putting a hand on Dominus's shoulder. "Inside of you."

"I'm nothing like you," Dominus spat, grabbing Conlan's wrist and yanking the man's hand off of him.

"Oh yes you are," Conlan retorted, that maddening grin still on his face. "And as long as you're alive, you'll never be able to get rid of me."

Dominus stepped forward, shoving Conlan backward with one hand. Conlan stumbled, falling onto his butt on the floor.

"You're a fool," Dominus growled. "You've always been a fool." He shook his head, glaring down at his son. "What have you accomplished in your life? Hmm? What great deeds have you done to earn that pathetic ego of yours?"

Conlan got to his feet, striding forward and shoving Dominus back. Or at least he tried to; Dominus dodged to the side, using Conlan's momentum against him and throwing him onto the ground. He pointed the butt of his cane at Conlan.

"You're a sad little man," Dominus muttered, watching as Conlan scrambled to his feet. "A pity you couldn't be more like Axio." He shook his head at his son. "He's more of a son to me than you ever were."

Conlan rose up to his full height, his chest heaving, his eyes moist.

"That's because you never wanted a son who could question you," he retorted acidly. "You never could stand to be challenged," he added bitterly. "You always needed to be the wise, know-it-all father...you never learned how to treat me as a man!"

Dominus snorted derisively.

"You?" he retorted. "A man?" he smirked. "You're not a man, Conlan." He pointed his cane at the large bed at the other end of the chamber. "*He's* a man. You? You're just an impotent boy, all talk and no action." He sneered at Conlan. "By the time Tykus was your age, he was already king."

"*I* am king!" Conlan shouted, jabbing a finger at his own chest.

"No Conlan," Dominus replied. "You aren't. You never will be." He smiled then, pointing at the bed again. "But he will be."

"Will he?" Conlan retorted, walking up to Dominus, his fists clenched at his sides. "Will he, father?" He stopped a foot from his father, his chest rising and falling, his eyes locked on Dominus's.

"Oh yes," Dominus replied, holding his ground. "And when he finally murders what little remains of your pathetic soul, I'll finally be able to be proud of my son."

Conlan stared at Dominus, his knuckles turning white. He turned away from his father suddenly, storming toward the leftmost wall of the chamber.

"I'm not dead yet father," he shouted, reaching the wall. Various weapons hung on hooks on the wall, and Conlan reached up for a warhammer, taking it from the wall. He turned to Dominus then, gripping it tightly.

"Are you trying to threaten me?" Dominus inquired, putting his thumb over the head of his cane, at a slight depression there. He pressed down, and the shaft of his cane separated from the head, revealing the cane-sword hidden within. He drew the blade outward, holding the shaft in his left hand, the sword in his right. He was hardly worried. The boy was a passable fighter, but nothing extraordinary.

"Not you, father," Conlan replied. He turned toward the bed then, striding up to it and kicking the mattress off of it, exposing a pure crystalline slab below. Suspended in that slab was a whole skeleton, its skull facing upward, its jaw agape in an otherworldly scream.

The bones of Tykus. The Ossae of the Legend.

"Conlan!" Dominus shouted, a bolt of sheer terror striking him. "What are you doing?"

Conlan ignored him, walking up to the side of the bed, then lifting the hammer high over his head. He swung it downward with all of his might, the head of the hammer smashing into the crystalline slab…right above Tykus's skull. The hammer bounced off, the crystal cracking with the force of the blow.

"No!" Dominus cried, hobbling forward. "Stop!"

"I'm not dead yet," Conlan shouted, raising the hammer up above his head again. "I still matter!"

He swung the hammer downward again, and this time the crystal cracked further, a chunk of the slab at the very edge breaking off and falling to the floor.

"Conlan no!" Dominus yelled, reaching Conlan at last. Conlan heaved the warhammer above his head a third time, his eyes wild, and Dominus cried out in horror. Conlan ignored him, bringing the hammer back, then grunting as he swung forward and downward.

Dominus lunged forward, thrusting his sword into Conlan's back. The blade passed through him, burying itself to the hilt in his flesh.

Conlan stumbled forward, the hammer slipping out of his hands and striking the far edge of the crystalline slab, chipping it. He gasped, falling forward to brace his hands on the slab, his eyes wide with shock.

Dominus stared at the sword in his hand, his breath catching in his throat.

What have I done?

He pulled the sword out quickly, as if trying to reverse what he'd done. But blood gushed from the wound, forming a rapidly expanding crimson stain on Conlan's robes. Conlan rolled onto his back, sliding down the side of the bed to sit on the cold stone floor. He clutched at his chest, blood oozing from between his fingers, staring up at his father in disbelief. He coughed, pink spittle dribbling down his chin.

Dominus stared at him mutely, letting go of his cane-sword. Or at least he tried to; when he glanced down at his hands, it wasn't there...he'd already placed it back in its sheath. Like the attack before it, it'd been pure reflex...the result of years of exposure to powerful artifacts.

What have I done?

He stared at his son again, then found his eyes moving to the crystalline slab, to the skull of Tykus suspended within. He breathed a sigh of relief, his shoulders slumping; the skull was still intact, as was the rest of the skeleton. He turned to face Conlan again, dropping his cane and kneeling before his son.

"Why?" he asked, shaking his head. "Why would you do such a thing?"

Conlan coughed again, blood spattering the front of Dominus's shirt. He shook his head.

"How," he asked, his breath coming in short gasps, "...could you...do this...to me?"

"You tried to destroy the Ossae!" Dominus protested, placing his hands over Conlan's wound and pressing on it. "What was I supposed to do?"

Conlan shook his head, a bitter smile on his lips.

"You could have...pushed me."

Dominus swallowed past a lump in his throat, shaking his head mutely. Tears blurred his vision, and he blinked them away.

"I didn't mean to," he said. "It just...happened."

"No," Conlan retorted, falling into another fit of coughing. "It didn't."

"It did," Dominus insisted.

"I always loved you," Conlan stated, grimacing as he shifted his weight. "It didn't matter...how angry I was. I still...loved you."

"I love you too," Dominus replied, tears streaming down his cheeks. He wrapped his arms around his son, pulling him into an embrace. He could feel Conlan's breath on his ear.

"Not as much," Conlan mumbled, "...as you love Tykus." Dominus frowned, pulling away and staring at Conlan.

"I had to protect the kingdom," he protested.

Conlan just stared at him, his breathing rapid, sweat pouring down his pale skin. His eyelids fluttered, and Dominus gripped the boy's shoulders tightly, shaking him.

"No Conlan," he cried. Conlan's eyes refocused on him.

"You saved him," Conlan mumbled, giving another weak cough. His eyelids fluttered again, and Dominus shook him a second time.

"Conlan..."

"You saved him," Conlan repeated, his breathing slowing. "You saved your...past," he added. The corner of his lips curled upward. "By killing your future."

And then, as his father watched, Conlan's eyes glazed over, staring off into nothing, his last breath rattling in his throat. Dominus stared at his only son, watching as the last wisp of life left his body.

Then he pulled the boy to his breast, embracing him tightly, and wept.

CHAPTER 34

Hunter groaned, opening his eyes.

He found himself in a small room with mortared stone walls, facing a single wooden door. He looked down, realizing he was sitting in a wooden chair; four huge black hands gripped him from behind, holding him fast to the chair by his shoulders and hips. He struggled against them, but it was hopeless; the hands were far too strong.

He looked forward, at the door not ten feet away, trying to remember how he'd gotten here. He vaguely remembered the hallway he and Vi had been in, the Ironclad grabbing him from behind. And then...and then...

He couldn't remember.

Clunk.

The door swung inward, something *huge* stepping through. A massive Ironclad, its head nearly brushing against the ceiling, with a glowing, pale blue mane of gel-filled membrane rising like a mohawk from its head, a broad, glowing tail hanging between its thick armored legs. It shut the door behind it, stepping forward and staring down at Hunter.

Hunter stared up at those horrible eyes, that grotesque face, and felt his breath catch in his throat. The beast looked identical to the one who'd attacked him at the Gate so long ago.

The thing bent over until its head was level with his, gripping two of its hands on the armrests of his chair. Its hot, putrid breath blew in Hunter's face, making him want to gag.

"WE MEET," it growled, its voice deep and guttural, each word forced from its lips as if it were painful to do so. "…AGAIN."

Hunter stared at it, his eyes widening, a chill running through him. It couldn't be the same Ironclad he'd met…he'd shot that one in the face, and Alasar had crushed its head. Twice.

"YOU ARE…THE ORIGINAL," the thing growled. It was a statement, not a question. Hunter hesitated, then nodded. He swallowed in a dry throat, realization coming over him.

This is their leader, he realized, his heart pounding. *The one we're supposed to kill.*

"YOUR…NAME?"

"Uh…" he mumbled. "Hunter."

The Ironclad made a low, guttural sound deep within its throat, its eyes locked on his. Hunter stared back at it, breathing through his mouth, the stench of its breath nauseating.

Where the hell was Vi?

"YOU CAME…THROUGH THE GATE?"

Hunter nodded, and the thing let go of the armrests of his chair, rising up to a standing position. It stared down at him.

"WHY?"

He blinked.

"What?"

"WHY DID…YOU GO THROUGH…THE GATE?"

"To find my mother," Hunter answered. The Ironclad just stared at him, and he cleared his throat nervously. "She found the Gate years ago, and went through it. I came after her."

The Ironclad leaned over again, its head inches from his. It rested its hands on his arms, making some sort of gesture with one of its other hands. The arms holding Hunter to the chair slipped away. Light from the lone lantern in the room reflected off the leader's eyes, embedded in wet, sunken sockets. Hunter resisted the urge to pull his arms away from its grasp.

"COME," it growled.

It stood up suddenly, letting go of Hunter and turning to open the door. It stepped through, using one hand to flash rapid signals to the Ironclad standing behind Hunter. Hunter hesitated, then stood from the chair, watching as the leader walked into the room beyond the doorway, its glowing tail swinging behind it.

He glanced back, seeing a half-dozen Ironclad standing at the other end of the room, staring at him.

"Guess I don't have a choice," he muttered.

He turned back to the leader, then walked through the doorway, following it into the room beyond. His eyes widened; a huge cavern opened up before him, a truly massive cave. The ceiling rose upward in a dome over fifty feet above his head, a circular hole at the very center. A large waterfall fell from this, cascading down into a large, shallow circular pool in the middle of the cavern. The waterfall obscured a small island in the center of this pool, the roar of water crashing into the pool almost deafening. Sunlight streamed through the hole in the ceiling, glowing beams striking the island below, dust swirling like fireflies in their light. The pool drained into a narrow stream that flowed rapidly down an incline in the cavern floor to the left, vanishing into a small tunnel in the rock wall.

And there, heaped up against the walls of the cavern, were bones. *Lots* of bones.

Hunter stared, hardly believing his eyes.

They were *human* bones, he realized. Countless skeletons piled several feet high against the walls. More bones were strewn across the cavern floor, but none were near the pool.

Jesus.

The huge Ironclad strode forward toward the shore of the shallow pool, stopping before it and turning to look at Hunter. Hunter hesitated, then followed behind the thing, glancing behind him as he walked. The half-dozen Ironclad behind him were walking through the doorway into the cavern, and more Ironclad strode through several tunnels hewn into the cavern walls. They formed a loose circle around Hunter and their leader, stopping to stare at them.

Then, to a one, they dropped to one knee, bowing their heads.

The leader's gaze swept across the kneeling Ironclad, then turned to face Hunter. It reached out with one hand, placing it on Hunter's shoulder.

"WELCOME," it growled, its voice barely audible over the roar of the waterfall behind it. "MY..."

And then its head snapped to the side with a loud *crack*, its hand slipping away from Hunter's shoulder. It stumbled to the side, barely keeping its balance.

Hunter stumbled backward, his eyes widening. There, sliding to a halt on the cavern floor beside the huge Ironclad, was a very familiar person.

"Vi!" he cried.

"Catch!" she shouted, tossing a sword at him. He caught it by the hilt, and she threw him his bow. He caught this too, slinging it over his back. The huge Ironclad turned toward her, its jaw caved in on one side, blood pouring from its mouth.

It roared, a horrible gurgling sound that echoed through the chamber. The Ironclad surrounding them got to their feet, rushing inward toward Vi!

"Watch out!" Hunter warned. He flipped his sword around so he was carrying it by the blade, stepping forward to intercept one of the Ironclad before it got to Vi. But the leader shoved him backward, standing between him and Vi. Vi sprinted toward the nearest Ironclad, dodging as it swung at her, then smashing it in the face with her mace. It stumbled backward, and she leapt at it, spinning around and back-kicking it in the chest. It flew backward, slamming into two Ironclad behind it. All three tumbled to the ground.

A fourth Ironclad rushed at Vi, reaching out for her with all four hands, and she ducked underneath them, swinging her mace into its knee. It tripped, falling face-first into the cavern floor. Vi chopped downward at the back of its head, cracking its skull, then switched to her longsword, thrusting the blade deep into its skull.

Hunter tried to step out from behind the Ironclad leader, but the massive beast barred his way with one arm. He gripped his longsword tightly, his heart pounding in his chest.

The Ironclad leader shouted something unintelligible, its mangled jaw hanging uselessly.

Two more Ironclad rushed at Vi, and she ran toward one of them, dropping to slide on her back at the last minute, passing right between its legs. She got to her feet, spinning around and smashing it in the back of the knee in one smooth motion. It fell onto its back, Vi's mace cracking it in the temple in mid-fall.

The other Ironclad reached her, kicking her in the flank.

Vi grunted, flying onto the ground and rolling on her side for a few feet. She got to her hands and knees, then stood, clutching her injured side.

"Little help here?" she called out.

Hunter hesitated, staring at the leader's broad back. Then he flipped his sword around, grabbing it by the blade in both hands. He grit his teeth, then swung it as hard as he could at the back of the leader's head.

The cross-guard slammed into the thing's armor, bouncing off harmlessly.

Shit!

It turned to face him, slapping his sword to the side, knocking it out of his hands. He froze, waiting for it to pulverize him…but it just turned back to watch Vi. Hunter hesitated, then reached down, picking up his sword by the blade.

The Ironclad who'd kicked Vi rushed her again, and she turned to it, swinging her mace at its head. But it blocked the blow, grabbing her by the front of her uniform and lifting her right off the ground. She reached out with her free hand, sinking her thumb into one of its eyes.

It roared, releasing her and stumbling backward, covering its injured eye with one hand.

Another two Ironclad rushed at her from either side, and she spun around, dodging one of the Ironclad's punches and smashing it in the temple. Hunter slipped out from behind the Ironclad leader, rushing toward the other Ironclad attacking Vi. Hunter swung the hilt of his sword at its head with all his might, the cross-guard smashing into its temple. It fell to the ground, sliding to a stop in front of Vi.

"Took you long enough," Vi grumbled.

"You're welcome," Hunter replied.

The leader tried to speak again, but only a gurgling sound came out. Vi turned to face the beast.

"Stay close," she told Hunter. Then she charged the leader, leaping into the air and swinging viciously at its head, so fast her mace was a blur. The Ironclad raised an armored forearm to intercept the blow, the mace bouncing off it with a loud *crack*. Vi used the momentum from the ricochet to spin around, dropping to a crouch and swinging at its knee.

Again, it lowered one forearm, blocking the blow. Then it kicked at Vi with one massive foot.

She dodged the blow, swinging straight upward, right at its chin. It blocked it with another forearm, reaching out with two other hands and grabbing the front of her uniform, picking her up and tossing her backward like a rag doll. She flew into the air, tucking her knees and executing a backflip…and landed right on her feet, her green eyes locked on the leader's. She smirked.

"Not bad," she admitted.

Another Ironclad ran at her, and she spun around, whipping her mace in a tight arc and smashing the thing in the temple. It dropped like a stone, sliding on his belly on the rocky ground. Without so much as a pause, she charged at the Ironclad leader, feinting with a swing at its knee, then spinning around in a full circle and clipping the leader's jaw again, snapping its head to the side. Vi followed with another low swing at the thing's knee, but it blocked it with one forearm, the mace bouncing off harmlessly.

Hunter saw his chance, and ran up to the leader, gripping the blade of his sword tightly and swinging the hilt at the back of the thing's knee as hard as he could. The blow struck true, and the Ironclad's knee buckled, sending it stumbling backward.

Vi leapt at the thing, smashing it in the face with a horrible *crack*.

The leader fell backward, landing in the shallow pool, water shooting upward and outward from the impact. It splashed Hunter, the icy water soaking through his clothes instantly.

"Watch out!" he cried, spotting two more Ironclad rushing at Vi. These had warhammers and carried two shields, like the ones outside.

"Take one," she ordered, turning to face the one to her right. Hunter ran at the other one, intercepting it before it could get to Vi. It stopped, facing him, its shields raised. It stared at him, its warhammer clutched in one big hand.

Then it lowered its weapon, trying to step around him to get to Vi. Hunter blocked its path, looking for a weak spot in its defenses. But with both shields raised, he didn't have much of a target.

He heard a *thump* behind him, followed by a loud *crunch*, and glanced back to see the other Ironclad on its back, Vi standing over it.

"Any time now," she pressed.

Hunter heard a splashing sound, and turned toward it. The Ironclad leader was standing in the pool near the shore, water streaming from its armored body. Its glowing mane cast the water around it in a pale blue hue.

"STOP!" it shouted.

Hunter felt an arm grab him from behind. It was the other Ironclad…the one who hadn't attacked him. He spun around, tearing away from its grasp. It reached again with its one free arm, trying to grab his sword. He jerked it out of reach, then ducked low, gripping his blade tightly and swinging under the thing's shields, hitting its right ankle with his cross-guard. It lurched to the right, and he ran right at it, slamming his shoulder into one of its shields. He bounced off, stumbling backward…but the Ironclad, already off-balance, toppled over, landing on its back.

Hunter sprinted forward, leaping on the thing's chest, then swung his sword overhead, chopping downward at the thing's face. The cross-guard crushed its left eye, sinking into its socket.

The Ironclad *howled*, swinging its shield at him, striking him in the left side. He was thrown to the ground, landing on his right shoulder…and nearly impaled himself with his own sword. He grunted, pain shooting through his left shoulder, and struggled to his feet.

The Ironclad leader stood there in the pool facing Vi, the water lapping at its lower legs. It raised one of its four arms, flashing a rapid series of hand signals to the Ironclad Hunter had felled. That Ironclad rose to its feet, backing away, clutching at its ruined eye.

Vi faced the Ironclad leader, her mace gripped in one hand.

The leader stepped backward until he was halfway between the island and the shore. More Ironclad ran out of the tunnels in the cavern, swarming toward Vi, but their leader made a motion with one hand, stopping them in their tracks. Then he gestured at Vi to come forward.

"Time for a swim then," Vi decided.

She stepped into the pool, the water up to her thighs, and strode slowly toward the Ironclad. The water glowed with the light of its mane and tail, blood dripping from its mouth, staining the water red. It waited, watching silently as Vi approached. She stopped a few feet away from it, circling slowly. Then she burst forward, swinging her mace!

…and stopped, pulling the attack back.

The leader didn't react to her feint, standing there with its arms at its sides. Vi smirked, continuing to circle. Then she feinted again, lunging forward to swing at his upper thigh, then pulling it back. But then she changed direction, swinging upward – right at its chin. The Ironclad managed to block the blow at the last minute, intercepting it with its forearm. The force of the blow knocked his arm upward, and she swung again, using the ricochet to swing her mace down, then up in a circle over her head, bringing it down on its face. It blocked the blow again, with the same forearm. The armor there crumpled inward, blood spurting from the exposed flesh underneath.

The leader grunted, backing up a step, then swung one arm through the water, creating a huge wave that struck Vi in the face and chest. It lunged forward then, its arms held out wide to grab her. Vi leapt to the side at the last minute, spinning around and swinging her mace.

It struck the back of the thing's head with a terrible *crack*, sending it face-first into the water.

She swung again, striking the back of its head, driving it into the water. She leapt up, chopping downward in another vicious swing, her mace smashing into its skull. Again and again she struck, water flinging off of her mace with each upswing, sparkling in the beams of light coming from high above. Hunter watched, his heart soaring.

Yes!

Then the leader burst out of the water, slamming into Vi and making her stumble backward. She caught her balance – just as it spun around, swinging wildly with two of its arms, using the other two to splash water at her face. At the same time, Hunter saw its leg burst out of the water, its foot slamming into Vi's chest…right as her mace smashed into its face. She flew backward, plunging beneath the water.

Hunter swore, grabbing his bow from his back. He drew an arrow, aiming for the thing's head. He let it fly just as the leader lunged at Vi, and the arrow struck its temple, bouncing off its black armor, but jerking its head to the side. The blow distracted the thing for long enough for Vi to get out of the way of the thing's attack.

She faced the beast defiantly, her green eyes almost iridescent as she stared the Ironclad down.

Hunter drew another arrow, aiming at the leader again. He saw movement in his peripheral vision, and turned, spotting more Ironclad entering the chamber. His heart leapt in his throat, half-expecting them to swarm toward Vi, but they just stood near the edge of the cavern, doing nothing.

Why aren't they attacking?

The leader circled around Vi, its eyes locked on hers. Neither of them made a move for each other, continuing to circle until the leader was standing near the island in the center of the pool, his back to the waterfall.

Hunter strode to the edge of the pool, keeping his arrow on the bowstring. If he could distract it again, while Vi was attacking…

He drew the bowstring back, then fired.

The arrow flew straight and true, shooting over the pool and striking the leader right in the forehead. Its head snapped back.

Vi rushed forward, leaping at the monster, her mace crashing down on its upturned face. The Ironclad fell back, its head vanishing into the waterfall behind it.

Vi swung again, her mace disappearing through the waterfall. Again and again she swung, the leader's arms jerking with each blow.

Then she brought her mace up above her head, heaving downward, her muscles rippling with the effort. Her mace struck with a horrible *crunch*, the sound echoing through the cavern.

The Ironclad's arms spasmed once, then again…and then went still.

Vi reached into the waterfall with one hand, pulling the Ironclad's head back out of it. Its face was utterly destroyed, the center crumpled inward. She stepped behind it, bracing her hips against the island, the waterfall falling around her shoulders. She reached into one of the pockets of her uniform, pulling out a large, serrated knife and bringing it to the thing's neck. She began sawing at it, the blade cutting slowly but surely into its armor there.

Hunter glanced back at the Ironclad in the room, expecting to see them charging toward the pool to save their leader. But still they just stood there, watching.

Vi's blade cut through the thing's armor at last, biting into its flesh, blood spilling down its neck and chest. Still she worked, sawing viciously until the blade was nearly through. Then she put the knife away, grabbing its head with both arms and twisting, then heaving upward.

The Ironclad's head tore off its shoulders, its body slumping forward into the pool, swallowed whole by the water. Vi stood there before the waterfall, holding its head high above her own, its ruined face displayed for all the other Ironclad to see.

And then her body jerked forward.

She looked down, her eyes wide, her mouth agape. There, protruding from her belly, was a long, silver blade. It glimmered in the sunlight, blood dripping from its edge.

"*Vi!*" Hunter screamed.

The blade impaling her lifted upward, taking her with it. She rose through the air, her feet leaving the water, blood pouring down the front of her uniform.

Then the blade jerked back, and she fell into the pool, vanishing beneath the water.

Hunter leaped into the pool. The ice-cold water enveloped his legs, a powerful current pulling him leftward toward the stream emptying the pool. He resisted it, striding forward toward her, his bow clutched in his hands. A bright blue glow appeared behind the waterfall, the blade retracting into the falling water. As he watched, something came out of the waterfall.

A face.

Its skin was jet-black, with all-black eyes supported by high cheekbones. Countless long black tendrils sprouted from its head like hair, rising upward and backward. Most were black, while others glowed bright blue, filled with the same gel as the other Ironclad's mane. These were much longer than the other antennae, falling backward and downward over its shoulder. As the creature stepped out from behind the waterfall, Hunter saw that it had four slender arms, a sword clutched in each hand. Its body was covered in black armor like the other Ironclad, but it was clearly female, with breasts jutting out of its thorax. The glowing antennae cascaded down its shoulders, draping over its breasts, casting its body in a bright blue hue. Tendrils of glowing blue membrane extended over its arms, even its legs.

The creature emerged from the waterfall, sheathing one sword and stepping down into the pool. It reached its free hand into the water, lifting Vi upward by the neck. Vi's feet dangled in the air, the other Ironclad's decapitated head dropping into the pool.

"No!" Hunter cried, nocking an arrow and drawing it back. The creature raised one sword high into the air.

He aimed, then released the arrow.

It shot forward, whizzing toward the thing just as it started its downswing. Then its head jerked backward.

It dropped Vi into the pool, stumbling backward, an arrow protruding from its left eye.

The creature let out a horrible roar, gripping the arrow and tearing it from its face. She tossed it aside...just as Vi leapt out of the water, swinging her mace at the thing. Taller even than the Ironclad Vi had beheaded, her mace struck its chest, knocking it back a step. Vi went to swing again, but the creature recovered quickly, swinging its three swords with terrifying speed. Vi backpedaled, barely managing to dodge the attacks, blocking a few with her mace before managing to get out of range. But the

Ironclad, being much taller, moved through the water more easily, the pool only reaching to its mid-calves. Vi circled, aiming toward the island.

Hunter drew another arrow, waiting for an opening, watching as Vi reached the waterfall.

The Ironclad lunged at Vi, unsheathing its fourth sword and whirling the other three so quickly they were a blur. Again, Vi got out of the way just in time, barely avoiding the rain of lethal blows. She plunged through the waterfall, vanishing behind it. The Ironclad followed, leaping out of the water and crashing through the waterfall.

"Vi!" Hunter cried, striding across the pool toward the island. He reached the waterfall, holding his bow with one hand and plunging the other through the wall of water. He felt the wet rock of the island beyond, and hauled himself through the waterfall, gasping as the ice-cold water drenched him. He passed through, seeing a circular island some fifty feet in diameter, surrounded on all sides by walls of falling water.

And there, in the center of it, the Ironclad faced Vi, its blades whirling in a murderous dance.

Vi stayed well clear of the Ironclad's swords, more agile now that she was out of the water. But Hunter couldn't help noticing that she was hunching over a little, blood still trickling from the wound in her belly. She was moving slower than usual, though still quick enough to outmaneuver the massive beast...for now.

Suddenly Vi lunged forward, dodging one sword, then blocking two others, somehow managing to get past its attacks. She ducked down, smashing it in the knee with her mace. It buckled, its head jerking forward and downward.

And Vi leapt up at that moment, smashing the Ironclad in the face.

The Ironclad stumbled backward, its arms flailing wildly. Somehow it managed to keep its balance. But Vi wasn't done; she charged, leaping and swinging her mace into its chest with a loud *crack*. Again the thing stumbled, and Vi swung again, hitting it in the chest a second time.

The Ironclad fell onto its back, its swords *clanging* on the rocky ground.

Vi rushed up to it, swinging her mace over and over, smashing it in the chest. The armor there cracked, then caved in, blood dripping from Vi's mace. Still she attacked, raising her mace high into the air yet again.

The Ironclad roared, kicking Vi in the belly.

Vi cried out, stumbling backward and landing on her back. She gasped for air, clutching at her wounded belly, her eyes wide. The Ironclad got to its feet, lunging toward her.

Hunter grabbed an arrow, nocking it and letting it fly.

It struck the Ironclad in the temple, knocking its head to the side just as it was about to slash at Vi. It stopped, turning to glare at him, its black eyes locked on his.

Vi got to her feet, stumbling backward, still clutching her side with one hand. Blood seeped from between her fingers, dripping onto the rock below. She turned to Hunter.

"Get out of here kid," she ordered, gritting her teeth. "Grab the head!"

"I'm not leaving you," Hunter retorted, drawing another arrow. He let it fly, aiming for the wound in its chest. The arrow missed the mark, bouncing off its intact armor.

The Ironclad ignored him, lunging at Vi, its blades whirling.

Vi got her mace up just in time, blocking a few blows, then dodging to the side, barely escaping the beast's attacks. She was moving much more slowly now, her wound clearly getting the better of her. Still, she managed to avoid the thing's attacks…until the Ironclad chopped downward with two swords at the same time. Vi raised her mace to block the attacks, but the force of the blows sent her reeling backward, her mace arm going wide.

The Ironclad lunged forward, thrusting her sword right at her!

Vi dodged out of the way with surprising speed, knocking the thing's arm out of the way, then running in and striking it in the chest with her mace. It howled, stumbling backward…just as Vi switched weapons, drawing her longsword and thrusting right at its heart!

The blade sank into its chest, burying itself deep into the Ironclad's flesh.

The Ironclad cried out, stumbling backward, somehow managing to keep its balance, its eyes wide, its mouth open in a perfect "O."

And then it chopped downward with one sword, cutting Vi's left arm off at the elbow. Her arm fell to the ground, blood pouring from the severed end.

"*No!*" Hunter screamed.

Vi stumbled backward, staring at the stump of her left arm in disbelief. Blood spurted from it, spraying the ground in front of her.

Hunter rushed up to Vi just as the Ironclad lunged for her, chopping down at her head with one sword. Hunter swung his bow to intercept the blade, managing to deflect it. But the impact knocked the bow out of his hands, sending him stumbling to the side.

The Ironclad's eyes went to him, and it stepped back, its arms dropping.

"Run!" Hunter cried, getting in between Vi and the Ironclad. "I'll hold this thing off!"

"But…" Vi began.

"Go, *now!*" Hunter ordered, shoving her toward the pool as hard as he could. She stumbled backward, striking the waterfall and vanishing beyond it.

He turned then, facing the Ironclad, drawing his longsword from its scabbard. He flipped it around, grabbing it by the blade and striding toward it. The Ironclad stared at him, taking another step back, its eyes going wide, its jaw dropping.

And then he attacked.

He burst forward, sprinting right up to the creature. It raised its blades, and he dropped to the ground at the last minute, sliding between its legs. He swung his sword, the cross-guard smashing into the back of its knee.

The Ironclad buckled, falling onto its back with a *thump*, its swords *clanging* on the rock.

Hunter leapt onto its belly, swinging his sword right at its chest. The hilt struck the cross-guard of Vi's sword, shoving the blade deeper into the Ironclad's chest.

The Ironclad *shrieked*.

"Time to die, freak!" he shouted, raising his sword up again. He chopped downward, but the Ironclad intercepted the blow with one forearm, deflecting his sword to the side. He grunted, raising his weapon a third time. The Ironclad held up one hand.

"Stop!" it cried.

Hunter ignored it, chopping downward, this time striking Vi's cross-guard again. Her blade sank even deeper into the thing's chest, and it bit off a scream.

"Stop," it repeated. Hunter raised his sword again.

"You tried to kill my friend," he retorted angrily, chopping downward. The Ironclad managed to block the blow again. "You tried to kill me!"

"No," the beast protested. "Hunter, stop!"

He swung his sword up, then froze, staring at the Ironclad. A chill ran down his spine.

"What?"

"Stop," it repeated.

"How did you know my name?" he demanded. It grimaced, clutching at Vi's blade. He kicked its hands away. "Tell me!"

It shook its head, staring up at him.

"Is it really you?" it murmured. It reached up with one hand, trying to touch Hunter's face. Hunter jerked away. "It *is* you," it gasped. "I'm so sorry baby, I didn't...recognize you."

"Who the fuck are you?" he demanded. "And why do you keep sending these...*things* to try and kill me?"

"I didn't send anyone...to kill you," it countered, trying to grab the blade again. He batted its hands away.

"One more move and I'll kill you, I swear to god," he growled.

"I sent them to *find* you," the creature said. "To save you from..."

It grimaced, its breaths coming more quickly now, blood spilling from the corner of its mouth.

"From what?" he pressed.

"From *them*," it answered. "From the...kingdom."

Hunter just stared at it.

"I knew they'd...get to you," it continued. "We had to get to...you first." It grimaced, gritting its teeth. White teeth, in stark contrast to its jet-black lips.

"What are you talking about?"

"That's why I sent...your...brother," it gasped.

Hunter lowered his sword, staring down at the creature. A chill ran through him, goosebumps rising on his arms.

"My what?"

"Your brother," it repeated. "I sent him...to the Gate," it explained.

"No," Hunter protested. "What brother? I don't have a brother."

The creature's lips curled into a smile.

"Yes…you do," it insisted, gripping Vi's blade with one hand. It tried to pull on it, but the blade didn't budge. "We never told you," it added.

Hunter swallowed in a dry throat, his body feeling numb, as if he wasn't really here. As if this were happening to someone else. He barely felt his sword slip out of his hands, falling with a clatter on the ground.

"No," he whispered.

The creature coughed, bloody sputum dribbling down its chin. Then it smiled up at him again, reaching up and placing one hand gently on his leg.

"I've waited…for this moment," she whispered, "…for so…long."

Hunter's legs wobbled, and he fell to his knees beside her, not even registering the pain as his knees struck the rocky floor. Tears blurred his vision, and he bit back a sob, his whole body trembling.

"I love…you," she gasped, her breathing slowing. She gripped Vi's sword again, trying in vain to pull it out. Her hands slipped from the blade, and she sucked a deep breath in, a horrible gurgling sound coming from deep within her throat.

"No," Hunter mumbled. "No no no…"

"Take…" she gasped. "Take…"

And then she let out one last breath, her eyes staring off into the void.

CHAPTER 35

Dominus let go of his son, grabbing his cane and rising shakily to his feet.

He stared down at Conlan, at the pool of blood growing around the boy, then glanced at his own hands. They were covered in blood. He wiped his hands on his shirt, but the blood was sticky, and wouldn't come off.

He stumbled backward, shaking his head slowly, his lower lip quivering.

What have I done?

Dominus heard a *clunk*, and turned to see the door to the Royal Chamber opening. He froze, his heart leaping into his throat. Two members of the Royal Guard rushed into the room, their swords bared. Their eyes went to Dominus, then to Conlan's body slumped against the bed.

"I can…" Dominus began, holding up both hands.

"Murderer!" one of the guards shouted, rushing at him. The guard slashed at Dominus, the blade arcing at his neck. Dominus stood a step backward, then blinked.

His cane-sword was already in his hands, the tip embedded in the guard's throat. The guard's sword flew to the side, striking the wall with a terrible clatter.

The guard slumped to the ground, dead.

The second guard stared at Dominus, his eyes widening.

"Wait," Dominus protested. But the guard cried out, thrusting at Dominus's belly. Dominus's sword intercepted the blade, and he counterattacked, slashing at the guard's throat. The guard blocked the attack, kicking at Dominus's belly. Dominus stepped to the side, slamming the pommel of his sword on the guard's knee, then slashing at his throat again.

The guard's head came clean off of his shoulders, toppling to the floor in a spray of blood.

More guards ran into the room, and Dominus stood before them, raising one hand.

"Stop!" he commanded.

The guards looked down at their two dead colleagues. At the two Royal guards, masters of warfare, considered the greatest warriors in the kingdom. Unmatched in skill, almost invincible.

Then they looked up at Dominus, the old cripple that had bested them. In seconds.

"As your Duke," Dominus ordered, "...I command you to stand down!"

"We answer to the king," one of the guards retorted. He gestured at the other guards, and they surrounded Dominus, forming a loose circle around him.

"There is no king," Dominus countered. "And my son is dead."

"You assassinated him," the guard argued.

"He went mad," Dominus retorted, pointing to the cracks in the crystal slab where Tykus's Ossae lay. "He was going to destroy the Ossae!"

The guards glanced at the slab, their resolve clearly wavering.

"I killed my own son," Dominus declared, his voice cracking. "I killed him to save Tykus. To save the kingdom." He stared at the guards, standing at his full height. "Is that not my sworn duty as Duke of Wexford?"

The guards glanced at each other, then lowered their weapons.

"Drop your weapon," one guard ordered. Dominus hesitated, then lowered his sword to the floor, standing back up with some difficulty. "Summon Duke Ratheburg," the guard commanded one of his fellows. The guard saluted, sprinting out of the room. Dominus stood there, surrounded by the Royal Guard. A part of him wondered what would happen if they attacked, if Ratheburg gave the order to kill him. He'd exposed himself to powerful artifacts – artifacts forbidden by the kingdom, most of which Vi

411

had provided him. His skills were clearly superior to that of a single guard, but if they all attacked at once…

He grit his teeth, knowing that Ratheburg stood to gain by having him murdered. The second most powerful duke in the kingdom, Ratheburg could kill Dominus, then install Axio as a puppet Duke of Wexford, molding the boy in Dominus's absence as he saw fit. He could sap power from the Duchy, until Ratheburg became the most powerful man in the kingdom save for the king. It could happen even if he *didn't* die today.

Dominus lowered his gaze, staring at the sword lying there.

If Ratheburg betrays me, he thought, *I'll have to kill him before the guards kill me.*

Dominus rejected the idea immediately, raising his gaze to the chamber door. He could not allow such an ignoble end to his family's reign. The Dukes of Wexford had served the kingdom selflessly for millennia. He would not be the first to betray their legacy.

If he was to die today, so be it.

Minutes passed, pain growing in his rotting, infected leg, and he clenched his teeth against the pain, sweat beading on his forehead. He refused to allow these men to see weakness in him. He had to be strong until the very end.

A man strode through the doorway suddenly, accompanied by more guards. It was, Dominus saw, Duke Ratheburg.

Ratheburg saw Dominus standing there, hands and uniform covered in blood, and he froze, his eyes widening. His gaze was drawn inexorably to Conlan's corpse, slumped against the violated crystal slab atop his bedframe.

"Dear God," Ratheburg blurted out, his eyes returning to Dominus. "What the hell happened here?"

"Conlan went mad," Dominus answered shakily. "He thought himself stronger than Tykus, and when he discovered he wasn't…" Dominus shook his head, the words catching in his throat. "He went insane, said he'd make his mark. He tried to destroy Tykus," he added, gesturing at the damaged slab.

"Unthinkable!" Ratheburg exclaimed, striding forward, ignoring the guards around Dominus. He walked up to Conlan's body, staring at it, then at the cracks in the slab. His shoulders relaxed visibly, and he turned to face Dominus. "It's intact, thank God."

"It is," Dominus agreed. "I tried to reason with him," he added, gesturing at Conlan. "But he wouldn't listen. He grabbed Tykus's warhammer..."

"I see," Ratheburg interjected. He sighed then, shaking his head. "To think of what would have happened if you hadn't acted...it's inconceivable."

"These guards attacked me," Dominus said, gesturing at the two dead Royal guards. "They thought I had assassinated Conlan, and would not hear my story."

"You defeated them?" Ratheburg inquired, his eyebrows rising. It was unheard of for any man to best a Royal guard...any noble, that was. The dukes, however, were exposed to powerful legal artifacts, Ratheburg knew.

"My family left me many fine artifacts," Dominus explained. "A blessing that the Dukes of Wexford never had to use their gifts until now."

"Indeed," Ratheburg replied. He sighed then. "I admit I was aware of Conlan's troubled mind, but I never thought he'd descend into madness so completely." He walked up to Dominus, putting a hand on his shoulder. "I, and the kingdom – indeed, humanity itself – will be forever in your debt."

Dominus swallowed past a lump in his throat, nodding back.

"It is my duty to protect the kingdom," he stated.

"And you have executed that duty today, at great personal cost," Ratheburg replied. He turned to Conlan's body, shaking his head again. "I'm truly sorry for your loss, Dominus."

"As am I," Dominus replied, his voice wavering.

Ratheburg glanced at the guards surrounding Dominus, and glared at them.

"Stand down," he ordered sharply. "You are in the presence of the heir to the crown of Tykus!"

The guards sheathed their swords immediately, turning about and walking out of the room, leaving Ratheburg alone with Dominus. Dominus hesitated, then shook his head.

"I cannot accept the kingship, Ratheburg," he declared. Ratheburg blinked.

"What?"

"I cannot accept it," Dominus repeated. Ratheburg's eyes narrowed.

"Why not?" he demanded.

"I'm not fit for it."

"Malarkey," Ratheburg retorted. "You're as fit as any man. Fitter, I'd say," he added, gesturing at the corpses of the guards. "Dominus, you cannot refuse the crown again. Once was suspicious enough, but twice?" He shook his head. "If it weren't for your actions today, I'd worry about your loyalty."

"I'm dying," Dominus stated bluntly.

Ratheburg stared at him silently, his jaw dropping.

Dominus bent down, ignoring the pain in his leg, and pulled off his boot, then his sock, exposing his mutilated foot. The entire foot was black, tendrils of necrotic tissue extending up past the ankle. Pus oozed from the septic flesh of his beefy red shin, a red streak winding up his leg.

Ratheburg drew a sharp breath in, jerking backward. His eyes widened, his hand going to his mouth.

"Oh god," he mumbled. "Please, cover it," he added, turning to the side and dry-heaving. Dominus obeyed, slipping his sock and boot back on.

"I'm dying," he repeated firmly. "The infection has already spread to the bone, and will go to my blood. The doctors say even amputation is unlikely to save me now."

Ratheburg nodded, still turned away from him.

"If I become king, I will die before the transformation is complete," Dominus insisted. "Or soon afterward."

"I understand," Ratheburg replied, finally turning to face him. The man glanced down at Dominus's foot, clearly relieved that it was covered once again. "Then I suppose we have no choice," he stated. "We must enlist your heir to ascend to the throne." He paused. "What was his name again?"

"Axio," Dominus answered, his jaw rippling. The thought of wasting such a perfect heir to the Duchy was heartbreaking. To think of how long he'd waited for a suitable heir, after his son had proven himself a failure...

"Axio, yes," Ratheburg replied. "He shall become king then."

"As you say," Dominus agreed.

"Very well then," Ratheburg sighed. He put a hand on Dominus's shoulder. "You should get back to Wexford, to get your affairs in order."

Dominus nodded, knowing the man was right. He had to choose another heir, and soon. It was unlikely he would find a candidate like Axio again. That meant the Duchy might suffer a

414

weak link in the long chain of dukes, a chain extending backward across the millennia. He would have to plan accordingly.

Ratheburg put a hand on Dominus's shoulder.

"I'm sorry, old friend," he murmured. "You're too fine a man to have suffered like this."

Dominus felt a lump rise in his throat, and nodded mutely. Ratheburg held his gaze for a moment longer, then walked out of the chamber, leaving Dominus alone. He watched the man go, taken aback by Ratheburg's generosity...and his selflessness. Far from taking advantage of him, Ratheburg had executed the duties of his office with honor and integrity. He was truly a fine man, bred and educated to be a paragon of virtue.

The kind of man the kingdom was *supposed* to produce.

Dominus sighed, glancing at the corpse of his son, then at the guards at his feet. It was only then that he realized how far he'd strayed from the ideals of the kingdom, dabbling in forbidden artifacts. They'd muddied his ideals, making him suspicious of others, suspicious of men that were beyond suspicion. It had all been for the noblest of causes...to give him the tools he needed to protect his people, their way of life. But in doing so, he'd stopped being like them. He was an outsider now.

He clenched his fists, turning to face the corpse of his son, knowing that Conlan had been right all along. The boy's will *had* tainted him.

Dominus turned away from his son's body, picking up his cane-sword and sheathing it, then limping slowly toward the chamber door, leaving Conlan behind.

But with each painful step he took, he knew that his son's will remained, living on within him.

CHAPTER 36

Vi plunged through the waterfall behind her, the ice-cold water drenching her instantly. She felt herself falling, then felt her back slam into the pool beyond. Water rushed in all around her, enveloping her. Her back struck something hard below – the rocky bottom of the pool. She felt herself sliding to the left, and reached out with her right hand, grabbing at the rock below. But her fingers slipped over their smooth, slick surface, and she continued to slide, gaining speed as the current grabbed her.

She kicked with her legs, rising up out of the water, her head bursting through the surface. She took a deep breath in, staring at the waterfall ahead.

Hunter!

Vi tried to get her feet under her, but the current swept her sideways, her feet sliding on the bottom of the pool. She saw a spray of red to her left, and turned, staring at what remained of her left arm. A stump just above the elbow, pearly white bone and rust-colored muscle visible there. Blood spurted from the artery there, her blood draining with every beat of her heart.

Fuck.

She grimaced, pressing the stump hard against her thigh to staunch the flow. Her feet slipped out from underneath her, her head plunging below the surface again. She pulled her feet underneath her again, feeling her left foot strike something. Opening her eyes, she saw a dark, round blur at the bottom of the pool, lined by a faint blue light. She reached out for it on an impulse, grabbing it and pulling it to her chest. Then she got her feet under her, standing up again. Her head emerged from the water, and she took another deep, gasping breath in, looking down at the object she'd grabbed.

It was the head…the Ironclad's head. Its mane glowed blue, the light reflecting off of the rippling water. She saw the waterfall pulling away as the current carried her toward the stream emptying the pool, toward the dark, gaping maw of the tunnel it flowed into.

She turned back to the waterfall, her heart leaping in her throat. *Hunter!*

Vi tried to get her feet under her again, tried to resist the ever-growing power of the current sweeping her away. But it was no use. She grit her teeth, staring at the waterfall, her heart sinking.

The damn fool.

He was as good as dead, she knew. That…*thing* would tear him apart. Probably already had. An emotion she hadn't felt in years came over her, a pain she'd promised she'd never allow herself to experience again.

That damn, beautiful fool.

Darkness fell over her then, the tunnel enveloping her. She felt the bottom of the stream fall away suddenly, and her stomach twisted into a knot as she entered free fall, her head plunging below the surface of the water. Her back struck something hard, and then she was jerked to the side. Her head burst through the water, and she took a breath in…right before she was plunged yet again below the water.

Her descent slowed then, her back scraping against the floor of the stream. She saw a dull light ahead, and kicked her legs, her head emerging from the water. It was shallower here, and she was able to keep above water. She slid downstream, spotting a lantern to her right. The same lantern she'd seen earlier, the first one she and Hunter had passed by.

The stream curved quickly to the left, and she saw another light ahead, approaching rapidly. The floor dropped out from her again, and she fell a couple of feet, landing on her back, light exploding all around her. She cried out as pain shot through her back, water flowing over her shoulders and head, shoving her further downstream. Her back scraped painfully against the rocky bed of the stream, the water shallower now. Eventually she stopped, water coursing around her.

She looked up, seeing blue sky, and the slivers of three crescent moons.

Vi rolled onto her right side, seeing the shore of the stream a few meters away. She logrolled toward it, eventually reaching the grass beyond. She rested on her back then, clutching the Ironclad's head to her chest. Looking around, she saw a familiar hillside nearby, the stream flowing from the mouth of the cave. She was outside the Ironclad back entrance…which meant that Traven and Edgar should be close by.

She groaned, looking down at the wound in her abdomen, then at the stump of her left arm, still shoved into her side. Blood oozed from the severed end, jelly-like clots sticking to the stump. She grunted, trying to sit up, but felt immediately lightheaded. She fell onto her back, feeling woozy.

You've lost too much blood.

Vi laid there, her heart pounding, her head swimming sickeningly. The inevitable pain of her wounds reared its ugly head then, the merciful numbness of shock abating. Her left arm felt like it was on fire, the pain in her abdomen sharp and excruciating. Every breath felt like someone was stabbing her there, like that…*thing's* sword was impaling her over and over.

So this is how it ends.

She groaned, staring down at the head still clutched in her right hand. She picked it up by the glowing blue membranes at the back of its skull, holding it above her face. Stared into those dead black eyes.

"Well *you* weren't worth it," she muttered.

She coughed then, pain lancing through her belly, her grip on the mane tightening reflexively. The membrane burst, a gush of cool, thick fluid splashing her hand. Globs of glowing gel fell onto her face, covering it. She gasped, bitter fluid flowing into her mouth and down her throat as she tried to take a breath in. She swallowed reflexively, then gasped for air, coughing again. Another gush of fluid fell on her, but she turned her head to the side too late. More of the awful stuff dripped into her mouth, forcing her to swallow again.

She gagged, then grit her teeth, her belly on fire as her abdomen tensed. If she threw up, it was going to be very, very bad. She suppressed the impulse, setting the head aside and wiping the goo from her eyes. Looking down, she saw herself covered in the stuff, the blue glow contrasting starkly with her dark uniform, covering the skull embedded in the leather at her chest like an otherworldly flesh.

She felt anger then, a sudden flash of rage that came out of nowhere. The analytical part of her mind reacted instantly, reciting the old mantra.

Emotion is temporary. Action is forever. Find the cause, suppress the effect.

She found herself examining the emotion, recognizing the suddenness of it, the lack of context. It was not hers, she knew. It was the Ironclad's, sudden and powerful by virtue of her having taken a part of its body into her own.

She let the emotion come, felt herself enter that dissociative state she'd mastered so long ago. Experienced the emotion as if it were happening to someone else…because it *had* happened to someone else. It was not hers. She would not claim ownership of it. Would not allow it to own *her*.

Slowly, it faded.

Vi heard a sudden *crunch, crunch* of footsteps approaching, of boots crushing twigs and leaves underfoot. Two sets of footsteps, walking in tandem, maybe twenty yards away. She turned her head, staring off into the tree line bordering the shore, spotting two men there. Relief coursed through her; it was Traven and Edgar!

"Hey!" she yelled, grimacing as another stabbing pain shot through her belly. "Over here!"

The two men strode up to her, and Traven bent to one knee before her, shaking his head.

"Damn," he blurted out. "What the hell happened to you?"

"I tripped," she deadpanned, rolling the head toward him. "Looking for this?"

Traven's eyes widened, and he stared at the head. Most of the glowing goo had drained from its mane, leaving small glowing streaks across its flesh.

"You did it?" he breathed. Edgar picked up the head, turning it around in his hands.

"This is him," he confirmed, turning to Vi. "Damn Vi," he muttered. "Heard you were good, but I never thought…"

"You're welcome," Vi interrupted. "Can we get me to a doctor now?"

Edgar and Traven stared down at Vi…at the bloody hole in her belly, and at her bleeding stump. Traven gave a low whistle, shaking his head.

"Damn Vi," he stated. "You're all fucked up."

"Yeah," Vi retorted, "…well no one happened to mention the bitch hiding behind the goddamn waterfall."

"What?"

"That isn't the leader," she explained, gesturing at the head Edgar was holding. "The real leader's a female Ironclad, bigger than him."

"A female?" Edgar asked. "Didn't realize they had any. How could you tell?"

"She had tits."

"Ah," Traven replied. He stood up then. "I take it the kid didn't make it," he added. Vi hesitated, then shook her head, swallowing past a lump in her throat. An image of Hunter being torn apart by that monster came unbidden to her mind's eye, and she shoved the thought away, blinking moisture from her eyes.

"Come on," she urged, trying to sit up. But the pain in her belly stopped her, and she fell onto her back, taking short, gasping breaths. She waited for the pain to subside a little. "We need to get back to Tykus." Traven hesitated.

"There's been a complication," he confessed, sighing heavily.

"What?"

"Well," Traven replied, scratching his head, "…as you know, the guild hasn't been too happy with you since you left. In fact, the High Seeker himself ordered your death oh, I don't know, a decade ago now?" He glanced at Edgar, who rubbed his chin.

"Eleven years, actually," he corrected.

"You know as well as I do that no Seeker is allowed to leave the guild," Traven continued. "Brilliant to get Duke Dominus as a client so he'd protect you."

"I don't need protection," Vi retorted.

"Probably true," Traven agreed. "See, now a guy like Dominus can get away with breaking the law, hiring non-guild Seekers. Not much the guild could do about it. Quite the conundrum for the High Seeker, don't you think?"

"Screw the High Seeker," Vi spat. "A deal's a deal. Dominus paid you to help me, and he'll be pissed if you don't."

"Oh really?" Traven murmured. He reached back, grabbing his warhammer and holding it in one hand, dropping the head of it down on the ground, inches from her head. "That's funny, isn't it Edgar?"

"Hilarious," Edgar agreed.

"The Guild of Seekers can't have someone knowing what *you* know running around," Traven continued, leaning both hands on the warhammer. "Can't have the kingdom finding out what we're really up to, can we?"

"I haven't talked yet," Vi retorted. "And I don't plan to. I don't give a shit about the kingdom," she added, "Or your damn cult."

"Oh, I believe you," Traven agreed. "Trust me I do. Unfortunately, the High Seeker doesn't see it that way. You're the only Seeker to ever break the covenant without being killed," he added. "And the way the High Seeker sees it, you're the single greatest threat to the guild...and our mission."

"Screw your mission."

"So the High Seeker himself made a deal with Dominus," Traven continued, ignoring her. "The guild would use all their resources to find the Ironclad base, and the good duke would look the other way if something...unfortunate were to happen to you."

"He wouldn't..." Vi began.

"He did," Traven interrupted, smirking at her. "Seems like he doesn't need your services anymore, Vi." He sighed then, shrugging his shoulders. "Anyway, that's the story," he added, lifting his warhammer up and resting it over his shoulder. "...and what'ya know, here we are."

Vi reached for the mace at her hip, but Traven lunged forward, bringing the heel of his boot down on her wrist...hard. She bit back a scream, trying to kick him, but he slid the butt of the warhammer down, dropping it on her belly.

She *howled*.

"Edgar, if you would," Traven prompted. Edgar reached down, unsheathing her sword and tossing it a few meters away. Traven turned back to Vi, giving her a rueful smile. "You know, damn if I can't help it, but I kinda like you," he admitted. "Scratch that...I *really* like you," he corrected. He lifted his warhammer, resting it on his shoulder again. "You know what?" he added. "I wanna know what happens if we let you go...if you're so damn good that you can make it out of all of this alive."

Vi groaned, clutching her belly, waves of excruciating pain radiating to her back. She tried to take a breath in, but couldn't. Traven nodded at Edgar, and then both turned away from her, walking toward the tree line. Then Traven stopped, turning around to look at her.

"You know what?" he said. "I've changed my mind."

He stepped forward, raising his warhammer high above his head, the metal gleaming in the sunlight. Then he grunted, swinging downward, right at Vi's head.

CHAPTER 37

Hunter stared down at the thing that had claimed to be his mother, at her inky black eyes staring lifelessly upward. He shook his head, tears streaming down his cheeks. Despite her inky black, armor-plated skin, despite the all-black eyes and the glowing tendrils cascading from her head, she *did* look familiar. The same high cheekbones, the same lips. Even her voice had been similar.

"No," he whispered, staring down at her…at the sword – *Vi's* sword – protruding from her chest. The one he'd shoved right through her heart.

What have I done?

He reached down, shaking her shoulders, then slapping her cheek, hoping beyond hope that she would wake up. That her eyes would focus on his, that she would smile at him again. But there was no life in her. It'd been snuffed out.

By her own son.

He shook his head, tears blurring his vision, and held her head in his arms, leaning over to press his cheek against hers. It was warm, if hard, the armor slick against his skin. A sob escaped him, the sound swallowed whole by the roar of the waterfall.

"No, mommy, no."

Hunter sat down, cradling her head in his lap, rocking back and forth. He ran a hand through the hair-like tendrils on her scalp, his tears dripping onto her cheek.

I'm sorry.

He closed his eyes, an image of her smiling up at him coming to him, the sudden recognition. The love.

I'm so sorry.

She'd tried to warn him, tried to tell him to stop. But he hadn't. He'd let his anger get the best of him, and murdered his own mother.

Oh god, he thought, a sickening feeling twisting his guts. *Oh god oh god…*

He hunched over, crushing his cheek against her bosom, gritting his teeth.

I can't do this.

He gave a low moan, raising his head, staring up at the blue sky visible through the hole in the ceiling far above. He took a deep breath in…and screamed.

The sound echoed through the chamber, the agonizing sound drowning out the roar of the waterfall. It faded, and Hunter lowered his gaze, his chest heaving.

I killed my own mother!

He stared down at his mother, at her beautiful face. Alien, but beautiful still. Because it was *her.*

She sent my brother to find me.

He closed his eyes, *seeing* the huge Ironclad that had attacked him after he'd gone through the gate. The Ironclad he'd shot in the face, right before Alasar and the other soldiers had killed it.

My brother!

Hunter stood then, his mother's head sliding off his lap, rolling to the side on the rocky floor. He stumbled backward, an image of him pulling the trigger – of his brother's face exploding – forcing itself on him. His brother had been trying to save him all along, to stop the kingdom from getting him. To take him to his mother.

And he'd killed *him* too.

His legs wobbled, and he fell to his knees, barely registering the pain as they struck hard rock. A wave of nausea came over him, and he leaned over, retching once, then again.

Dark shapes appeared through the waterfall.

Hunter scrambled to his feet, turning in a slow circle. Dozens of Ironclad stepped through the waterfall surrounding him, water cascading down their armored bodies. They stepped toward them, their black eyes on him.

He glanced down at his mother, then at them, clenching his fists.

"Kill me," he ordered.

They stopped, standing around him silently. Staring at him.

"Kill me!" he repeated.

Still, they did nothing.

He unsheathed his sword, walking toward one of them, pointing the tip at its chest.

"Do it!" he shouted, flipping the sword around and grabbing it by the blade. He swung it over his head, aiming for the thing's face. It raised four arms, blocking the blow, his sword bouncing off harmlessly. He stumbled backward, nearly dropping the blade, expecting the Ironclad to lunge at him.

But it just stood there.

Hunter stared at it, his heart pounding, his chest heaving with each breath. Then, in a fit of madness, he gripped the blade tightly, pressing the point of the sword under his breastbone. He grit his teeth.

"Fine," he muttered. "Fine!' He closed his eyes, steeling himself. "I'll do it myself then."

Something tore the sword out of his hands, and he opened his eyes, seeing an Ironclad standing before him. It flung his sword backward through the air, and it vanished beyond the waterfall.

Hunter backpedaled, then tripped on something behind him, falling onto his butt. It was his mother, he realized; he'd tripped over her body. He got to his feet, and the Ironclad strode toward him, reaching for the hilt of the sword embedded in mom's chest.

"No!" he cried, lunging for the sword and grabbing it before the Ironclad could. He yanked on it once, then again, the blade finally pulling free. He stumbled backward, then turned in a slow circle.

The Ironclad were all around him, forming a veritable wall of armored flesh. He saw them flashing rapid hand signals to each other.

"Get back!" he ordered, glancing from one of them to the next, continuing to turn in a circle. He spotted a gap between them, and burst forward, sheathing Vi's sword. He feinted to the left, then leapt rightward through the gap, sprinting up to the waterfall and leaping through.

He gasped as the icy water coursed over him, then felt a second chill as he fell into the pool beyond, his head plunging below the surface. The current grabbed him, pulling him forward, and he swam for the surface, his head bursting through. He gasped for air, seeing a dark tunnel in the distance, the water flowing toward it. He looked around, but Vi was nowhere to be seen.

She escaped through that tunnel.

It was the only possible route, Hunter knew. At least one that wasn't crawling with Ironclad. She *had* to have taken it.

He swam forward, working with the current, the tunnel swallowing him whole. Utter darkness enveloped him, the current carrying him swiftly forward. His guts lurched as the stream dropped suddenly, angling sharply downward. He jerked to one side, then fell again, the current plunging his head underwater.

And then, mercifully, the current slowed. He felt his back scraping against the floor of the stream, and kicked upward, breaking through the surface of the water. He noticed an orange light to his right, but it passed by too quickly for him to get a good look at it, the stream curving leftward.

Then he saw it: sunlight, shining through the end of the tunnel ahead!

Hunter slid toward it, the stream becoming steeper as he drew closer. At last he burst into the light, the floor of the stream dropping out from under him suddenly. He dropped onto his back into the stream as it continued below, water gushing over his face and shoulders.

Hunter grimaced, rolling to the side as the stream carried him toward the larger stream ahead. He made it to the shore, rising unsteadily to his feet. He was, he realized, right back where he'd started…at the rear entrance to the Ironclad lair.

He stared at the mouth of the cave, at the stream spilling from it, hardly believing his eyes. Realization came over him; if he'd made it out, that meant that Vi had, too.

Vi!

He turned, scanning the shoreline, and spotted something lying there a few yards from the stream. His heart leapt in his throat; it was a person, lying on their back in the grass, covered in glowing blue liquid. He walked toward it, unsheathing his sword slowly, holding it out in front of him, stopping a foot away and staring down at it.

His heart skipped a beat.

"Vi!" he cried, sheathing his sword and kneeling before her. It *was* her. Her head was covered in glowing goo, and he wiped it away, uncovering her eyes. They were partly open, staring off into nothingness. "Vi," he repeated, slapping her face lightly. But again, she didn't respond.

A bolt of fear shot through him.

"Vi?"

Hunter slapped her face again, but she didn't respond.

"Come on, Vi," he urged, slapping harder. He shook his head, tears welling up in his eyes. "No Vi, no," he pleaded. "Don't do this to me!"

It was only then that he saw the large dent in her skull, covered by the glowing gel.

"Oh god," he mumbled, tears flowing down his cheeks. "Oh god no. Not you too, Vi. Not you!"

He put a hand on her cheek, feeling the warmth there. Surprisingly warm; she must have just passed.

"Come on Vi," he pleaded, shaking his head. "I need you."

He stared at her, wiping the tears from his eyes, waiting. Hoping beyond hope that she would come back to him. That everything would be okay.

She lay there, unmoving in the grass. Gone.

He grabbed her shoulders, shaking her, but it was no use. He stared down at her, at those exotic eyes. At her lips, so often curled into a smirk, but now set in a straight line, parted slightly.

Dead.

At length he sighed, leaning forward and kissing her forehead.

"I love you," he whispered.

And it was true. In the vacuum left when his mother left so many years ago, he'd dreamed of what it would be like to have her back. To have a mother again. And in the brief time that he'd been with her, Vi had been that for him. A mother, a sister…and his best friend. He'd never allowed himself to care about anyone like he'd cared about her. Not his father, not even his friends. He'd never seen the point, after all…not after Mom had died. He'd never wanted to care about someone enough for them to hurt him when they inevitably left him.

And now she, and his real mother, were dead.

He closed his eyes, lowering his forehead to hers, not caring as the warm gel covering it touched his skin.

A flash of light appeared in his mind's eye, and a bolt of anger and fear. Pain in his left arm, in his belly…and an image of a man standing above him, smirking at him.

Traven.

He saw a hammer swinging toward his head, and then felt a flash of excruciating pain…and then darkness.

Hunter jerked his head away, staring at Vi's lifeless body.

How the hell?

He hesitated, then lowered his forehead to hers again, closing his eyes. Again he saw Traven's face in his mind's eye, knew that the Seeker was going to kill him. No, not him...*her*. She knew too much, after all. The Seekers had been wanting to kill her ever since...

Hunter pulled away, feeling a chill run down his spine. He recalled the day after Vi had saved him, when they'd gone back to the broken-down carriage. How he'd touched one of its wheels, feeling the fear it had absorbed. And how he'd imagined himself sitting in the carriage when it was attacked, hurtling sidelong into the door as the carriage tipped over.

I wasn't imagining it, he realized. It'd been someone's memory, absorbed by the carriage. He remembered Vi's lessons, what she'd said about absorbing traits.

A few people in the past could even absorb memories.

He closed his eyes, seeing Traven standing over him. Over Vi. He felt her fear as if it was his own, the terror as that horrible hammer swung down toward her head.

Traven!

He stood then, turning around to where he'd seen Traven standing in his vision, spotting footprints there. He tracked them, just as Vi had taught him, seeing them extending off across the shore, toward the tree line. He recalled the anger he'd felt as Traven had attacked, the sense of betrayal.

Traven killed her!

Rage burned within him, and he broke out into a run, following the footprints toward the tree line. He reached the trees, weaving around them, his eyes on the ground, his heart hammering in his chest. He knew without a doubt that the Seekers had ordered her death.

The footprints went deeper into the forest, and he followed them quickly, feeling something trickling down his forehead. He wiped it, seeing glowing fluid on his hand. He wiped it off on his pants, jogging ever forward. Minutes passed, then what felt like an hour, but he didn't slow, even as his legs started to burn. The image of Traven's smirking face, the feeling of fear and anger as the man's hammer descended...

He grit his teeth, going faster.

Eventually he saw the King's Road in the distance through the trees, maybe a half-mile away...and two men walking toward it. A tall man and a shorter man, warhammers on their backs. Hunter picked up his pace, grabbing his bow from his back and an arrow from his quiver. He slowed, then stopped, aiming carefully, then firing.

The arrow whizzed through the air, passing just over Traven's left shoulder.

Damn!

He grabbed another arrow, seeing Traven turn, then look backward. Traven's eyes widened, and he and Edgar broke out into a run. Hunter aimed, letting fly with another arrow. It arced through the air toward Traven, even as Hunter started running forward again.

Traven fell, slamming face-first into the ground.

The man cried out, and Edgar slowed, glancing back at his fallen comrade. Then he continued forward, sprinting toward the King's Road in the distance.

"Son of a...!" Traven shouted, scrambling to his feet and limping after Edgar. Hunter pumped his legs hard, grabbing another arrow, then stopping to fire at Edgar's retreating form. The arrow struck the man in the shoulder, nearly toppling him. But Edgar kept his balance somehow, running toward the ladder rising up the side of the King's Road, leading to the carriage waiting twenty feet above.

Hunter aimed again, shooting another arrow at the man. But it went too low, slamming into the ground a few feet from him. Edgar reached the ladder, climbing upward frantically.

"You bastard!" Hunter shouted, reaching for another arrow. But there were none left...he'd shot the last one. Edgar reached the top of the ladder, vanishing into the carriage.

Damn it!

"Hey!" Traven yelled after the carriage as it rolled away, waving his arms wildly. "Hey!"

Hunter stared at the departing carriage, then saw Traven – about fifty feet away – turn to face him. He put his bow away, unsheathing his sword. Cold fury burned within him.

"Hey asshole," he greeted, striding toward the man. Traven turned to face him, his eyes widening. The Seeker drew his own sword, leaning his weight on his good leg.

"Vi said you were dead," Traven accused, pointing his sword at Hunter. "I'd hate to make a liar out of her."

Hunter lunged at Traven, thrusting his sword at the man's chest. Traven dodged to the side, batting Hunter's sword away and countering with a slash at his face. Hunter barely dodged in time, backpedaling rapidly.

"Careful *boy*," Traven sneered. "You're fighting a real Seeker now."

Traven lunged forward, slashing at Hunter's neck. Hunter blocked the blow, but Traven attacked again, thrusting at his chest. Hunter leapt to the side, the blade barely missing him. He slashed back at the Seeker, but Traven blocked his attack easily, ducking down and swinging at Hunter's legs. Hunter backed away, but too late; he felt a sharp sting as the man's blade sliced his thigh.

"You're slow," Traven observed, lowering his sword and smirking at him. "That bitch didn't teach you much, did she?"

"Shut up," Hunter growled, backing away. He glanced down at his thigh; there was a cut in his pants. Blood poured down his leg from a small, gaping wound there.

"Why don't you try shutting me up?" Traven retorted. "Come on, show me what you got boy." But he lunged forward right as he finished speaking, attacking again with another series of blows. Hunter backpedaled, barely blocking the flurry of attacks. Then he felt a sharp pain in his injured thigh as Traven's blade nicked it again.

"Damn it!" Hunter swore, limping backward. There was another gaping wound in his thigh, right below the first one. Traven smirked, shaking his head.

"Damn boy, you just take it," he observed, leaning his weight on his good leg. "Just like Vi did before I finished her off." He grinned then. "I don't wanna get into details, but if you ask me, I think she liked it."

"Shut the fuck up," Hunter retorted.

"Guess you could say I pounded her twice," Traven quipped, his grin widening.

"Shut *up!*" Hunter shouted, lunging at him. He slashed furiously at Traven, but the man blocked, their swords ringing as they clashed. Hunter swung again, and Traven dodged out of the way, kicking Hunter in the thigh.

His injured thigh.

Hunter howled, falling to his knees on the ground, pain shooting through his leg. He stumbled to his feet, backing away from Traven.

"Hell, you even moan like her," Traven mused. Hunter glared at him, limping backward, his leg throbbing. He wanted nothing more than to smash the man's face in, but he suppressed the urge, realizing that Traven was baiting him…just as Vi had done during their sparring matches.

Emotion is temporary. Action is forever.

He grit his teeth, forcing himself to calm down. He studied Traven, noting how the man was leaning on his good leg. If Hunter could injure Traven's good leg…

"What's the matter boy?" Traven asked. "Scared?"

Hunter ignored him, remembering what Vi had told him. He had to pay attention to what Traven was doing instead of focusing on what *he* wanted to do. He hesitated, then feinted, thrusting at Traven, then pulling back. Traven swung up and to the right to deflect the blow. A full swing; he didn't pull it back.

Interesting.

Hunter tried again, feinting with the same thrust. Again, Traven swung up and to the right.

"You *are* scared," Traven observed.

Hunter kept out of range, his eyes on Traven's. Seekers trained by absorbing traits, not by practicing like Vi. That meant everything they did was a reflex…no strategy. He either had to figure out what those reflexes were and take advantage of them, or he had to do something unique…something Traven couldn't have developed a reflex to.

Or maybe…

He glanced down, spotting dirt and leaf litter all around him. He hesitated, then feinted again, pretending to trip as he stepped backward. He fell onto his left hand, grabbing a clump of dirt and twigs. Traven took the bait, lunging forward to attack. Hunter blocked Traven's thrust one-handed, throwing the dirt right into the man's eyes.

Traven swore, lurching backward, his sword hand automatically rising to cover his face.

Hunter gripped his blade in the half-swording technique Vi had taught him, then lunged forward, thrusting the tip of his blade right at Traven's chest!

The blade bounced off harmlessly, shoving Traven backward.

Hunter backpedaled, staring at his sword, then at Traven's chest. Traven wiped the dirt from his eyes, looking down at the small hole Hunter's sword had made in the leather armor covering his chest.

Then he reached under the neck of his shirt, pulling out a silver medallion. There was a small dent in its surface.

"Well well," Traven stated, giving a rueful grin. "It was a nice try, I'll give you that." He gripped his sword two-handed, his smile fading. "Too bad. I was hoping to play with you a bit more. Now I'm just gonna have to kill-"

He lunged forward, slashing at Hunter!

Hunter blocked just in time, the force of the blow knocking his sword back, nearly throwing him off his feet. Traven attacked again, bringing his sword up high, then chopping down at Hunter's head. Hunter barely managed to get his sword up to block it, but the blow knocked his blade out of his hands, sending it flying backward. Hunter swore, dodging out of the way of yet another strike, then turning to run. But his injured leg gave out on him, and he stumbled, grimacing as pain shot through his thigh. He heard footsteps behind him.

"Time to die," Traven growled.

Hunter spotted his sword lying in the grass next to a nearby tree, and went for it. He heard Traven curse, turned just in time to see the man limping toward him. Traven swung his sword just as Hunter reached the tree, and Hunter ducked at the last minute, feeling the wind of the blade whipping through his hair. He heard a *thunk* as Traven's blade struck the tree, burying itself into the bark.

Hunter spun around, seeing Traven standing over him, his medallion hanging from his neck. The Seeker yanked at his sword, pulling it free.

Hunter grabbed Traven's medallion with both hands, yanking it as hard as he could.

Traven's head lurched forward, his forehead slamming into the tree trunk.

Hunter lunged for his sword, grabbing it and spinning around to face Traven. The Seeker stumbled backward, a dazed look on his face.

Hunter thrust his sword right into Traven's gut.

The blade sank into Traven's flesh with startling ease, and the man's eyes widened, his sword dropping from his hands. He stumbled, then fell onto his back on the forest floor, Hunter's sword slipping out of his belly. Hunter limped forward to stand over him, glaring down at the man.

"Lucky little fucker," Traven spat, trying to get to his feet. Hunter planted one boot on the Seeker's wounded belly.

Traven *howled*.

"You murdered my friend," Hunter accused, pointing his sword at him. "You *murdered* her!"

Traven grimaced, clutching at Hunter's boot. An expanding red circle stained his leather armor.

"She was dead anyway," he retorted, sneering at him. "I just put her out of her misery."

Hunter ground his heel into the man's belly. Traven cried out, then swore, shoving Hunter's boot away.

"You're full of shit," Hunter shot back. "You Seekers wanted her dead all along!"

Traven glared at him.

"You're next," he growled. "Duke Dominus wants you dead," he added. "Just like he wanted Vi dead. Who do you think she was working for, huh?" He smirked at Hunter. "You're a dead man."

"You first," Hunter retorted, aiming the tip of his sword at the man's heart. He paused, then flipped the sword around, gripping it by the blade with both hands. He raised it high over his head, then swung down with all of his might, aiming right for Traven's skull.

CHAPTER 38

Dominus sat at his desk, shifting his weight in his wheelchair. A humiliating necessity now that his leg had failed him. It'd been comfortable enough at first, but after hours of sitting he found himself wanting nothing more than to get out of it. A symbol of his body's failure, the rot consuming him from within. He could no longer hide his body's betrayal, its weakness.

He sighed, staring down at the paper on his desk, a quill pen in his hand.

"Last Will & Testament," it read.

Dominus's gaze fell to the bottom of the page, his pen hovering over the place where he was to sign. He pressed the tip of the quill against the parchment, watching as a circle of ink appeared there. He'd chosen an heir from within the family, a man of modest talent, patriotic and of reasonably strong will. Nothing compared to Axio, but serviceable. The man would be a mediocre duke, a placeholder for the next generation.

Dominus sighed again, then penned his signature in brisk, precise strokes. He dropped the pen in a bottle of water, then grabbed a pinch of sand from a nearby bowl, scattering it on the paper to soak up the excess ink. Then his hand began to shake.

He frowned, willing his hand to stop, but the tremors grew stronger, traveling up his arm. His whole body began to shake then, his teeth chattering, the wheelchair creaking beneath him. He grit his teeth, knowing it was futile to resist this. That it was impossible to control.

Slowly, after a few minutes, the shaking subsided.

He sat there, wiping his forehead with his hand, feeling the tremendous heat radiating from his skin. The infection was spreading, he knew. Slowly but surely, it was taking over his body.

The doctor had insisted on surgery, of course. All doctors were possessed of the idiotic compulsion to intervene, to *do* something, even when there was nothing left to be done. He was dying, he knew. No doctor could save him.

It wouldn't be long now.

He called out for Farkus, watching as his old, trusty servant walked into his study. The man bowed.

"My Duke?"

"Take me out to my gardens," Dominus ordered.

"But of course, your Grace."

Farkus got behind him, pulling Dominus out from behind his desk, then pushing him out of the room. Dominus was glad that it was Farkus who was pushing him; he wouldn't have tolerated anyone else seeing him so helpless. They made their way out of the castle and into his gardens. The sun shone brightly in the sky, the warm beams feeling marvelous on Dominus's skin. A slight breeze danced over him, bringing the sweet smell of flowers and grass. He closed his eyes, treasuring the sensation.

"I want to die out here, Farkus," he decided. "Even if I'm no longer in my right mind. Will you do this for me?"

"I will do anything for you, your Grace."

Dominus smiled, his eyes still closed.

"I know you will."

He felt the wheelchair stop, and opened his eyes, spotting his beehives in the distance. He pointed at them.

"Bring me to my hives."

Farkus wheeled him dutifully forward, until they were only a meter away from the boxes standing on their wooden platforms. The servant hesitated.

"Shall I retrieve your beekeeper uniform?" he inquired.

"No," Dominus answered. He was no longer concerned about getting stung. The meager discomfort would pale in comparison to the pain in his leg, to the infection coursing through his blood. And he would hardly suffer any stings for long; if he didn't die tonight, it would certainly be tomorrow. He would lose his mind eventually,

435

succumbing to merciful delirium before the end. Even now, he felt distractible. Scattered.

He felt his arms shaking again, and grit his teeth, feeling another wave of tremors come over him. Violent, awful tremors, wracking his body. He waited for the spell to pass, sweat dripping down his forehead, stinging his eyes. He wiped it away with one hand, shaking his head. To Farkus's credit, the servant did not ask if Dominus needed help, did not hurry away to summon a doctor. He knew Dominus too well for that. Indeed, there was likely no other man who knew Dominus the way that Farkus did. Decades of allowing the servant near him, years of having absorbed Dominus's superior will, had made Farkus so much like his master that they understood each other implicitly.

"Thank you, Farkus," Dominus stated suddenly.

"For what, your Grace?"

"For taking care of me all of these years."

"I took care of us, your Grace."

Dominus paused, staring at his hives. Then he sighed.

"If you were my blood," he stated quietly, "...I would have made you my heir."

"I know, your Grace."

Dominus leaned forward then, gripping one of the wooden frames from the nearest box and pulling it upward. Bees buzzed around him disturbed by the movement, but he paid them no mind. He peered at the honeycomb, at the cells within, but saw far too many drone cells.

He lowered the frame, picking up the next one...and smiled.

There, at the bottom of the frame, was a large, domed cell hanging downward. A queen cell, already sealed. After he'd killed the failed queen, the nurse bees had been alerted. A larva had already been fed the royal jelly, that mysterious, powerful essence. It alone had the power to make a queen, and make a queen it had.

Dominus stared at the cell, wondering if this queen would be strong.

He replaced the frame carefully, grimacing as a bee stung his hand. He ignored this, wheeling himself away from the boxes, bees crawling over him. He waited for them to leave, which of course they did. Then he sighed.

His hives would not survive in their current state, he knew. The next duke would not be interested in maintaining them, not well anyway...and Farkus could do it, but he was too old to live much longer. The integrity of the hives would become compromised, losing their carefully bred excellence over time. Their neglect would lead to the loss of their fine qualities, to the inevitable descent toward mediocrity.

Dominus stared at the boxes, the product of a lifetime of care, countless hours of work. That they would all be lost not to destruction or disease, but to sheer entropy, was almost too much to bear.

He had the sudden urge to destroy them.

He turned to Farkus, and nearly told him to arrange for it. But then he saw one of his guards walking into view, striding through the long grass toward them. He frowned.

"What is it?" he asked as the guard stopped before him, bowing deeply.

"A visitor, your Grace," the guard replied. "A Seeker."

"Bring her here," Dominus snapped. "At once." The guard hesitated.

"It's a man, your Grace."

"Then bring *him* here," Dominus commanded impatiently. The guard bowed, leaving them. Dominus saw movement to his right, and glanced to the side, realizing that Farkus was holding his cane, offering it to him.

"In case you feel like…walking, your Grace," Farkus explained with a slight smirk. Dominus took the cane, holding it in his right hand.

"Thank you, Farkus."

Moments later, the guard returned with another man at his side. Somewhat shorter, with broad shoulders and short brown hair. A mutt; hardly representative of the great people of the Acropolis.

"Duke Dominus," the man greeted, bowing deeply.

"Edgar," Dominus replied. He glanced down at the man's hands, in which a sizable obsidian box was clutched. Obsidian, formed of molten rock deep within the earth, what some called neutral stone. It was the standard container to carry an important artifact in.

"Show me," he ordered, gesturing at the box. Edgar complied, unlocking the lid, then opening it. He hesitated, glancing at the guard, then pulled something out of it.

A head.

Dominus stared at it, his breath catching in his throat. It was an Ironclad, that was clear. But a thick, translucent membrane sat atop its skull, traveling down to the back of its severed neck. The membrane was collapsed, folded on itself, but faint blue light came from it, the thinnest film of luminescent fluid held within. His heart skipped a beat, and he felt the faintest glimmer of hope.

"Put it back," Dominus ordered. "Hand the box to me."

Edgar complied, and Dominus set the box on his lap, resting his cane against his wheelchair. He looked up at the Seeker.

"What of the others?" he inquired. Edgar fidgeted.

"Traven is dead," he stated. Dominus's brow furrowed.

"Who?"

"The Seeker I was with," Edgar clarified. "That kid killed him. Almost killed me."

"The Original?"

"Yeah," Edgar confirmed.

"So he's still alive," Dominus deduced. Edgar nodded silently. "What of Vi?" Dominus pressed.

"She came out of the cave before the kid," Edgar answered. "Gave us the head. She was hurt pretty bad," he added. "Arm was chopped off. She said something about an Ironclad…something bigger than that one," he added, gesturing at the box on Dominus's lap. "A female."

"A female?" Dominus inquired, raising an eyebrow. He frowned then, gazing at the hives nearby. "And what of Vi?"

"Dead," Edgar answered. "Traven killed her."

"You're sure?" Dominus pressed. Edgar nodded.

"Saw it myself," he confirmed. "Squashed her head like a melon."

"And you burned the body, of course," Dominus stated. Edgar stared at him.

"Uh…"

Dominus sighed, rubbing his face with one hand. It was moist with sweat.

"You didn't, did you," he muttered.

"No your Grace," Edgar confessed.

"I *specifically* stated that her body was to be burned if she retrieved the head," Dominus pressed. Edgar swallowed visibly.

"We couldn't," he protested. "She pulled herself out of a stream…she was soaking wet."

"Ah," Dominus replied. "I see." He lifted the box from his lap then, twisting around and placing it on the ground beside him. Then he turned back to Edgar, smiling at him. "Thank you for your services," he stated. "You've done well."

"Thank you, your Grace."

"You are dismissed," Dominus stated. Edgar hesitated, then bowed deeply.

And Dominus reached for his cane, pressing the button on its head with his thumb. He unsheathed its blade, slashing the man's throat in one smooth motion.

Edgar stood up from his bow, not even realizing what had happened. His head continued to fall back, the severed muscles at the front of his neck unable to counteract those on the back. The wound on his neck gaped open, blood spurting from it in long, crimson jets.

Edgar fell to his knees, clutching at his throat, his eyes wide with shock.

Dominus watched as the man struggled in vain to staunch the bleeding, crawling over the ground on his hands and knees. Terrible choking and gurgling sounds came from his throat, blood spraying on the grass beneath him. Edgar made it a few meters before collapsing, before his life was finally snuffed out.

Dominus sighed then, reassembling his cane and setting it aside, then picking up the box and putting it back on his lap, ignoring the blood that had spattered his clothes. He glanced up at his guard, who was staring at Edgar's body mutely, his face pale.

"Dispose of the body," Dominus requested. The guard turned to him, bowing deeply.

"Yes your Grace."

Dominus nodded at Farkus, gesturing at the castle. The servant picked up Dominus's cane, then got behind him, wheeling him through the grass. Dominus glanced at the body as he passed, then eyed the guard.

"And burn the body," he added, giving the guard a tight smile. "Please."

CHAPTER 39

Sukri sat in her wheelchair in the great hall of the Guild of Seekers, a huge two-story room as big as a large chapel. Gammon stood at her side, looking rather handsome in his crisp white initiate uniform. Over a hundred Seekers stood behind them, with Master Thorius standing a few meters to the side. One story above, at the front of the great hall, was a large, white marble balcony. She glanced up at it, feeling ill at ease. It wouldn't be long before the ceremony began – their formal ascendance to apprentices of the Guild of Seekers.

It was a moment she'd dreamed of ever since she was a little girl. While others had pined for a "normal" life, she'd dreamed of adventures in the wilderness, exploring ruins and finding powerful artifacts. Of absorbing their powers and becoming something more than normal...more than human. Of being *superhuman*. It was a dream she'd had to keep to herself; in Tykus, being human was the pinnacle of achievement.

But she'd always wanted more.

Her mother had tried to steer her away from these ideas. Foolish dreams, she'd called them. A woman should find a good man, start a family. Women were nurturers, after all, not fighters. But in the end, Sukri had been, well, Sukri. She'd never known how to be normal, and frankly, never wanted to be.

Sukri glanced at Master Thorius, who gave her a slight smile, nodding at her. She forced herself to smile back, knowing that she was supposed to be happy now. Her lifelong dream was finally coming true, after all.

But she didn't feel happy.

She glanced sidelong at Gammon, who was staring up at the balcony above. They hadn't spoken much since the night of their final Trial. Not of anything substantial, anyway. She felt guilty, knowing how hard it must be for Gammon. He'd finally confided in her, revealing his terrible secret, and she'd rejected him. Thrown it back in his face. He'd sacrificed everything for her. *Killed* for her.

The sudden, low beat of a drum sounded from above, like the heartbeat of a great beast echoing through the great hall. Sukri returned her gaze to the balcony, spotting a man walking up to the edge, tall and regal. He was dressed in the typical black and gold uniform of a Seeker, but with countless rows of medals on his chest. A black and gold cape flowed behind him, so long that it touched the floor. He had snow white hair, long and wavy, with a full beard and striking silver eyes. He must have been in his sixties, but few lines marred his face.

Everyone in the room bowed deeply. Sukri and Gammon followed suit, having been prepared by Master Thorius.

"Good evening," the man greeted, resting his hand on the ornate stone railing. His voice was deep, almost hypnotically so, and it carried across the huge room effortlessly. "I am Zeno, High Seeker of the Guild of Seekers."

The drums stopped.

"We are here today to celebrate our newest candidates for the Guild of Seekers," Zeno stated. He smiled down at Sukri and Gammon. "Congratulations on passing your Trials."

The gathered Seekers applauded, and Zeno allowed this for a moment, then raised one hand for silence. The crowd hushed.

"Becoming a Seeker is a great honor," he continued. "And a grave responsibility." He gazed at the two. "As a Seeker, your allegiance is to the guild, and the guild only. There can be no other."

"Yes High Seeker," Sukri stated, Gammon doing the same. Again, as Master Thorius had instructed.

"You must trust that the wisdom of the guild is greater than your own," Zeno stated sternly. "That *my* wisdom is greater than your own." He paused. "Do you swear allegiance to the guild?"

"Yes High Seeker."

Zeno gave a tight smile.

"Prove it."

Sukri heard shouting from behind, and she turned, seeing two Seekers entering the room through double-doors at the rear of it. They were escorting two boys, each dressed in white and blue uniforms...the regalia of lower nobility. They looked like teenagers, maybe thirteen or fourteen, with long blond hair and blue eyes. She realized that their hands were bound behind them...and that they were the ones who'd been shouting.

"Release me!" one of them ordered, trying to shove the Seeker holding him. The Seeker pushed the boy forward, making him stumble, falling flat on his face on the marble floor. He cried out, and the Seeker strode forward, grabbing him by the hair and yanking him up to his knees. Blood poured from the boy's nose, dribbling down his chin and dripping on the floor. He spat, turning to glare at the Seeker. "When my father..."

"Shut up," the Seeker growled, slapping the boy's ear...hard. He fell to his side, his head bouncing off the floor. This time he lay there silently, looking stunned.

The Seeker hauled him to his feet, bringing him to stand in front of Gammon, forcing him to his knees before the big man. The other boy was placed similarly before Sukri. Sitting in her wheelchair, his eyes were level with his. Sukri stared at him, swallowing in a dry throat.

He looked frightened. No...he was scared shitless.

"These minor nobles," The High Seeker stated, gesturing at the two boys, "...were declared missing a few weeks ago." His eyes went to Sukri and Gammon. "They are good boys, both of them. Upstanding citizens of the aristocracy. Their families assume the worst, and have already begun preparations for their funerals."

"Traitors!" the boy with the bloody nose shouted, glaring at the gathered Seekers. Though on his knees, he stood tall, ignoring the blood dripping down his face. "When the king finds out about your treachery, you'll all be hung!"

High Seeker Zeno ignored this, gesturing at the boys.

"These boys are innocent," he declared. "They have committed no crime, done no great wrong. They are fine representatives of the kingdom."

His gaze turned back to Sukri and Gammon.

"Kill them."

Sukri stared at Zeno, at first not registering what the man had said.

Then her blood went cold.

442

She glanced sidelong at Gammon, who glanced back at her. She saw him swallow, saw him turn back to face the boy in front of him. She did the same, staring at the poor boy. His eyes were wide, sweat glistening on his forehead. He shook his head mutely, his eyes moist.

Master Thorius walked up to Sukri, handing her a dagger. Then he walked up to Gammon, handing the big man a sword. He stepped away then, returning to where he'd stood previously.

Sukri glanced up at High Seeker Zeno, who was staring down at them impassively. She lowered her gaze to the boy before her, the handle of her dagger slippery in her sweat-slicked hand.

"Don't," he pleaded, his voice cracking.

"You can't do this," the other boy complained, spitting blood that had dripped into his mouth. "We haven't done anything wrong!"

Zeno gestured at the boy.

"He is correct," the High Seeker agreed. "If you kill them, you will be committing capital murder. But in doing so, you will be removing a threat to the guild. For if these boys were to escape and tell the Acropolis of our treachery, we would all be put to death."

"So you'd kill us for the crime of being illegally kidnapped?" the boy retorted incredulously. "You're nothing but terrorists!"

"You murdered your colleagues during your third Trial," High Seeker Zeno stated, "…in order to save yourselves." He raised an eyebrow. "Would you not do the same for your guild?"

"This is madness!" the boy shouted.

"You have your choice," High Seeker Zeno stated, nodding at Sukri and Gammon. "Make it now."

Sukri looked down at the dagger in her hand, surprised at how calm she felt. There was no fear, no horror. She'd chosen this, to become a Seeker. There was no turning back now.

She glanced up at Master Thorius, remembering his words to them on the day they'd been accepted as initiates.

I suggest you enjoy your self today. Treasure your final moments as you. I guarantee you they are your last.

If only she'd known what that meant.

Sukri took a deep breath in, letting it out. She was not fully herself anymore, and never would be. She was part of something greater than herself now. She was a Seeker…and so was Gammon.

She glanced up at the big guy, her gentle giant, catching him looking back at her. He put a big hand on her shoulder, but she didn't feel the usual sense of calm radiating from him. She was already calm…that was *her* emotion. A wave of affection came over her, and Gammon smiled at her. She smiled back.

That was hers, too.

She nodded at Gammon.

Gammon lunged forward, slashing at the boy's throat.

The blade cut cleanly through his neck, his head falling from his shoulders and striking the floor. It rolled to a stop, blood seeping from the neck, while the boy's body fell forward, striking the marble floor with a *thump*. Blood spurted from the stump in pulses, shooting across the floor and spraying Gammon's legs, staining the pure white fabric a brilliant crimson.

Gammon backpedaled, standing well clear of the deluge, his eyes on the boy's disembodied head. Then he looked upward, nodding at the High Seeker.

Zeno's gaze turned to Sukri.

"Don't do it," the boy before her cried, tears streaming down his cheeks. He shook his head. "Please, I didn't do anything, I didn't *do* anything!"

The Seeker behind him kicked him in the back, sending him face-first into the floor, his arms still bound behind him. He was hauled to his feet then, his face a bloody mess. He groaned, spitting blood onto the floor…and a tooth.

Sukri set the dagger in her lap, gripping the wheels on either side of her and pushing them forward. She wheeled herself up to the boy, a fraction of a meter away. She stared at him for a long moment, her eyes level with his.

She wanted to remember his face. *Had* to remember his face.

"Please," the boy whimpered.

Sukri grabbed the hilt of her dagger, then grabbed his hair with her left hand, yanking his head back, exposing his neck. He screamed, the sound going straight to her soul, goosebumps rising on her arms. She ignored it, pressing the edge of the dagger against his neck, then slicing it with one vicious jerk of her arm.

Hot fluid sprayed on her neck and face, and she flinched backward, dropping the dagger. She felt her wheelchair being pulled backward, and knew without looking that it was Gammon. He pulled her clear, and she wiped her face with her sleeves, her heart pounding in her chest. She stifled a sob, gritting her teeth against it, refusing to let her body betray her.

Then, her face as expressionless as stone, she gazed up at High Seeker Zeno. He nodded approvingly, his lips curling into a smile.

"Our initiates have chosen," he declared, throwing his arms up in the air, his voice booming over the crowd. "Please welcome our newest apprentices to the Guild of Seekers!"

The gathered Seekers burst into applause, and Master Thorius strode up to Sukri, removing the Seeker medallion from around her neck, then placing a new medallion there. This was made of a silver metal, and was remarkably heavy for its size. The medallion itself was shaped into a triangle, three symbols engraved into its surface near each of the three points: an eye with rays shooting out from it, a skull, and a human heart.

"Well done," Thorius murmured, giving her a smile. She nodded, unable to smile back. Thorius turned to Gammon, doing the same for him. That done, he stood before them, a proud look on his face. "You're one of us now."

Sukri swallowed, glancing down at the body of the boy she'd murdered. Master Thorius was right, she knew. She *was* one of them now. A Seeker. And to become the thing she'd dreamed about for so long, she'd had to murder three souls. Lucus's. This boy's.

And her own.

* * *

High Seeker Zeno walked down the hallway leading away from the second-story balcony overlooking the great hall, glancing at the man waiting for him a few meters away. It was Jarl, one of his active Seekers. A man far more suited to scouting than to combat or artifact retrieval, which was just as well. Every Seeker had a role to play in the guild, one appropriate to their strengths. Jarl bowed deeply as Zeno drew close, and Zeno gestured for the man to walk beside him. He felt a slight pang of anxiety, and realized that Jarl was nervous...disturbingly so.

"You have bad news," he observed, eyeing the man critically. Jarl hesitated, then nodded.

"Unfortunately so, High Seeker."

Zeno waited, knowing the profound power of his silence.

"I have news of the mission," Jarl stated. "The one co-sponsored by Duke Dominus." He hesitated. "There's bad news," he confessed. "And good news."

"Tell me the good news first," Zeno commanded.

"Vi is dead," Jarl replied. "And Edgar retrieved the head of that Ironclad…the one that took Traven."

Zeno nodded. That *was* good news. Vi had been a thorn in his side ever since she'd left the guild, violating her oath and abandoning her family. A shame, considering what she'd accomplished. She'd nearly become the very thing the Guild of Seekers had struggled so long to create.

"And the bad news?" he inquired. Jarl grimaced.

"Seeker Traven is dead," he answered. "Killed by the Original."

"The Original is still alive?" Zeno pressed. Jarl nodded. "Interesting," Zeno murmured. The boy was an anomaly…one that he was as yet unsure how to handle. If Master Thorius was right about the Original, then he could represent an enormous threat to the guild…or an invaluable weapon.

"Edgar retrieved the head," Jarl continued, then hesitated again. "He was seen going toward Wexford a few days ago, but he managed to escape our scouts." He swallowed visibly. "He hasn't returned."

Zeno stopped walking, turning to stare at Jarl, his jawline rippling. He resisted the urge to snap at Jarl, knowing that the man could feel his anger radiating from him…and that that was enough. Indeed, Jarl paled.

"Edgar was supposed to return here immediately," Zeno stated, knowing that Jarl already knew this. "He was *supposed* to tell Dominus Vi failed to find it."

"I suspect the duke bought Edgar out," Jarl replied apologetically. "He must have promised him protection from us, as he did with Vi."

Zeno took a deep breath in, letting it out slowly. He forced himself to unclench his fists, forced himself to relax, to push away his emotions.

Emotion is temporary. Action is forever.

Calmness returned, that placid neutrality every Seeker strove to achieve. It came easily to Zeno, steeped as he was in the will of the Founder. Indeed, he suspected that he was Zeno in name only now; the Founder had all but taken over his soul.

He resumed walking, and Jarl continued alongside him. That head – containing the skull of that most intriguing Ironclad – was potentially the single most important artifact the guild had ever come across. With it, they could finally achieve their sacred mission with impunity. No more lurking in the shadows, secretly tainting artifacts to slowly and carefully corrupt the nobility, controlling their wills from afar. No more hoarding stolen, illegal artifacts in secret, fearing a surprise raid by the Acropolis.

They could finally emerge, nearly invincible, able to heal from any wound. The Guild of Seekers would usher in a new era. The ascension of Man…and the resurrection of the Founder.

"Thank you," Zeno stated, nodding at Jarl. "You are dismissed."

Jarl bowed, leaving quickly, no doubt relieved to get away. Zeno sighed, continuing down the hallway, lost in thought.

Dominus was in possession of the head, that much was certain. The old man was close to death, at least according to his doctor – a useful mole, that one. There was a chance that Dominus still wouldn't survive, but there was no guarantee of that now.

Ah, the law of unintended consequences, he mused.

The campaign against Dominus had worked too well, it appeared. Corrupting Dominus's son had been relatively easy, slowly introducing forbidden ideas into the boy's head. Ideals cherished by the Seekers. With the boy's will being slightly stronger than Dominus's – admittedly the only quality the boy had possessed that had eclipsed his father's – he'd then transferred these ideas to Dominus. And how effective that campaign had been! After all, Dominus, the very paragon of the kingdom's misguided virtues, was now dabbling in illegal artifacts. And with this Ironclad's head, he'd transitioned – in his desperation – to using *wild* artifacts.

Unfortunately, Dominus had proven stronger than Zeno had anticipated, retaining the vast majority of his will. The duke still believed in the kingdom, in its ideals. He only resorted to forbidden methods to preserve them.

Zeno sighed again, shaking his head. If Dominus survived, the longer the duke spent with the Ironclad's Ossae, the more difficult it would be to kill him. They needed to retrieve the head…and that would require dealing with Dominus once and for all. And then Zeno would gain power his predecessors could've only dreamed of.

Zeno smiled to himself, touching the medallion resting on his breastbone.

Centuries of planning…and it would all come to fruition soon.

CHAPTER 40

Hunter stood perfectly still, his eyes drawn upward to one of the many tree branches in the distance. A large bird with white feathers and a golden plume atop its head was perched there, facing away from him. He grabbed an arrow, slowly drawing it from his quiver, then nocking it on the bowstring. He drew the arrow back, feeling considerable resistance as he did so, the back of his shoulder burning with the effort. He took his time, ensuring that his feet were pointed perpendicular to his target, his shoulders square, just as Vi had taught him.

He aimed, taking a deep breath in, then letting it out slowly...and let the arrow fly. It flew toward the bird, slamming into its side precisely where he'd been aiming.

He limped forward, watching the bird fall to the ground with a *thump*. It flapped its wings frantically, spinning in a circle, using the last of its life to rail against its death. He stopped a few feet from it, placing his bow on his back and watching as it struggled.

Slowly, painfully, it died.

He stared at it, at the soft white feathers, the golden plume, noting faint blue quills at the tips of its wings. He reached down, yanking the arrow out and putting it back in his quiver. Then he grabbed the bird, turning around and walking the other way. It wasn't long before the forest ended in a sheer cliff, a huge canyon opening up before him. He walked right up to the edge fearlessly, staring down at the lake hundreds of feet below. At the island in the

448

center, a long wooden bridge connecting it to the shore along the edge of the canyon.

He turned left, limping down the spiraling ledge hugging the wall of the canyon, following it as it curved rightward and downward. Eventually he reached the bottom, walking across the long wooden bridge toward the island. He saw Vi's house in the distance, the front door smashed in. The storehouse nearby was a mess, holes smashed into its walls.

Hunter reached the end of the bridge, walking up to a pile of sticks near the house. Leftovers from the campfire he'd made for them so many days ago, before the Ironclad had come for them.

For *him*.

He tossed the bird on the ground, plucking the feathers and then making an incision with the tip of his sword, opening its belly, being careful not to puncture the intestines. He removed the intestines, pinching them at the top and pulling downward, then took out the rest of the organs. That done, he plucked the rest of the feathers, packing the abdominal cavity with clumps of grass to soak up the blood.

He set it aside, getting to work building a fire, which only took a minute or two. Once that was done, he got to work extracting the meat from the bird, then puncturing each piece with a sharp stick and roasting them. He smiled then, remembering how Vi had made fun of him for being useless. Learn to hunt or starve, she'd said…and she'd meant it. He almost *had* starved after she'd refused to hunt for him again, before he'd managed to kill his first prey. Hunger had been a very effective motivator.

He bit into a piece of meat, closing his eyes. An image of Traven's hammer coming down at him, of Vi's lifeless body, came to him. He opened his eyes, staring into the fire. Now he was hungry for something else entirely.

Revenge.

He finished his meal, then stood, walking up to Vi's house and stopping before the shattered front door. Despite everything, it felt wrong to even consider stepping inside. This had been Vi's, a shrine to her personhood. Only she had slept here, among the things she'd collected in her lifetime. Now that she was dead, her home *was* her…where her will lived on.

Hunter hesitated, then stepped through the doorway into the room beyond.

He stared at the bed in the corner, covered with stuffed animals and dolls. At the bookcase on one wall, knick-knacks set atop it. He walked up to the bed, picking up one of the dolls, feeling a sense of peace and comfort as he did. A memory of a woman smiling down at him flashed in his mind's eye.

Vi's memory.

He set the doll back on the bed, taking a deep breath in, then letting it out. Looking up, he spotted a few weapons mounted on one wall. He walked toward them, putting a hand on the handle of a mace. He could feel Vi there, somewhere inside of it...and something else. He closed his eyes, a vision coming to him. One of tall spires of black stone rising from a forest far in the distance, vines crawling up their walls.

He opened his eyes, staring at the mace for a long while. Then he grabbed it from the wall, holding it in his hands. It was heavy – far heavier than his longsword – but it felt right somehow. He held on to it, gazing at Vi's room, feeling suddenly overwhelmed.

She's here, he thought with a smile. *She'll always be here.*

He turned then, walking out of the house and gazing across the canyon, at the many waterfalls cascading down its sides. It reminded him of the waterfall in that cavern, falling all around him as his mother had gazed up at him lovingly, smiling as she'd recognized him. He felt an all-too familiar depression come over him, so awful he wanted to lie on the ground and curl up in a ball.

Instead, he stood there, taking a deep breath in, then letting it out. Vi's words came to him then.

Emotion is temporary, action is forever. Don't let your temper control you, or you'll regret it.

He shook his head, a bitter laugh escaping him.

If only I'd listened.

Hunter sighed, rubbing his face with his hands, tears threatening to well up in his eyes. He grit his teeth, refusing to give in to them again. He'd cried enough. The time for mourning was over.

Emotion is temporary, he thought. *Except when it isn't. Then you should act on it.*

He pictured Traven, smirking up at him right before he'd killed the man. He'd knelt over Traven's corpse afterward, pressing his forehead against Traven's. Just as with Vi, images had appeared in his mind's eye...memories flooding into him. Traven's memories. Within seconds, Hunter had known that Dominus had ordered Vi killed. That the Seekers had wanted Vi dead ever since she'd left the guild. And that the Guild of Seekers were hiding a dark secret…a secret they had killed so many to protect.

A secret that could destroy them.

Hunter pictured Master Thorius, his supposed mentor, the very man who'd sent him to be killed, letting Kris be torn apart. Imagined an old man sitting atop his throne in the castle Wexford, a place he had never heard of yet somehow knew about. The Duke of Wexford, the man who'd been behind it all, sending Vi to her death, and nearly killing Hunter.

Hunter gripped the mace in his hands so hard his knuckles turned white, then secured it to his belt opposite his longsword. No, not *his* longsword.

Vi's.

He touched the hilt of her sword, feeling her presence there…and a hint of something else. Some*one* else…someone both alien and all-too familiar. He closed his eyes, seeing his mother lying before him, a smile on her lips. Hideous and beautiful at the same time, a monster yet still a woman.

Then he opened his eyes, turning back to Vi's house, his mouth set in a grim line. He'd thought he had nothing left to live for, right before he'd tried to kill himself with his own sword, before the Ironclad had torn it from his hands.

I'm not going to leave you, Vi had said. *I'm not your mother.*

And yet that's exactly what she'd done.

Another wave of despair came over him, grief so powerful it nearly brought him to his knees.

I can't do this.

He had the sudden urge to go back inside of Vi's house, to surround himself with her things. To wait for her powerful will to start changing him, making him into someone else so he wouldn't have to feel this way again. Maybe his will wouldn't be powerful enough to resist her. Maybe he could *become* her, so he wouldn't have to be himself anymore.

He opened his eyes, staring at her home.

Don't give up on yourself, she'd said.

But how was he supposed to live with himself, after everything he'd done? What did he even have to live for anymore?

He sighed, turning away from the house to gaze across the lake. The water glimmered in the sunlight, as if countless jewels were floating on its surface. Then he turned to the campfire, at the carcass of the bird he'd killed. Feathers of white, gold, and blue…like the kingdom of Tykus set against the endless sea. He pictured Duke Dominus, a faceless aristocrat who'd been behind it all.

Hunter grit his teeth, clenching his hands into fists.

He *did* have something to live for. To become powerful enough to take on the Guild of Seekers. Powerful enough even to take on the duke himself…the man who'd driven his mother out of Tykus, who'd brutally ended the war she'd started. Who'd ordered Vi's death, and Hunter's…and had gotten Kris killed.

Yes, he thought, turning to gaze upward, at the top of the canyon walls hundreds of feet above. He would become a Seeker, like Vi…the greatest Seeker alive. Absorbing the skills from Vi's weapons would only be the beginning. He needed more…to hunt down the artifacts and bones of the most powerful men and women who'd ever lived. He would become the world's greatest hunter.

A hunter of Legends.

EPILOGUE

Xerxes stepped out of the mouth of the Ironclad cave, bright starlight shining down on the grassy field before him. He took a deep breath in, savoring the sweetness of the air, so fresh compared to the musk of the tunnels. It was all the sweeter to his newly regenerated nostrils, which were still incredibly sensitive. Each sensation was familiar, yet new somehow.

He glanced up at the sky, squinting at the three crescent moons high above, their light almost blinding after hours spent underground. He sighed, lowering his gaze to the tree line beyond the field. Footsteps approached from behind, and he felt a hand on his left shoulder, long, black fingers resting there.

Xerxes grunted, then turned left, pulling away from that touch and walking close to the short rock wall. His bare feet *thumped* rhythmically on the grass, not even feeling the twigs and small pebbles underfoot through his armored soles. He heard the footsteps behind him, following him as he went. Several minutes passed, until he saw a stream ahead, its waters glittering silver in the light of the three moons. He strode toward it, taking his time. He was still weak, after all. Regenerating so much tissue had sapped a great deal of his strength, robbing his limbs of their muscle.

At last he reached the grassy shore before the stream, glancing to the left. The mouth of another cave opened up at the base of a cliff there, water streaming from its mouth, falling in a short waterfall. He raised one hand, flashing rapid hand signals.

"They came through there," he signed.

He turned away from the cave, spotting something lying on the ground a couple of meters from the shore. A body covered in faintly glowing blue gel. He grimaced, striding up to it. It was the woman who'd beheaded him. She lay there motionlessly, a small dent barely visible in her forehead, her left arm ending at the wrist.

Xerxes stopped, staring down at her, an all-too-familiar anger rising within him.

"He went north," a female voice stated, gentle but firm. He nodded, spotting footprints leading from the shore toward the tree line, and raised one hand.

"I'll take a few men," he signed. "I'll find him."

"No," the voice behind him retorted. "You need to finish healing first. Then go."

Xerxes grunted, raising one hand to his neck, feeling the sharp indent in the middle of his neck, his fingers dipping into the soft flesh there. Though his new head was fully formed, the armor covering it hadn't finished regenerating; he needed to eat more to fuel his recovery.

"They'll come after him," he signed. "The humans."

"I know," came her reply. She sighed. "They'll come after him…and us."

Xerxes nodded, not for the first time wishing he could speak fluently like her. It hadn't always been like this, of course. He'd been able to speak quite well in the past. But every minute he spent with his people, and amongst the countless beetles living in those damn tunnels, he lost more of his humanity. The worst part was that he was starting to prefer it, that alien part of him slowly taking over, year by year.

Eventually he would become like the others. The Lost.

"We'll protect him," he signed. "We've survived this long."

"This time will be different," she warned. "They'll bring everything they have."

"We should attack first then," he signed, making quick, angry motions. "Kill them before they can kill us. We're stronger than they are."

Another sigh.

"Perhaps," she conceded. "But there may be a better way."

He frowned.

"What way?" he signed.

She didn't answer, pointing to the woman lying on the ground.

"Take her," she ordered. "Bring her inside."

He stared down at the woman, feeling frustration mount.

"Why?" he signed.

He felt the hand on his shoulder again, felt it squeeze him gently. His frustration immediately ceased, overpowered by her legendary will. She rarely touched him, and only when he was in danger of becoming one of the Lost, for fear of robbing him of his soul.

"In due time, my son," she soothed. "In due time."

The following is an excerpt from

SEEKER OF LEGENDS

Book 2 in the Fate of Legends series

PROLOGUE

Countless stars shone down on the King's Road, a seemingly endless series of stone slabs suspended seven meters above the ground by massive wooden posts. The three moons of Varta, nearly full now, cast their pale glow on the forest the road cut through, casting soft shadows on the forest floor. A cool wind whipped through the trees, a prelude to menacing clouds approaching slowly from the west.

And on the King's Road, a lone carriage rolled steadily northward toward the Kingdom of Tykus, pulled by two burly horses.

Seeker Dante shifted uneasily in his seat inside the carriage, his buttocks aching from the days-long ride through the forest. The carriage was old and worn, the seat cushions stiff and uncomfortable. It was far from the usual luxury the Guild of Seekers provided. No one who managed to spot the carriage would think it was owned by the guild...or that it carried such precious cargo.

And that, Dante knew, was precisely the point.

He glanced to his right, at the other man seated in the carriage, a younger man with light brown hair and a pencil-thin mustache. It was Seeker Murin, a low-ranked Seeker Dante was mentoring. The man – practically a boy – was still green, fresh out of his apprenticeship. As with most fresh graduates, Murin's confidence far exceeded his competence. With experience, that would change.

If it doesn't, Dante mused, *he'll be dead.*

Dante sighed, looking down at the large wooden music box sitting between them on the seat cushions. It was well-made, with intricate designs carved into every inch of its exterior. A convincing counterfeit; anyone lifting the lid would find a fully functioning machine inside. But hidden within that machine was a sealed secret compartment, nestled between its gears. And in that compartment was an obsidian container containing a very valuable artifact.

A very *illegal* artifact.

What the artifact did exactly, Dante didn't know. That was often the case with the guild when they acted as their own client. Most Seekers retrieved artifacts for private clients, giving a percentage of their profits to the guild. A few of the more skilled – and more trustworthy – Seekers ran missions for the guild itself, retrieving artifacts that High Seeker Zeno felt were necessary to strengthen the guild. These artifacts were sacred indeed; the traits stored within them were almost guaranteed to increase the powers of all the Seekers, making them stronger, faster, or smarter.

Each artifact brought them one step closer to the Founder's grand vision: the Ascension.

Seeker Murin stirred, glancing at Dante.

"That was some weird shit, huh?" he said, shaking his head. "The Kingdom of the Deep, I mean."

Dante said nothing, not meeting the man's gaze. He recognized the statement for what it was…a banal conversation-starter. Silence made Murin nervous. It was a weakness of the young, and it betrayed a lack of self-confidence. All signs of a low-level Seeker. Assuming he was ever promoted, Murin would be exposed to a stronger form of the Founder's will, through an upgraded Seeker medallion. This would cure his weaknesses eventually, even if experience did not.

"If you ask me," Murin continued, "…they're all a bunch of freaks." He smirked then. "Ever wonder how they, you know?"

"No, I don't," Dante grumbled.

"How they do it," Murin continued. "Especially the guy who sold us that," he added, gesturing to the music box. "I mean come on, the guy was *huge.*"

"Like I said," Dante stated coolly, "…I don't."

"They're not even human anymore," Murin pressed, oblivious to Murin's unspoken sentiment – that he didn't want to talk. "They're like…*animals* there."

Dante ignored the younger Seeker, closing his eyes and resting his head back against his seat. They'd traveled from the Kingdom of the Deep, passing through the Glade of the Deep to reach the King's Road. Then they'd taken the road all the way to the Fringe, the last few kilometers of forest before the Deadlands…and the Kingdom of Tykus. A vast wasteland, the Deadlands was all that remained of the old Outskirts, a city once filled with peasants. Peasants that, under the leadership of the Original, had risen up to start the great Civil War a half-century ago.

Tykus had driven the peasants – and the Original – out, laying waste to the old Outskirts, digging the tainted earth of the ruined city up and tossing it into the ocean.

Dante stifled a yawn. It would only be another hour before they reached the Deadlands, and not much longer than that before they made it to the great wall surrounding Tykus. Going through customs would be risky, as usual; if they were caught transporting illegal artifacts, they would be tried and convicted of treason. Thus the necessity of building the music box around the obsidian container housing the artifact; customs officials would not break apart such a delicate machine to find the artifact, and the wood of the music box would insulate the traits emitted by the artifact, making them difficult to sense.

Dante had been through the process countless times, and had never been caught. A skilled smuggler like himself was exceedingly valuable to the guild…a fact that had made him a wealthy man.

Customs would use the guild's own Seekers to test the artifacts, as was the protocol. These Seekers were trained differently than the rest, of course. None carried the Founder's will. The kingdom tested each of these "false" Seekers by having mentally deficient, weak-willed people called Testers spend time with them, absorbing their wills. Then the Testers were extensively questioned by the kingdom. Any anti-Tykus sentiments a person might have would be absorbed by the Testers, and as they were simple-minded, they would not think to hide them.

A *real* Seeker would not stand up to such scrutiny.

"Wonder what that thing is," Murin mused, breaking the silence. His eyes were on the music box.

"If you're smart," Dante grumbled, "…you'll never find out."

"Why's that?"

"You should know why," Dante retorted. It was well-known that artifacts from the Kingdom of the Deep were often *wild* artifacts, those containing traits that weren't human. In the Kingdom of the Deep, humanity was not valued as it was in Tykus, and it was perfectly legal to expose oneself to wild traits. In Tykus, such a thing was forbidden. Preservation of one's humanity was the sacred mission of the Acropolis, the great fortress where the highest nobles lived…and King Tykus himself.

"I wonder if this came from the Deep," Murin mused. Dante glanced at him.

"Doubt it."

"Why's that?" Murin pressed. "What is the Deep, anyway?"

Dante sighed.

"What did I tell you about asking questions?" he stated wearily. Murin grimaced.

"Don't ask more than one at a time."

"You know it," Dante stated. "So *do* it."

"Right," Murin muttered. He shifted uneasily in his seat. "So what is the Deep?" he pressed.

"No one knows," Dante answered. "Except maybe High Seeker Zeno. All I know is the Great One went there a long time ago."

"What was what, a hundred years ago?"

"Hell of a lot longer than that," Dante corrected.

Suddenly there was an ear-splitting shriek.

Dante's gaze jerked forward, and he spotted the horse on the right through the front window of the carriage. It reared up on its hind legs, then bolted leftward, slamming into the other horse. The driver shouted something unintelligible, yanking back on the reins. But the horse ignored the driver, breaking out into a gallop, veering off to the left...and bringing the carriage with it.

"What the hell?" Murin blurted out.

Then Dante saw what'd spooked the horse: an arrow was sticking out of its right flank.

"Get out," Dante ordered, shoving Murin toward the rightmost door of the carriage. "Go!"

Both horses veered to the left, bring the carriage rolling straight toward the leftmost edge of the King's Road...and the sheer, twenty-foot drop to the ground below.

"Get out!" Dante shouted, shoving the music box off the seat and diving rightward toward Murin's door. He grabbed the door handle and pulled it, shoving the door open...just as the carriage's front left wheel rolled off the edge of the road.

Shit!

Dante scrambled over Murin's lap toward the open door...and felt the carriage tilt to the left, making him slide toward the opposite door. His back slammed into it, and he grunted, bracing himself. He saw the horses plunge off the side of the King's Road, then felt his stomach lurch as the carriage entered into free-fall.

His Seeker instincts kicked in.

He curled into a ball, ducking his head in his arms, every muscle relaxing, going limp. He felt the carriage accelerating downward, time slowing as it careened toward the ground seven meters below. The carriage driver leapt from his seat outside of the carriage, falling to the right of the horses. As Dante watched, the horses slammed head-first into the ground, the driver hitting moments later. The driver's seat struck next, disintegrating as it smashed into the forest floor. The front of the carriage *exploded*, pieces of wood and stone flying toward Dante. He closed his eyes, remaining limp.

And then there was darkness.

* * *

Dante groaned, opening his eyes.

He found himself lying on his back, staring upward at the seat cushions of the carriage. He frowned, wondering how they'd gotten up there…then realized that he was lying on the ceiling. The carriage had flipped upside-down.

He heard groaning, and turned to see Murin lying beside him, a deep gash in the man's forehead. Blood poured from the wound, forming a puddle under their heads. Dante grimaced, sitting up, feeling pain in his back and arms as he did so. He looked down, seeing pieces of glass and wooden splinters jutting out of his forearms…and his legs. Sharp, stabbing pain shot through the left side of his chest with each breath, and he grunted, putting a hand on his ribs there. The merest touch brought him agony.

What the hell happened?

It took him a moment to remember, and when he did, he swore.

"Get up," he ordered Murin, rising to a crouching position, ignoring the pain the movement caused. He lent the younger Seeker a hand, pulling him to his feet. Murin looked dazed, his eyes glassy. Concussed.

"What…" he began, but Dante cut him off.

"They're coming," he growled. "Go out that way," he added, gesturing to the still-open door nearest the man. "I'll go the other way."

"Who-"

"Shut up and go!" Dante hissed, shoving Murin toward the door. He turned to *his* door, yanking at the lever to open it. But it didn't budge. He swore.

461

They're watching, he knew. Whoever had shot the horse. If they saw his door open, they'd know he was trying to escape. Hopefully Murin stumbling out of the carriage would be distract the enemy. The kid was useless now, except as bait.

Dante waited for Murin to get clear of the carriage, then braced himself, kicking his door just below the handle. It burst open.

A fresh jolt of pain shot through his ribs, and he held his breath, his eyes watering. He waited for the pain to lessen, taking shallow breaths. Eventually it did.

He peered outside.

Pieces of the shattered carriage were strewn across the forest floor, lined by pale moonlight. The carriage had struck front-first, then tipped over onto its back. Which explained why it was upside-down. He spotted a man lying in a broken heap nearby…the driver.

If the man wasn't dead, he would be soon.

Dante drew his longsword from its scabbard slowly, turning so that his body was blocking the blade from view. Otherwise whoever had shot them down might see the moonlight flashing on the blade. He peered into the darkness, seeing nothing but trees and bushes.

Then he heard footsteps behind him.

Crunch, crunch.

Dante spun around, then relaxed. It was Murin; the man was limping into the forest, his sword in plain sight, moonlight shimmering off the blade. Exactly as Dante had hoped.

Idiot.

Murin jerked back suddenly, an arrow protruding from his chest.

Dante broke out into a run toward a large tree ahead. He reached it, ducking behind it, keeping his sword down low. He felt panic rising within him, and suppressed it, trying to focus. Panic would get him killed. He needed to think.

The arrow came from straight ahead, he reasoned, recalling the angle it'd struck Murin at…and the horse earlier, on the King's Road. That meant that the archer had to be to the right of the road. Dante circled around the tree trunk until it was between him and the carriage. His ribs hurt terribly, and his hands were slick with the blood trickling down the countless wounds in his forearms. The hilt of his sword felt slippery, and he wiped his hands on his pants one at a time, then gripped the hilt of his sword tightly.

He had to kill whoever ambushed them, he knew. If he didn't, whoever it was would get their hands on the artifact. His hand went to his chest, reaching for his Seeker medallion, but of course it wasn't there. He'd left it at the guild, as he always did when going out to transport illegal artifacts. Couldn't have the enemy getting ahold of his medallion, after all.

There could be more than one archer.

The thought made the hair on the nape of his neck stand on end, and he glanced out from behind the tree, peering into the woods. He still couldn't see anything; a dense mist hung in the air just above the ground a few dozen meters away. There was no way the archer could have shot Murin through that haze. Which meant...

Pain lanced through his left leg, and he cried out, dropping his sword and falling onto his back on the hard ground. He looked down.

An arrow was sticking out of his shin.

He scrambled to his feet, then saw something burst out of the mist ahead. A man in a black cloak, their face hidden in the shadows thrown by the hood over their head. Holding a bow, sprinting right at him!

Shit!

Dante reached down, retrieving his sword. The cloaked man dropped the bow, unsheathing a sword from their hip in one smooth, quick motion. Moonlight danced off the silver blade, and the man reached Dante within seconds, swinging their sword at him with terrible speed!

Dante felt his Seeker reflexes kick in, and he blocked the blow, their blades ringing with the impact. He counterattacked without thinking, without needing to think. He'd spent years absorbing the skills of the finest Seekers who'd ever lived, some of the most skilled swordsmen in the world. He thrust at the cloaked man's chest with perfect technique, aiming unerringly for their heart.

The man dodged to the side at the last second, then slashed at Dante's neck!

Dante parried the blow...or tried to. The man pulled the attack back at the last minute. But the feint caused the enemy to lose his balance, stumbling backward. Dante lunged forward, slashing at the guy, but the man dodged easily, scooping dirt from the ground and flinging it right into Dante's face. He closed his eyes automatically, turning his head to one side...

...and felt a horrible pain in his belly, shooting right through to his back.

Dante gasped, opening his eyes and looking down. At the sword buried to the hilt in his abdomen. He gasped, staring at it in disbelief, his sword slipping out of his hands and falling to the ground beside him.

The cloaked figure lifted one black boot, kicking Dante in the hip. Agony burst through his belly as he lurched backward, the sword sliding free from his body. He fell onto his butt, his back slamming into a tree trunk behind him. He stared up at the cloaked figure, clutching his belly with both hands. There was a dagger at his hip, but he didn't bother reaching for it. It was futile, he knew.

He was already dead.

Dante stared up at his attacker, feeling hot blood pour from between his fingers. The cloaked man stood there, facing him silently. Then they reached up with one hand, grabbing the edge of their hood and pulling it back.

Dante's breath caught in his throat.

It was a young man, he realized. With skin nearly as dark as the night sky, and black eyes that glittered in the moonlight. His hair was so short he was almost bald.

"You've just attacked two Seekers," Dante growled, grimacing as a fresh wave of pain shot through his belly.

"Damn right," the man agreed. He raised the tip of his sword, pressing it against Dante's breastbone.

"You must have a death wish," Dante muttered. "They'll find out about this," he added. "You'll have to face the entire guild now."

The man's lips curled into a smirk.

"That's the idea."

"You're a dead man," Dante promised. When the man didn't respond, he grimaced, shoving the tip of the man's sword away from his chest with one hand. "What are you after?" he added. "The artifact?"

"That," the man answered, "...and information."

"What information?" Dante pressed. Not that it mattered...he wouldn't live to relay the information. But he was curious.

"About the guild," he replied. "And a certain artifact they stole."

Dante gave the man a smug smile.

"Over my dead body," he muttered.

The man shrugged, flipping his sword around so he was carrying it backward, gripping the blade with both hands.

"Works for me."

464

And then he swung his sword over his head, chopping downward at Dante's face.

Printed in Great Britain
by Amazon

37545878R00270